RUBY OUT OF RUINS

THE SEZNA SEER SERIES
BOOK FOUR

KIERSTEN LILLIS

First edition December 2025
Cover design by Blue Raven Book Covers

ISBN 978-1-7336178-8-8 (paperback)
ISBN 978-1-7336178-7-1 (ebook)

kierstenlillis.com

CHAPTER 1

MARGOT

Margot could have practiced the spell inside.

Even if Penny or her father caught her attempting Manipulation magic, what could they say?

Nothing that would change her mind.

Not now that she'd figured out how to control the illusions more carefully. And not now that she was the oldest Bridgestone daughter in the house.

Talullah, the eldest of the three, had gone yet again, searching for the final stone in her necklace that denoted her as a Sezna Seer, one with all four Sights.

Margot didn't necessarily envy the magnitude of her sister's powers. Seeing the past, present, potential, and certain futures was a heavy burden to carry. She *did* envy being special.

For a while, she thought the cinnamon smell she sometimes created in her home was just an accident, or something her mind had conjured. An illusion only she could experience.

But then, she'd done it on purpose. Multiple times.

When her family had commented about the whereabouts of the cinnamon bread which she'd supposedly been baking, Margot smiled to herself. Her own power had finally risen to the surface.

And until she'd gotten a fair handle on things, she wanted some privacy.

Golden leaves stuck to the bottoms of Margot's boots. They'd softened in the rain that had paused in the past ten minutes after hours of unrelenting drops. Breath puffed from her chilled cheeks and disappeared into the dawn air as she walked to the edge of her family's yard.

The pink sunset sat atop the largest hill in the distance, its rays guiding Margot to the spot she'd chosen: her mother's hazelnut tree.

A fitting place to practice, considering her mother's genes had given Margot this new magic. And considering Margot had few memories of the woman. Maybe learning these skills would help Margot learn about her mother and herself.

Her father talked about her mother often, but never about her disappearance or anything since. It was all just reassurance that her mother loved her.

Well, if she loved them all so much, why hadn't she come back?

Surely, if her mother had died, her father would have told her that, at least. Then, she could properly grieve the woman she barely knew but who had left a giant hole inside Margot's heart. It was hard not knowing half of herself.

Margot's magic was still just a whisper beneath her skin, not reaching her veins just yet. Not formed enough to flow through her body. She hadn't told anyone about what she could do. With Talullah's discovery and subsequent quest to find her gemstones, and all the terrible things that had happened since the first day she'd left looking for them, there hadn't been enough room for Margot to reveal a secret of her own.

Magic had torn the Bridgestones apart in the last year, and as much as Margot relished having something powerful building inside her, she also felt conflicted about it. Talullah was the responsible one, of course. No one was surprised by that. Becoming a mother-figure to two young sisters at seven will do that to a person. And Pennilyn, though not that much younger than Margot, was the carefree spirit who never had to worry about a thing. Margot was the middle child.

She still hadn't found her identity within her family.

Now, she pulled her blond hair up into a bun on top of her head and spread the old, worn star-print quilt on the wet grass. It wouldn't take long for it to be soaked through, but it was either this or have a conversation about magic with her father. She got the feeling he understood more than he let on about Talullah and her gemstones. Maybe he would be happy that Margot had Sight powers, too.

Or maybe he'd forbid her using it so she couldn't be another loved one he'd lose to magic.

That wasn't a risk Margot could take at the moment.

So, wet grass, it was.

Margot sat cross-legged on the quilt and laid the notebook she'd stolen from Talullah's room open in her lap. She bit the inside of her cheek while staring at the cover. Was it wrong to read her sister's class notes?

She shook the thought away. If Talullah had cared about the notes from her time on the Isle of Salire, she would have shoved them in her knapsack the last time she came home. As far as Margot was concerned, anything left behind was fair game.

She flipped to the section about Manipulation. That's what the cinnamon smells she'd conjured were—illusions caused by Manipulating the surrounding environment. Smells could be useful, but visual Manipulations would be even more so.

Margot skimmed the notes. She'd try changing the color of a hazelnut. It was small, so it shouldn't prove too difficult. She plucked one off the ground at the base of the tree and set it on top of the open notebook.

Closing her eyes, she concentrated on controlling her breath: deep, even inhales and exhales. Then she opened her eyes and focused her gaze on the hazelnut, zeroing in on every detail she possibly could notice. She willed it to change for her.

Come on. Change. Turn white.

Nothing happened.

Already frustrated, Margot picked up the nut between her thumb and forefinger, narrowing her eyes at it.

She threw it as hard as she could at the tree trunk.

Did she think she'd get it right the first time? Okay, maybe she did.

Was it fair to put that much pressure on herself? Maybe not.

Still, Margot pushed herself to standing and sighed at the sky.

The back of her neck prickled. Even during the most extreme sunrise or sunset, it had never looked like that. *Wrong.*

Her mouth dropped open in shock. Sweat ran down her forehead. Luckily, she was alone.

She wouldn't have been able to bear it if James or any of her other friends had seen her gaping like a fish.

But she couldn't help it. It looked like someone had sliced open the sky and made it bleed.

Did I do that?

Was it possible her spell had misfired? That, instead of turning the hazelnut white, she'd turned the whole sky crimson?

Adrenaline pumped warmth through her in anxious tingles.

If that were the case, it was good she hadn't been inside her home. She might have turned her sister into a chicken or something equally ridiculous.

The thought pulled a choked laugh from her throat. If she could do that, what else was she capable of?

I have to turn it back.

Margot breathed in and out. "Turn the sky back to blue."

It stayed as it was.

"Turn back." She spoke the words to the sky itself. "Come on. This isn't funny. If I did it once, I can do it again."

The sky shimmered, iridescent, like a rainbow caught underwater.

Look at the barrier.

The voice entered her mind so seamlessly Margot would have sworn it was her own subconscious. But there was something different about it. Something mysterious and sharp as a fox's teeth, and familiar, like she'd heard it before in a dream.

Once more, Margot pleaded with the sky to change back. "If it was my doing, you have to change back now." Never mind magic couldn't simply be told to obey.

The sky continued to shimmer in shades of red, purple, blue, and green.

Margot's stomach folded over on itself, trying to hide the panic growing there.

The barrier, Little Seer. It will show you the truth.

Had Margot made the sky change? Or had someone else?

She had to know.

She ran to the edge of the forest, to the closest part of the barrier. When she reached it, she understood. The magic that had altered the sky couldn't be Margot's.

It had to belong to a Sezna Seer.

Recently, she'd started noticing the threads of magic around her. At first she'd thought something was wrong with her eyes or her brain, and she'd tried to rub the images away with her palms over her eyes. Now, she recognized them for what they were: the threads of time magic.

The barrier glistened with a new layer made from threads of all four Sights.

Margot reached out and grazed a finger along the barrier. It zapped her.

She swore and shook her hand. It had never done that before. The Founders of River Hill had constructed the barrier when they'd fled the First War. The magically Gifted had spelled it to protect the town, to conceal it from view, not to keep people in.

Gritting her teeth, she tried again. The second time, Margot's hand got through the barrier to her third set of knuckles before flinging her whole body backward. She landed on her bottom with a thump.

Look and see. The voice again. Decidedly not her own.

Could it be her mother's voice, finding her across space and time? The barrier itself? Maybe a spirit guide taking pity on her?

She shook her hand again, her anger boiling up. If anything set Margot apart from her sisters, it was her attitude and temper. She stood with a huff and blew her bangs out of her face. She glared at the barrier. It wouldn't let her out. But why?

Look and see.

"I am looking!" Margot yelled. "I'm looking and seeing! What do you want from me?"

Look and see, the voice repeated in a sing-song tone.

Margot was about to yell at no one again, but something caught her eye. The place where she'd pressed her hand on the barrier. She leaned closer. It was a thread, glistening and red.

If she pulled it, would the barrier let her out? Would it unzip whatever magic had trapped her there?

Only one way to find out.

Margot gripped the thread and tugged.

Red light flashed across her vision, blinding her for a second. When her eyes cleared, she certainly wasn't behind the barrier anymore.

The forest and River Hill were gone.

Margot pivoted in a circle. The room was large—a cavern, it seemed. Dusty stone lay beneath her feet. She looked up. A brilliant night sky made of black tiles and bright white dots made it impossible to know how far above the ceiling hovered. White carved marble pillars guarded each of the four doorways. Instead of doors, though, twisted tree roots obscured the exits.

A thin veil of red colored everything, as if Margot peered through sheer fabric. Her heart pounded against her ribs.

A bird screeched overhead and dove toward her.

Margot's eyes darted around the room, desperate for an escape. She ran to the nearest doorway and tugged at the roots. A sharp pain lanced through her hand. Blood ran down her palm. Panicked, she gripped the roots again, pulling as hard as she could.

Crackling sounds echoed in her ears. Beneath her fingertips, shapes pushed upward as if growing out of the tree roots.

Margot's vision went blurry. She blinked, trying to clear it. But her eyes caught on a woman wearing a long silky gown. She was thigh-deep in a pond made of rainbow water. Her light hair rested in a braided crown atop her head. "You have been a scourge on my life ever since your birth, Talullah Bridgestone. And I will waste no tears at your demise."

"Wait!" Margot tried to say.

The scene wavered again. Margot stumbled to the side, bumping into a wall made of rough rock.

Out of the corner of her eye, she spotted something glimmering on the ground.

A knife?

She snatched it.

The object was too small to be a knife, too soft. She looked at her palm. A blood-red feather streaked through with gold.

The woman took two steps toward her, still in the rainbow pool. Then she froze. And screamed.

Margot blinked, but she couldn't dispel the number forty-seven from the back of her eyelids. Now she stood alone in the dark. Anticipation buzzed in her blood as she searched for something. But what? She blinked again. The number forty-seven rewrote itself in the air in front of her in golden light.

A musty smell filled her nose. Just as soon, it disappeared. She stared up at the ruby sky. Water seeped through the back of her pants. Her eyes saw two of everything. Double tree. Double cloud. Double fingers held in front of her face.

She rolled onto her knees and wretched into a bush.

Sweat stung her eyes as she tried to make sense of everything. Her body was unharmed. She was back at the edge of the forest near the barrier, which still shimmered innocently in front of her.

"Lies," she said aloud to the magic.

You looked, Little Seer. But did you See?

Margot grasped at the vision. Because she understood now. That's what it had been. A premonition.

The woman had called her Talullah.

Margot's skin prickled. Someone was going to try to kill her sister.

Margot hadn't Seen the end of the scene. Was that because of what she'd done while in it?

The feather. Was that important somehow? Would it help Talullah escape?

Margot's head spun. It was as if she'd experienced multiple events all at once. Were they all part of the same event or different ones that her magic couldn't yet separate? What did the number forty-seven have to do with anything?

Only one thing was clear: Talullah was in danger.

And Margot had to help her.

CHAPTER 2

TALULLAH

Talullah and Dhal stepped out of the transport tree and into a world unlike anything Talullah had ever imagined. Magic exhaled and inhaled at a different pace here.

Praeteriti, the world of the past, breathed slowly, in measured, even, confident turns. The Isle of Salire's cadence swelled and broke with the ocean tides, alternating between slow and fast, echoing its inhabitants.

Here in Calla, magic hyperventilated, as if there wasn't enough time or space for it all to exist. It grasped at her consciousness, each Sight's unseen aura fighting for Talullah to notice it.

Talullah touched her sapphire. The cloud of overwhelm that had settled in her mind dissipated.

If she was going to get any clarity here, she and Dhal needed help.

"Let's Scry Jothi," Talullah said.

She removed her gold reusable Scry bracelet from her wrist and pressed its inlaid sapphire, thinking of Jothi. Watery film stretched across the bracelet, filling the hole. Jothi's face appeared.

Their forehead wrinkled under their smooth brown skin, but a relieved smile found its place between their high cheekbones.

"About time you called," they said.

"We're in Calla," Talullah said. "And the Scry works both ways, you know."

Jothi laughed and then raised a black brow. "I assume this isn't purely a social visit. Where are you?"

Jothi's directions led Talullah and Dhalian past the ships in port, the ocean breeze caressing Talullah's hair. She almost wished they could have traveled the distance by sea instead of transport tree. The journey would have given her more time to process what had just happened, to let sink in the fact that she'd just cut herself off from her family, maybe forever.

And taunted an evil sorceress to chase her.

Talullah let Dhal take the lead this time, with his multiple maps furling and unfurling while he mumbled to himself. He'd been many places with Master Norr, so his version of traveling was much different from Talullah's. Hers had been borne of necessity and, in the case of her first visit to Praeteriti, a willingness to survive and escape danger.

Now, more than ever, she was glad Dhal was there with her to help her through it, to ground her, and to be a link to home, despite her best efforts to convince him to stay behind.

If she hadn't been too scared to try to use her ruby to See the Certain Future without help, they wouldn't have needed to come to Calla.

Jothi was the only other Sezna Seer Talullah knew. Hopefully, they could help her bring her powers together, or at least lead her to someone who could.

Her mind wandered to the ruby. Again she asked herself how

much her father knew, how much her mother had known before she'd disappeared. What would happen when she added the ruby to her necklace, effectively completing her power? Or at least completing her *potential* for the power. She still had a lot of work to do to figure out how to use all her Sights individually, as well as together.

She wanted so badly just to get it over with, to pop the ruby in and see what would happen. But now more than ever she had to be careful with power she didn't understand. Renevelda would be looking for her. Any misstep could lead the sorceress to her.

The briny wind reminded Talullah of the Isle of Salire and the people she'd lost there. Beck's round face always sported an easy smile. His passion for magic had inspired Talullah. Lynx had been the best female friend Talullah had ever had. She'd welcomed Talullah immediately, without condition. Her pale freckled skin had cloaked a difficult past. But she hadn't let her hardships define her. She'd been warm and kind and, unfortunately, too trusting.

Talullah's throat tightened at their memory. She had failed her friends in the worst way. They'd died because she hadn't been smart enough to figure out Master Eliya's corruption in time to save them from being sacrificed to the Isle's dark spirit.

Talullah sucked her tears back in. She promised herself to use her grief as fuel in avenging her friends, as well as everyone else who had perished at the hands of evil.

She'd been so caught up in her thoughts, she hadn't paid much attention on the walk to the café where they met Jothi.

Her friend leaned against the building's thick white wooden planks, which glittered with threads of magic. Now that Talullah knew to look for the threads, she noticed them everywhere. Maybe these were meant to protect against the wind and salt.

"You hungry?" Jothi asked, smoothing their cream linen pants.

"Not really," Talullah said.

"We should eat anyway," Dhal said, rubbing his wrist.

He was right, of course. But grief had a way of stealing appetites, for food and for other things.

They sat at a wrought-iron table under a large red umbrella on the edge of the patio, which overlooked the port.

"You okay, Dhal?" Talullah's brows knitted together.

"Yeah. It's just my scar."

Jothi leaned closer to take a look. They whistled. "That's quite the mark."

Dhal rolled his wrist. "Yeah, well. Turns out the sorceress likes inflicting pain."

"Have you had anyone check that out?" asked Jothi.

"Haven't had a chance to. It just flared up. Started tingling when we left the castle grounds. I'll be fine." Dhal picked up his glass of water and chugged half of it. "Seriously. I'm fine, you two. Stop staring at me and let's focus on what's important."

Talullah knew Dhal better than anyone else. His pain ran deeper than he was showing. As soon as they figured out what to do, she'd convince him to see a medic.

After a few moments of perusing the menus, Jothi broke the silence. "I'm sorry, Talullah." They sighed.

"For what?" Talullah glanced at them. Her heart squeezed at the look of distress on their face.

"Leaving."

"The Isle? I left too. Why would you have stayed?"

They shrugged. "It just felt sudden, you know? I've been trying to figure out a way to reach out to you that didn't seem contrived or self-serving. But." Jothi clasped their hands in front of them on the table, wholly uncomfortable in a way that Talullah had never seen from them.

Talullah placed her hands on Jothi's. "You are the only reason any of us made it off that Isle alive. You know that, right? I am so grateful to you. I should be the one apologizing. I hope you've been well."

"As well as one can be at the moment."

"What has been going on in the community?" Dhal asked after they ordered their grilled pork and rice.

Jothi took a measured drink of lemonade. "Where to start? Well, there has been a lot of talk about a change in magic. From a potential change to the timelines." They gave Talullah a pointed look. "But you already know about that, I imagine?"

Talullah shifted in her seat. Her fingers scrunched the silky cloth napkin. "You have to understand, it was my sisters' lives at stake. I had no other choice. And trust me, I've paid for it. My loved ones have, too."

Jothi smiled. "Relax, Talullah. I'm not judging. We all have to do the best with what we've got, right? That's kind of the deal with being a Sezna Seer. But I won't lie. Some of the community isn't happy about what you've done."

"What are they saying?"

Jothi faked a cough. "Ah, well…" They sipped their drink again.

"Just tell me. It can't be any worse than what's happening with Renevelda."

"The thing is…the Sezna Seers, and even the Ceserites, if I'm being honest, have enjoyed a comfortable life in their hidden communities. It's a shock to realize that things might be changing. They don't know what to do or what's going to happen now. Some of them think Talullah is working with Renevelda."

Now it was Talullah's turn to be indignant. "Are you serious? There's no way I would ever side with her. She threatened my family multiple times. She invaded my home. The nerve of these people! I have half a mind to march to their houses and demand an explanation about why I'm suddenly a villain when I've been trying to stop her all this time, while *they've* been hiding."

"Don't shoot the messenger. I want you to be prepared for what you're walking into. There are also whispers of some Sezna Seers who might be sympathetic to Renevelda's cause. They believe that if she's in power, like ruling the territories, life will be better for them, because they won't have to hide their power. That she'll allow them to be themselves and they won't have to worry anymore."

Talullah scoffed. "Then those Seers are naïve. Renevelda cares about herself, and that's it. She doesn't care about any other Seers, whether they share her power or not." She ripped a recently-delivered dark brown roll in half and dropped it on her plate.

"You don't have to convince me. But you can't blame them for wanting to believe that a world exists in which they could truly be seen again for who they are, without the threat of exploitation or demonization."

"I understand the desire. But I think there's got to be a different way to achieve that goal. One that doesn't involve bowing to the sorceress. Exploitation is her number one tactic. If she's in power, no one will be safe. Not even Sezna Seers. *Especially* not us. We're a threat to her."

They ate while they discussed. Talullah pushed her food around her plate but took a few bites when she caught Dhal watching.

At the end of the meal, fatigue had steamrolled Talullah's body and brain. How had it only been a few days since she, Dhal, Maeve, and Silas had hatched and executed their plan to infiltrate Castle Viltresor? Renevelda had only just sacrificed Corinne, Prince Alexander's mother. Talullah hadn't even been able to say goodbye to Kai or to clarify whether their friendship was more than that.

She took a sip of her sparkling water and tried to push down the dread. What if she never saw him again?

And what had happened to Maeve and Silas? If Renevelda had captured them, Talullah would never have forgiven herself.

She pressed between her eyes, where a headache had formed.

She couldn't break down now, even though every bone in her body begged her to.

The sun sparkled orange as it set over the water. It was nearly night. They needed a place to rest and regroup.

"Do you have any ideas for safe places to stay?" Talullah asked Jothi.

"A few. But one trumps them all. Come on." After they paid for the meal, Jothi led them through the city center, pointing out the lighthouse, their favorite bakery, the best place to hear live music.

It was a distraction tactic, and Talullah appreciated Jothi's effort. She was sure the city was lovely on a regular day. But all Talullah wanted was a cozy bed.

They continued into the outskirts of the city and to an A-frame cottage made of light brown wood and dark gray stone. Rose bushes lined the cobblestone path walkway to the front door. "This is where Ma and I live."

"I feel so much power here," Talullah said in awe.

"There are a few Seers about. We try not to live in concentrated numbers just in case something goes wrong. The Ceserites, though, tend to stick together. There's a rumor that a bunch of them live in a compound up there." Jothi pointed to the mountain range.

"How does one even get up there?" Dhalian asked, his head tilted back.

"With pluck, luck, and a death wish." Jothi laughed. "In all seriousness, it's possible. But most people don't bother. There are a few guides who take people on excursions up there. Some tour companies even claim to have a tour that looks for the Ceserites' secret worship place, but as far as I know, that's just a scam for collecting tourists' money."

Talullah turned over this information in her mind. The Ceserites didn't want to be found, then.

But to fulfill her power, she'd have to find one willing to train her.

CHAPTER 3

KAI

They'd been in the tunnels for so long that Kai almost couldn't remember what fresh air smelled like. He couldn't believe that people used to live in the tunnels, not just pass through them on their way to escape war or famine or other terrible methods of destruction. He, along with Theresa, Edouard, and Zinni, had been making camp for the better part of a week in the abandoned caverns, some of which held remnants of artifacts from people who had lived there.

Luckily, his companions had been just as keen as he was to skip over the ones that still had bones.

The whole thing gave Kai the creeps. Maybe if he'd been an Urtharian Seer, he could have appreciated the history and the connection to people long forgotten.

He wasn't, though.

He was a Katamian Seer cursed with the anxious tendencies of a Dunamarian.

All he wanted was to get above ground, take a scalding hot bath, and blow the dust out of his sinuses.

Alas.

As they passed yet another of these graveyard caverns, Kai looked away. He had to actively stop himself from thinking about what would happen if they were lost and never made it out.

Would anyone ever find their bones, or would they be lost to history like the rest of these people?

A flush rushed through his body. Kai took a sip of the meager portion of water he had left in his canteen. If they didn't get out of there soon, they would all dehydrate to death. He ruminated on whether that would be worse than starving or being attacked by a wild animal or falling off a cliff or—

Zinni interrupted his spiral of thoughts by nudging him in the side with her sharp elbow. "Don't get lost in your head on me now, Kai. We may have a little while left to go, and if you leave me here with these two, I'm going to do some things my mother would be ashamed of. Please don't make me into that person."

She batted her lashes at him, and Kai couldn't help but laugh out loud. A layer of gray-brown dust, glowing blue in the light from the group's magic, clung to her eyelashes. Kai's laughter echoed off the cave walls.

Theresa turned around abruptly. She shot him a look so severe that if eyes alone could kill, he would have keeled over on the spot and saved himself the agony of comparing the merits of ways to die. "Be. Quiet," Theresa clipped.

"Why?" Zinni asked, her tone reflecting her annoyance.

"Someone could hear," Theresa bit back.

"Who?" Zinni replied. "Nobody else is here. In case you hadn't noticed." She spread her arms wide and looked around the tunnel as if searching for anyone. But of course, they were alone. As they had been since they had descended into the tunnel beneath Castle Viltresor.

"Don't bicker," Kai said. "We'll be quiet. Sorry, Theresa." He shot Zinni a warning glare. She returned it, then rolled her eyes and folded her arms across her chest.

Kai had never wished for varied company more in his life. Normally, he loved being alone. He found it relaxing. And he loved Zinni.

But this was too much.

He'd considered many times over the past few days turning around and walking back the way they'd come just to avoid Zinni and Theresa's jabs at each other as well as Edouard's unhelpful grunting and ambivalence about everything.

Theresa had assured them she knew the way to a safe place where they could rest while they figured out their next move in opposing Renevelda's rise to power. The tunnels were supposed to shield them from the sorceress until they arrived at the utopia Theresa had promised.

By Kai's count, they should have arrived days ago. It seemed like they were walking in circles.

Kai didn't mind the walking. Being so physically tired kept his mind from spiraling into the depths of the terrible places it ached to go. The first two days had been the worst of that. Of thinking about Talullah and where she'd gone and if she was alright. He'd tried unsuccessfully to Scry her. Had she ignored his attempts, or was the reception so poor down in the tunnels that they never went through at all?

At least she hadn't been alone as she fled Castle Viltresor. Though the thought of Talullah and her friend—Kai wouldn't let himself think more of Talullah and Dhalian's relationship than that now—on the run from the sorceress couldn't be comforting at all.

Traveling had been hard. Much harder than he'd ever thought it would be. And their meager rations were running out. They needed to get to a safe location to rest properly and refuel and, hopefully, meet up with some other Seers who could help them formulate a plan.

Despite everything, Kai was grateful that he wasn't alone. The only thing worse than being stuck in a seemingly endless series of tunnels underground would be weathering it solo. Though Kai wasn't claustrophobic, thank the goddesses.

Not like Zinni.

He'd caught his best friend shivering a few times as she tried to breathe expansively in the small spaces they'd traveled through. He'd counted with her as they walked and helped her keep her breath.

Though, if Zinni didn't stop baiting Theresa, Kai didn't know what would happen.

"Let's rest for a minute," Kai said, trying to break the tension between them and to redirect to something more positive. "We have to have made some good progress."

They all shuffled into what looked to have once been a room and pulled out some food rations.

Kai swallowed the tough bite of bread that tried to lodge itself in his throat. He washed it down with a swig of stale water and winced.

"What food are you looking forward to the most when we get out of here?" he asked Zinni.

She closed her eyes and licked her lips. "You know that white cake with the berries your mom always made for my birthday?"

Kai's stomach grumbled in response. "The one with the fluffy cream in between the layers?"

"Yes, that one. If we ever get out of here, I want to eat that for every meal for a week." Zinni opened her eyes and ripped off a bite of stale bread, smiling even as her jaw worked to break down the inferior food. "I'm just going to pretend this is cake."

If we ever get out.

Kai trusted Theresa. He did. In the general sense, at least. He didn't believe she'd willingly let harm come to them. But the longer they spent together, the more he realized how little he knew about her. He had no idea if her planning skills would translate well into leading a rebellion, but it might be a bit too late to be questioning that.

After Renevelda seized control of Castle Viltresor and forced King William and Prince Alexander into hiding, there wasn't much time to think about anything beyond survival. It was either join Theresa and Edouard or stay and be used or killed by the sorceress.

Had Talullah asked him to come with her, he would have in less than a heartbeat.

But she hadn't asked.

Now that they'd been walking so long, Kai didn't know how to get out of the tunnels alone even if he did want to leave the group. He was stuck. At least until they reached a place the sun touched.

Which he hoped would happen soon. His eyes had started playing tricks on him in the dark. Despite his and his companions' magic light, the tunnels still conjured shadows that made him question his own sanity.

"You sure you know where you're taking us?" Zinni asked. She peered over Theresa's shoulder as the older—by a few years—and shorter group leader studied the map.

"Of course, I do," Theresa snapped. Her round eyes softened. She adjusted her bright purple headscarf, which, like everything else, had turned gray with filth. "Sorry. I'm just hungry." It showed. Her normally golden skin had turned ashen with fatigue.

"Same," said Edouard, who, if Kai wasn't mistaken, had already lost a few pounds. A hulking boulder of a man, Kai assumed Edouard needed to consume at least twice, if not three times, as many calories per day as Kai himself. He couldn't possibly be getting nearly enough. None of them were.

"We're all hungry," Zinni said. "But that doesn't change the fact that it feels like we're nowhere nearer to our destination than when we started out. Let me see this." Zinni grabbed the map before Theresa could protest, but then the leader just waved her on.

"Go ahead. Maybe you can make more sense of it. I'm going to close my eyes for a minute." She leaned her head against the nearest wall.

Kai moved to Zinni's side and, along with Edouard, peered at the map.

Its lines were wavy, like it had been drawn in haste. No wonder they hadn't gotten anywhere. The map was incomplete.

"Where did you get this?" Kai asked, careful to keep any judgment out of his voice. The last thing he needed was to anger her.

Theresa sighed deeply, her eyes still closed. "If I tell you, you're going to hate me."

"Theresa. Where?" Zinni asked.

"I guess it can't do any more harm than what I've already done." She leaned forward and opened her eyes. "I saw it in a dream."

For a moment, the tunnel went deathly silent. Kai's own mind whirred.

Zinni spoke first. Well, more like seethed. The words pushed out like the first flow of magma before a volcano erupts. "You. Saw. It. In. A. Dream. A *dream*? And you thought this was a strong basis for building a rebellion?" She shook the map.

"I saw a way out of that castle, a way to get out alive, and I took it. I've been having this same dream for years. Piece by piece this shape came to me. I'm a Dual, with both Katamai's and Cesera's blessings. My inevitable visions always come to me in dreams, though I can clarify and amplify them by using Cesera's tools. When King William asked Kai and Edouard to make the ledger, I knew we'd need an escape route. This was the best I could come up with.

"And my dreams kept coming, kept clarifying. I don't think it was just my Future Sight helping us escape. I think it's speaking to something bigger. Ceserites have been reading messages in the sky for centuries, predicting big changes reflected in the pattern of the stars. I've been seeing this same pattern of constellations for years. There's the big dipper, a bird, and a few others I haven't deciphered yet."

"You think this map isn't just a map of the physical tunnels," Edouard said. "You think it's a prophecy?"

"Yes." Theresa bit her lip.

"What else aren't you telling us?" Zinni asked. She ran her hands through her poofs of black hair that were also covered in dust.

"C'mon, Theresa. We have to be able to trust each other. Otherwise this isn't going to work." Kai tried to put as much calmness as he could muster into his voice.

Theresa looked up at the ceiling, muttering something to herself, before meeting the group's attention again. "Okay." She blew out a breath. "The map doesn't always stay the same."

"What does that mean?" Zinni asked. "Didn't you draw it?"

"It means, it changes. Sometimes, I'll look at the map, and we'll be following a straight path and then suddenly there's a fork that didn't exist an hour ago. I drew the original, but my lines keep shifting."

Kai choked on his water. "Is it just the map that's changing, Theresa? Or are the tunnels changing, too?"

"Impossible to know for sure. I didn't say anything because I didn't want to freak anyone out. But now *I'm* kind of freaking out, and I have no idea what to do." She pressed her fists to her eyes. Tears streamed from them freely. How long had she been holding them in?

"We'll figure it out," Kai said. He touched the tips of each of his fingers on his left hand to his thumb in succession, a way to focus his brain and not let himself spiral. "Could it be an illusion? A way for the tunnels to protect themselves? Or to protect something within them? Maybe we can think of a different way to navigate."

Theresa sniffled. "It's possible it's reacting to my Future Sight, since the image came in a dream. Or the Sights might be crossing each other. Like, my Present Sight is trying to keep us in the moment or fight the illusion, but my Future Sight won't let it. Maybe they're trying to lead us to two different endpoints."

"Why don't you let someone else hold it for a while? We'll see if that helps. I'll go first. Since I only have Present Sight, maybe that will keep us grounded in our goal of escape instead of wherever else your Future Sight may want us to go." Externally, Kai projected confidence, because what else could he do?

Internally, his brain was on fire. All the alarms sounded. Begged him to evacuate.

We're going to die here.

CHAPTER 4

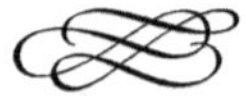

RENEVELDA

The Davabere Needle was a good start to her plan. And now that Talullah had confirmed the goddesses' tapestry wasn't just a myth, Renevelda was determined to find and use it to locate the Source of Sight magic.

The natural well that gave the goddesses themselves their powers, which trickled down to everyone else.

Whoever controlled the Source could use the power to create the world they wished to live in.

Unfortunately, though she was already more powerful than most Seers, Renevelda needed more magic to ensure she could control the Source. Legend said it could consume a person who was unworthy of wielding it.

Renevelda was many things. *Unworthy* would never be one of them.

The sorceress swept through Castle Viltresor, past the

unlucky servants who hadn't managed to escape during her takeover.

One such girl flinched as the train of Renevelda's deep plum dress grazed her worn leather boots.

Renevelda rolled her eyes and touched the girl's shoulder, speaking a Manipulation spell over her. "Go make yourself useful."

The girl bowed, her eyes swirling blue with the spell, then fled down the hall in the opposite direction.

"Now, where would he keep it?" Renevelda asked herself. King William had been up to his own kind of mischief before Renevelda had stolen his throne and his home. And it was just the kind of thing that could help the sorceress get what she wanted.

Renevelda shuffled through the papers in the king's office and private chambers but didn't find what she sought.

The ledger was a record of those who possessed Sight magic in Viltresor. And, as it turned out, she needed to locate some Seers. Stealing their magic was the quickest way to amplify her own and prove her worth to the Source.

After a few moments of fruitless searching, Renevelda retreated to her favorite divination room to gather supplies for her memory access spell. Doing things manually was so tedious she didn't know why she even bothered.

Magic was always quicker.

She closed her eyes as a breeze blew through the cracked window, bringing with it the scent of summer. She'd never liked the heat, and her magic had always thrived better in the cooler months.

For now, she placed one hand on the table and the other on the bronze hourglass she used for grounding. Renevelda closed her eyes and invited the castle's memories to reveal themselves to her.

Pulling memories from a living being was more straightforward than reading a place. To permeate someone's mind was as simple as inserting a key into a lock. There was only one layer of defense to get past: the person's will. Often, their will was so pathetic it took merely a suggestion to convince them to let her in.

Places worked differently. With so many histories tangled together, Seeing and making sense of those memories was more like untying a series of knots or chiseling away sediment one layer at a time.

At least, that's how it worked for her. She'd never bothered to ask about anyone else's experience.

Renevelda let her mind sink into the castle's recent history housed within the walls and searched for any sign of the ledger. With each layer she removed, Renevelda's annoyance grew.

"Boring, boring, boring," she mused as she swiped the useless memories aside like cobwebs.

Until one caught her attention. Its energy sparked with something special. Renevelda's brows lifted as she recognized the boy she had nearly killed, the one who seemed enamored with Talullah for some unknown reason. Well, the *other boy*. Alexander's assistant. In the memory, he wrote in a large book with sparkling paper.

The magic reverberated even through the memory.

Renevelda focused her energy on the paper's contents. It was a list. A smudgy, glittering fingerprint had been pressed next to each name.

The purple tint of the past made it impossible to tell whether the fingerprints were made with ink or something else. Though their glittering quality made the corners of Renevelda's lips turn up.

She'd bet anything they'd been made with blood. Which meant this was what she'd been searching for. The record of magic users, complete with their type of magic, indicated by the spelled paper that reacted to their blood.

This book would make her work much quicker. She needed to pursue those with the highest concentration of magic, and the more Duals and Triads and, if she was lucky, Sezna Seers she collected, the quicker she could siphon their power with the Davabere Needle.

"Where did you hide it?" she asked the boy in the memory. He couldn't hear her, of course.

She searched through the castle's memories until she came to one where a young woman wearing a headscarf and a burly-looking man talked together. They'd wedged themselves in a crowded corner of an office. The ledger lay open between them, poised on a marble table and hidden behind an arrangement of lilacs. As if the flowers could conceal a man of that stature.

Then the burly man closed the ledger and shoved it in a leather bag before the two people fled the room and parted ways.

Renevelda's chest tightened. She recognized the young woman. She'd fought against the sorceress during the wedding celebration.

If only she'd known then they possessed the ledger, she would have made sure to take it.

It would take time to track them down. Cleo, her faithful hawk companion, could do that. And there was still the matter of finding the tapestry. Talullah—ever the needle in Renevelda's shoe—had flaunted a piece of it. Renevelda would need to collect it from her eventually.

Even if the sorceress amassed enough power to appease the Source, she still had to find the sacred place.

In the meantime, perhaps she could convince the Seers to come to her.

Inviting weaker beings to share her home gave her shivers. But, she needed to fight against her usual desire for isolation and instead build her own army from the bits that King William had already collected.

Was that the former king's plan when he'd ordered the ledger to be made? Or had he desired to snuff out all the power that was right under his nose?

What a waste, if so.

His fear would be his undoing.

While Renevelda didn't hold as strong a vendetta against him as she'd had for his brother, her ex-husband—may he rest in pieces at the bottom of the sea—she wanted to eradicate the whole family line. William's queen Corinne's power had started Renevelda on this path, and there was no looking back.

Cleo soared through the door and landed on the table.

"What news do you bring, my dear?" Renevelda stroked the bird's head.

Cleo dropped a shell onto the table. Renevelda picked it up, studying it. Then, she used the same spell to sink into its memories.

The ocean breeze. Ships at port. The mountains in the near distance.

Renevelda smiled as she came out of the memory. "This confirms my suspicions. They're in Calla. Good work." She offered Cleo a little treat from her hand. "Rumor has it the Ceserites live in those mountains. I wonder if the young Seer seeks a mentor."

The bird squawked, then flew off again, probably to find a more sustainable dinner.

Renevelda tucked this information away in her mind and then went down to the cellar.

The prisoner sat where Renevelda had left her. The Seer had proved herself to be a challenge. She hadn't wanted to come, of course. In the end, Renevelda had broken her with the one weakness that Renevelda herself would never succumb to. She'd threatened the woman's family.

The woman greeted her with a harsh stare that Renevelda could almost respect.

She spat at the sorceress's feet and didn't say a word as

Renevelda unlocked the gate of her cage. Cuffs on the woman's arms kept her magic inaccessible. A flicker of fear crossed her stoic expression when Renevelda pulled the Davabere Needle from its pouch.

"Do you know what this is?" Renevelda asked. The woman just stared, not giving her the satisfaction of an answer.

But Renevelda didn't need the ego boost. She didn't dawdle. Instead, she closed the short distance between them and, as she'd done with Corinne, pressed the tip of the needle against the Seer's shoulder.

The magic seeped from the captive into the needle, making the object glow. Renevelda didn't know what kind of magic this woman had, but at this point it didn't much matter.

The brighter the needle grew, the dimmer the light in the Seer's eyes became. The life drained from her face, making her already light skin even paler. She collapsed to the floor with one final groan.

A raspy breath rattled out of the woman before she lifted her head off the floor just enough to speak her last strangled words. "Sacrifice, Seer, and master of flight, in unity prevail. And transform magic with immortal light, in control of threaded grail."

A shiver ran up Renevelda's spine.

The Seer collapsed onto the floor, unmoving.

Prophecy, then, a Ceserite Gift. Good to know.

Renevelda headed toward the stairs, already wondering how much power the Needle could hold. "Guards?" she called, focused on the needle in her hand without a spare thought for either the Seer she'd just killed or the woman's final words. She gestured to the dead woman on her way up. "Take care of that."

CHAPTER 5

TALULLAH

Talullah and Dhalian spent the next morning exploring Calla while Jothi went to the market for their mother.

Jothi hadn't left them empty-handed, though.

Dhalian whistled as he flipped through the book of maps, each page with varying degrees of detail.

While he studied a page of the capital city, Talullah took in the natural surroundings. Two mountains loomed high overhead, both imposing presences, but not altogether unwelcome ones. They simultaneously made Talullah feel as small as a grain of sand and alive with possibility. If the rumors were true, somewhere in those mountains was a Ceserite Seer compound, and she and Dhal were determined to find it.

Stopping Renevelda depended on it.

Talullah marveled at the fact that while it was warm in the foothills, snow glistened atop the highest mountain peaks.

"It rarely gets above forty degrees up there," Dhal said.

"According to these notes." Jothi had also given them a traveler's guide full of factoids and tidbits about the area, including local shops, restaurants, and inns that would be interesting to tourists.

But Talullah didn't care about any of that. "Does it say anything about the magical community?" Other parts of the world had less strict views on magic than her home country, with its divided rulers, one of whom had despised and feared magic so much he'd oppressed an entire community, and the other who'd tried to collect as much magic as possible for himself, to the near detriment of society.

"Not much here about that," Dhalian said. His hazel eyes sparked. "Though, it could be in code. There have been other communities throughout history who used secrets to help their citizens find safety."

"It's possible. I assume if the Ceserites wanted to be found, they wouldn't have situated their community on a mountain. We'll just have to be smart about how we go about looking for them," Talullah said. "We don't want to draw attention to ourselves. Like Jothi said, I don't know which of these Seers might be sympathetic to Renevelda or which might think I'm on her side."

Dhal nodded. "Let's go to the market first. Get something to eat and see what we can find out."

Public events were a great way to observe people and to try to understand how they functioned as a society. Did people haggle, or were the prices firm? What kind of quality goods did they sell, and were there places to get specialty or rare items? Communities traded in goods, but the real value was in information. The kind that wouldn't be in a travel guide.

It was strange not to have to worry about covering her magic here. It hung thick in Calla's air, like a natural perfume. Everyone's magic auras mixed, and all of the scents complemented each other.

Each kind of Sight magic had its own distinct quality. Though she couldn't see the colored auras like some others could, Talullah could appreciate how overwhelming it must be to sense magic in that way.

Even with her own limited ability to notice it, fatigue had already set in, and they hadn't yet crossed into the market in earnest.

Stalls and merchants enveloped the entire city center. More densely-packed than the Hidden Market, there was no space to slip between the stalls divided by thick, taupe canvas tarps. Rather than a mélange of goods, these stalls were organized by category. One corner housed the food, where vibrant orange and yellow citrus shared tables with plump berries and crisp lettuce.

Headless fish stacked three high shone silver atop the fishmongers' tables. The fresh catch of the day, just hauled up from the boats docked in the harbor, scented the air.

Ten barrels of dried legumes in all shades of brown, fried dough dipped in sugar, live chickens strutting in pens.

Textile workers and other artisans set up in another corner selling patterned skirts, soft tunics, and bold, beaded jewelry.

Pottery, housewares, linens, shoes.

The market went on forever. Anything a person could want—and afford—was available. The bustle reminded her of the festival she'd attended with Kai in the square at Viltresor City.

Talullah's heart squeezed with worry for him. She'd tried to Scry a few times, but she'd never gotten through. Was he okay? Did he and Theresa and the rest make it out of the castle? When her mind wandered, it was easy to let the uncertainty take control. She pressed her sapphire and remained calm. If they'd retreated underground, the earth could interrupt the Scry signal. No news was good news in this case.

Maybe if she kept telling herself that, she'd start to believe it.

"Look at this," Dhal said, pointing to a puffy overcoat lined with fur. "And those boots are huge."

"Going up the mountain?" the merchant asked. He nodded toward the peak. "If so, you need to stay warm. I'll give you a good price."

"Not today, sorry," Talullah said. She forced a smile. "But I'm sure we'll be back. Can you recommend a tour guide?"

The merchant's gray eyes brightened. "Of course! What do you want to see? Waterfalls? Hot springs? The meadows are beautiful this time of year. Perhaps a romantic getaway for the young couple?" His smile stretched wide.

"Oh! No. It's not like that," Talullah said, flustered.

"Right. Yeah. We're not—" Dhal added.

The merchant held up his hands, still smiling. "Sure, sure. I understand." He winked at Dhal, who shifted on his feet.

"So," Dhal said, "We heard there might be a Ceserite community up there somewhere."

"Ah," the merchant replied. His smile faded. "Unfortunately, the tour is on hiatus for now."

"Why's that?" Talullah asked.

"Too dangerous right now. I'm sure you understand."

"Has something happened?" Talullah pressed. "We've only just arrived. We've been traveling for a while. Didn't get much news on the way."

"I'm sorry. I have some other customers to tend to. If you'll excuse me." A mischievous glint returned to his eyes as he met Dhal's gaze. "And just let me know if you change your mind about any of the excursions. I know a great guide." He winked again.

"That was weird, right?" Talullah whispered as she and Dhal passed the rest of the clothing merchants and popped into a food stall to order breakfast.

Talullah couldn't help but notice the way Dhal had tensed when the merchant had mentioned the romantic getaway. Was he embarrassed to have the merchant mistake his relationship with

Talullah? Or had he—like Talullah—imagined what it would be like if their stroll through the market *was* a date?

"So," Dhal said, after swallowing his final bite of his spiced meat hand pie, "what if we start over here?"

Talullah had forced down her own, despite her nerves still being heightened.

He pointed to a spot on the map, but Talullah's attention was drawn to the group of people sitting close to them who spoke in loud whispers. Three were male-presenting, two female.

"Wait, Dhal. I heard something."

Talullah traced her eye charm and pressed on her sapphire to dial up her sense of hearing so that she could more clearly make out what they were saying. She refused to call it eavesdropping. Because if she had heard the word "assassinate" like she thought she had, this could have something to do with Renevelda. Or whatever the merchant had alluded to earlier.

"You're sure?" one man asked. He raised a brow so blond it nearly blended into his pale skin.

"Yes. Nadine DuPoint has been missing for days now," a deeper voice answered. His back was to Talullah, but he tossed his long white hair over his shoulder as he spoke. "Didn't show up to the treaty council meeting. And she's not the only one. People are saying it was the Katamians."

"No!" Two more shocked voices responded together. In tandem, the two young women—they looked like twins—lifted teacups to their deep brown lips.

"They wouldn't. Especially not after what happened on The Isle," the blond man said.

"Or maybe that's exactly why they did it," White Hair argued.

"But why target the Ceserites?" the woman with the long black braids asked.

"Why not?" White Hair answered. "Only takes one to break the treaty."

"Wouldn't she have Seen them coming, though? Seems risky to kidnap someone with Future Sight, right?" The second woman pursed her lips and tucked her sleek black bob behind her ears, revealing dangling gold earrings.

"Doesn't matter one way or the other, does it? Fact is, she's gone. And people are pointing fingers." The white-haired man took a large bite of a thick biscuit.

Talullah's heart sped up. Had the factions turned on each other already?

"Are the Urtharians worried?" Gold Earrings asked.

"As much as anyone," White Hair replied. "It wasn't us, by the way. We remember what happened all too well. There's no reason for us to start any trouble now."

These people weren't all from the same faction, then. That was good. At least some of them were still being civil. But for how long? What would it take for this group to turn on each other?

"Such a shame. You think she's...dead? She's got a family." Pity filled Long Braids' brown eyes.

"I hope not," White Hair said. "But honestly, it's not looking good."

Gold Earrings swallowed hard and addressed the last of the group, the man with light blond hair that was shaved to the upper tips of his ears and longer on top. "You think the sorceress will help?"

Wait, what? No. They couldn't want Renevelda to rise. It would be catastrophic for everyone. They couldn't believe Renevelda wanted to help anyone, could they? What did the rest of the world even know about the sorceress? Most had never met or even seen her. What kind of persona had she invented to gain trust?

If enough people believed her, that lie might prove more dangerous than the truth.

The man had been quiet throughout the whole conversation

until now. He placed his palms flat on the table and answered in a calm, smooth voice. "It's about time one of our own came into a position of power again. It's what we've been waiting for. A true chance to reunite."

The factions wanted to come back together? That was good. It's what the goddesses wanted when they'd bestowed their Gifts.

The last man rubbed the back of his neck, where black ink swirled in a shape Talullah couldn't make out from her position. "We could take our true place in society."

Talullah drew a sharp inhale. *Take our place in society.* Did that mean he thought the factions should rule?

"Well, I think it's ridiculous." Gold Earrings sipped her teacup again. "There's no way she's as powerful as they're saying. And even if she was, how can we be certain that she would do what she promises?"

Long Braids nodded in agreement. "I think we need more information before we start pledging allegiance to anyone."

That's a relief. They didn't seem totally convinced. Talullah strained to listen as another group of people passed, their chatter interfering with Talullah's magic.

"You really think having a Sezna Seer in high command is a good idea? You know what they've done in the past. It'd be much better, in my opinion, to have a council made up of all four Sights. Much more balanced, like the goddesses wanted." White Hair spoke with conviction, like someone who'd thought about it for more than two minutes. Maybe there was still time to show Seers who Renevelda truly was.

"She's already making moves." Blond Brows waved a piece of parchment in the air. He cleared his throat. "By royal decree, any Seers who feel threatened by the recent attack on the Ceserite community may seek asylum at Castle Viltresor. The Castle will provide lodging and necessities in exchange for light service. All Sight factions are welcome. Many open positions and rooms are ready to be filled."

Talullah wobbled, dizzy all the sudden. Renevelda would never take care of anyone without another motive. Why would she invite Seers to the castle?

It hit her like lightning. Her stomach swooped as if she'd missed a step.

The Davabere Needle.

Renevelda needed more power. What she'd taken from Corinne hadn't been enough. And now she'd lured in unsuspecting Seers with the promise of protection.

The voices faded as the group paid and moved out of Talullah's range of hearing.

"So?" Dhal said. His leg bounced up and down. "What's the big news?"

Talullah told him what she'd overheard. "What concerns me the most is the argument that Renevelda could be good for the Sight community. They clearly don't know who she is, what she's done, or what she's capable of."

Talullah wanted to follow the group, to tell them they shouldn't trust Renevelda, that they didn't know the death and destruction the sorceress had caused.

Then she remembered what Jothi had told her. That some people thought *Talullah* was the one to blame.

She couldn't reveal what she knew without compromising her identity. It wouldn't be safe to do that until she had a plan in place to take down Renevelda and had figured out who else wanted to stand against the sorceress.

Though Talullah didn't know the extent of Renevelda's plans, she was certain they wouldn't benefit anyone but the sorceress herself. The more she thought about it, the more sense it made that the sorceress's invitation was a way to lure Seers to the castle so she could steal their power.

The tapestry square burned a hole in her pocket. Talullah

had seen a similar image on Gillie the Wood Faerie's wall the first time she'd been in his tree house. Could it be the same one?

Renevelda wanted it too, for some reason. What could it do for her? And how did it connect to the power the sorceress wanted to collect?

Dhalian touched her wrist gently, and Talullah snapped her attention up to his face. "If there are already rumblings about Renevelda's dealings on this side of the world, we have bigger problems than we thought."

Word had traveled faster than she thought possible to the other continent, across the ocean.

What if Renevelda's plan was to position herself as the only one who could bring the Sight factions together and offer them the status they thought they deserved?

The sorceress wasn't known for her desire to create peace among anyone, nor was she particularly interested in having a strong community. She'd always looked out for herself, preferring to burn bridges rather than build them.

If Talullah could build a bridge between the Sight factions, maybe she could convince them to turn against Renevelda.

There were so many things to figure out. And not enough time to do so.

Dhal seemed to understand. "What do we do first?"

Start with the past, Aurinia had written in her journal. It had been advice meant for finding the emerald, but it rang true in this case, too. Maybe even more so.

She had to go all the way back to the beginning. To the tapestry.

"We need to figure out what this tapestry is and why Renevelda wants it."

"I think we need to go see Gillie," Dhal said.

Talullah sighed. Gillie wasn't exactly her biggest fan. "What if he hasn't forgiven me?"

"We won't know until we ask. He's the only one we know who's seen a tapestry like this."

Dhal was right. Still, the thought of laying herself at the mercy of the Wood Faerie once again was humiliating. He'd already done so much. Could she justify asking more of him?

"Tules. Let's just try."

"Fine. But if he turns us away, you owe me the biggest bowl of ice cream we can find."

CHAPTER 6

MARGOT

Margot entered the River Hill Library and laughed to herself. Never in her wildest dreams did she think she'd be spending most of her free time at the library. That was more her older sister Talullah's style, not Margot's.

She preferred to be out in the sunshine or in the kitchen, but there she was among the books that made her sneeze. Ever since she'd noticed something strange with the town's protective spell, she hadn't been able to let go of the thought that her sister had had something to do with it. It couldn't be a coincidence that Margot had experienced a vision of Talullah at the exact moment she'd tugged the barrier's loose prophecy thread.

Something weird was going on. There had been fewer visitors to the town recently. There never were many, but often families who lived there had some contacts on the outside who would occasionally, after being sworn to secrecy, come to visit. That had pretty much stopped.

Talullah had done some incredible things over the past year, but Margot couldn't help but think if the situation turned more dangerous, she could lose her sister as well as her mother.

That was why, she had to remind herself, she was spending her free time researching the barrier to figure out what had changed and why.

Because something had changed.

The barrier's magic no longer only reached for her when she neared it, as she did on her way home from school every day. Now she sensed it in the air, like an impending storm she could perceive but couldn't see.

It had all the hallmarks of Sight magic, which interested her less because of her sister and more because her mother had had magic as well.

As Margot entered the thick wooden doors, she waved hello to the front desk librarian, whose dollop of white hair reminded Margot of whipped cream atop a sundae.

Margot adjusted the pack on her back. It was mostly empty now, but she imagined that by the end of the morning, she would have many books to look through.

She'd done well, so far, to hide her own abilities, which had bloomed later than Talullah's, a fact that made Margot grumpy.

She wanted to explore them on her own for a while first, and she couldn't help think that maybe her powers were coming to light now because of the barrier. That perhaps the two events were connected somehow.

Margot had become obsessed with the barrier in the past week. Scraps of the vision of Talullah in danger had haunted her dreams. She missed her older sister—though she would die before ever admitting it—but that couldn't be the cause of the dreams. The barrier had communicated to Margot. Had maybe even chosen her to help.

Maybe it was a silly theory, but she had to find out. Besides, reading wouldn't do any harm. Talullah was always droning on and on about how powerful books were. How information was the strongest currency. How it built up societies or let them fall.

Information was another kind of power. Margot had promised herself she would do everything she could to ensure her survival no matter what happened.

She headed to the history section of the library in search of books on the history of River Hill. The town had to have records detailing the way the Founders had found this uninhabited piece of land and had claimed it as their own. How the magic users among them had protected the town to hide it from both kingdoms, which were at war at the time.

Margot didn't necessarily find the history of her town's founding particularly riveting, but maybe she could learn about the original protection spell, and from there, discern what had changed.

A few hours passed. She'd skimmed through a stack of nearly twenty different books without a single mention of the stuff she was looking for.

Then she remembered the special book Talullah had brought back from the realm of the past. *That* was where she needed to go. She needed the unedited and true record of the historical events. Plus, that library would likely have more information about the magic that was used.

Her hopes crumbled immediately. She didn't have a special amulet like her sister, so she couldn't travel through the Four Worlds the way Talullah did. Not that Talullah had ever mentioned exactly how she did it in the first place.

Maybe Margot could find a historian in her own realm. That could work. Maybe there was someone in Viltresor City who had Past Sight who could help her. But how would she even find such a person?

That wouldn't work if she couldn't get past the barrier.

Margot tugged her blond hair out of its bun and shook it loose. She raked her hands through it, thinking. Everything came back to the barrier. If she couldn't break the spell, she couldn't get out to warn Talullah.

She groaned, drawing a glare from a gangly library assistant in suspenders shelving books across the room.

Margot glared right back. There was no one else around her. Her frustration wasn't bothering anyone but her.

He continued to stare, so Margot smirked and slammed her book closed. She relished the way he winced at the sound. Satisfied that her pettiness had hit its mark, Margot headed back down to the reception desk to ask the head librarian.

"Excuse me," she said, coating her voice in as much sugar as she could manage.

"Oh, hello there," the librarian replied. She slid her red wireframe glasses down to the tip of her thin nose. "How can I help you?"

"I'm looking for some books for a school project. About the founding of River Hill."

As the librarian nodded, the dollop of white hair bobbed back and forth. "Yes, yes, of course. We keep the original manuscripts back here in the archive. Is that what you're looking for?"

"Yes, that'd be great, thanks."

"We don't allow these to be taken home. Have to preserve their integrity, of course. But you're welcome back there while the library is open. Follow me." The librarian, a woman barely taller than Margot, ambled to the door behind her. She used a black skeleton key to unlock it and ushered Margot inside the room, which could have been confused for a storage closet.

Dust tickled her nose, but she stifled her sneeze. By the looks of these books, the slightest breeze might destroy them. The oil lamps in the corners were nearly out of fuel, but they provided enough light to see by.

"Let me know if you need anything else, dear." The librarian closed the door behind her, leaving Margot alone.

More than a hundred wooden drawers were set into the walls.

"Better get started," Margot groaned to herself. She pulled the handle of the drawer nearest her and slid it out. Inside, a single tome of at least six hundred pages glared up at her. Muscles straining beneath the weight, Margot hefted the book out and onto the table, trying not to let it slam on the square worktable.

She peeled back the sturdy cover and thumbed through the delicate pages, which were covered top to bottom in tiny script. "This is going to take forever."

Why wasn't there a spell for finding what she was looking for?

Magic.

Of course.

Why hadn't she thought about using her new skills before?

She tapped her fingers on the table as she thought. But what use would Manipulation magic be? She'd succeeded in changing the color of small items, but that would only be good if she were trying to hide something not find it.

Margot wet her lips and paced up and down the aisle. She opened each drawer and peered at its contents. The same style book, each as thick as the last, filled them all.

Maybe she needed to use her other Gift. But prophecy would only help if she was destined to find a useful book in that room.

Things would have been so much easier if she'd had Urtha's Gift of Past Sight.

And she'd only ever had that one prophecy, about Talullah.

Forty-seven.

That part of the vision still made less sense than the rest. But the smell she'd experience then…it was so similar to the one tickling her nose now.

Margot studied the drawer nearest her again. This time, a brass plate at the bottom right corner caught her eye.

8.

She scanned the other drawers. A numbered plate was affixed to each one.

Margot moved until she found the number she sought.

47.

Margot eased open the drawer, daring to hope. It was empty. Of course it couldn't be that easy.

But she wasn't ready to give up yet.

She reached into the drawer, expecting to find only air. But her fingers grazed something her eyes couldn't see. Smooth, maybe leather?

Warmth spread through her fingertips, as if something inside her was searching the object for recognition. Or maybe the opposite was true. Maybe the hidden object was searching *her.* Perhaps for worthiness?

Now it was time to practice revealing illusions. Gently, Margot rested her fingertips atop the item and coaxed her power forward.

"Come on," she whispered. "Show me your secrets."

The drawer flickered. And then it was no longer empty.

Margot gasped.

The leather-bound book was half the size of all the others. A gold scripted title covered most of the brown cover, but Margot couldn't read it. It wasn't written in the common language, which was strange. Once again, Margot rolled her eyes. Talullah would be useful to have around about now. Her sister had been obsessed with languages ever since she was a child.

Maybe some of Talullah's knowledge had seeped into Margot's own subconscious. Founders knew Margot had heard Talullah practicing enough.

Did the librarian know the book was there? Had she been the one to hide it from view? Or had someone else, and regardless, why?

Margot ran her fingers across the front of the book. A spark of curiosity ran through her. Everything had been written in the common tongue since River Hill's founding. Why not this? Unless, of course, it was not supposed to be in this library at all.

Fire lit inside her at that thought. At the thought that maybe someone had placed this book here on purpose. Maybe it had been left for her to find. Maybe this was where *her* destiny began.

Excitement and fear ran through her. She'd never felt called to do anything. But this book called to her as if it knew her. She would indulge it in whatever secrets it wanted to share with her.

Margot took a deep breath and opened the front cover of the book. She couldn't quite make out all the words, but the longer she stared at the pages as she flipped through them, the more her brain adjusted. Was the book translating itself for her? Or maybe this was another part of her magic.

That thrilled her enough to unfold a smile from lips.

Or maybe she was fatiguing, and her mind was filling in things that seemed to make sense but were nonsense. She'd almost given up hope that this would bring any sort of clarity when she turned another page.

A folded piece of parchment was tucked inside. It wasn't attached. Had someone made notes and left them? When Margot unfolded it, she furrowed her blond brows. It was a star chart about the size of a few dinner plates put together.

Margot's Sight magic tingled as it recognized the magic that had been used to create it. In the back of her mind, a red image flashed.

Talullah grabbing the red feather.

As quickly as it came, the image was gone. Margot looked back at the star chart. In the corner, a hand-drawn feather stared back at her.

A zap of intrigue ran from her fingers down to her toes.

That had to mean something. There was a connection between the star chart and her vision, and possibly the barrier.

Now she was getting somewhere.

Through the window, the sky darkened. It was getting late. Her father didn't like it when she stayed out past dark.

Again, Margot groaned. She'd finally found something inter-esting and potentially useful. She wasn't ready to leave her research, but she couldn't miss curfew if she wanted the ability to test her theories.

Glancing around, she bit the inside of her cheek. The librarian had said she couldn't check out the archives. But… nothing on the book indicated it belonged in these archives or even this library. No markings or stamps of ownership or anything. No one would miss it. No one was supposed to even know it was there.

She folded the star chart, placed it in the book where'd she'd found it, and nestled the book into her knapsack beneath her extra sweater.

If it didn't belong to the library, there was no reason to tell the librarian about it. It was none of her business what informa-tion she learned from it. And she couldn't risk anyone confis-cating her only lead.

Later that night, beneath her magenta and aqua striped quilt, she pulled out the star map and studied the symbols. What would it be like to be able to read someone's destiny based on the posi-tion of the stars at any given moment? Would her own chart reveal she was as average as she felt when she compared herself to her older sister? Or could there perhaps be something else waiting for her, a grander design than she'd ever thought possible?

Margot stared at the stars on the chart. Was this a person's birth chart? Did it map an event?

What if this was a sign from her mother, left especially for Margot to find?

She couldn't even remember what her mother looked like. She'd disappeared when Margot was barely a toddler and Penny was still a baby. They only had a few portraits of her in the house, and it made Margot's heart ache so much not to know that part of herself. She'd wanted for so long to be in contact with her mother. A wish buried deep in Margot's soul whispered she was still alive somewhere.

But if that were true, why hadn't she come home? Why had she stayed away so long?

Margot wanted to believe with her whole heart that her mother had left her something, anything. Talullah had gotten the Eye necklace and the loom. What had Margot and Penny got?

Absence.

Whether or not the star chart was from her mother didn't matter in truth. All that mattered was figuring out its connection to her vision and to the barrier.

Margot would figure it out. And maybe, just maybe, *she* would be the hero for once.

CHAPTER 7

KAI

"The main tunnels are still the same." Kai studied the map for the zillionth time, aching to be out in the sun with the fresh air beating him in the face.

Theresa had delegated navigation duties to him over the past few days. It helped quell his anxiety, sort of, to have a tangible task to focus on.

Not dying was a bit too ethereal.

"As long as we stick to this route, we should be fine," he said, rolling it up. As long as Theresa didn't touch the map, the pathways didn't change. A fact that annoyed Theresa to no end, since she'd been the one to create it. Relinquishing control didn't come easily for her, but she'd trusted Kai without too much hovering. "We're almost there."

Edouard's stomach growled, filling the tunnel with a sound loud enough that it could have come from a grown dragon.

That was one thing Kai could be thankful for. No dragons in the tunnels.

Katamai taught that gratitude helped keep the worries at bay. Kai had been grasping for something to be grateful for lately.

No dragons. Check.

Edouard shrugged. "Hungry," he said, matter-of-factly, as if no one else could have deduced the reason for the sound.

"Let's keep moving," Kai said. A thin white beam caught his eye not far down the path. His heart jumped, daring to believe it might be a way out. Finally. "I think I see light up ahead."

"Is that it?" Zinni asked. "Have we finally reached the outside world? Or am I destined to die a cave person?" She strode ahead. "I'm going to check it out. I need to get out of here."

Kai and the rest sped up to catch Zinni, just as she turned into a small cove.

To Kai's disappointment, it wasn't an exit.

It was, however, littered with artifacts. That wasn't any different from the countless others they'd passed. But many of the objects in this one were nearly whole. One was even fully intact. It looked like a large metal serving spoon of some kind, and it was shinier than Kai would have expected.

And was it his imagination, or was it emanating a soft glow?

Edouard started toward it, but Theresa clapped him on the shoulder. "Are you crazy? Don't touch anything. We don't know what that is or what it does. It could be cursed, for all we know."

Edouard tilted his head and assessed the object with his steely gaze. "A cursed spoon?"

"Could be."

"Cursed by whom?"

"I don't know. The ancient people." Theresa folded her arms over her chest and glared at the object.

"Hmm," Edouard said. "How long ago?"

Theresa threw up her hands and sighed. "Again, Edouard. I.

Don't. Know. We have known about this object for the exact same length of time."

"Would be helpful to have an Urtharian with us," Edouard said.

"Yes. That would be convenient. Unfortunately, we didn't have as much time to plan this as I would have liked."

"Maybe we could take it to one," Zinni said. "We have a whole book of people in Viltresor City we could contact."

Kai's stomach clenched. "I'm with Theresa on this one. I don't think stealing a potentially magical, potentially cursed object from an ancient cave network is a good idea. Plus, what if someone needs it for their soup?" The joke fell flat, but Kai had to try. His insides churned like a pot about to boil over.

"Why would someone curse a spoon?" Edouard asked, inching closer, his gaze still assessing it. Maybe he was reading the object's aura. Kai had always wanted that ability. It would have saved him a lot of anxious moments to be able to figure out whether or not someone meant him harm without having to run through every possibility in his mind. "The Ceserites are known for their potions. Especially the ancient ones."

Zinni stepped closer. She tilted her head in thought. "Yeah, and I remember my uncle Silas telling me stories of the Seers who lived in the tunnels during the First War and how they set up stations for taking care of people. Hidden meal houses, that kind of thing. Do you think that's where we are now?" She looked around, and Kai followed her gaze across the crumbling rocks, trying to imagine the cove as a serving zone for refugees.

Edouard reached out.

"Edouard. Don't," Theresa said.

One corner of Edouard's mouth twitched up. That was the closest thing to a smile Kai had ever seen on the stoic man's face.

Ignoring Theresa's warning, Edouard stepped forward. He

was too strong for the three of them to hold him back, even if they'd tried.

He grabbed the object and tried to lift it. Only the handle raised. The cup part of the ladle pivoted, but only just.

A loud boom echoed through the tunnels.

"What was that?" Zinni shrieked, covering her ears with her hands.

"Hmm," Edouard said again, seemingly unbothered. He peeked back out into the hallway. "I don't think the spoon is for soup." He winked at Zinni.

"Let's get out of here," Theresa said. "Before everything collapses."

Kai took one last look at the map. "This way!" He had to raise his voice because another sound flooded the area. In his panic, it sounded like feet pounding pavement. Large, heavy, powerful feet.

Maybe there are dragons here, he thought vaguely. *Maybe this is their nest.*

It was a ridiculous thought. There hadn't ever been dragons on this continent. But his mind didn't care about logic or historical accuracy.

It felt like something was pursuing them, and maybe that, too, was all in Kai's mind. He and the group ran as fast as they could, just in case.

Don't look back. Don't look back. Kai repeated the refrain over and over. If there were dragons back there, he didn't want to know.

They took a sharp left and an immediate right, following Theresa.

Edouard let out an "oomph" somewhere ahead.

"Take deep breaths, Zinni," Theresa called back.

"Don't worry," Edouard added. "I can fit. Mostly. Ouch. You'll be through just fine."

Uh oh. That meant there was a narrow passage ahead.

Zinni groaned and grabbed Kai's hand, squeezing until Kai's pulse beat in his fingertips.

"It's going to be okay," Kai assured her. Zinni whimpered as she and Kai both turned sideways to fit into the passage opening. "Edouard is probably twice your size. If he can get through, you'll have no problems. I'm right here with you. At least if this is a dragon lair, they won't be able to get us in here."

"Dragons? What in the Four Worlds are you talking about?" Zinni hissed between ragged breaths.

Right. He hadn't mentioned anything about the dragons aloud. "Never mind. Just keep going."

They side-shuffled through the grimy rocks, which, if Kai wasn't hallucinating, seemed to be turning a lighter shade of gray.

"You're almost there," Theresa said. "And I have a surprise you're going to like!"

"It better be an aboveground hot springs resort with cloud-like beds and an all-you-can-eat buffet." Zinni ground out the words as she pushed through the end of the passage and into a larger chamber.

Kai followed, his hand still stuck in her vice-grip.

"It's not a resort," Theresa said. "But it is aboveground."

Another boom shook the ceiling. Kai wobbled on his feet.

"Look!" Zinni shouted. She pointed up ahead.

Kai half-expected a dragon's open mouth full of razor-sharp teeth.

It was a flight of stairs.

Theresa led them up the crumbling steps. At the top, they found a giant hole in the rock wall. It looked as if it had exploded. That would explain the loud noises.

They burst out of the tunnels in a sobbing heap, from exhaustion and terror at whatever—if anything—had come after them, and also with relief at finally being free of the tunnels.

At long last, everybody took greedy gulps of air. Zinni and

Kai lay down in the grass and waved their arms and legs back and forth as if they were making snow angels.

"This was worse than the bit we used at the castle," Zinni said. "Remember how young and naïve we were then, thinking the small portion we walked would never end?"

Kai just laughed hysterically. He couldn't form a coherent thought for lack of water and food and real rest. He coughed as the dust made its way out of his lungs.

Theresa rubbed between her eyebrows and pointed at the weathered sign that had fallen off the outside of the stairwell, her mouth dropping open. "Dip Down Tavern. I think…Edouard, I think you were right. This had to be used as a secret hideout. Maybe an underground safe place for people to rest. The ladle triggered the escape hatch. It must have been concealed better when the place was in use."

"Like I said, who would curse a spoon?" Edouard said.

Theresa rolled her eyes, but a thin smile broke through her scowl. "I'm sorry I doubted you."

"I forgive you." Edouard gently patted Theresa's shoulder.

Kai almost hadn't noticed it was night. They'd spent so long in the tunnels that time had become nebulous. Day was the same as night was the same as every other moment in which he thought they were going to die.

Somehow, they hadn't.

He looked up at the night sky. Here, in a big open field, the stars sparkled like diamonds sewn into black velvet.

And right above the little stone building they'd burst from blinked the Big Dipper.

CHAPTER 8

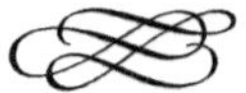

TALULLAH

The journey to the Wood Faerie's tree house was quick. Talullah and Dhal didn't talk much, both absorbed in their own thoughts.

Finally, Talullah broke the silence. "Based on my brief experience of seeing the inside of the tree house, I think the tapestry might be hanging above Gillie's fireplace or somewhere near there."

Dhal looked up at her. "And you think it matched the one we're trying to find?"

Talullah squinted in an attempt to conjure the memory. "It definitely had trees in the corners. The rest of the details are fuzzy. But it's the only lead we have."

"You think he'll help us?"

"I hope so." Gillie had taken their horses when they'd escaped the castle and the sorceress, but his loyalties didn't lie with humans—Wreckers, as he called them. She couldn't begrudge the nickname he'd given her kind. Humans did tend to ruin things. She herself had made a mess of everything since she'd discovered her Sight powers. And though her intentions were always good, she still made mistakes. Big ones. Would Gillie forgive her this soon…or ever?

"I just hope he tolerates our presence and answers our questions. Renevelda has caused him pain and suffering, too. I'm just not sure if his hatred of humans cuts deeper than the wounds she's inflicted."

They passed by two rivers, the blue River Ketslane and the orange River Lethe. Being there reminded her of the first time she'd met Gillie. He could have easily let her drink from the River Lethe and wipe away all her memories. But he hadn't. He'd warned her. Had saved her. Despite hating humans. Talullah clung to that knowledge like a lifeline.

Maybe he had some kind of tip from the future that told him she'd be worth saving. Whatever the reason, she owed Gillie more than she could ever repay him.

And she was about to add one more line of debt to her ledger.

Finally, the tree house came into view. Its deep brown bark was damp with late fall rain. A string of tiny lanterns hung from the lowest branches in lieu of porch lights. Talullah imagined Gillied perched on the porch as the sun set, a mug of tea grasped in his long fingers, his large ears fanning out to listen for danger as Kahu curled at his feet. It was too quaint a picture to reconcile with the short, brusque creature Talullah knew.

But it was impossible to know all sides of someone unless they offered to show her.

Talullah took a deep breath. The last time she'd come to ask for help in finding her sapphire and in learning how to use her Present Sight, Gillie had dismissed her and called her selfish.

He'd been right.

She'd been so focused on her own pain and desires that she hadn't reached out to him to see how he was coping after the battle with Renevelda. This time, however, she had come prepared.

The largest jar of elderflower honey she could find at the market in Calla weighed down her bag. It was Gillie's favorite. The tiniest of gestures, but it was all she could think of.

"What if he says no?" Dhal asked her.

Talullah adjusted her knapsack on her shoulders. "Then he says no. And we'll have to come up with another plan."

They were halfway to Gillie's front door when a flash of white raced through Talullah's vision. It circled five times and then skidded to a stop in front of them. The wolf's tail swished back and forth and tickled Talullah's arms.

Kahu licked Talullah's hands and jumped up, leaning her paws on Talullah's shoulders.

"Kahu, heel." Gillie's gruff voice came from the front door where he peeked out. His round orange eyes locked with Talullah's. Talullah held her breath, waiting. If she jumped ahead too far, Gillie would slam the door in her face. She needed to be patient and in control of herself. She pressed her sapphire to help her calm down and to ease the worry rising in her mind. Worry that he wouldn't help. Worry that he would, but it wouldn't matter.

Gillie looked from Talullah to Dhal. He shook a leaf out of his wild red hair and then called Kahu back inside. The wolf ambled toward Gillie and glanced at Talullah and Dhal over her shoulder a few times. "Kahu, come now," Gillie said. She trotted the rest of the way to the house.

Gillie's gruff voice called from the threshold. "I'm not interested in what you're selling."

"We're not selling anything," Talullah said. She took one step forward.

"I'm not interested in anything you have to say."

"We were hoping you could do the talking."

Gillie stared at her. "About what?"

"I'll tell you if you let us in, please. I have a large jar in here, and it's incredibly heavy."

"Weak human bodies." Gillie raised his eyebrow. "Jar of what, exactly?"

Talullah allowed herself a hint of a smile. "Elderflower honey. Turns out I don't love the stuff, and yet I seem to have an abundance of it. I thought maybe you might know someone who could take it off my hands."

Cautiously, she approached. She handed the jar to Gillie, satisfied at the way his eyebrows lifted.

His long fingers wrapped around the glass. He glanced from the honey to Talullah.

Then he went inside and closed the door behind him without another word.

"Well, that could have gone better," said Dhal.

"It also could have gone worse. We'll wait."

Talullah understood why Gillie was mad. She couldn't blame him for that. If she were in his position, she probably would have felt the same way. She might have even been less polite than the Wood Faerie had been.

Unfortunately, she couldn't do as Gillie wished. She couldn't just leave him in peace and disappear. There was too much at stake.

"For how long?"

Talullah sat down on the ground with her back pressed to the rough bark of Gillie's tree house. "For as long as it takes."

Dhal sank down beside her. Whatever questions he had remained unspoken, though Talullah could guess they were the same ones she refused to let her own tongue release.

What if Gillie refuses to help?

What will become of magic?

Of the world?

If she gave these thoughts oxygen, they would catch fire and burn her last shreds of hope to ash.

He had to help.

There was no margin for failure.

And without him, she had no idea what to do next.

Dhal squeezed her hand. He could always sense when she needed reassurance. The gentle pressure brought her back from the edge. If she allowed herself to spiral, she wouldn't be able to think clearly. Instead, she focused on the one thing she could control: her response.

Before, when she'd asked the Wood Faerie for help, she'd allowed Gillie's gruffness to push her away. She'd given up too easily. This time, she would show him he was wrong about her, that she wasn't just some dumb Wrecker.

She was strong of mind and heart and body. She could be patient.

Darkness descended on Talullah and Dhal as the sun drifted off to sleep in Nainehta Forest. Talullah always forgot how quickly time changed in the enchanted forest.

Talullah's teeth chattered. Last time she'd spent the night in Nainetha, it was late summer, still weeks before the first frost.

Now, in late fall, the chill of the air seeped into her lungs, threatening to freeze the air inside.

She pulled her mother's old cloak tighter around her on one side and allowed Dhal to snuggle in next to her on the other, so he could share the cloak's warmth. Not for the first time, Talullah was grateful for the spelled cloak that protected its wearer from external threats.

Talullah relaxed almost immediately in Dhal's proximity. They'd been sitting close before, but not *this* close. Not close enough for her to count the golden flecks in his hazel eyes. Not close enough to feel his forearm muscles pressed against hers.

Nervous tingles tightened her nerves like brand new violin strings. If Dhal noticed a change in her demeanor, he didn't mention it.

Hopefully Gillie would change his mind before true night

fell. If not, she'd stay in the forest all night. It wouldn't be comfortable, but the cloak would ensure she and Dhal survived.

The sun was nearly gone when Dhal inhaled. Talullah turned to look at him, though in the near pitch dark she could barely see his silhouette. The moment their eyes locked, his breath hitched, but he didn't speak.

"What?" Talullah asked. "You think it's stupid of me to keep us out here in the dark and the cold, on the slim chance that Gillie will change his mind?"

"No," Dhal said, his voice rough and gravelly. "I—look. The window."

Talullah glanced up. The curtain, lit by the spelled lamps inside Gillie's house, fluttered behind the glass. For a second, Talullah's hopes lifted.

A black nose parted the fabric. Kahu's white snout, gray eyes, and pointy ears followed. Her fur shone like a beacon.

The wolf cocked her head to the side and howled, as if asking Gillie to come to the window. Talullah held her breath, her heart beating a steady, pleading rhythm.

Ten agonizing seconds later, Kahu's face disappeared. There were no signs of any other movement.

The tiny spark of hope snuffed out. "Maybe we should just go home," she said. Her nose, unable to be covered by the cloak, had gone partially numb.

The door to the treehouse clicked open.

"You two must be even more insane than I thought," Gillie said. "Never mind. Why am I surprised? Of course you're insane. You're goin' to freeze out there." He sighed. "I can't have your dead bodies ruinin' my aesthetic. Get inside."

Talullah stared at him, daring to believe it was real.

"I won't ask a second time." Gillie turned and went inside, leaving the door cracked.

CHAPTER 9

TALULLAH

*T*alullah and Dhal scrambled to follow Gillie into his tree house. Warmth hugged Talullah as soon as she stepped inside.

The atmosphere swept her back into the memory of when she awoke there after being trapped in Igdrasil, the largest transport tree in Nainehta Forest. That was the second time Gillie had saved her life. Without him, she probably would have died inside that tree. Back then, she had no idea her cloudy visions were evidence of her Sight powers trying to surface or that her heirloom necklace would amplify them.

She'd ended up inside the tree by accident, and again, Gillie had gotten her out and to safety. She'd originally thought he'd kidnapped her for Terrapese. Luckily for Talullah, he'd hated the rulers more than he hated her.

Now, the hearth emitted a fire only felt, not seen, as did the white tapered candles spread through the home. Knitted blankets and patchwork quilts lay folded in a basket near the sofa.

The air held a slight tang of sourdough. For a Wood Faerie who preferred to be alone, Gillie had a knack for creating a welcoming, homey space.

Gillie gestured for them to sit at his small wooden table. Like the other times Talullah had sat there, Kahu flopped down on her feet. Talullah patted the wolf's head under the table while she addressed the Wood Faerie.

"How are you, Gillie?" she asked.

"Been better, been worse. Why are you here?"

Gillie set a loaf of bread on the middle of the table. Large oven mitts concealed his hands. He must have baked the bread while Talullah and Dhal were outside.

Wordlessly, the Wood Faerie set down two plates, the massive jar of elderflower honey Talullah had gifted him, a smaller jar of orange marmalade, and two spreading knives next to the bread. "Eat. Unless you're as determined to starve as you are to freeze to death." Gillie nodded at the food as he slid into one of the chairs.

Talullah and Dhal each cut themselves a slice of bread and spread orange marmalade on half and elderflower honey on the other. Talullah hadn't lied when she told Gillie she didn't have a taste for elderflower honey. It wasn't her favorite, but she wanted to prove her gratefulness for his hospitality and that she hadn't given him tainted goods.

Had he heard the rumors that Talullah was working with the sorceress? If so, he couldn't believe it. He'd never have let them in if he suspected she'd defected to Renevelda's side.

Talullah took a bite of her bread, the side with the elder-flower honey.

"Thank you very much," Dhal said, nodding to Gillie.

"Please put aside your feelings about Wreckers, and me, specifically, for a few minutes," Talullah said. She pulled the square of tapestry out of her bag and unfolded it, placing it flat on the table in front of Gillie. "This is bigger than any of us. I need to know everything about this tapestry. Why it was created, who created it, when and why and how it was destroyed, and why the sorceress wants this piece so badly."

Gillie snorted. "Oh, is that all you need?" He sliced himself some bread and slathered it with elderflower honey. He ate the whole piece before speaking again.

"Renevelda is looking for the rest of the pieces. She already knows I have this one."

Gillie stared at it for a second or two, blinking with his expression blank. He slowly raised his eyes to meet Talullah's. "And you came to me because?"

"I thought you had a tapestry similar to this one. Or perhaps they're one and the same?"

Gillie gestured around his home. "Look around. Do you see it anywhere?"

The spot above the fireplace was bare. Talullah could have sworn it was hanging there before. "Just because it isn't here now doesn't mean it never was."

Gillie grunted and sliced another hunk of bread. "The one I have isn't exactly the same."

"Then this isn't a piece of your tapestry?" Talullah asked, pointing at the square on the table.

Gillie shook his head. "Mine's a sister. It's a less-detailed map to the Source."

"The Source?" Talullah asked.

"Of the Suditzas' magic. Obviously." Gillie blinked at her as if she should have known this. "Where did you think they got it?"

"I've never thought about it, to be honest."

Gillie scoffed. "That's the problem with Wreckers. Never questionin' anythin'. Unbelievable." He leaned closer, his mossy scent washing over Talullah. "The Suditzas' magic, my magic, yours, all the magic in the world comes from the Source."

"Right," said Dhal. "Of course."

"If Renevelda's looking for the pieces of the tapestry, then she's trying to find the Source," Talullah said.

Gillie's nostrils flared. "She's not just tryin' to find it. The Suditzas' original tapestry—the one the Elder Council destroyed—when united, gives the bearer the power to control the Source."

"Control it?" Dhal swallowed hard. "So, if, for example, Renevelda, the most evil sorceress we've ever met, had the original tapestry and found the Source, she could basically do whatever she wanted."

"You are clever indeed." Gillie's eyes darkened to the same rich amber as Dhal's skin. "The second tapestry can't be used to control the Source. It reflects the state of magic, like a weather barometer."

"Is that why the Elder Council destroyed the original?" Talullah asked. "They wanted to prevent someone from having control of the Source?"

The Wood Faerie nodded. "There's an old prophecy. They thought it predicted the rise of someone who'd use the Source's magic for dark means."

That sounded like Renevelda.

"How does the prophecy go?" Dhal asked.

Gillie grumbled again. "Ask an Urtharian or a Ceserite for that. I don't keep track of Wreckers' history."

Dhal shifted in his seat. "Well, if it did talk about a dark sorceress, it could be Renevelda. Her goal has always been to gain more power. And we know from the story we found in Praeteriti that she's a demi-goddess. Taking the Source's power could be a way for her to win her place in the Realm of the Divine."

"Should we hide this piece?" Dhal nudged the scrap of fabric on the table like it might bite him. "Make sure she can't find it?

Even if she finds the others, it won't work unless she's got the whole tapestry."

Gillie shook his head. "Unless a Seer with positive intentions unites the tapestry, there will always be the risk that the sorceress or anyone else with unsavory ones will find it. Are you prepared to guard that scrap for the rest of your life, always lookin' over your shoulder and wonderin' when the sorceress will come?"

Dhal's brows scrunched. "Why keep the tapestry at all, then, if it can be used for such evil? Why not destroy them both?"

Gillie growled. "By that logic, why don't we melt down every sharp tool? Bury every heavy stone? Pick and burn the plants that can be made into healing tonics just because they can also be turned to poison?" He leaned closer. "The Suditzas' legacy and magic run through every fiber of our world. If we destroy the instructions for how to care for it and use it, that magic will disappear. Permanently. The elder council members were fools." He snorted and shook his head. "Wreckers."

"So," Dhal said, "to recap. We can't destroy it, because then magic will die for good. And we can't just sit back and wait for Renevelda to find all the pieces."

"Looks like there's only one way forward." Gillie's round orange eyes fixed on Talullah. "Find the pieces, repair the tapestry, prevent Renevelda from using it, and end her reign for good."

"But how am *I* supposed to do that? And why does it have to be me?" Talullah heard how whiny she sounded, but this was the literal fate of magic on her shoulders. They were valid questions.

Gillie stared at her until she lifted her head and met his eyes. "I think the better question is, if not *you*, then *who*? Seems you've done okay findin' those gemstones your great-great-grandmother hid for you."

A few beats passed.

"Did you know this was going to happen? Did she come to you? Did my family tell everyone else secrets about my life that they hid from me?" With each question, Talullah's passion burned hotter.

"Are you finished havin' your tantrum?" Gillie asked in a calm tone.

"No, I'm not, thank you very much." Talullah stood and paced around the room. "My mother kept my powers a secret, disappeared for half my life, and as soon as I found her, she got zapped by magic, and I don't even know if she's still alive. My great aunt Mirella lied to me about my mother's disappearance. My great-great grandmother set up this quest for finding my gems for some unknown reason. And who even knows how much of this my father knows?"

Gillie watched Talullah with uncharacteristic patience. Dhal nodded along with Talullah's rant.

Talullah stopped. "And you're now telling me I have to go on another quest to put together this tapestry and then, what? Try to control the Source of magic to finally get rid of the sorceress who'd happily kill us all? I honestly don't think I'm being that dramatic. This is kind of a lot." She breathed heavily. "Now I'm done."

A slow smile stretched across Gillie's weathered face. He steepled his fingers together atop the round kitchen table. "Have you considered, perhaps, that the quest to find your gems and the quest for the tapestry are one and the same?"

Talullah blinked, letting the suggestion sink in.

Gillie continued. "That, just maybe, Aurinia knew a few things you don't. And that, maybe, she set this task to help you."

Dhal's eyes lit up. "Tules, what if the pieces of the tapestry are in the same places you found your gemstones?"

"So," Talullah responded slowly, "finding my gemstones was a test run?"

Gillie shrugged. "Only Aurinia knows for sure. But, I'd say it would be a decent place to start."

"If I'm going to retrace my steps, I could have just gotten the stones and the tapestry pieces at the same time. I could have saved so many more lives."

"Or," Dhal offered, "Aurinia knew you'd need time to learn. Can you imagine your reaction if you'd found out about your Sight, Renevelda, the prophecy, reuniting the factions, the lost tapestry, and the Source all at the same time?"

Just the thought of it made Talullah's mouth dry and her breath stutter. "I would have run away," she whispered. "Gillie, you never answered my question. Did you know this would happen when you first saved me in Nainehta Forest, that I'd have this chance to oppose Renevelda?"

Gillie sliced himself another bit of bread and slathered it with elderflower honey. "No."

"Then why'd you do it? Why'd you save a Wrecker? Twice."

"Because I was the only one who could." Gillie polished off the bread, then stood, peeking out the window. "Sun's comin' back up. Should be safe for you both to travel now. You've got your work cut out for you, so you best get started. Make sure to find a Ceserite to teach you to control your Future Sight. Now that you have the ruby, you're probably goin' to have more prophecies asking for your attention. Maybe an Urtharian historian, too. They should be able to answer the thousands of questions I don't have time or patience to answer."

Talullah's lip quirked up. "I'll do that."

Dhal and Talullah headed for the door. Kahu nuzzled the side of Talullah's leg.

"Thank you, Gillie," Talullah said. "For everything you've done. I wouldn't be here without you."

"Until we meet again," Gillie replied. "I have a feelin' this isn't the last time we'll see each other."

CHAPTER 10

MARGOT

"Please tell me again why I have to come out here with you. It's freezing." Penny shivered and pulled her knit cap further down over her ears.

The edge of the forest was quiet except for the faint chirping of the early birds. A thin crust of frost coated the dead brown leaves on the ground.

Margot sighed and looked at her younger sister. "Because it's stupid to do something like this alone. This kind of magic requires an extra person, just in case something goes wrong." She swallowed the lump in her throat and tried to put on a brave face.

Margot stared at the hand print still visible on the shimmering barrier. Visible to her, at least. Her sister couldn't see the strands of magic making up the barrier, Margot's hand print, or the discoloration in the sky.

She shuddered at the memory of how forcefully the barrier had rejected her.

She'd been caught off guard. But she was better prepared this time.

Penny paused. She batted her long eyelashes at Margot, her emerald eyes sparkling with sudden fear. "What kind of things could go wrong?" She squeezed the huge stuffed bear Margot had asked her to bring.

Margot shrugged. "I don't know. This is the first time I've tried this, and if something bad happens, I'm going to need you to tell Father what's going on. And you'll have to get in contact with Talullah and figure out what else we can do to get rid of this barrier."

Penny tugged on one of her low braided pigtails. "Nothing bad is going to happen. You're good at your magic. I've seen you practicing."

Margot had spent every evening since she'd discovered the change in the barrier waiting for Penny to fall asleep in their shared room so she could sneak out into the yard to practice her spells. Night had faded to twilight and then to sunrise while she pored over the materials she'd borrowed from Talullah's room, her mother's old potion book, and the few books she'd managed to sneak from the library. Countless mornings, she'd returned to bed just minutes before Penny woke. She'd told her father bad dreams had kept her up and that's why she'd nearly fallen asleep on her breakfast plate.

Maybe he believed her, maybe he didn't. But he never challenged her.

Weeks passed in which Margot finally succeeded in changing the color of the hazelnut, and then a walnut, and then a small stuffed turtle. Once, she'd successfully made her shoes invisible only to be unable to reverse the spell for an hour.

Margot studied magic like she'd never cared to study anything else before. She thought about it while she ate and brushed her teeth and raked leaves away from the front path. Stolen naps kept her energized enough to spend her nights immersed in the possibility of her powers.

Despite Margot's efforts at secrecy, Penny had caught her reciting the illusion spell one night. There had been no denying what she was up to, so she'd confessed. Releasing the secret lifted a weight off her back. She needed someone's help anyway, if she was going to attempt to fool the barrier into letting her out.

"Thanks, but thinking I'm good at it and *being* good at it are two different things entirely. I've mastered some less complicated things, but this is on another level."

"Why do you want to go outside the barrier?" Penny asked. "It keeps us safe."

"I used to think so, too. But now I think that, while well-intentioned, it's a hindrance. I think we need to be able to go out in the world, whether it's scary or not. We don't need to run from the same things the original Founders did. And Talullah needs my help."

Behind Margot's eyelids, the image of a burning feather glittered. The vision had haunted her in different ways over the past few days, but the feather always remained.

Penny nodded, nearly eye-to-eye with Margot after a growth spurt, and considered. "What do you need me to do?"

Margot took a deep breath and exhaled loudly, glad that she wouldn't have to argue with Penny to get her to help. While Penny sometimes annoyed her—most of the time, if Margot was being honest—her younger sister was loyal to a fault. She'd support Margot unconditionally. For better or for worse.

For better, in this case, Margot told herself.

She didn't understand the full weight of the decisions Talullah and their mother had made, but now that Margot faced similar ones, she smothered the ember of anger she'd held on to for so long.

Maybe they'd just been doing their best.

"I need you to hold this." Margot handed Penny the silver hand-mirror. "The goal is to convince the barrier I'm still on this side while I sneak through a gap." She uncapped the vial of black powder she'd concocted from household ingredients under the direction of a recipe from her mother's old book. "The powder is supposed to create a fissure in a spell. I'm not powerful enough to break it completely, but if I can crack it enough, I should be able to sneak through."

At least, that was her theory.

"You stand back and point the mirror so it shows me and the bear. Once the illusion is set, I'm going to say the words and throw this onto the barrier. If anything bad happens to me, go get Father immediately."

Penny swallowed hard, her eyes widening again, but she nodded tersely.

Margot closed her eyes and focused on the desire to replicate her image. She opened her eyes and locked her gaze on the reflection, concentrating. "A trick I need for just a while, makes this reflection exact in style, from hair to face and limbs to smile, bewitch this bear and all spells beguile."

Slowly, the bear's image transformed. Its fur receded, leaving smooth tan skin. Its ears hid beneath a white knit hat. The rest of its features elongated, stretched, and changed until Margot saw not one reflection of herself, but two.

"By the Founders," Penny whispered.

"It worked." Margot laughed. "I can't believe it worked."

Penny bit her lip. "Better hurry, Mar. It's flickering. I don't know how long the illusion will last."

Margot concentrated on holding the spell. She just needed a few seconds. She tossed the black powder onto the barrier where her handprint glittered.

For a long moment, nothing happened. She and Penny stared into nothingness and held their breath. They gripped each other's hands so tightly Margot's knuckles throbbed.

"Is anything going to happen?" Penny whispered.

Margot tamped down the initial urge to snap at her sister. It was a valid question, and Penny wasn't questioning her abilities so much as just wondering exactly what Margot was thinking. "Maybe I got everything wrong. Maybe the proportions were wrong, or the recipe wasn't designed for spells like this."

A cross between a buzzing and a ringing sound filled Margot's ears.

"Do you hear that?" Penny asked.

The noise grew louder until it scraped her eardrums, like metal sliding against metal. Like how Margot assumed a sword might sound when being unsheathed.

She thought, as she turned, for just a horrific moment, that maybe she'd broken down the barrier only to let their enemies straight in, as if they'd been waiting on the other side for her to do something foolish.

But no.

Where Margot had tossed the powder, a black slash like spilled ink colored the barrier.

"What is it, Mar?" Penny asked, sensing her sister's fear.

"That sound. It was the barrier tearing open. I—we—did it. I have to go now." She threw her arms around Penny, nearly knocking her sister to the ground. "Thank you for helping. Tell Father I'll be back as soon as I can."

She grabbed her pack and approached the rip.

"Be careful, Mar," Penny said. Fresh tears shone in her bright green eyes.

"I will. I love you."

"I love you, too."

Margot stole one last glance at her sister, biting back her own tears. Then she slipped through the fissure in the magic and left River Hill behind.

CHAPTER 11

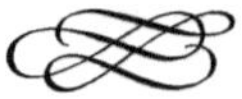

TALULLAH

Talullah pulled on her cloak, then topped it with the fur-lined coat Jothi had let her borrow. Dhalian dressed in his borrowed warm layers, too, lacing up the boots with delight.

"Thanks for letting us borrow these," Talullah said to Jothi.

"Don't mention it. It'll be good to get some use out of them. We don't do much mountain exploration these days." They wound a yellow wool scarf around their neck and waved Talullah and Dhal along.

"I can't imagine this is going to amount to much," Talullah said. "But it's the only idea I have right now."

Taking a guided hiking tour to look for the Ceserite compound felt ridiculous. But Talullah was desperate. She needed to find a Ceserite to train her in Future Sight, and it's not like there was a registry floating around that she could use to look one up.

"It will be fun," Jothi said. They leaned in conspiratorially. Their black hair glimmered with freshly applied styling oil and smelled of coconut. "Can I tell you a secret? I've always wanted to do the tour, but it felt lame since I live here. Now that I have actual tourists to show around, I'm excited."

"We're happy to make your dreams come true, Jothi," Dhal said.

Jothi led the way to the kiosk at the trailhead. It was a small cabin just big enough for a few people to stand in. Behind a thin glass window sat a tour guide. He popped up as soon as Talullah's group entered.

"Here for a tour?" he asked. Thick brown twists of hair grazed the shoulder of his bright red tunic. Beads of sweat dotted his deep mahogany forehead. He swiped them away with a cotton handkerchief.

"We do indeed," Jothi said. "Three for the Mystical Mountain Tour, if it's running again."

"Really?" the guide's large eyes widened. "Oh, this is my lucky day. I love giving this tour, but attendance has been lacking lately. Well, I'm sure you've heard the goings-on."

Dhal nodded. "We have."

"Such a shame about that poor woman." He tsked as he counted Jothi's change. "And if you ask me, something's up at Castle Viltresor. I can't put my finger on it, but I shouldn't be spouting politics when you nice people have come for a tour! I see you're all geared-up already. That's great. Let me do the same, and we can leave right away. Lucky for you, today's an open schedule."

He whistled as he pulled on a turmeric-colored parka and hat, then grabbed a few folded parchments. "These are maps of the area. Shouldn't need 'em, but just in case. Everyone ready? Follow me."

Talullah was sweating by the time they made it to the start of the actual trail.

"I know it's hot now, but you'll be grateful for the layers in a few moments," the guide told them. "By the way, I'm Orleone. Friends call me Leo. Please ask any questions you have as we go."

A few minutes later, the air turned chilly out of nowhere. One second Talullah was wishing for a refreshing lemonade, and the next the tip of her nose burned with cold. The atmosphere crackled with something else, too. Magical energy.

"Katamian magic?" Talullah whispered to Jothi and Dhal.

Jothi nodded. "Feels like it to me. Which is strange. Supposed to be a Ceserite community, right?"

"But Maeve said over the years some of the magic has bled into each other. So maybe the Ceserites have learned to adapt some of the Katamian spells," Talullah said.

"Or maybe there are Duals, Triads, or even Seznas up here," Dhal replied.

"Here we are," Leo said. He gestured grandly to a hand-painted wooden sign, smiling wide enough to show the charming gap between his top front teeth.

"World-famous Magic Trail," Dhal read aloud.

Behind the sign, a dirt path led through a modest copse of evergreen trees.

Leo looked sheepish. "Alright, so maybe not world-famous. But people do come from all over to see if they can find the fabled Ceserite community."

"Ceserites do exist, though," Talullah said. "They're not merfolk or dragons. They're real people."

"Yes, yes, of course," Leo said. "It's just, they tend to keep to themselves. Like much of the Sight community, the Ceserites fled during the First War, fearing their Gifts would make them targets for the people in power. Whether to be used as pawns to do evil biddings or to be executed out of fear they would use their Gifts to harm others."

"But why the fascination with finding them?" Jothi asked.

Leo scratched his chin, which was completely devoid of hair. "I think it's the thrill of seeking something. Of the possibility of finding something rare and exquisite."

"But if the Ceserites wanted to be found, they wouldn't be in hiding, right?" Jothi pressed.

Leo expelled a humorless laugh. "Right you are. I'm going to play it straight with you, because I sense you all know more than you let on. The thing about this tour? No one's ever found the Ceserites, have they? It's not about the finding. It's about the potential. It's about adventure. And the bond you form with your companions along the way."

Jothi nodded. "Of course."

"So, it's rumored that the Ceserites have concealed the entrance to their community somehow. But how? No one knows for sure," Leo said.

They passed through the trees and started up the path's incline. Fingernail-sized flowers in a rainbow of colors lined the path. Talullah kept her eyes peeled and her body poised to receive any kind of magical information. Jothi's brows furrowed in concentration. They must be doing the same. Dhal studied the map as he walked, a sight that brought a smile to Talullah's face. If anyone could find hidden meaning in a collection of lines, it was Dhal.

Leo continued his narration, explaining various foliage and wildlife. "We have many types of birds up here, too. I even heard a rumor that someone saw a phoenix once."

"Aren't phoenixes a myth?" Jothi asked.

"Could be," Leo said. "A lot of things are myths…until they aren't."

Talullah knew that all too well. The murderous sand jellies and the Sapphire Wall from the Isle of Salire had certainly been real.

"Plus," Leo continued, "phoenix feathers are supposed to have protective powers. Legend says ancient Ceserites used bits of phoenix feathers in potions, sewed them onto clothing, or forged them in metal to hang above their doors to ward off danger or aid in recovery from bad luck or illness. One myth even says holding a phoenix feather can save a person from death."

Dhal snorted. "That sounds a bit far-fetched."

Leo grinned. "Maybe, maybe not. Only way to find out would be to find a phoenix feather and try it. Not something I'd recommend, of course, on the off-chance it *is* a myth." He winked. "But it's fun to think about that kind of magic existing. Follow me."

Talullah's breath exhaled in cloudy puffs, as the air temperature had dropped significantly since they'd started. They reached a fork, one side of the dirt path leading further up the mountain and the other veering right through a meadow.

As she and the others followed Leo to the right, Talullah read the sign posted at the fork. On the wooden sign were the words, "Keep Right." Talullah blinked, her vision growing blurry. Maybe she was dehydrated.

She swigged her water, blinking at the sign. Her vision cleared, but instead of the original words she knew she'd seen, they changed. Shifted right in front of her eyes until they formed different words altogether. It looked like a different language. An ancient language, even.

Talullah moved closer to the sign and stared at it, trying not to blink, fearing if she did so the words would go back to normal.

A group of stars arranged in an interesting pattern had been carved beneath the words on the sign. Talullah thought first of the sorceress's mark that never appeared, the one with three stars enclosed in a circle. But the next was the pattern of dots her friend Lynx had marked on her Alleviation stone.

Talullah knew Lynx was a pure Katamian Seer, but perhaps there was something more to these markings.

Talullah touched her amethyst and called upon her magic to remember the words and markings. Her blood hummed with unanswered questions. That usually meant she was onto something.

"Leo?" she called.

"Yes?" He stopped a few paces ahead.

"Could you tell me about this sign?"

"This one?" He backtracked to meet her, and Dhal and Jothi also gathered around it. "Nothing special about this one. Make sure you stay on the right of the path instead of taking the left fork."

"Where's the left path lead?" Dhal asked. He alternated looking between the map and the path.

"Waterfall and cliffs," Leo said. "It's too dangerous to climb up there these days. There was a rockslide a few years back that took the safe walking path and a few tourists' lives with it. The rangers won't let anyone go up there."

"Right," Talullah said. "Anything else interesting about the sign?"

He looked at her as if she were maybe a little crazy. "Not that I can see." He shrugged. "Do *you* find anything interesting about it?"

The weight of his gaze reminded Talullah that it was dangerous to reveal her true Gifts to strangers, especially here and especially now. "No. I thought I saw something, but it must have been a trick of the light. I think the altitude might be getting to me."

"Let's wrap it up then. No need to make anyone sick." Leo led them to a small black stone cabin, its yard covered in a thin layer of snow. "This is Stars Align. You can warm up with a hot beverage and snacks and rest in front of the fire. When you're finished, there are carts with drivers that will take you the rest of the way down the mountain. It's a smooth ride down from here."

"Thanks so much for your time and knowledge today, Leo," Talullah said.

"My pleasure. It's always nice to see young people interested in culture."

"And adventure," Dhal added.

"Indeed. Well, I'll leave you to it. Come find me at the kiosk if you think of any more questions. I'm there most days."

He headed down the path, and Talullah, Dhal, and Jothi entered the café.

Pinpricks of light drew Talullah's eyes up to the ceiling. She inhaled a surprised breath. It was painted black with bright white constellations. A circular glass lantern glowed at the center of each star.

Fire crackled in two simple iron grates along one wall. Plush sofas covered in deep purple velvet hugged close to the warmth. On the other side was a gray stone counter and four light wooden tables with mismatched, spindle-legged chairs.

They were the only people in the place, so they chose a table and removed their outer layers. Talullah's eyes immediately locked on the bookshelf behind their table. It was full of books about astronomy. The owner had committed to the theme.

"So, what was up with that sign?" Jothi asked.

"Did you see it, too?" Talullah replied.

"I didn't see anything strange, but I saw how you looked at it," Jothi replied.

"It changed," Talullah whispered. "I think my Gifts saw through the spell somehow." She told them what it had looked like.

"Draw it," Dhal said, handing her his map and a charcoal pencil he always kept with him.

Talullah pressed her amethyst to recall the memory and drew the sign as she'd seen it, complete with the star arrangement.

"It looks like a constellation," Jothi said. "I'm not sure which one. I'm a bit rusty on my astronomy. But we can look it up. There are plenty of resources at the compound."

Time was running out. Renevelda had already made moves to bring Seers to the castle for some reason. She had a plan. And Talullah had nothing.

"Cold out there today, isn't it?" A short, stout woman with bright blond hair toddled out from a door behind the counter. "You kids take a tour?"

"Yes," Dhal said. "It was great, but cold."

"Well, better warm you up then! My name's Edda. What'll you have?"

CHAPTER 12

KAI

Once out of the tunnels, guided by the stars and a map of the country aboveground, Theresa easily navigated the group to their destination.

Zinni kept her comments to herself, though Kai could sense her disgruntled attitude toward Theresa hadn't subsided. Edouard's stomach grumbled, but the large man voiced no other complaints. Maybe he was as relieved as Kai to be in the real world again.

Kai didn't even mind walking a few more miles. Breathing fresh air strengthened him from the inside out.

"This is it," Theresa said. Weariness coated her words like a thick layer of honey.

One circular window of Theresa's mentor's house peeked through the hundred foot tall evergreen trees like an ivory-lidded eye beneath a curtain of dark green hair.

Theresa whispered a couplet—perhaps a password—then waved them on. "We're safe to enter now."

Kai's magic tingled as he passed through what he assumed to be a concealment spell. Extra precautions couldn't hurt. He liked that the owner had taken this seriously.

Approaching the cottage reminded Kai of his first time seeing Castle Viltresor. This cottage was nowhere near the size of the castle, and instead of outlandish, sparkling details, the small home offered the opposite. It camouflaged into its surroundings and emanated a quiet, commanding power.

Perhaps that was the point. To be unseen and underestimated could be an advantage.

"You made it," said a smooth voice.

"Veylan!" Theresa sprinted toward the young man who'd just come out of the house's black front door.

Veylan caught Theresa, picked her up, and spun her around. He leaned in to whisper something in Theresa's ear, but Kai wasn't close enough to hear. The words didn't seem to be for him, anyway.

Edouard cleared his throat, and he and Kai approached Theresa and Veylan.

Veylan beckoned them forward. "Please come in. My father has been expecting you for quite some time." His gaze lingered on Theresa for a long second before he turned and led them inside.

Warm lantern light bathed the entryway, finally giving Kai a better look at their host, Veylan. He stood eye-level with Kai, so just over six feet. The bottom half of his white-blond hair was shaved close to his head, while the top fell in tousled waves over his forehead.

"Hmm." Edouard looked left and right, sniffing the air from his position next to Kai.

Kai raised a brow at him in question, but Edouard shrugged.

They followed Veylan's lead and removed their shoes, leaving them by the door.

Kai's feet ached at their newfound freedom as he padded across the polished birch floor and into a sitting room. He'd been wearing his boots for over a week straight.

A man who looked older than Kai's father sat in the bay window seat. He had the same white-blond hair as Veylan, but the older man's was pulled into a sleek knot atop his head. "Come in, come in. I have been waiting for you for a long time, Kai Lin." He stood with some difficulty as Kai approached and immediately held out his freckled hand for Kai to grasp.

"Oh," Kai said in surprise. "How do you know my name?"

The man chuckled in a good-natured way. "There are many mysteries in the universe, Kai. This is but one." He paused, then a sly smile broke his serious expression. "I'm only kidding. Theresa wrote about you in her letters to my son."

"Ah, I see." Kai looked at Edouard, whose gaze was fixed to the trinkets decorating the stone mantle.

Kai's expression remained neutral despite the thoughts darting through his mind like a scattered school of fish.

How long had Theresa been writing to Veylan? What had she told him about Kai? And, more importantly, *why* had she mentioned Kai?

"Thank you for inviting us into your home, Master Marquet," Theresa said, nodding her head in a deferent bow.

"Yes, please let us know what we can do to contribute," Zinni added. "We're happy to help."

"Call me Quentis, please. 'Master Marquet' makes me feel like I'm on my deathbed. Which, as you can see, I am not." He did a funny little dance and ended with his arms spread out, his lips stretching in a wide smile.

"Alright, father, I think they understand you're the epitome of good health." Veylan folded his muscular arms over his broad chest and rolled his bright blue eyes at Theresa, who stifled a laugh.

"Veylan, my boy, show these lovely people to their quarters. We'll reconvene in a bit for dinner, after you've all had the chance to bathe. I can imagine you've had quite the journey."

Veylan bowed to his father. "Of course."

Kai caught a flash of ink at the base of Veylan's neck as he dipped forward. It was a tattoo of some kind, but Kai couldn't see enough to figure out what it was.

If he'd known Veylan better, he could have asked. Given they'd only met five minutes ago, Kai would have to be content with his curiosity. He always wondered about the things people valued enough to make permanent on their skin. Though now that the group had finally reached their destination and was once again within reach of modern comforts like food and hygiene and sleep, Kai doubted his mind would be able to focus on anything other than regaining the strength that had been shed in the tunnels.

He still hadn't fully processed the confrontation with Renevelda.

Yes, there were many more important things to worry about than their host's body art.

The first being a nice, long, hot bath.

IT WAS a shocking experience to wake up and not feel like he'd slept with a sharp rock beneath his shoulder blade. The mattress in Kai's assigned guest room at the Marquets' cottage had embraced him all through his dreamless night, the faint scent of lavender lulling him into the rest he so desperately needed.

Now, he sat with the Marquets, Theresa, and Edouard, while Zinni luxuriated in sleeping late. They breakfasted at a wrought-iron table in a small but picturesque garden out back. A large umbrella shaded them from the early morning sun, and glasses full of fresh-squeezed lemonade quenched his never-ending thirst. Kai couldn't help but wonder if he'd entered some sort of alternate universe.

An anxious tingle ran up his arms at the thought.

Please don't let it be a dream.

He pinched his leg under the table and found that, *Ow. Yes, that hurt,* and so he must be awake. He took another sip of the refreshing drink and had to force his brain to calm down. Maybe things were going to be okay after all. He had no reason to believe that Quentis Marquet, Theresa's mentor, would cause them any harm. Quentis had personally invited them to come and had offered to house them while they got their bearings.

Renevelda wouldn't look kindly on Seers protecting fugitives. The Marquets had put themselves at risk by helping Kai and his friends. Theresa trusted them, and she clearly knew them better than she'd let on.

She sat close to Veylan, laughed at his jokes—which weren't *that* funny—and rushed to help him at every turn. If Kai were a gambler, he would have wagered a hefty sum that they had a history. Possibly a romantic one. Or maybe it wasn't so far in the past.

The thought made Kai's insides twist like a pretzel. On the one hand, good for Theresa. On the other hand, it reminded him of the fact that Talullah had left him behind.

Kai forced himself to break the thought pattern and studied Quentis as he talked.

"So, what is it exactly that you want out of this?" He directed the question at Theresa as he popped a bit of cherry turnover into his mouth.

Theresa smoothed her now-clean headscarf and, with a conviction Kai had never heard, spoke aloud their demands. "We want to be able to practice our magic in the open and without consequence, assuming we do no harm to others. We want to be able to work in any job we choose, regardless of the proprietors' feelings about magic."

"Essentially," Quentis said, "you want to reverse the edict that King William put into place before the sorceress attacked the castle."

Theresa straightened in her seat. "We don't want things to return to the status quo. We want to redefine our place in society. We deserve the same opportunities as everyone else, everywhere in the world, and we want to be recognized for who we are."

Quentis sat back in his chair and tipped his head. "Those sound like reasonable requests. And you don't believe the sorceress can provide that?"

Kai flinched. "She's despicable." Why would he even mention Renevelda?

"She's done horrible things," Theresa said. "We don't want to align with her." The defeat in her voice broke Kai's heart a little bit. As long as he'd known Theresa, she had been a solid, strong force. She always had a plan and always knew the details.

"Hmm. Alright. How, then, do you intend to achieve these goals since you reject the sorceress's power and status, now that the king and prince have gone into hiding?"

Theresa continued while staring at her hands. "That's kind of why we're here. I don't know what to do next. The original plan was created to oppose the king, not Renevelda."

Seeing Theresa falter made her more human in Kai's eyes. It made him truly notice that she wasn't that much older than he was, only a handful of years. "I never anticipated the sorceress showing up and throwing a wrench in everything. Now that the castle is compromised, I don't know how to adapt the plan to oppose her. The prince would have been our preferred ally. And we do intend to locate him."

"We do?" Kai asked. This was news to him.

"Of course. We'll need his support if we're going to over-throw Renevelda."

Kai snorted. "Alexander doesn't have any magic. How do you expect him to oppose a sorceress?"

Theresa sighed. "Not on his own. We'll need to build support. We need to be able to convince people to come to our side. And for that, we need a charismatic leader."

"You mean Edouard isn't going to be the face of the rebellion?" Kai deadpanned.

"You think I'm not charismatic?" Edouard asked, just as drily. He bit a cherry turnover in half and let the filling ooze over his lips without cracking a smile.

Theresa rolled her eyes. "You know as well as I do, Kai, that the people love Alexander. And once they hear that he's convinced his father to give him the throne—"

"Hold on, hold on." Kai's head was starting to hurt. "Since when did he say that? Have you been communicating with them in secret all this time? Because this is the first I'm hearing of it."

Alexander told Kai everything. If he'd been working on this plan with Theresa, Kai would have known about it.

Though Alexander hadn't mentioned being in possession of the Davabere Needle, an ancient artifact that could steal or gift magic, which the sorceress stole from him. Maybe he had more secrets.

Theresa huffed. "You're missing the point. We desperately need allies. People will want to follow Alexander. And you saw King William. He's no longer fit to rule. He'll abdicate. And Alexander loves the people, too."

"Alexander never wanted to rule," Kai said.

"Well, he doesn't have much of a choice now, does he?" Theresa said. She gesticulated with her hands, nearly knocking over the blue glass teapot. Edouard steadied it without missing a beat, while Theresa continued her rant without noticing. "Everything's going up in flames, and someone's going to have to step up so the sorceress doesn't destroy everything."

"Who says she wants to destroy it?" Quentis asked.

Kai clenched his jaw. Any mention of the sorceress not being evil raised his hackles. He'd encountered her, endured her torture. There was no hope of a world in which Renevelda in power didn't raze everything good and rebuild to her preference.

Quentis held his palms up. His bright eyes softened as he regarded Theresa. "I'm not on her side. I want to make sure you're not jumping to conclusions that haven't been proven. Just playing devil's advocate so we run through every possibility. We need to be prepared."

"Renevelda only cares about herself," Kai said. "She'll use any and everyone to get what she wants." He turned his attention to Theresa. "And it sounds like you want to do the same."

Theresa's expression hardened. "Don't be naïve. We're all well aware of the instability of the political sphere. Neither of the territories has a real leader at the moment. The sorceress has assumed control of Castle Viltresor. How long do you think it will take her to claim the one in Terrapese, as well? If we don't act now, we've already lost. Can you think of anyone better to unite the Sight community?"

"Talullah." Kai said her name without hesitation. An ache formed in his heart. He hadn't spoken to her in so long. Didn't even know if she was still alive.

Theresa looked up at him now, her eyes aflame. "I don't know if you realize this, but we are in quite a delicate situation. We can't afford mistakes."

"But she's on our side," Kai said.

"Is she?" Theresa said. "Do you know that for certain? Or is your heart blinded by affection?"

"Of course I'm sure she's on our side." He ignored the jab at his feelings. Affections or none, he still believed Talullah stood with them. "Did you see how she fought Renevelda at the castle?"

Edouard and Veylan watched Theresa and Kai's verbal sparring match with opposing expressions. Edouard, as usual, looked bored. But at the mention of Talullah's name, Veylan's eyes had sparked with interest. With hope. Maybe he'd side with Kai on this.

Theresa folded her arms. "She's a Sezna Seer. Like Renevelda."

"So?" Kai's anger bubbled higher now, threatening to spill out. He pushed his chair back and stood, pacing the cobbled porch. Too much energy pushed through him. He needed the physical release or his head might explode.

"How do you know she won't align with the other Sezna Seers who have been campaigning to take over for years now? They believe that we're less valuable than they are because we have fewer Sight powers. Even though we're stronger in those powers than they could ever be."

Kai swallowed before answering, making sure his tone was calm. "Not everyone thinks that way, Theresa."

"It doesn't take everyone. It only takes a few radicals to change everything."

"I understand your hesitation and fear—"

She cut him off. "It's not fear. It's rage. Rage that we have been deemed as lesser, both by those without magic *and* by those leaking it from their pores. Being stuck in the middle hasn't served us well. We can't win unless we take the power for ourselves."

"Talullah isn't like those other Seers. She's only recently come into her own power. She's probably feeling the same way that we are. I don't know why she took that tapestry square from Renevelda, but I do know that her intentions are good, whatever she means to do with it.

"I sort of envy your confidence." Theresa sighed. "I don't

know if I can be as trusting as you. For your sake, I hope you're right. But, do you think people would follow her? Risk their lives for her?"

I did. And I'd do it again.

"Actually," Veylan said, his expression now composed and thoughtful. "I think Kai's right."

"What?" Theresa whirled on him. The ends of her dark brown hair whipped across her chin from beneath her headscarf. "You're supposed to be on my side."

"I am." Veylan's tone turned gentle, soothing, almost like how one might speak to a child. It sparked an urge in Kai to punch him in the jaw, even though Veylan agreed with him. "If what Kai says is true, and I don't doubt it is, Talullah would be a strong asset to our cause. She's fought against Renevelda previously, knows the sorceress's strengths and weaknesses. And she has a piece of the tapestry."

"Whatever you decide to do," Quentis said, "I'd suggest doing it quickly. Theresa is right that the sorceress is gaining power." He pulled out a piece of parchment and unfolded it. "A friend passed this along to me this morning."

Kai read it aloud. "Any Sight magic users who wish to be granted amnesty in the rising conflicts, should come and declare their loyalty to Renevelda Anaideia at Castle Viltresor." Kai looked up. "She's offering preemptive protection. Which means she's planning something." His mind spun in a thousand directions at once.

"Most people don't know anything about her," Theresa said quietly. "She's offering them exactly what they want and need during this time of uncertainty. It's not like anyone has been telling the citizens everything the sorceress has done in her pursuit of power. She could easily amass a following that would be unstoppable."

"Would they truly believe she wants to protect them?" Kai asked.

"If this is all they know of her, why wouldn't they?" Theresa replied.

"They're walking into a deathtrap," Kai said slowly, remembering the way he felt with the Davabere Needle so close to him and how Alexander's mother's skin had turned gray as Renevelda drew the magic and life force from her. "What if she's luring them in so she can steal their power?"

He imagined all the innocent citizens who would flock to the castle at the prospect of securing a sustainable and comfortable life for themselves and their families, how they would be so full of hope and gratitude. The sorceress would wipe them from existence without blinking.

Unbidden came the image of the little girl and her brother, whose house Kai and Edouard had gone to on their first day of creating the ledger that now sat in his bag, taunting him and telling him he'd made a horrible mistake.

What if Bo and his sister went to the sorceress for help? What if their parents thought they were doing the right thing by sending their kids to the castle, like so many who'd sent their kids to the Isle of Salire in hopes of making a better life for them?

Talullah's pain, as she'd explained the Isle's sacrifices, had scorched his body. It radiated through him just as intensely now as he recalled it. He didn't need an amethyst or Urtha's magic to experience that pain.

"How are we going to protect them?" Kai asked, his voice gravelly with fear. "We can't let all those people go into the castle. Even if they don't know about Renevelda, we've seen what she's capable of and is willing to do to claim whatever power she believes is rightly hers. It doesn't even matter if she thinks it's *rightly* hers. She'll take it, regardless."

"Unless someone stops her," Veylan said.

"Unless *we* stop her," Theresa amended. "No one's coming to save us. We have to save ourselves."

Veylan cleared his throat as he laced his fingers through Theresa's. "It's time to build up our forces from the king's ledger. See how many people we can bring to our side. And Kai, contact Talullah. Ask her to come here. I think you're right. She's going to be integral to our success."

CHAPTER 13

MARGOT

As soon as Margot was far enough from the barrier that she could no longer see Penny, her stomach sank like a botched soufflé. She hadn't thought this far ahead, hadn't considered how she would find Talullah if she managed to get through the barrier.

Part of her hadn't truly believed she *would* get through the barrier. Now that she had, she needed to pull herself together and come up with a plan. Planning ahead was, of course, one of Talullah's strengths. Margot worked better on the fly, making things up as she went along. She reminded herself of this as she trudged along through the woods.

She pulled out the map she'd stolen from Talullah's room. It was crumpled from her haphazard folding job, so when she took it out, she had to smooth it down against a tree. Lucky for her, Dhalian was always leaving random maps behind. This one had come from a rather large stack piled in the corner of her sister's closet.

It showed both continents, as well as the islands that surrounded them. She knew Talullah had gone to Calla to visit Jothi. At least, that's what Talullah had told her family.

Margot grazed her shaking pointer finger across the map until she located the black dot labeled *Calla*. She groaned. Why did it have to be so far away? And across the sea.

Suddenly, Margot wished she'd paid more attention in World Geography class at school. If she had, she might have thought twice about leaving home.

She breathed in the cold air and let it warm in her chest.

That was the best lead Margot had to go on. She had to hope her responsible sister hadn't lied about where she was going.

Calla's unfortunate location—all the way across the sea— meant Margot would need to somehow get herself on a ship and sail for at least a few days to travel to the other continent. A few days seemed like enough to cross that little bit of water. It looked more like a river than an ocean. It couldn't take that long.

Margot's jaw clenched. She didn't love the idea of spending multiple days on a vessel that could sink at any given minute.

Never mind the fact that she didn't know where the nearest port was. The map would show her that, at least.

Margot leaned against the tree and pressed the map to her chest, inhaling in the scent of looming snow and exhaling the thoughts of impending doom.

Was this a terrible idea?

Had she already screwed up?

Why did she think she could be the one to save Talullah?

Because, to her knowledge, she was the only one who'd been having visions of her sister in trouble. She couldn't stand by and wait for something bad to happen without giving it her best effort to warn her sister.

Margot thought for a long minute, counting the iridescent starlings swooping from tree to tree. A normal ship at a port wouldn't exactly invite her, even if she managed to make it there. She had no travel documents, barely enough money to feed herself, and no one to vouch for her.

But…

She might be able to find someone to vouch for her. To help her gain access to a ship. Someone to pretend to be her guardian or to falsify documents for her.

Her soufflé stomach deflated further. She was already turning to illegal options.

But what other choice did she have?

She had to get to Talullah.

Resolved, Margot refolded the map—more carefully this time, creasing the edges and everything—and put it back in her bag. She wouldn't need it for the next step.

She didn't go to the Hidden Market often. That was always Talullah's job as the eldest. Nonetheless, Margot remembered the way. She straightened her shoulders and rolled her neck, gearing herself up.

If there was a place she could find what she needed, it was the Hidden Market.

She counted the tree stumps and stepped between the sixth and seventh. The tingling warmth of magic enveloped her. Unlike the barrier around River Hill, the Hidden Market's magic invited her in, guiding her with one hand in hers and the other on her back.

A wave of scents mingled together and washed over her. Something salty, something pungent. Something a little sweet, yet bitter, like licorice lingered beneath it all.

Margot glanced back and forth. Her eyes struggled to land anywhere for long, jumping from the woman carrying a hissing basket to the red-bearded man bartering with a merchant to a small boy reaching for a bracelet on the edge of an orange table-cloth. Tents stood in rows, each blanketed by thick canvas.

Now that there were no kings to hide from, banners outside

each tent advertised exactly what they were offering, savory or otherwise.

As she forced her legs to carry her into the river of people, Margot noted signs for love potions and protection spells, objects claiming to curse one's enemies or disguise one's appearance. She gripped her bag tighter and tried to project confidence. Her pulse pumped in her throat.

The nerves wouldn't show on her face, though. If Margot had anything going for her, it was her ability to shield her emotions. Maybe that was part of her Katamian Gift, an ability to illusion herself.

Margot wandered through the stalls with cautious purpose. Coins jangled in her bag, the meager savings she'd compiled throughout her eleven years. She only hoped it would be enough.

A black tent with silver words scrawled on the outside caught her eye. "Documents, etc." She mouthed the words to herself. "Not a very clever name." But it might be what she needed. Fake papers would be less risky to deal with than saddling herself to a stranger.

She'd put her fingers on the tent's flap when arguing voices burst from inside. Margot recoiled. She wedged herself in between that tent and its neighbor. The tone of the voices conveyed an urgency and displeasure that intrigued her.

"You have the rings, right?" the first voice asked in a voice so slippery Margot's ears struggled to hang onto his words. Was that some kind of magic?

"Of course, I do. I'm good at my job, regardless of your opinion," said the second. His deeper tone rasped with annoyance. "You think I'm stupid? I know how important they are."

Important rings?

Maybe they could help her find her sister. Stuff like that existed. Margot strained to listen, wishing she'd learned enough Katamian magic to dial up her senses.

"No, but I do think, on occasion, a pretty face can beguile you," said the smooth voice.

"I can appreciate a woman's aesthetics without being taken advantage of. She's too young for me anyway."

Margot's breath hitched. Could he be talking about Talullah? Had she come to the market looking for a magic ring to help her defeat Renevelda?

The deeper voice continued, "And that spider she always wears gives me the shivers."

Spider? No, that couldn't be Talullah. A sigh of relief escaped Margot's lungs. She was desperate for any sign of her sister, but she didn't want to think about Talullah on the dark side of the market.

"Make sure you keep on your guard," the first man said. "I don't trust the criminals from the Isle. And now that they know we have the rings, I expect they'll return." He spat the words like spoiled milk. "They're worth way more than they'll ever deign to pay. Plus, I kind of like having one over on them. But if I find out who told them…"

The back of Margot's neck prickled. The Isle? Could it be the same one Talullah went to? How many Isles were there? She *really* needed to brush up on her geography. Who knew it was this important?

The first man grunted. "Are you finished lecturing me, Veylan? Some of us need to work for a living."

The second man—Veylan—snorted. "By all means." He stormed out of the front of the tent, flinging the curtain so hard it nearly hit Margot in the eye. She held her breath, but he didn't notice her as he stalked away.

The air tasted like scheming. What did the mysterious rings do? Why did the criminals want them? What would happen if they didn't get them?

Margot shivered. She was way out of her league here. Veylan had called the other people criminals, but Margot got the sense that the guys operating this tent didn't exactly operate by the book, either.

Her head swam with second thoughts. She had no idea what to do when faced with men of this sort.

Would she even be able to convince them to give her papers?

She took a walk around the market to let herself mull it over. Was asking them worth the risk?

Of course, it was. Talullah wouldn't let her fear get the best of her, not if the roles were reversed and it was Margot in trouble.

Margot returned to Documents, etc. She steeled her features to make herself look older, more capable than she felt.

She peeked in the tent, her breath shallow.

It was empty.

She crept in. "Hello?" She hated how meek her voice sounded. "Anyone?"

But no one answered.

She darted her gaze around the tent. Along the ceiling sparkled circular mirrors strung together like lights. Long black tables filled the space, but all were empty.

Looks like he'd already closed up. She'd have to come back.

She was halfway out the door when a low voice rumbled in her eardrums. "Whatever you're trying to steal, put it down and I might let you keep your hand."

Margot squeaked in surprise and turned around, hands held up. "I'm not stealing anything. I promise."

The merchant had to be at least six-and-a-half feet tall. His biceps bulged as if he were smuggling boulders beneath his skin. He smiled at her, revealing two missing teeth, the rest a bit yellow. "Lying costs the other hand. You sure you want to gamble?"

He stood and stalked toward Margot, whose feet had picked the worst time to forget how to move.

She swallowed hard but remembered her purpose. Forcing all

the moxie she could muster into her eyes and voice, she replied, "I like my odds."

The merchant raised a nearly-nonexistent eyebrow. The hair was so pale it blended into his skin. "Give me your bag."

Margot thrust it toward him. He dumped the contents onto the nearest table and brushed through the bits and bobs Margot had packed for her journey.

Satisfied, the merchant swept the contents back into the bag and handed it to Margot. "If you're not stealing, why were you sneaking around?"

"I wasn't sneaking! I was looking."

"For?"

This close, the merchant's smell of sweat mingled with the licorice-like one Margot had noticed upon first entering the market.

"Documents. Have any of those by chance?" She was pressing her luck being so sassy, but Margot couldn't help it. This guy had accused her of being a criminal, and now he was looking at her like she was a whiny toddler. It was annoying. And offensive.

The merchant laughed. "What kind do you need?" He snapped his fingers.

Margot's vision blurred. The smell of licorice burned the inside of her nose. When her eyes cleared a second later, the previously empty tables overflowed with crates full of parchment rolled into scrolls. Margot gasped.

"If you're impressed by a simple illusion spell, little girl, I'd say you need to get out more. Now, what can I help you find?"

Margot choked down all the questions she wanted to ask. She wasn't there to bother scary men about their magic. "I need to board a boat."

"Follow me." The merchant waved her to a crate in the middle of the room. A ship had been burned into the wood. "Destination?"

Margot took a deep breath. Last chance to change her mind. "Calla. Please."

The merchant withdrew a scroll. "You got money?"

Margot nodded. "How much?"

"Fifty pewters." He gestured for her to follow him to the desk near the entrance.

Panic squeezed Margot's lungs like hands wringing a sponge. She only had fifty-five. She wouldn't be able to afford a place to stay or much food. But this was her only shot at finding Talullah.

She reached into the bag and counted out the money onto the desk in front of the merchant. Each clang of metal on wood sounded like something lost.

Goodbye ham biscuit. Goodbye lemonade. Goodbye inn room.

He watched her with a curious yet oddly gentle expression. Margot drew a ragged breath as she pushed the coins toward him.

"Sign here," the merchant said. Margot did. She watched in awe as he traced his own finger across the page, signing with magic instead of ink.

He rolled up the paper, tied it with a thin black ribbon, and handed it to her. "Your ship leaves in three days from the port at Adeline Square. You know how to get there?"

"Yep." Margot kept her answer short. She'd check her map and figure it out.

The merchant nodded and stepped back. "Stay safe." It was a strange thing to say to a customer, but Margot didn't want to dally any longer. She'd gotten what she came for.

Probably even more.

"It's been a pleasure," Margot said as she sped from the tent, though it had been nothing of the sort.

The merchant's breathy laugh followed her all the way out of the market.

CHAPTER 14

TALULLAH

While Talullah, Dhal, and Jothi waited for Edda to bring their tea and snacks at Stars Align mountain café, Talullah perused the bookshelves that took up nearly an entire wall.

Talullah always found something magical about books, even if they were ordinary ones. The potential gave them powers of their own in Talullah's mind. Books had never failed her.

She leaned into the familiarity amidst the chaos of the unknown. Wandering around the city, she'd felt unmoored, like a ship being blown by the wind without oars or anchors or any method of steering.

On the contrary, book research grounded her. It gave her confidence that if an answer existed, it would be on a page somewhere. It made her feel like she could take as many steps forward or back as she needed, but she'd still be on the right path.

She dragged her finger gently across the spines at eye level, reading the titles scrawled in varied lettering styles.

Recipe books specializing in cakes or bread or soups were all bound in thick burgundy covers with clean, white blocky titles.

Countless volumes told stories of tea plants behind evergreen spines with golden scripted names like *A Thousand Ways to Use Tea Leaves* and *The Healing Power of Tea.*

Finally, Talullah reached an entire case dedicated to the stars. Matte black tomes, each with a star at the top of the spine, stretched ceiling to floor, almost a continuation of the mural painted overhead.

The sight stole her breath. It was a stunning, visual, yes. But it was more than that. It was a thread to tug, an opportunity to dig deeper, to see if she could make sense of the constellation she'd seen.

Talullah pulled as many books as she could carry off the shelf and brought them to the table.

"Find a little light reading?" Jothi asked.

Talullah rolled her eyes, though her friends would barely be able to see the gesture behind the books stacked up to her nose.

Dhal laughed. "We're on a mountain in a small, secluded café, and still you find a library." He shook his head and grinned at her so brightly that Talullah's heart quickened. "You have many talents, Tules."

Her face flushed both from the attention and the teasing, but she let her excitement take the lead.

Talullah shrugged, tucked a stray bit of hair behind her ear, and sank into the chair.

She pulled the stack in front of her and turned it so Dhal and Jothi could see the spines. "As luck would have it," she said, "Edda is interested in the stars. Or at least she thinks her patrons might be."

The first few books held no information about the star pattern she'd seen on the trail sign, but the fourth one in the stack made her eyes light up. It held nearly a hundred star maps, a record of all the constellations that astronomers had currently discovered.

"If this truly is a constellation," she said, tapping the drawing she'd made from memory with fingers that refused to stay still, "it will be in here."

Dhal and Jothi scooted their chairs closer. The wooden feet scraped against the floor and echoed through the otherwise empty café. All three of them huddled over the book as Talullah flipped through the pages one by one.

"Wait," Jothi said. They picked up the parchment on which Talullah had drawn her version of the pattern. "It looks kind of like this one."

"Or that one," Dhal said. He pointed to another constellation with a similar number of dots and similar positioning.

"Maybe I should try Scrying Captain Caprico," Talullah said. She didn't know why she hadn't thought of it before, but Colfax Caprico, the man who'd assisted her in both saving her sisters from the sorceress and in escaping the Isle of Salire, had mentioned his love of the stars. "I bet he'll know what this is. I'm going to go outside and try to Scry him now." She took the parchment with her so she could show him.

Talullah found a spot near a fragrant juniper tree out of sight of the café windows. Despite the ubiquity of magic in Calla, Talullah wanted to keep the extent of her powers to herself. The conversation she'd overheard in the market returned to her—*that poor woman.*

Until she knew for certain who was trustworthy and who wasn't, she had to be careful.

The gold and silver bracelet Scry sat cold against her wrist. She glanced around and found herself alone in the rocky side yard. Still, better make it quick.

Talullah pressed the sapphire on her necklace to dial down the high-pitched, syncopated bird calls foreign to her ears. Then, she touched the sapphire on her reusable Scry and waited.

It had been a little while since she'd spoken to either Captain Caprico or his wife, Gwendolyn. But she hoped they'd answer.

Bubble-like film stretched across the circle Scry. Talullah readied her questions.

Then the Scry beeped twice. The sapphire flashed black. The film popped.

Talullah flinched. That had never happened before.

She turned the Scry over. The sapphire had returned to normal. She tried again, but the same thing happened.

Something must be wrong with the Scry. She wondered if there was a repair place in town she could take it to be fixed. Would anyone look at her with suspicion if she did?

Disheartened, she returned to her friends, prepared to deliver the bad news, and found Jothi bent over Dhal's wrist on the table.

Dhal's breaths came in measured waves that Talullah recognized as a concentrated effort to ignore the pain. His eyes were squinted while closed, and he had covered his wrist with a black linen napkin. The exposed skin had turned pale brown from the pressure.

"It's happening again?" Talullah asked. She dropped the drawing on the table and placed her hand in Dhal's.

Dhal nodded, keeping his eyes closed. He took a few deep breaths in and blew them out.

"We need to find you a medic," Jothi said.

"Do you think that's safe?" Dhal asked through clenched teeth.

"I think it's safer than doing nothing," Jothi replied, looking at Talullah.

"Let me see it." Talullah peeled back the napkin despite Dhal's insane proclamation that he was fine.

The R-shaped scar throbbed red, raised off the skin even more than usual. A faint red glow made it look like it was bleeding, though no trace of actual blood was visible. "Yes, we definitely need to find you a medic." She pulled Dhal to standing.

At that moment, Edda came out of the kitchen balancing a tray laden with tea, muffins, and sausage. "Sorry about the wait." The smell of salty, nearly-burned meat and baked blueberry muffins swirled around.

Edda paused. Her eyes darted from Dhal's exposed wrist to Talullah and Jothi, and then to the open books and the star drawing on the table. Her gaze lit with recognition. She looked between all of them and the paper and the book in rapid succession twice. Dhal hurried to cover his wrist, but Edda reached out. "There's no need to hide here," she said quietly. "This is a safe place for you."

She slid the food and tea onto a neighboring table.

"May I help?" Edda gestured to Dhal's wrist.

It might be too late to find a medic. Edda might be their best chance to help Dhal. If she knew how.

A sensation like the brush of butterfly wings touched the exposed skin of Talullah's face. At the same time, a scent like spiced cherries washed over her.

Magic.

A new kind Talullah hadn't experienced before. Talullah's heart skipped.

Edda locked eyes with Talullah. "I promise I won't hurt him. I can't heal it completely. This is a temporary fix. But it will ease the pain."

"Dhal?" Talullah would let her friend decide.

"Okay," Dhal said, breathing heavily.

Edda laid a gentle hand on Dhal's wrist. Immediately, he stilled. The tension that had held his jaw taut melted like butter in a warm room.

Dhal blinked his eyes open. The crinkles holding pain at the corners dissolved. "Thank you."

"You're welcome. Though, you will need to treat that regularly. How'd you come by an injury like that, anyway?"

"Made the wrong enemy," Dhal grumbled.

"Easy to do these days," Edda said. Her sharp gaze returned to the books on the table. "Interesting pick of books."

"Oh, yes." Talullah rushed to grab the parchment with her star drawing. "Just doing some reading."

"Funny thing about this place," Edda replied. "Nonmagical folks never seem to order the muffins. Or notice the books."

Talullah froze. Dhal met her gaze, questions firing from his eyes.

Should they tell her? Should they deny it?

"We're not—" Jothi started.

Edda held up a hand and smiled. "It's hard to disguise a Gift like that." She nodded at Talullah. So she'd sensed Talullah's magic. And she'd invited them to stay. But to what purpose?

Talullah's eyes found the bookshelves again. They seemed to wink at her, pleased they'd played their part in the facade.

Recipes.

Tea.

Stars.

Those were all tools the Ceserites used. The only section Talullah hadn't seen was—

"Palmistry's over there." Edda pointed to a shelf half the size of the others. "Couldn't fit it all in one place." She shrugged as if to say, *what can you do?*

"Are you a Ceserite?" Talullah asked, her voice breathy, her palms sweating.

Edda laughed. The half-cackle showed she was missing a few teeth. "Guilty."

Relief flooded Talullah's senses, releasing the breath trapped inside her.

"Why put yourself at risk like this?" Jothi asked.

"People see what I want them to see," she replied. "My son, Leo, does a good job of steering the right clientèle to my door."

"He knew too?" Talullah asked. "That I'm—wait. What—or who—do you think I am?"

Edda glanced again at the drawing of the constellation in Talullah's hand. "You're exactly who we've been waiting for, Sezna Seer."

CHAPTER 15

TALULLAH

As it turned out, the entrance to the Ceserite compound was *not* hidden behind the rock slide site and waterfall. It was, more surprisingly, through a broom closet in Stars Align Café.

Talullah turned the bronze teaspoon over in her hand. The five-pointed star on top poked into her palm.

Edda had given it to Talullah. "The key, of course," she'd said.

Of course.

Edda had gone ahead to prepare whatever tools she'd need to teach Talullah how to effectively use her ruby. And she wanted to make sure Talullah, Jothi, and Dhal would be able to find their own way.

"Are you ready?" Dhal squeezed her hand. A jolt of nerves, among other things, whizzed through her body. She'd been waiting for this moment ever since she'd discovered her visions weren't simply dreams.

Truthfully, she'd been anticipating this moment since that first vision when she was seven, and when she'd first received the necklace from her mother.

She hadn't known then what kind of journey she would go on to discover her Gifts. She was glad she hadn't known. Maybe she would have made different decisions.

Jothi nodded at her.

"Here goes nothing." Talullah inserted the spoon into the door's keyhole and then took a step back.

Dhal squeezed Talullah's hand again. In front of them, the door flickered and disappeared. The spoon fell out. Talullah caught it, stuffing it in her pocket. The three of them stepped through into a short stone tunnel.

The further they walked toward the light, the stronger the scent of cinnamon and woodsmoke became.

Their boots made no sound on the spongy moss, which covered the ground instead of stone. The tunnel opened onto a plateau that stretched further than Talullah could see.

To their left, a mountain rock wall reached for the clouds. Dwellings with windows, doors, and narrow porches had been carved out of its face. Purple and white flowers spilled out of red wooden window boxes, which hung below each window.

Talullah's brown eyes widened as she stared open-mouthed, awestruck at the craftsmanship. At being privileged enough to witness the extraordinary skill these people possessed.

A maroon shutter burst open on a window two levels up. "You made it!" Edda leaned the upper half of her body out the window and waved with a deep brown hand. "Come on up!" She pointed to a winding staircase that had also been chiseled out of the mountainside.

Talullah looked at Dhal, but he wasn't paying attention to Edda. His eyes were locked on Talullah.

He inhaled sharply when she met his gaze, then looked away, shaking his head and smiling.

Jothi tugged them forward. "Let's go."

They climbed the stairs, Talullah and Dhal still holding hands, though it wasn't necessary. Talullah liked how their fingers intertwined. She felt safe in Dhal's presence. She wasn't ready to let go.

Edda rushed them through her white front door and into a sitting area. The floor was made of the same stone as the walls, but that's where the similarities to the mountain ended. Talullah had imagined a dark, cold space, but Edda's home burst with warmth from a wood stove in the corner.

"Glad to see you navigated the spoon alright." Edda fluttered through her space, dodging pots of aloe and jade large enough for a person to bathe in. She touched a diamond-shaped mirror the size of her palm, and the whole space brightened.

Talullah, Jothi, and Dhal loitered on the scratchy, braided rug by the door.

"Well, come in, come in. We can't do much work from there."

The magical energy crackled in the air. It raised the hair on Talullah's arms as she and her friends followed Edda through the living area into a back room.

A star chart covered the entire back wall. It looked like many more had been hung behind it, so that one could flip back and forth between them. A white wood hutch housed four tea sets and sat against the wall to their right. Tallulah couldn't help but wonder where the tea sets had come from and what Mabel Miller would think of them.

Edda had already moved to the hutch and pulled open the drawer. She muttered to herself as she moved her hand over the tins of tea within.

Talullah stepped closer so she could get a better look.

Symbols she'd never seen before adorned each tin. Labels, perhaps?

It was another language, certainly.

"Sit, sit," said Edda, gesturing behind her to the oblong table in the center of the room. Scattered pieces of parchment covered the surface.

Out of necessity, Talullah let go of Dhal's hand. He glanced down at it, then quickly grabbed the chair in front of Talullah and pulled it out for her.

"Oh. Thanks," she said, flustered. She sat. Warmth that had nothing to do with Edda's wood stove climbed her neck like ivy.

If Edda noticed the awkwardness of the exchange, she kept it to herself. Dhal, too, remained cool and calm. He flashed her a smile and whispered, "We're here."

Edda took a seat across the table. She shuffled the papers into a semi-neat stack at the far end and slid a tea tray next to it. Talullah wet her lips. This was it. What she'd come all this way for.

The older Seer tilted her head toward Talullah and clasped her hands together in front of her on the table. "Now, I know there are many questions swirling in that head of yours. I can feel them in the air, and I will answer as many as I can. But first, I think you need to have all your tools at your disposal. So why don't you go ahead and put that ruby in its spot so it can be reunited with its sisters? It's calling desperately to them."

"It is?" Dhalian asked, and his gaze dropped to Talullah's satchel, where she still had the carved handle of her father's cane with the ruby in its eye slot. She'd been afraid that if she removed the ruby, she would drop and lose it before she got a chance to put it in the frame.

"Do I need to know anything that might happen once I put it in?" Talullah asked.

Edda laughed, a musical sound. "Oh, dear, there is so much to tell you, but in these matters, experience works much faster than lecture alone. I will say you're going to be incredibly thirsty afterward, and you may feel a bit faint. That is completely normal. I assume you had a strong reaction when you first put in your amethyst?"

"You could say that," Talullah said, remembering how the rush of past events had overwhelmed her senses and made her feel like she was spinning in circles and trying to watch multiple things happen at once. It was like being in the middle of a tornado of thoughts and feelings and experiences.

"The amethyst and ruby are quite alike in this regard, so don't be surprised if you get a similar rush of visions all at once, which makes no sense to you."

"Okay," Talullah said, breathing deeply. She pulled the fish handle out of her bag and handed it to Dhalian with only a slightly shaky hand. Tears welled, unexpected, in her eyes. Her heart ached to see her father, to tell him thank you for keeping the ruby safe for so long, for trusting her to use it. She imagined him wrapping her in a warm hug. His trimmed blond beard would catch in her hair, but she wouldn't care.

I'm proud of you, my Talullah, he said in her mind.

Once the thought of home had broken through, she couldn't stop the images of Penny and Margot barreling through the house and catching her between them. If Talullah managed to stop Renevelda—no, *when* she did—when this was all over, she wasn't leaving her family for a long time.

With care and precision, Dhal pressed the tip of his pocketknife blade under the two pointiest corners of the gem. With a gentle *pop*, it released from its hold. Dhal placed it in her palm.

The distinct warmth Talullah associated with her Sight magic radiated through her hand.

She looked between Dhalian and Jothi for encouragement. They both nodded and Dhal squeezed her other hand, once again leaving it in hers. Talullah found the ruby's place in her necklace and pressed it in.

All at once, Talullah's vision went red. Everything around her in the mountain dwelling faded to a red hue until it all blurred together. All she saw was a solid block of color. Then, an explosion that felt like a blow to the head made her eyes open within her. A burst of white flashed, then faded to a glimpse of a scene.

A room beneath the ground. Objects strewn haphazardly about. A rush of adrenaline.

As with the amethyst, her vision cycled through many different visions of things that were to come, but none lingered long enough for her to understand what they were. Her body shifted through fits of pleasure and fear, elation and dread. She felt disconnected from her own body.

Though she couldn't see him, she leaned into Dhal as his arms wrapped around her. The scent of morning dew and honey trickled in through the cracks in the vision.

As quickly as it had appeared, his presence faded. The air around her turned cold. So cold, she struggled to breathe. She looked for him in the hazy red vision. "Dhal!" she heard herself shout, and the words bled raw and desperate, like they'd been cut from her throat.

Damp air swirled around her. It smelled of dirt and iron. Constellations circled overhead. A wetness drew her attention to her palm, which bled freely as twisted black tree roots crackled in front of her, raised symbols pushing up from beneath the bark. A clenching in her stomach made her want to vomit.

Talullah blinked.

And the whole scene disappeared.

~

TALULLAH OPENED HER EYES. One of Edda's quilts tickled her chin. She shifted in the small arm chair and pulled the blanket down off her shoulders. The fabric was well worn, but in a way that made it softer than almost anything she had ever felt before.

She vaguely remembered mentioning she was tired. After the visions her ruby had provided, her whole body ached and her eyelids hadn't been able to stay open.

"Rest a while," Edda had said gently.

Someone had moved her. Her cheeks burned a little bit at the memory of Dhal carrying her.

"Move slowly, dear," Edda said from a rocking chair in the corner of the room.

"How long was I asleep?" Talullah's tongue stuck to the roof of her mouth as she spoke.

"An hour or so. There's a mug of tea next to you, if you're thirsty."

Thirsty? There wasn't a word in the entirety of *Ancient Languages of the World* strong enough to describe how thirsty she was. Talullah gulped it down. It was the perfect temperature. Not hot enough to scald her tongue and throat, but not cold either.

Jothi waved at her from across the room. "Welcome back."

"Where's—"

"Right here," Dhal said. He appeared at her side. The sight of his face nearly made Talullah weep. She'd been so desperate to find him, but he'd been here all along. But had that been real, or part of the vision?

"Just whipping up some sustenance." He offered her a plate full of bread, cheeses, and sliced fruit.

Talullah blinked away the visions she'd Seen when she'd added the ruby to her necklace. Ignored the distress fluttering in her belly. Lied to herself that she'd misinterpreted it. That she hadn't lost Dhal and smelled blood.

"Thanks." She sat up and nibbled on some bread slathered in butter and a berry jam. A satisfied sound escaped her mouth.

After a few moments, she'd eaten enough to have regained some strength.

Dhal watched her, concern tugging at the corners of his mouth. "Edda said we could have been here all night. But, look at you, surprising me yet again." He gently tucked a piece of her hair behind her ear, his fingers lingering longer than was strictly necessary.

Talullah addressed Edda. "That's not going to happen every time I try to use this magic, right?"

"No, no, that will be the worst of it, and not a moment too soon."

"What do you mean?" Talullah asked.

"I've just received word about some suspicious activity happening at Castle Viltresor."

Talullah still hadn't heard from Kai. She'd try to Scry him again as soon as they left Edda's. "What's going on?"

Instead of answering, Edda nodded to Talullah's tea. "Drink up. And better finish that snack while you're at it. You're going to need as much strength as possible."

Jothi refilled Talullah's mug from a white ceramic teapot patterned with purple irises.

"What are we doing?" Talullah asked.

Edda straightened up and folded the blanket Talullah had been huddled under. "As soon as you're fit, I'm taking you to Ragnatri, the Forest of the Future."

CHAPTER 16

TALULLAH

Talullah followed Edda up the winding mountain path. Labored breaths puffed in and out of her lungs, though she was the only one struggling. Edda surged ahead as if the high altitude bore no effect on her. Talullah gave herself the benefit of the doubt. Edda lived up here all the time. Her lungs were used to it.

Already Talullah missed Dhal. Edda said only Seers with the power of Future Sight could go to Ragnatri, so Dhal was stuck waiting at Edda's house. Jothi had graciously kept him company.

"How much further?" Talullah asked. They'd already passed countless forks in the red dirt path, each marked with a wooden sign like she'd seen on her tour with Leo. White-barked trees as thick as three of Talullah's whole body dotted the landscape, towering hundreds of feet overhead.

Edda glanced over her shoulder and adjusted her slate gray shawl. "Not far."

Talullah grumbled under her breath, but she continued on, following Edda until they passed through a thick row of plum-colored bushes with leaves as small as fingernails.

The cave beyond, scooped from the side of the mountain, opened like a mouth frozen in a half-yawn.

"Come now. We're going to have to do this part together." Edda waved Talullah forward. Bats hung sleeping in secluded corners. Talullah tread carefully to avoid stepping in the shallow puddles beneath rose-pink stalactites. They reached a set of stairs at the back of the cave.

The opening seemed barely big enough for a child to slip through, but when Edda touched the ceiling, the opening widened enough for the two of them to go up together. There were few crevices to use as hand holds, so the Seers supported each other as they walked up and back into the cavern.

"Do people live in here?" Talullah asked. "Or did they at one time?"

Edda nodded. "They were temporary residences at various points in history, but now they're for the Seers to use."

When Talullah thought she couldn't go another step, her lungs filled with fresh air as her head broke the surface. "Are we on top of the mountain?"

She gulped the air greedily as she pulled herself through the hole after Edda and sat down on the dusty earth.

"Indeed we are." Edda filled her lungs with a deep breath, too.

"And we couldn't have gone up the regular path?" She pointed to a clearly marked trail head.

Edda shrugged. "I suppose we could have. But what fun would that have been? Also, it would have taken much, much longer and been more dangerous."

Talullah balked inwardly, but she sighed in relief and looked around. "It's beautiful here."

She'd never been on top of a mountain before. It was

different from how she'd imagined it. Instead of only expansive sky, large, aged deciduous trees with thick trunks and nearly as thick branches surrounded them.

"Welcome to Ragnatri, the official grounding place of the inevitable future." Edda stretched her hands wide. "Still gives me goosebumps all these years later."

"Only those with Cesera's Sight can find this place?" Talullah asked.

"Not only are they the only ones who can find it, they are also the only ones who can enter it. If someone were to accidentally travel up here, or if someone were to come up here with another Seer, but the companion did not have Cesera's Sight, the companion would see no stairs at the bottom of the cave. It would be a solid wall and they would be unable to ascend."

"Ah, so this was also a test." Talullah smirked slightly.

"Can't be too careful these days." Edda shrugged. "Though, I never doubted you."

"I wouldn't blame you if you had. I know it hasn't been easy for your community ever, but especially not now."

Edda nodded. "I would not have brought you to Ragnatri if I did not trust you. This is a sacred place full of sensitive information."

"These trees are so unique," Talullah said.

Edda studied them. "They are home to every inevitable future that has been accessed. Each branch of the tree contributes something to the web of the future."

Talullah gawked at them. She'd always been in awe of trees, their strength and their ability to grow in the most hostile of places, as well as to flourish when other things couldn't. To rebuild themselves and regrow after disaster. It seemed fitting that they held the secrets of the future. "And what about the leaves?"

The trees' leaves reminded her of Nainehta Forest, where

metallic gold and silver leaves adorned the trees. "Did the ones in Nainehta Forest originate from these?"

Edda nodded. "You are a quick study, Miss Bridgestone. All these trees as well as the ones in Nainehta Forest are related. Their magic came from the same source, and thus they grow in a similar fashion. Though their powers vary, they are similar at their core. The roots of all the magic trees connect just as the magic waterways all connect to the Source."

"The Source of the Suditzas' magic?"

"Yes. The shared connection is what makes the trees, waterways, and the magic itself so powerful. But it also makes them vulnerable. If someone were to poison the Source, it would affect all the magic given to us by the Goddesses."

A shiver ran up Talullah's spine. "And what would happen if someone with unsavory motives controlled the Source?"

Edda watched her carefully, her gaze trained on Talullah. "Devastation."

Talullah cleared her throat. "Can I get a closer look?" she asked.

"Sure. Be prepared. You never know what the trees want to show you."

Talullah inspected the bark of the tree nearest her. At once, the tingle of familiarity rolled over her skin. It was covered in runes. The same kind of runes that she'd seen on the transport trees. "What language are these written in?"

"The language of magic, of course."

Talullah laughed a little at that. But as she leaned closer, Dunamai's Eye warmed against her collarbone. "Is it possible for my amulet to translate the runes?"

"Ah, there's an idea. Come to think of it, that seems like something that might be possible. Why don't you give it a try?"

Talullah's breath grew shallow as she leaned forward and did her best to calm herself. She traced her amulet and pressed on the ruby in her necklace, calling forth the power of the inevitable to help her find the words that the runes represented.

The runes were arranged in a straight line down starting midway up the trunk, at eye level. She touched the topmost rune and closed her eyes while dragging her fingers down the rest, like she might touch the spine of a book.

Her vision went black, then flashed red.

When it cleared, she was no longer atop the mountain with Edda. She was in a circular room with a black ceiling. Pinpricks of light winked from above. Real stars or magic? Was this the café?

"Hello, Little Seer." The Spirit Fox appeared, lit by torch-light. Her black boots struck the stone of the floor in a pattern as she hopped across the floor.

No. Not the café. Somewhere new.

"Zeri." Talullah's voice strained against the gritty texture lodged in her throat, the pressure on her chest like she'd dived too deep in water. She hadn't been this anxious before, so why was she now?

"We're nearly finished with our business together. But I have one last gift for you."

The flames dancing behind Zeri froze in place, though their light remained. The air itself paused, everything so still that Talullah feared to breathe. Zeri's yellow cat-like eyes crinkled at the corners and her red ponytail swung, carefree, the only thing in motion.

In her mind's eye, sentences formed from the tree's runes. They sparkled gold and silver. Then, they translated into the common tongue.

Through the fire blazing bright, trust yourself, harness your might. Inner struggle blinds your eyes, let it go and win the prize. Use your heart, keep your mind, and what you seek, you shall find.

When the reflected light shines brightest, the imprisoned

must be freed. The power of two shall return what was stolen from the sea.

Destiny spelled in cards. A secret leads to the beginning and the end. What was hidden is no longer. Dark and light in equal measure. A powerful duo brings both ruin and ascension. When she with three breathes violets under the harvest moon, the cat that's not a cat will chase the mouse that's not a mouse. Silver water makes a red sky in sacrifice.

Twisted roots like night, four in harmony convene. With blood shed on stars of sleight, power taken as foreseen. Sacrifice, Seer, and master of flight, in unity prevail. And transform magic with immortal light, in control of threaded grail. Death relinquished by a heart of might, an ancestor restored. The sky weeps its blight, then will rise a new sense of accord.

The words caught flame and burned until they were merely ash on the ground.

Talullah shuddered in recognition. It was the same prophecy that Zeri had spoken to her in parts over the past year, plus the addition of a new stanza.

"Is this about Renevelda?" Talullah struggled to say. The pressure on her chest strengthened, threatened to crush her ribs to dust. "Is she going to control the Source?"

Zeri grinned, showing her pointed white teeth. "I'll see you again, Little Seer."

The flame torches flickered with motion once more. The Spirit Fox cocked her head, snapped her fingers, and disappeared, taking the rest of the vision with her.

Talullah stared at the light blue sky overhead, focused on the rustle of the leaves, tried to slow her racing heart.

Did the Spirit Fox receive her prophecies from these trees, too? Had she received Cesera's blessing?

The trunks of trees were the oldest parts. How long ago was this foretold? Could this be the same prophecy that divided the Seer factions all those years ago?

"So?" Edda asked as she came to stand next to Talullah. Her round brown eyes widened in curiosity.

"Edda, do you worry about the Source? About what could happen to it?"

"The Suditzas were optimistic in allowing humanity access to their power. They did build in some precautions to protect it."

"Like how my necklace cannot be stolen, only freely given?"

"Exactly like that. Many people believe that they have protected the Source so well that we needn't ever worry about it. We shouldn't assume the Suditzas would leave us vulnerable. That Cesera would know any bad thing that might happen, and they'd be prepared for it." Edda sighed.

"I'm sensing there's more to your opinion."

"I believe there is no such thing as fail-proof."

The prophecy's words returned, slamming against Talullah's mind. "Someone I trust believes Renevelda wants to control the Source."

"I agree. And that is why *you* must find it first."

CHAPTER 17

TALULLAH

Talullah pressed her palm to the matte black bark of Igdrasil, feeling the raised symbols beneath her fingertips.

She could read them now, if she wanted, with the help of her ruby. But she didn't have the mental capacity to absorb more prophecies.

The books Edda had let her borrow stretched her canvas bag and dragged her shoulders down. She hadn't had time to study all the ways Ceserites accessed and interpreted their prophecies. So now she had homework on top of everything else.

After Talullah had told Dhal everything that had happened in Ragnatri, he'd suggested they rest for the night and then leave immediately for Praeteriti. They needed to locate the other three pieces of the tapestry to find the Source, and they didn't have any time to lose.

The door appeared in the trunk at once. Talullah pushed it inward, revealing black nothingness.

"Exactly like last time, right?" Dhal questioned with a sly raise of his brow.

"Better than last time," Talullah responded. "Because this time, we don't have soldiers chasing us, and I won't have to cut off my hair." She ran her hands through her hair. It hung to her shoulders now.

Dhal brushed his thumb softly over the scar that ran from her cheekbone down to her earlobe, where the soldier's blade had kissed her, leaving a mark that not even changing the past had erased. She was glad of that, though. She wanted the reminder of what had happened before and didn't want to forget the pain that everyone she loved had endured both because of the sorceress and because of her own decisions.

Maybe it was Urtha, the Suditza of the past, influencing her to remember. Either way, she guarded her memories closely. Even the difficult ones. She had become the person she was today because of everything that had happened to her.

"Ready?" Dhalian asked.

And also because of the people who stood with her.

Dhal dropped his hand from her cheek and grabbed her hand instead. He rubbed his thumb over hers, and a zap of electricity ran through her body. They had never crossed into being more than friends, but these days, Talullah wondered if that was a possibility. There had been moments when she thought something lingered in Dhal's eyes, that he'd swallowed words she also wanted to say. For so long, she'd harbored these feelings and had been too afraid to do anything about it, fearing that she would lose one of the people closest to her in the process. So far, that risk hadn't been worth taking.

Could she cross that line now?

It would be so easy to lean forward and press her lips to his.

So easy, and yet the most difficult thing she'd ever done.

She'd cut herself off from her father and sisters and wasn't even sure if her mother was still alive. Dhalian was truly the last strong relationship she had. She needed him more than she cared to admit.

Maybe once all of this was over, there could be something more between them. But right now, she couldn't bring herself to do anything other than squeeze his hand and pull him with her down into the tree.

They slid down, more slowly this time, under the influence of Dunamai's Eye and the four stones within.

That first time, they'd gone too fast, pushed by adrenaline and untamed magic, for Talullah to catch more than a glimpse of the markings that had been written on the wall inside the passageway of the tree. But now, her amethyst glowed on her necklace, illuminating the symbols which she'd guessed were stories of the past.

Memories flowed into her mind, translated by her amethyst. One specific set of drawings caught her attention, and without knowing why, she threw her arms out to the side. Surprisingly, their forward progress halted, so she and Dhalian sat on the slide, but no longer moved downward.

"Whoa, that was cool," Dhal said. "Did you know you could do that?"

"No. I had a feeling I needed to look at this drawing more closely." She gazed at the drawing, which was of four large trees in separate corners of a rectangle. In the center of the drawing, the trees' roots tangled together in a knot. Other shapes surrounded the drawing, but their meaning wasn't obvious. "This is it, Dhal. This is what the tapestry is supposed to look like."

"I'll sketch it so that we can reference it later. Or, I guess so I can reference it later, since I assume now that you've seen it, your amethyst will remember."

Gillie hadn't shown them his, and Talullah couldn't access an image of it since she'd seen it before she had the amethyst. But the threads of magic inside her hummed with recognition.

"There's another drawing next to it," Talullah said. "It's the same, but the trees are less prominent. There are words weaving through the branches."

Talullah waited until Dhal had sketched both drawings on a square of parchment with a charcoal pencil. It was lucky that some things never changed. He always had parchment and charcoal on him, no matter the occasion. When he had finished, he nodded at Talullah.

She brought her hands together, and down they went again. Down, down, down the slope, though in a much more controlled fashion than the first time they'd come. When they made it to the bottom of the slope, they both glided out of the chute gracefully and landed on their feet. Still, bits of lavender dust clung to them as they exited into the closet of the library in Praeteriti.

About a year ago, they'd arrived in a rush of fear and tangled limbs. Talullah had met the teenage version of her mother, whom she hadn't seen since that day in the maze.

Talullah shoved aside those memories for now, because she needed to focus on the present. Even while she was in the world of the past. Maybe especially then.

She touched her sapphire and inhaled the scent of cinnamon that always seemed to ground and calm her because it reminded her of home. Then she and Dhal made their way out of the closet, which had a new, unlocked door.

The closet no longer housed books with the tortured souls of the Unforgiven. Once Tallulah had released them from her mind, they'd finally moved on to the actual afterlife, having served a purpose and forgiven themselves for their past faults.

Now, Talullah entered the main area of the library and inhaled its ever-present scent of old parchment. She walked along the black-and-white checkered floor with Dhalian right beside her. He hadn't visited since then, though Talullah herself had many times over the past year. More recently, she'd seen Cecilia the ghost in a potential future. The ghost had teased her with the promise of information about Talullah, her mother, and Aurinia. But Talullah couldn't follow Cecilia on that path without risk of becoming trapped in the Between.

Maybe the information was important.

Maybe it never existed.

Now would be the perfect time to ask, if only they could find the ghost. Out of the corner of her eye, Talullah noticed the twirling lace parasol and the honey blond curls, forever perfect, on the ghost's head. At the sight of Dhalian, Cecilia perked up and squealed. She floated over and tried to give Dhal a big hug. But, being that she was a ghost, and he was not, she went right through him.

Dhal shivered and hugged himself, clearly affected by the ghost's temperature.

"Sorry about that, doll," Cecilia drawled. "I couldn't help myself. And I thought maybe, since you have a bit of power now, things might have changed."

"Sorry, Cece," he said. "But for what it's worth, it is nice to see you." He nodded in her direction, and though a twinge of something shaped like jealousy rose in Talullah's chest, she waved it away. She couldn't be so desperate as to be jealous of a ghost. Especially not when they had important work to do.

"Cece, you are just the ghost we were looking for," Talullah said. Delighted by this, Cece fluffed her hair. "What can I help you with, darlin'? You know, I've got nothing but time."

Talullah elbowed Dhal in the side. "Show her the drawing. We can see if she knows anything about it, since she knows pretty much everything that goes on around here." Was Talullah laying it on kind of thick in the flattery department? Yes. Did she need Cece's total and utter cooperation? Yes. Was the ghost prone to fickleness and a bit of pettiness? Absolutely. So, Talullah wasn't going to take any chances. She would bend down and kiss the ghost's toes—or attempt to—if she had anything important that could help them defeat the sorceress once and for all.

Dhal took the fresh drawing out of his pocket and showed it to Cecilia.

Cece leaned around him, clearly trying to make some kind of contact, though it was impossible. Talullah stifled a laugh as Dhal stood there, the hairs on the back of his neck and his arms raising up at the coldness of Cece's nearness to him. But he didn't flinch, to his credit. He also understood how to play to his audience. "Have you ever seen anything like this before?" he asked her, and he tossed her a half smile.

Talullah rolled her eyes at the flirtation, though she did wish it was directed at her. The ghost stared at the paper for a long while before she raised her large doe eyes toward Talullah and nodded.

"Oh yes," she said. "Not for a long time. But there have been whispers about this around here in the last few months. I wasn't sure if it was real or not, but now I've been hearing so much about it, and you brought this picture to me. Where did you say you saw it again?"

Talullah explained how it had been etched in the passageway from Igdrasil down into the world of the past. The young ghost nodded again, her face solemn. "If it's what I think it is, it's an old representation of the Suditzas' map of the Source."

"Yes, exactly," Talullah said.

"I heard the map was destroyed a while ago."

"Right again, Cece." Dhal smiled wider. "And"—He leaned closer to whisper in her ear. "We're looking for the pieces. Rumor has it that there's one hidden here, in Praeteriti."

If Cece could still blush, her cheeks would have been the color of summer cherries. The ghost twirled her parasol and tilted her head in thought. "You know, I think I might have an idea. There are some highly esteemed people here, of course.

Some were quite well connected in their lives. But only one I can think of who would have been trusted with something like this."

"Please, Cece. Give us their name." Talullah masked the desperation in her voice.

Cecilia smiled widely. "This is exciting, being part of the most important piece of gossip to reach Praeteriti in nearly a century."

"And once we find the pieces and defeat the sorceress, everyone will remember the ghost who made it possible," Dhal said. "You'll be famous, probably. Even up above."

Cece stilled. Her eyes focused on something in the background. Imagining her impending celebrity, most likely. "Of course, I'll help you. Not for the fame or anything. Because it's the right thing to do."

"Of course," Talullah said.

"You'll want to talk to Huber Feinwright. He comes from a long line of Urtharian Seers. Was quite the big-wig back in his day. If the community was going to trust anyone with such a precious artifact, my money would be on him. Not exactly my taste, his house"—She wrinkled her button nose— "but to each their own. I wouldn't go so far as to call it garish, but it does have a certain *off-putting* aesthetic."

"You've been there?" Talullah asked.

"Oh, yes, darlin'. What Huber lacks in exterior design, he makes up for in delectable canapés. Tell him I sent you, and you shouldn't have a problem. He's trustworthy. He'll help you with whatever you need."

"Thank you, Cece. You've been amazing." Dhal laid the gratitude on thicker than the apricot jam he liked on his toast, but Talullah didn't mind. The ghost had provided their best lead.

"Don't mention it, sugar. You'd better get goin'. If that sorceress is as bad as you say, there's no time to lose."

CHAPTER 18

KAI

The next few days at the Marquets' estate all blurred together. Theresa and Veylan became a team and had assigned jobs to everyone. She and Veylan wrote letters to the people in the ledger they'd stolen from the castle to try to recruit them.

Kai couldn't help but feel relieved that he'd mercifully been spared from that task. Compiling the ledger in the first place had nearly sent him into a bedridden anxiety spiral.

Meanwhile, Edouard had reinforced the security spells around the property, which took him half a day. The rest of the time he'd spent eating, sleeping, and scowling.

The latter was generally directed at Veylan. For the first time, Kai wondered if maybe Edouard harbored feelings for Theresa, as difficult as it was to imagine Edouard having any sort of emotion. It would explain Edouard's sour mood. Kai could relate. Any time he thought about Talullah with Dhalian, Kai's jaw popped from clenching.

Kai slouched in the light gray wingback chair in his room, ignoring his emotions and his grumbling stomach. He could go find Zinni in the kitchen, where she'd been spending much of her time assisting with food preparation for the growing coalition. Quentis had been teaching her some of his favorite recipes.

Going out into the crowd sounded worse than being hungry. Kai gulped some water from his canteen instead.

He'd been avoiding his own assignment. Contacting Talullah and convincing her to join them wasn't as singular a thing as it sounded when Veylan said it.

It's not that Kai didn't want to talk to her. He did. More than anything. Which, despite sounding counterintuitive, was why it was so difficult for him to do it.

Thinking about what he would say kept him from pressing the sapphire on his pocket Scry mirror.

They'd parted on strange terms, what with Talullah literally fleeing the castle and goading the sorceress to chase her. There hadn't exactly been a proper moment to discuss what they were to each other.

He'd built up this reunion in his mind so much that he couldn't help overthinking how it could go. On the one hand, having the conversation through Scry might soften the blow if she rejected him. On the other hand, he couldn't completely stifle the bit of lingering hope that maybe she felt the same way. If that were the case, he'd prefer to have that conversation in person so he could hug her—maybe even kiss her, finally.

And on a third hand, an evil sorceress was trying to take over both territories, potentially more. Against that reality, his relationship with Talullah couldn't be more insignificant.

Of course, his job wasn't to figure out their feelings for each other. It was to convince Talullah to join them.

That made his blood itch for an entirely different reason.

Kai stared at the mirror in his palm, searching his reflection for a wrinkle of courage.

Nope. None to be found.

Talullah could help them. His confidence in that fact didn't waver. He had to get over himself first.

And what if she said no?

Theresa would no doubt want to default to her original plan of bringing Alexander out of safety to become the face of this rebellion.

The acid in Kai's stomach sloshed.

He didn't know what it said about him that he was more protective of Alexander and his physical well-being than of Talullah's.

Maybe he thought Talullah was stronger than Alexander. Strong enough to handle whatever came her way. She'd already proven as much during her previous conflicts with the sorceress.

Kai needed longer to digest these feelings, to rip them apart and see what was inside.

But that was time he didn't have.

In the hallway outside his room, the newest group of recruits clomped across the birch floors in search of a bath. People had arrived on each of the last four days.

Unlike Kai, Theresa and Veylan had jumped into their task immediately, contacting everyone in the ledger they could reach.

Many had already sought asylum in the castle. For them, Kai's heart squeezed. They might never make it out again.

Those that remained seemed keen to join an organized group —or one that presented an organized face—rather than weather the coming days alone.

Consequently, the Marquets' cozy cottage had already become cramped. Edouard and Zinni had moved their things into Kai's room, leaving two other rooms free for newcomers.

Even still, all the beds were now full. New arrivals had been set up with tents in the yard.

The whole situation had given Kai a permanent dull headache. He needed quiet in order to think and to process, longed for his secret library at the castle.

He would probably never see it again.

Enough of this.

He forced himself out of the chair, shaking his legs to reawaken them. Slipping the Scry into the pocket of his dark green pants—borrowed from Veylan—he pushed his way through the throng of people in the living space in search of the backyard.

Makeshift drying racks made of fallen tree branches held wool shirts and pants in every corner of the room.

The clank of pots and pans echoed from the kitchen, no different from any other time of day. There was always someone eating. Everyone had contributed a few pewters to the collective pot, but surely it wasn't enough to feed this many people for long.

A delighted roar rose from the crowd behind Kai as someone played a good hand in whatever card game they were playing. Kai didn't know how they could be so nonchalant about the whole thing, as if they were on a vacation instead of planning a potentially deadly revolution.

Maybe, like Zinni always said, Kai needed to learn how to relax.

Kai pinched between his eyebrows and left the chaos behind, moving into the yard. He breathed in the scent of grass. He sneezed. Late-fall pollen always irritated his allergies. And his constitution in general.

Passing by the three new canvas tents that had been constructed that morning, he walked to the edge of the property and sank down to the ground. The tall oak tree trunk he rested against supported him much better than the too-soft chair in his room.

He breathed deeply in and out, in and out, with his eyes

closed. From this far away, he could barely hear the noises from the cottage. Away from the chaos, his lungs pushed and pulled in an easy rhythm. The simmering in his blood cooled to stillness.

Where Zinni's claustrophobia triggered in physical spaces, Kai's activated in crowds. But outside, he could breathe again. He could think again.

An audible sigh escaped his lips.

When he heard footsteps approaching, he opened one eye, thinking it would be Zinni coming to scold him yet again for skipping breakfast.

Without input from his brain, his mouth turned to a frown as his eyes locked on Veylan.

"It can be a lot, can't it?" Veylan gestured over his shoulder toward the house.

Kai nodded.

"It's good to find a quiet place to be alone. I won't intrude for long. I just wanted to check in and see how your job is going." Veylan assessed him with cool blue eyes.

"It's going," Kai said vaguely.

"Has she agreed to come?"

"I haven't been able to reach her yet. The Scry connection has been unstable." Not an outright lie. It had been unstable the one time he'd attempted to contact Talullah in the tunnels.

"I heard some interference has been coming from Castle Viltresor. Keep trying. You'll get through, eventually."

Kai fidgeted with the pinprick of a hole in the knee of his borrowed pants. He traced it with his pinkie finger, resisting the urge to poke through the hole and make it bigger. "I'll do my best." Even he could hear how half-hearted the words were. But did he want to delay contacting Talullah because of his own personal issues, or was there something else deeper inside him that was telling him not to do so?

"Do you mind if I sit for a minute?" Veylan's expression warmed.

Kai gestured to the spot next to him. "Sure. It is your house, after all."

Veylan sat. He watched Kai for a moment, then took a breath before speaking. "I know what it's like, you know."

"What's that?"

"To be unsure. To wonder, *does she feel the same*? To play everything over and over and over again, wondering if I'm a fool." Veylan looked out toward the edge of the garden where Theresa chatted with Quentis. He'd dropped his normal air of confidence, letting a pinch of insecurity shine through. He ran a hand through his hair. Was it Kai's imagination, or was the blond darker today, edging on brown?

"Oh?"

"Yeah." Veylan turned his attention back to Kai. His eyes, too, seemed to be darker blue than usual. "But you can't let that stop you from going after what you want. I know we haven't known each other long, but if Talullah doesn't truly see you, you have to do something to get her to notice."

Shame flushed Kai's tawny neck. "Oh, that's not what this is about—"

"Kai." Veylan placed a steady hand on Kai's shoulder and looked him straight in the eye. "I'd like to think we're becoming friends. So, be honest with me, please."

Kai sighed. Pressed his fists over his closed eyes. "Fine. Yes, that's what it's about. I'm sorry. I know I'm holding everything up."

Veylan squeezed his shoulder gently. "It's okay. But you can do this. I know you can." He released his grip and stood. "I'll check in with you soon. Be brave."

"Yeah. Sure." Kai watched Veylan swagger back toward the house. Was it that simple?

CHAPTER 19

MARGOT

One step onto the ship, and Margot knew she had been played for a fool. The merchant who'd sold her the false papers had seriously overcharged her for these accommodations.

Crime really did pay for the criminals. She'd probably financed a horse or something for that guy, while she was stuck aboard a cargo ship.

She probably shouldn't have expected anything nice, because, criminals.

But still. She'd hoped for more than splintered railings and fraying ropes and peeling paint.

And the smell.

By the Founders she'd be lucky to ever get the smell of fishy seawater out of her hair.

As she filed down the creaking set of stairs into the belly of the ship, she considered asking one of the other five passengers what they'd paid for their ticket. By the looks of things, she wouldn't have been surprised if they, too, had been swindled by the merchant at the market.

Kindred spirits, maybe. But she wasn't there to form connections. Better to keep a low profile.

Lucky for her, it would only be a two-day journey across the sea to Zenzhari Cove, the closest port to Calla according to her map. From there, she'd have to walk.

The vessel itself was large and had an expansive cargo hold. The guest accommodations, on the other hand, lacked charm and basic comfort. She didn't have to share her cabin, thankfully. Though calling it a cabin was quite a generous way to describe the literal closet that her tiny, inch-thin mattress had been shoved into. It was lifted off the floor at least and secured to the wall.

A finger-sized lantern was bolted to the back wall. She flipped the switch. It flickered on and cast a dim ray of light across the sad excuse for a bed. A pancake of a pillow and a nearly threadbare blanket had been tossed without care.

Margot hoisted herself up and lay on her side, curling her legs to her chest and wrapping her arms around them. She slid the pocket door closed, engulfing herself in the near-darkness. She breathed for the first time since she'd handed her papers to the stern-faced, yellow-mustached attendant checking them. Her pulse had stuttered in her throat. He'd asked her purpose for travel, and she'd barely been able to cough out the words "visiting family." She'd added, "Sir," as an afterthought.

Behind rectangular black wire-framed glasses, he'd glanced twice between the papers and her face.

She'd tried to project confidence, but the longer he stared at her, the more convinced she was that he would have her arrested. In the end, he'd nodded and told her "cabin three" and proceeded to check the papers of the people behind her in line.

Now, in the safety of her musty closet, Margot still didn't know whether he bought her story or felt sorry for her. Maybe he'd thought, *What harm could an eleven-year-old cause, anyway? And if she's fleeing across the ocean, she probably has a valid reason.*

Margot hoped she wouldn't cross paths with him again.

She would, however, have to leave her cabin to get any sort of food. If general cleanliness wasn't on the menu, room service certainly wouldn't be.

Her stomach grumbled, but Margot curled tighter into a ball under her blanket and breathed. She would get food eventually, but right now, she wanted to congratulate herself for making it on the ship.

Two big obstacles overcome.

And she'd done them both alone.

Well, mostly.

Her thoughts drifted to Penny. She should try to contact her somehow. Maybe there was a mirror onboard she could use to Scry her sister and father to let them know she was okay.

Margot pictured her father's face. How his twinkling eyes would have flared with anger once Penny revealed what Margot had done. His pale cheeks would have flushed beneath the gray-blond stubble.

The thought made her queasier than the rocking of the ship.

But she sucked her brimming tears back in. She'd made it this far. She could do it. Find Talullah.

She only hoped that her sister would still be in Calla when she arrived. Margot hadn't worked out exactly how to find her sister in such a large city, but that was a question for Margot two days from now. In this moment, her only objective was to survive.

Mercifully, her papers stated she'd prepaid for a few meals on the ship. So, Margot exited the comfort and safety of her closet cabin and went in search of the food.

She pushed open the kitchen's rickety door, which hung

loosely on its squeaky, rusted hinges. Pickings were slim. Not that she expected fine dining. Not anymore.

She settled on a filet of crispy fish tucked into a semi-soft roll. The fish, at least, smelled freshly seared in butter and spices she couldn't name but which made saliva pool in her mouth.

She hadn't realized how hungry she truly was. She added a berry muffin for tomorrow's breakfast. "Thanks." Margot nodded at the kitchen attendant, a lithe redheaded woman with a scar that bisected one thin eyebrow.

"No problem, doll," she called in a husky voice.

Margot intended to take the food back to her cabin to eat, but halfway there, she realized she'd already devoured the sandwich.

Voices caught her attention, and she paused, listening. Had she heard correctly? Were they talking about the sorceress?

Margot inched closer to the voices. They'd carried down the hall. She tread lightly on the plank floor, pausing when she stepped on a creaking board.

No one was around to notice, though.

Still, she didn't want to get caught sneaking. Especially if it turned out the people in the room were in league with Renevelda.

Margot shivered, but chased away her nerves. Now would be a great time to practice the spell she'd been working on. It was a concealment spell meant to shield her from outside view.

She ducked into an unlocked broom closet and steadied herself. She didn't know how other Seers grounded themselves or accessed their magic, but Margot had found recently that if she closed her eyes and took three breaths, in and out through her nose, then clasped her hands together with the fingers interlaced, it centered her in a way nothing else did.

The stringent scent of cleaner burned the inside of her nose as she breathed. She didn't have a book of spells to recite. Instead, she reached within herself to find the spot where her magic simmered. She imagined dipping her hands into the bubbling water of magic at the center of her being.

The tingling warmth began in her ribcage and then spread through her body to the tips of her toes, the follicles of the hairs on her head, the edges of her fingernails.

It was working.

To test it, she stepped out of the closet, looking for anyone in the hallway.

She came face to face with a steward in dark green trousers and tunic, a broad middle-aged woman with two limp brown braids. Her hand was extended, reaching for the handle of the door.

The woman's mouth dropped open. "Oh!"

Margot held her breath and resisted the urge to apologize.

"Paul!" the steward shouted. "The darn lock is broken again. Get the toolkit, would you? Need to fix it."

Margot's gaze landed on the young male steward at the end of the hall. He spun on his heel and headed in the opposite direction. The steward in front of Margot looked right through her, her delicately-tamed brows furrowed.

Margot smiled to herself, pleased that her magic had worked. She sidestepped the steward and headed down the hall as quietly as possible. She still hadn't mastered the art of silencing her footsteps or breathing, so she would have to be careful.

Down the hall, voices and laughter spilled out from behind a plain white door with no window. It stood slightly ajar. Margot eased it open a touch more so she could listen and peek inside.

Uniformed stewards sat around a shabby, white washed table in mismatched wooden chairs. Cards and coins sat in the middle of the table. It looked like they were gambling on some kind of card game.

"I heard she's blocked Scry communications," a steward said. He looked like he was near Talullah's age, with no facial hair to speak of and a round, light brown face.

Wait, what? If that was true, that could explain why Margot hadn't been able to reach her sister. The comfort wasn't complete, though. If the sorceress could block Scrys, what else was she capable of?

"Well, I heard that she's kidnapping people and feeding them to a dragon." The young woman next to the first speaker flashed timid brown eyes around the table.

An older steward with half a cigar stub sticking out of his lips, puffed the disgusting thing, then laughed. "I think you all have been listening to too many scary stories."

"Tell us more about the Scry communications," the young woman said. "I haven't been able to talk with my cousin in weeks. The whole DuPont estate is out of touch."

The older man grunted. "My Scrys have been working just fine."

The young man cleared his throat. "Well, I heard if she knows the location of the Scry, then she can block the signal. Wouldn't be concerning to most people, right? But if she finds someone she's not too fond of, that could be an issue."

The cigared steward laughed again and slapped his thigh as if this was the funniest thing he'd ever heard. "The stories you young people come up with." He put his cards on the table. "I believe that pot's for me."

The two young stewards groaned and pushed their coins forward. The older man raked them in with his arms, which were covered in black hair and silver tattoos. "Better luck next time, kids. Break's over. Those dishes aren't going to wash themselves."

Margot speed-walked to her cabin and shut herself in, panting both from the pace and the adrenaline from the story she'd overheard.

If what the young steward said was true—that Renevelda could block Scrys for which she knew the location—then she might know where Talullah was. She might be blocking communication to her, which was why Margot hadn't been able to reach her.

Dread sloshed around Margot's stomach.

It also might mean Renevelda had already captured Talullah.

Margot might be too late.

She tried to sleep, hoping the rocking of the ship would lull her into relaxation.

But all she saw when she closed her eyes was Talullah holding a red feather while the sorceress laughed in the background.

CHAPTER 20

TALULLAH

Dhal pointed toward the left once he and Talullah said goodbye to Cece and made it outside the library. "Think it might be that one over there?"

Talullah squinted. A black-gabled roof was barely visible atop a hill in the distance. "I think it looks like the exact opposite of what Cece would like, so that's a great place to start."

Dhal referenced the map of Praeteriti they'd used on their first trip to the world of the past. Bless him and his love for maps. He never threw any away. "We should be able to cut straight through this neighborhood once we get past the main commercial strip."

They walked side-by-side on the cobbled street. Overhead, the sky remained a cool, consistent gray. There was no weather in the world of the past, just a continuous air of plainness.

They'd made it a few steps when Dhal winced and grabbed

his wrist. His pained expression soaked through the normally calm demeanor he wore.

"Are you okay?" Talullah asked, putting a hand on his forearm.

He grimaced and pushed his palm harder onto his wrist. Covering his scar yet again.

"Let me see." She gently pulled Dhal's fingers away and bit her cheek so she wouldn't cry out in surprise. The scar tissue shaped like the capital letter R flamed angry red on Dhal's amber skin.

The sorceress couldn't come to the world of the past, as far as Talullah knew. Then again, she'd learned to be wary of trusting any information she thought was fact.

Dhal winced again. Sweat droplets ran down the sides of his face. The scar pulsed, the edge visible even beneath his hand.

Talullah grabbed a fistful of Dhal's tunic and tugged him in the opposite direction.

"Where are we going? We need to find Huber," Dhal protested.

"We will. First, we're getting that checked out. No more pretending it's nothing. If anyone can help make it better, it's the apothecary, Mr. Miscian." Talullah practically dragged Dhalian down the street, ignoring the sidelong glances the ghosts tossed her way as they passed. Whispers followed them past the tailor and the grocer and around the corner until they reached the apothecary's pink paisley door.

Talullah knocked three times then pushed the door open. "Mr. Miscian, are you here?"

He appeared from behind the counter, scrubbing a cloth over his bronze wire-frame glasses before plopping them on his nose. "My goddesses. If it isn't the Keeper of the Keys."

"I'm sorry it's been so long," Talullah said.

Mr. Miscian looked over them with concern. "I'm not

worried about that. What's wrong? You look panicked." He came out from behind the counter and beckoned them closer.

They rested on the cushioned stools, and Dhal lay his arm on the counter, his face still pinched in pain.

"It's his wrist," Talullah said. "He has a scar that's inflamed. It's happened multiple times over the last few days, and it seems to be getting worse. Do you have anything that can soothe it?"

"Well, let me take a look," the ghost said. He couldn't touch Dhal's arm, suffering the same problem—being non corporeal—as Cece. But he leaned over to inspect it. Mr. Miscian grimaced, his bushy white brows inching closer together. "How long have you had this, my boy?"

Dhalian squinted as he did some mental math. "Over a year? Wow, has it been that long?"

Mr. Miscian stood up, knocking over his three-legged stool, and rushed to the back of the store. He returned with an arm full of hand-sized bottles of ingredients. "You have quite the magical infection to deal with. Though I'm not certain what's causing it to flare up."

"Can you help?" Talullah asked.

"Oh, yes, I have no doubt I can help control it, but you're going to have to be diligent about applying this."

They took the ingredients to a back room where Talullah had never been and observed while Mr. Miscian mixed his ingredients in a large black cauldron over a stove.

Talullah watched with awe, remembering how her mother used to mix potion ingredients. Another pang of missing rose in her. Did her mother's potion book have recipes for healing?

She made a mental note to check, and then she turned her attention back to Mr. Miscian who had ladled the bright blue potion into a collection of vials. It had thickened from liquid to paste.

Dhalian wrinkled his nose at the smell of it.

"The stench will die down as it ages," Mr. Miscian assured them. "Now, let me see your wrist." The apothecary slathered Dhalian's scar with the potion. Immediately, Dhal's pained expression relaxed. It must have already started working.

Mr. Miscian wrapped a thick bandage around Dhal's wrist to keep the solution on, wrote instructions on a piece of parchment, and gave it to Dhalian. "Without knowing exactly what the curse is, I can't heal it completely. But this should at least keep the inflammation at bay. Though if you want to heal it, you're going to need to figure out what's causing this flare-up. If you've had it as long as you say and it's only started to give you trouble, something must have happened recently to irritate it."

"The sorceress gave it to him," Talullah said, dry-mouthed. She shrank a little further in herself. It was her fault the sorceress had gone after Dhal in the first place. Because he had been close to her, and the sorceress had wanted to exploit him to find her and her necklace. "What if it's her doing? What if she's figured out a way to cause you pain from afar?"

Dhal set his jaw. "Then she's going to be disappointed I'm not so easy to break. Thank you for the salve, Mr. Miscian."

"Happy to help." Mr. Miscian cleaned up the workstation as he talked.

Talullah gazed at the leftover light blue liquid in the bottle on the table. "That's water from River Ketslane, isn't it?"

Even through the glass, she could smell the faint scent of blueberries. That was the river she'd drank from when she was lost in Nainehta Forest. Gillie had yelled at her to drink from it instead of the orange River Lethe.

"Ketslane is part of the sacred rivers?" Dhal asked.

"Oh, yes," Mr. Miscian said. "All of the magical rivers stem from the Source. The magic flows through the rivers and into lakes and other bodies of water and imbues them with magical properties. Some places' power are more concentrated than others. We call those locations the nexuses. Those are where people usually built strong fortresses, either to protect themselves or to guard the magic from others."

Talullah and Dhal shared a look of understanding. "That must be why Renevelda wanted the castle. It's the only reason that makes sense. It must be built on or near a nexus of power," Dhal said.

"If that's the case," Talullah continued, "then we might be in more trouble than we originally thought. She already has the Davabere Needle. If she's stationed on a nexus and manages to find the Suditzas' tapestry, then she can do whatever she wants. She'll have complete and unchecked power."

Dhalian stood up, a little shaky now, but he thanked Mr. Miscian again. "Tules, we should get going. We have a lot of work to do if we're going to find the rest of the tapestry before the sorceress does."

"Let me know if you need anything else," Mr. Miscian said.

"Could you give us a few vials of that water from river Ketslane? Its healing properties might come in handy," Talullah asked.

"Of course." Mr. Miscian handed over a few vials, which Dhal divided, putting some in his knapsack and a few in Talullah's. "I'll throw in a few other things too. Some healing salves, muscle relaxer, and some other concoctions to keep you safe on your quest."

Dhal surreptitiously slid a handful of silver Meitats, a mid-value marble used as money in Praeteriti, onto the counter behind Mr. Miscian and winked at Talullah.

The apothecary would argue with them if they tried to pay. They said their goodbyes, then stepped back out onto the sidewalk so Dhal could get his bearings and figure out which way to go.

Talullah's hair stood up on the back of her arm.

Dhal touched his bandage. "It's throbbing now."
"Do you need more of the salve already?"
A deafening screech drowned out Dhal's answer.
A hawk circled above them.
Then dove.

CHAPTER 21

TALULLAH

Talullah and Dhalian hit the ground and covered their heads with their arms as the giant bird swooped down over them.

"Is that Renevelda?" Dhalian asked, his voice muffled under his arms.

"I can't tell," Talullah said. She lifted her head to get a better look at the bird as it flew back up and circled above them. "I don't think so. I think it's Cleo."

"So, the sorceress can't get into Praeteriti, but her pet can. The bird figured out where we are and will report back to the sorceress. She might try to trap us here again. We need to get out of here."

But they couldn't go anywhere yet. Not while the huge hawk loomed above with her razor sharp talons, ready to rip them to shreds.

"Renevelda must have sent her after us to get the square of tapestry. We need to move. We can't stay here." They crawled along the cobblestones, scratching their hands and knees as they tried to stay low.

"Head toward Huber's house. I'll try to shield us." Talullah fumbled for Dunamai's Eye and pressed her sapphire. Her heart beat too wildly to channel any semblance of calm, but her magic sparked to life around her and Dhal, anyway.

Above them, Cleo circled, drawing the attention of two passing ghosts dressed in floor-length gowns and silk gloves.

Talullah grabbed Dhal's uninjured hand and pulled him to standing. "I think it's working. Let's make a run for it."

They bolted through the street. The smell of vanilla wafted through the bakery door but vanished the next second. Talullah chanced a glance behind them. Cleo was nowhere in sight.

Breaths thick with adrenaline burned Talullah's throat and chest. She stared up at the stone gargoyle keeping watch from a perch above Huber Feinwright's front door. Black wood trimmed the one-story white clapboard home.

Cleo screeched.

"She found us," Talullah said. Her attention elsewhere, she'd dropped the focus on the illusion hiding them.

Dhal fumbled for the door knob. "It's unlocked. Come on." They scrambled inside and locked the door behind them.

Talullah's breaths came in ragged pants as she leaned her forehead against the closed door.

"Breaking and entering is still a crime in the world of the dead," a voice said from behind them. Talullah whirled around.

A ghost stood with his arms folded and assessed them with raised eyebrows. His bushy mustache covered his lip completely, and though his voice was stern, his eyes twinkled, as if in jest.

"We're so sorry," Talullah said in a rush. "It was an emergency."

"Potentially life or death," Dhal added. "Seems to be a theme with us lately, unfortunately."

"Oh? What got you two spooked?" the ghost asked.

"Ever heard of a massive hawk with a sorceress for a master?" Dhalian asked.

The ghost dropped his transparent arms. All mirth faded from his pale face. "Forget what I said earlier. You can hide here as long as you need."

"So, you've heard of Renevelda?" Talullah asked.

The ghost nodded, rubbing his bald ghostly head and gesturing for them to come further into the home. "Had a run-in or two with her in my living days. None of them pleasant."

"We can't figure out how the hawk even found us in the first place," Dhalian said.

The ghost snorted. "Well." He nodded at Dhal's wrist. A black *R* had seeped through the bandage. "Looks like you've got a tracker on your arm. Probably led her right to you."

"My scar. Is that what kind of curse this is?" It was still covered by the bandage, but the skin higher up on Dhalian's wrist had swelled and turned a reddish purple.

"I see she hasn't changed her ways." The ghost's voice was as brittle as a dry branch ready to turn into kindling. "The apothecary give you something for that?"

Dhalian nodded. "The first dose was supposed to last for a week."

The ghost whistled. "Looks like it flares up when the sorceress's magic is near to you."

"Cleo must have been following us since we were in Nainehta Forest," Talullah said. "Which means Renevelda knows we went to Calla and the Ceserites' compound."

Dhal clutched his wrist. Talullah placed a gentle hand on Dhal's forearm, careful not to touch his injury. "We need to figure out how to disable this tracking curse."

Dhalian scrunched up his face. "I'd do almost anything for you, Tules, but I'm afraid I can't let you cut off my arm."

"I wasn't thinking anything that extreme. Maybe there's a long-term illusion I can try."

"In the meantime, we're already here. And as long as she can't break through Huber's house, we should stick to our plan."

Huber scratched his chin. "How do you know my name? Why *did* you burst through my door?"

"Cece sent us. She told us you're an Urtharian Seer."

Talullah winced as Cleo screeched outside the door.

Huber crossed to the bay window and closed the black velvet curtains. "Ah, Cecilia. Yes, she is quite the character. Loathsome taste in decor, always with the yellows and the pinks and the flowers and lace *everywhere*. But she's a good friend."

"She complimented your canapés," Talullah added.

Huber cracked a smile.

"And she mentioned you're quite famous. Are those all Nemosyns?" Dhalian nodded toward the cherry wood curio in the corner of the sitting room. Two white leather slipper chairs and a matching sofa were arranged near it, facing out the bay window.

"They are. And I don't know if I'd say *famous*. But I did have a positive reputation in my living days," the ghost said. He stroked his mustache as he floated around the sitting room. "You looking for a story?"

"We want to know more about the conflict between the Sight Factions. The one that made them destroy the Suditzas' tapestry," Talullah said. "I'm Talullah, by the way. And this is Dhalian."

"Talullah, eh? You wouldn't happen to be the same Talullah that freed the Unforgiven, saved the Isle of Salire, and prevented the collapse of the Between, would you?"

A hot flush warmed Talullah all over.

"Looks like Huber's not the only one with a reputation," Dhal said, winking at Talullah. "Why, yes, she is."

Huber whistled again. "Information gets around down here, but I never thought I'd meet the Keeper of the Keys in my own home." He bustled about, fluffing pillows that didn't need fluffing and checking the fake hydrangeas.

"We don't mean to impose, Mr. Feinwright," Talullah said, finding her voice. "But the magical world is once again in trouble. And Cece said you might be able to help us save it. We need to know what tore apart the factions so we can reunite them. Just like we need to reunite the Suditzas' tapestry. Renevelda is looking for it. And we think if she finds it, she's going to use it to control the Source. That's why the hawk has been following us."

Talullah stepped closer to Huber. "I wouldn't trust random people who barged into my house. But can I prove I am who I say?" She pulled Dunamai's Eye out from under her shirt.

Huber's eyes went wide as dinner plates. "Is that what I think it is?"

"Dunamai's Eye. I can show you my memories of Renevelda to prove we're not on her side."

Huber eyed the amulet with suspicion.

"What have you got to lose?" Dhal added. "We can't hurt you. You're already dead."

Huber grumbled. "As if I need reminding. Alright, fine."

Talullah couldn't touch the ghost, but she settled as close to him as possible, the chill of his aura seeping into her skin like morning fog. Hopefully, it would be enough. "Ready?"

"Go on, then."

Talullah pressed the amethyst and called forth the image of Renevelda trying to steal Dunamai's Eye in the midst of the Firefall of the Unforgiven. She showed Huber how Cleo had held down both Dhal and Aunt Mirella. How the sorceress had fought them on the Isle of Salire and how she'd used the Davabere Needle to steal Corinne's power.

"Enough!" Huber roared. He moved to the far side of the room.

"I'm sorry," Talullah said softly.

"Enough," Huber repeated, in a whisper this time. "I believe you." He sighed and scrubbed his palm down his face. "I think you'd better sit."

Talullah and Dhal settled onto the sofa.

Huber perched on one of the slipper chairs.

"The Sight factions have attempted to reconcile their differences over the last few decades. They have differing opinions on magic and different methods of using it, but their purpose is the same. They seek to use their powers to create the best life they possibly can and to enhance the lives of others around them. Unfortunately, beliefs become more complicated when they move from theory to reality. The problem comes when one's personal ideals conflict with another's ideals. We can agree that certain things make our lives better, but oftentimes it is the method of getting there that can muddle everything and cause confusion. Sometimes, irreparably so.

"My family swore to protect the tapestry. My vow lasts even in death. I can see now that keeping it safe means I have to let it go."

Talullah drew a sharp inhale. "You have the Urtharian square here?"

Huber nodded. "It seems as if the prophecy is already coming true," he muttered to himself. "Lot of good it did separating the thing."

"Your ancestors were part of the group of Seers that tore it apart?" Talullah asked.

"They thought they were doing what was best." Huber floated to a spot in the narrow hallway, which led to the kitchen. Deep green and purple flowered wallpaper covered the walls from floor to ceiling where Huber stood. He tapped on two spots at once. A compartment in the wall folded down. If he hadn't brought it to her attention, Talullah wouldn't have noticed it at all.

The ghost removed a simple silver tin and brought it over to Talullah. "I'm trusting you, Keeper of the Keys. With my family's legacy. Save magic once and for all, will you?"

CHAPTER 22

RENEVELDA

$\mathcal{A}$ soft, timid knock came on Renevelda's divination room door.

"Come in," she called out in a sharp tone. She had no time for pleasantries.

A shaking Seer accompanied her guard, whose eyes still swirled with the light blue Manipulation spell that kept him under her will.

"Ready for another one?" he asked. The Seer shook next to him but walked into the room. She pushed her shoulders back and lifted her head high, as if any show of strength might save her from what was about to come. Snarled tufts of auburn hair clung to the sheen of sweat coating the middle-aged Seer's round face.

"Yes," Renevelda said. "I think I'm quite ready." She'd already spent five Seers that morning with no further information to show for it. But this one had promise. There was something about the way her magic shone that made Renevelda optimistic that she would have something useful to share. "Leave us." She shooed away the guard, who ambled out the door and closed it behind him.

"What's your name?" she asked the Seer. At first, the woman pressed her cracked lips into a thin defiant line.

Renevelda relaxed her features and offered a gentle, icy smile. "There's no need to be afraid. Plus, if you don't want to tell me, I can figure it out on my own. It's more work for me, but more painful for you."

It was a thinly veiled threat that the Seer clearly understood. She straightened her spine even more and spat out her name. "Nadine DuPont."

"Was that so difficult?" Renevelda said. She realized now why she'd felt such a surge of optimism when this Seer had entered the room. She was related to Corinne, the poorly departed. A cousin on the dead woman's father's side. Royal blood. They would likely have been told similar tales as children.

Renevelda steepled her fingers and leaned across the desk, resting her elbows on the solid cherry wood. "I've heard great stories about your ancestors."

The Seer cocked her head. "I wouldn't know. I know almost nothing of my family history."

"Is that so?" Renevelda tasted the lie—earthy like moss—on the woman's words before she'd even finished the sentence.

Renevelda laughed inwardly at the impotence or stupidity it took to think she could get away with lying to a sorceress as powerful and cunning as she. For that, Renevelda would play this out longer than was strictly necessary. Make her suffer and understand the grave mistake she'd made. Had she only cooperated, Renevelda could have let her live. For a little while, at least. But the Seer had sealed her own fate.

"Such a shame not to know one's heritage. Especially one as storied and as highborn as yours."

The girl shifted on her slippered feet. She had to know she was caught. Still, she kept up the charade.

To what purpose, Renevelda didn't know. But she pried further.

"Oh," the woman said. "And you know of my heritage and my family?"

"I do. I would be obliged to tell you."

"Of course. I would be honored to know anything you could tell me to help me better understand my ancestors."

"It is my pleasure." She gestured for the Seer to sit in the chair next to her divination table. It wouldn't take much to draw out exactly what she needed to know. Renevelda luxuriated in the anticipation of finding what she wanted. "This may sting a little."

She pressed her fingertips to Nadine's temple and called her magic forth to dive into the Seer's mind. Nadine's eyes flew wide open. The shallow gasp of surprise was nearly a good enough reward.

But there was more to be had.

Renevelda dove first into the last few moments to confirm that Nadine had indeed lied to her. Then she cycled further through the woman's past.

A spark of glee ignited in the sorceress when she stopped on a memory of Nadine as a young adult. She stood in a cottage with birch floors and large windows that looked out onto the garden.

"It's imperative that you keep this information safe," an older man said.

"I don't understand, uncle," the young Nadine answered. Her full red-brown brows scrunched together.

An older woman leaned close to Nadine and placed a long-fingered hand on the girl's shoulder. "You deserve to know who we are and that we have a history of strength, even if our current status doesn't show it."

"Okay," Nadine said. "But what does this have to do with strength?" She unclenched her fist to reveal a square piece of tapestry with a tree embroidered on it.

Her uncle's lips turned down. "Our family has been trusted with guarding it. You needn't worry about it now. We'll place it back in the vault, protected by spells. But you need to know that it's here. In case anything happens to us."

Renevelda didn't need to See any more. Her magic had recognized the cottage.

She came out of the memory and loosened her hold on Nadine, who gasped as if she'd been held underwater for the last few minutes. "The magic does have its consequences."

"So?" the Seer asked in a shaky voice. But the defiance had returned to her eyes. "What did you find?"

"Exactly what I was looking for. There is one more tiny thing I need from you." Renevelda pulled out the Davabere Needle and held it in her palm.

Nadine's eyes widened. She tried to run, the poor, desperate thing.

Renevelda froze her in place with her Manipulation magic. She touched the tip of the needle to the woman's shoulder and drew the magic from her body. It throbbed its way into the center of the needle and coalesced in the diamond that Renevelda had added.

Nadine's eyes fluttered closed, and she slumped onto the floor.

"Guard," Renevelda called, admiring the way the golden magic swirled in the clear gemstone. "Take this body down to the communal holding room. Add it to the burning pyre this evening."

Once the body and guard were gone and Renevelda was satisfied that the magic had all been captured in the Needle, she settled into her silk-cushioned chair in the throne room.

"Guard," Renevelda called. Another Manipulated Seer

appeared to her right. "Tell Bodhi and Ivo to prepare for a little trip."

If everything went to plan, Cleo would return from Praeteriti with two pieces of the tapestry, the one from the world of the past and the one Talullah took from the castle. Bodhi and Ivo would bring the one from Nadine's family's cottage. There was only one more left to locate. She would have them all soon.

Renevelda wouldn't need Dunamai's Eye any longer. She would take the power on her own terms. She would control the Source.

And it would make her victory that much sweeter.

CHAPTER 23

TALULLAH

Talullah lifted the top of the tin and peered inside. She glanced at Huber for confirmation that this was what he wanted to do. She needed the tapestry, but she wouldn't take it by force.

He nodded at her.

Talullah carefully withdrew the folded piece of fabric. Dunamai's Eye hummed, and its amethyst glowed, the magic in it recognizing the tapestry square. She unfolded and laid it flat on the coffee table. Like the one she already had, a tree was embroidered on this one, but with dark purple thread instead of red. It was well-kept and free of dirt.

"You've upheld your vow, Huber," she said. "You've kept it safe. I promise to do the same."

"Yes, well. You'd better get going if you want to find the rest before the sorceress. No doubt she has other spies searching for the pieces."

Talullah grazed her thumb over the crimson threads. "Why are you trusting me with this, Mr. Feinwright?"

"Ah, well." Huber fidgeted. "There might be something else I should have told you."

"What?"

"Aurinia, your great-great-grandmother, belonged to the group of Seers tasked with protecting the Suditzas' tapestry. Our relatives were friends, Miss Bridgestone." He paused for a careful moment. "There are traces of her in you, you know. A person's history lives on in their kin."

Huber's words sank deep into Talullah's bones. Aurinia was supposed to protect the tapestry, but she'd failed. It had been destroyed anyway. Did Talullah have any hope of righting the wrong, or would she follow in her great-great-grandmother's footsteps?

"Right. Well, thank you, Huber, for everything. Tules, you ready to try the concealment spell?" Dhal asked.

He was trying to refocus her, to get her out of her own head. She cleared her throat. "As ready as I'll ever be. I think she can out-wait us. The spell is the best shot we have of getting out of here alive," Talullah said. "Thank you, Huber. For the information, hospitality, and this." She grabbed the tapestry square and folded it, placing it in her knapsack with the other one. "We need to get aboveground now."

Talullah used her sapphire to ground herself and imagined a bubble forming around her and Dhal that would be impervious to outside view. She'd be more careful this time, more concentrated on the task.

"Good luck," Huber said.

"So, what happens if this doesn't work?" Dhal asked as he grabbed the doorknob.

"We die." She laughed to dispel her own nerves and to ease Dhal's worries. The sentiment felt foreign to her. Usually, he made light of the dark situations.

"If the bird does kill you both, you can always come hang out here with me in your spirit form," Huber said, rocking back and forth on his ghostly feet. "The more, the merrier."

"Thanks, Huber," Dhal said. "But I think we'd like to live a bit longer."

Dhal grasped Talullah's hand under the spell. The scent of morning dew and honey filtered in through Talullah's nose. She snuggled in closer to him to make sure the spell covered them all the way—that was the *only* reason—and then they walked out the door.

They took a few tentative steps first, checking for any sign of Cleo.

"There she is," Dhal said from the corner of his mouth. He pointed to a lamppost the giant bird had perched atop. Cleo scanned the sky and the ground, but she hadn't made a strong move toward them yet.

"I think it's working," Talullah said. "Let's go forward a bit." They walked until they were off the ghost's porch, and Huber had shut the door.

Dhal looked back over his shoulder. "Oh, I thought he might leave it open for us in case we need to make a run for it."

"It's going to be fine," Talullah said. She held her breath all the way to the portal.

Cleo had followed, but not close enough to get them, and she didn't make any moves to attack them. Either she was simply spying or she didn't see them. They made it back into Nainehta Forest and breathed a tandem deep sigh of relief.

"Is it bad that I'm more comfortable in this dark, creepy forest than I was with the dark, creepy bird watching over me?" Dhal asked.

"I think all kinds of fear are acceptable in this situation," Talullah said. "Come on. Let's head back to Jothi's. I don't like the idea that more of Renevelda's spies might be lurking around here."

They stepped through the transport tree in Calla, the seaside air cleansing the last of the lavender dust from Talullah's nose.

"Tuley?"

Talullah froze. Tingles ran through her whole body. She whipped her head around, searching for the source of the small, tired voice. It couldn't be her sister. It couldn't. She'd reinforced the barrier.

But if her sister wasn't there, she was hallucinating. Because the voice called again, louder this time.

"Tuley! It's you!" A short but strong force collided with her hip and wrapped around her body. The smell of rosewater soap lingered beneath the stench of sweat and seawater.

Tears flooded Talullah's eyes, hot and wild. "Margot?" She squeezed her sister tighter. "Mar, how did you get here? How did you get out of the barrier?"

Margot leaned back, glaring at Talullah. "So it *was* you. I knew it." She stepped back. "Turns out you're not the only one with Sight powers in this family."

"You took it down? Alone?" Suddenly, Talullah was too hot. She fanned herself with her hand, but her chest still constricted with each labored breath.

Dhal offered her a canteen and encouraged her to drink. When she had, he locked eyes with her. "Breathe, Tules. Breathe. Slow. In and out."

Talullah closed her eyes and focused on her breath. She half-expected her sister to be gone when she opened them, that Margot was a hallucination.

But no. When Talullah had regained composure, her sister still stood in front of her, albeit a little less sassy than before. A hint of worry crept into her green eyes.

"I didn't take it down. I...made a hole. Penny helped." Margot dragged her foot back and forth in the dirt. "And I had a good reason! I had to find you."

"Why didn't you ask Aunt Mirella to Scry me?"

"I did. *Obviously,* that's the first thing I thought of. But you never answered. It was like something was blocking me from getting through."

"But how did you even get here? How did you get papers to pass on the ship?" Talullah's head swirled with questions and concern and disappointment in herself. She hadn't been strong enough to secure the barrier after all. And if Margot had gotten out, Renevelda would definitely be able to get in.

"It doesn't matter, does it?" Dhal asked. "She's here now. And she's safe. Unharmed. Right?" He addressed Margot during the last part, scanning her.

"I'm fine. But if you don't let me tell you what I know, it's all going to have been for nothing." The challenge in Margot's gaze bloomed conflicting emotions inside Talullah. For one, her sister had put herself in danger. Talullah had to bite her tongue to keep from scolding her, from yelling about how Talullah had tried to protect her. But for two, Margot was clever enough to outsmart the magical barrier and to get herself across the sea. *Proud* didn't even begin to describe the forceful warmth chasing away her initial anger.

"Fine. But not here," Talullah said. She paused, then bent, so she was eye-level with Margot and pulled her sister into a tight hug. "I'm so happy to see you, Mar."

CHAPTER 24

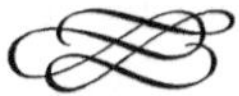

KAI

Kai returned to the cottage after taking yet another brisk walk around the property to clear his head. He missed the pond at the castle. There were no such water features out here, so when he had to Scry to dispel his headaches, he used his pocket-size mirror, which had collected a layer of dust in the tunnels that he hadn't been able to fully wash away.

Despite Veylan's encouragement, Kai still hadn't Scryed Talullah. Something about the situation still gave him pause.

He let himself in the back door, his thoughts wandering.

It was quiet in the cottage. Too quiet for the over fifty people now living in and around it. Come to think of it, no one had been outside either.

Strange.

"Zinni?" he called out. "Theresa?" He didn't bother calling for Edouard. The man wouldn't answer even if he were around.

Kai stepped through the house in a quiet panic he couldn't explain.

He hadn't been gone that long. Where could they all have gone?

Maybe they were resting?

An empty teacup sat next to a saucer full of wet tea leaves. Kai had never learned to read leaves—that was a Ceserite trade —but Quentis Marquet was a Sezna Seer. He must know the practice.

The undercurrent of worry that always surrounded his subconscious mind flooded. It was too coincidental that every single person on the premises would be sleeping or away at the same time.

He glanced again at the tea leaves. A destiny card lay next to them. Maybe it was a prediction. But of what? Danger?

The front door rattled. The way the metal clicked in the lock, it sounded like something other than a key had been inserted.

Kai shoved the armchair in the corner out of the way and flung open the trapdoor beneath it, which led to a cellar. He dragged the corner of the gray rug over as much of the door as he could before slipping through the crack and into the musty space.

He tried not to think about how much the smell reminded him of the tunnels.

The door opened.

Kai swallowed. He focused on keeping his breathing steady and silent instead of on the millions of new questions that shoved against his brain.

He didn't recognize the two people who entered, but they had to be under Renevelda's control. Their expressions matched the glazed swirl of the guards' at Castle Viltresor when they'd escorted Kai, Prince Alexander, and King William to the dungeons.

Then, Kai had been able to access his knowledge of their

personal lives to sever the spell and replace it with his own Manipulation magic. It had saved their lives.

But he didn't know these guards. His magic wouldn't work the same this time.

The guards moved through the cottage. Their thick black leather boots struck the floor with heavy thumps, leaving crumbles of dirt everywhere.

What were they searching for?

For him and his companions? For Quentis and Veylan?

Or for some*thing.*

The largest guard muttered out loud to himself. He brushed bright red hair off his freckled forehead. "Where is it?"

"She didn't say." The female guard swung her long blond ponytail as she pivoted.

Kai shrunk further into his hiding spot. His hips, and knees, and ankles protested the uncomfortable crouch. But he needed to see. To hear.

Use your Sight powers, dummy.

Kai waited until the guards had turned their backs on him, then he lowered the trapdoor the rest of the way. He flipped open his pocket Scry mirror and pressed the sapphire. Mirrors decorated nearly every room in the Marquets' home. It shouldn't be too hard to keep tabs on the intruders.

A deep breath of musty air filled his lungs as he focused his energy and dialed up his hearing. A cough caught in his lungs.

A smashing sound came from outside. And again. And again.

Kai risked letting the cough loose. His lungs couldn't hold it in any longer.

Were there more intruders?

Kai focused on the reflection in the Scry. The guards still stood in the living area, but they'd moved to the glass windows.

"What in the Four Worlds?" the redheaded guard grumbled.

"Ignore it." The blond guard rifled through the sideboard

drawers. "Check the kitchen." She moved down the hall. Toward the bedrooms where Kai and his companions had been sleeping.

Please let them not be there.

Twice Kai connected to mirrors in the wrong room before he found the female guard again.

She was in the room he now shared with Zinni and Edouard. A quick glance told him neither of his companions were there. There weren't many places to hide. Zinni couldn't conceal herself with magic, and even if Edouard had, the guard would surely bump into him.

What is the guard looking for?

She stepped directly onto Kai's freshly-made pallet and smeared dirt from her boots all over his blanket as she opened the closet door. With strong yet careful movements, she swiped her hands across the wall of the closet. Her pale pink lips turned down at the corners.

She scanned the walls of the room with her swirly blue gaze. One thin eyebrow ticked up. She moved to the tapestry hanging next to the lone window and touched each of its four corners.

The edge of the tapestry glowed blue.

With a swift, sure tug, the guard yanked the tapestry clean off the wall, revealing a white wooden panel.

Kai blinked in surprise. How many times had he stared at that tapestry? He hadn't realized why it drew his eye, but he should have known. He'd hidden the entrance to the castle's secret passageway behind a tapestry.

It wasn't exactly a secure guise.

The guard felt along the grooves of the panel's frame, then peeled it from the wall. Kai watched with a thumping heart as she removed a wooden cube. It looked solid, like a whittled block. But the guard tapped it with her fingers. Seams appeared.

The guard pried the box open.

She dipped her black-gloved fingers into it and pulled out a square of fabric.

Kai's stomach turned.

The square looked all too familiar. Instead of red thread, the embroidered tree was green.

The guard smiled. "Gotcha." She put the square into a small leather satchel which hung across her tight black tunic. "Bodhi, time to go."

Kai switched back to the living room mirror on his Scry.

Outside, another sound, louder than the first ones, banged and clanged. This time, both guards stepped into the backyard.

As soon as they were out of the house, Kai breathed.

Then he panicked again.

They'd stolen the tapestry square.

And he'd *let* them.

But what was he supposed to do? He couldn't fight off the two of them alone. And where in the Suditzas' names was everyone else?

A loud grunt reached his ears from outside. Kai climbed out of the cellar, his legs prickling as feeling returned. He peeked out the window. The large male guard lay on the ground.

Edouard appeared out of thin air holding a tree branch nearly the size of Kai.

"Did you hit him on the head?" Theresa shrieked, appearing next to Edouard.

Edouard shrugged. "Best option at the time."

Kai ran outside. "Thank the Suditzas you're alive."

"Kai!" Zinni jumped out from behind a bush and enveloped him in a hug. "I was so worried. The card and then the leaves and we didn't know where you were—"

"I'm okay, Zinni," Kai said. "A bit shaken, but I'll live." His gaze dropped to the prone, motionless body. "Is he dead?"

Theresa searched for his pulse. "No, just knocked out."

Thank the goddesses for that. Kai didn't want to add murder accomplice to his list of crimes. "Where's the female guard?"

Edouard looked up. "Ran away. She was too fast."

The color drained from Kai's face. All his previous hopes turned to ash. "There was a piece of the Suditzas' tapestry in the cottage," he said. "The guard found it. It was in her satchel. And now it's gone. And if I'm right, both are on their way to Renevelda right now."

Theresa's brown skin paled. She inhaled slowly, her eyes fixed on a spot in the distance. "I'm going to be sick. How could we let them get away?"

"We didn't know." Edouard patted her gently on the shoulder with his meaty hand.

"Where is everyone else? Where are Veylan and Quentis, by the way?" Kai asked. "Didn't he See this was going to happen?"

"No, he didn't," said Theresa, drawing herself up taller. "I did."

"But you're not a Dunamarian."

"So? Magic has been bleeding into each other for the last century. Not being born with it doesn't mean I can't learn. And I do have Cesera's Gift. The card was a guess, but the tea leaves were for real."

"So, the Marquets aren't here?" Kai looked around the yard.

"Nope," Edouard said.

"They left shortly after you did," Zinni said. "To go to the market. And the others are working on various projects off-campus. Recon. Gathering supplies. That sort of thing."

"Timing seems highly suspicious, don't you think?" Kai asked.

"You think the Marquets invited the sorceress's underlings to rob their own house?" Theresa said. "That sounds ridiculous."

Kai pressed a hand to his aching head. "No, you're right. That does sound dumb."

"Doesn't matter how it happened," Zinni said. "It happened. And if Kai is right, and the guard took the tapestry square back to the sorceress, that means she's one step closer to getting what she wants."

"We have to stop her," Kai said.

Theresa furrowed her brows. "What we need to do is stay focused on our mission, which is building a strong army of opposition that can fight against her. If we go now, alone, we'll get nowhere. Scratch that. I'm sure we would get somewhere, but that somewhere would be dead."

Kai agreed, begrudgingly. "I still don't understand how she knew to come here. Someone must have betrayed the Marquets and us. Can we even stay here, or will Renevelda send more guards to get rid of all of us?"

"We were all hiding," Zinni said. "And this guy didn't see anyone because Edouard knocked him out before removing his Concealment spell."

"You think we're still safe here, after this?" Kai asked. The swirling in his stomach disagreed.

"I think we need to talk to Quentis," Theresa said. "We can't disappear without letting him know what's happening. It's his and Veylan's home. They'll be in danger, too."

"Fine," Kai said. "What do we do with him?" Kai nodded at the unconscious guard.

"Contain him," Edouard said.

At Kai's look of disgust, Theresa rushed to add, "Only until he wakes up and we can talk to him. Maybe the Manipulation magic will have worn off and we can get some answers."

"I'm going to lie down," Kai said. "And I want it on the record that I do not endorse keeping this guy prisoner."

CHAPTER 25

TALULLAH

"*I* had a dream about you. I think it was a prophecy." The words spilled out of Margot's mouth as soon as she, Talullah, and Dhal crossed the threshold of Jothi's house.

Jothi popped up from the sofa, tossing aside a book. "A prophecy?"

Talullah's eyes widened as she stared at her sister. "Jothi, this is my sister, Margot. She arrived unexpectedly. I hope it's okay I brought her here."

"Of course. Any family of yours is family of mine. I think this calls for food. Mama's in town, but I'll be right back." They hurried into the kitchen. The sounds of flatware being unstacked filtered through the door.

Talullah turned to Margot. "A prophecy, Mar? That means—"

She nodded, her eyes shining. "I have some Gifts, too, but—I can't believe I'm saying this—that's not the important part, here.

The dream scared me, Tuley. It seemed so real." Dhal guided Margot gently to the squishy cream sofa as she talked. "You looked like you were in a cave or something, but kind of a nice one with tile and stuff and a rainbow pool. A woman in a silk dress started coming toward you—saying she wouldn't shed tears at your death. I was you in this scenario and instead of grabbing a weapon to defend myself, I picked up a bright red feather."

Talullah lowered herself onto the cushion next to her sister. Her brows drew together. "A feather?"

"Yeah. I thought it was a weird choice, too."

"Could be a symbol, right? What happened next?" Dhal asked.

Margot shook her head. "Nothing. I woke up. I tried to Scry you right away, but I couldn't get through. And—that's another thing I have to tell you. On the ship, I overheard some stewards talking. One of them said Renevelda can block Scry signals if she knows their location. Does she know where you are, Tuley?"

Talullah's nerves buzzed. She glanced from Dhal's bandaged wrist to his face. Guilt swam leisurely laps in his hazel eyes.

"Unfortunately," Dhal said, "I think she does."

The anxiety in Talullah's stomach doubled like dough left to rise in a warm room. They would have to figure out what to do about that soon. To tease apart why, if Renevelda knew her location, the sorceress hadn't come to kill her. Instead, she'd sent Cleo, kept tabs on her, blocked her attempts to contact her loved ones.

But for now, Talullah needed to focus on Margot. On what her sister had been through and what her vision might mean.

Because Talullah knew Margot wouldn't have risked so much for nothing. And she understood deep in her soul the confusion and fear visions could bring, especially when they were new.

Over mugs of tea and slices of freshly-baked cinnamon braid

at Jothi's square maple kitchen table, Talullah listened as Margot told her, Dhal, and Jothi the rest.

Outsmarting the barrier. Leaving home. Going to the Hidden Market. The passage across the sea on the cargo ship.

With each new obstacle Margot had faced, Talullah's admiration for her sister grew. She'd always known Margot was tough, but now her sister had proven it to herself.

Color returned to Margot's pale cheeks now that she'd eaten a decent meal and had hydrated. She spoke now, mouth half-full of cinnamon braid, with animated gestures as if she'd experienced the thrill of her lifetime. As if the earlier exhaustion and unease had been imagined.

But Talullah could see behind the sparks of excitement in Margot's eyes to the last lingering crumbles of fear. She knew that conflict intimately.

Being capable of weathering a storm didn't mean you emerged unscathed.

"Chew, swallow, then speak," Talullah corrected half-heartedly. Then she sighed. "Never mind. I don't care about manners." After listening to Margot's tale, Talullah's eyelids pulled down, her limbs aching to rest as if she were the one who'd endured it. She pressed her thumb and forefinger to the inner corners of her eyebrows.

"Any chance I could…take a bath?" Margot asked, when she'd answered everyone's questions and there were no remnants of the cinnamon braid. Anticipation and hope glimmered in her eyes above the dark circles unrest had wrought.

Jothi took Margot down the hall to get set up while Talullah stared at her empty plate.

"What are you thinking?" Dhal asked after a few minutes of silence.

"She can't stay here." The words foamed with betrayal. Talullah knew how much Margot had gone through to get to her, to tell her about the prophetic dream. She appreciated all her sister had done. But she also couldn't take Margot with her to find the other pieces of the tapestry, and she couldn't ask Jothi and their mom to look after her. Plus, their father would be so worried. He was probably already tearing his hair out.

Talullah deflated even more. If what Margot had overheard was true, she couldn't even Scry to tell him Margot was okay. In case, she slipped off her bracelet and pressed the sapphire.

The iridescent bubble stretched across the Scry circle. Nothing else happened.

Jothi returned and sat down next to Dhal. "She's all set. Should be in there for a while if her enthusiasm about the soap selection is any indication. I can take her home, if you want."

Talullah looked up. "You'd do that?"

They shrugged. "Your family is my family."

"No," Dhal said quietly. "It should be me. I'll take her." He stared at his wrist, then clenched his jaw. When he looked up, his expression had turned stoic, resolved. His eyes said not to argue. "I know I pressed to come with you, even though you didn't want me to—"

Hot dread bubbled in Talullah's stomach. "It's not that I didn't want you to. I thought that by pushing you away, I would be able to keep you safe."

"You were half-right." He said it so softly, she almost couldn't hear him. He ran his other hand through his curls. "If the sorceress can use this mark and whatever bond there is between us to track you, then I am effectively leading her right to you. You'll be safer without me. And you'll be able to communicate again. Maybe you can finally get a hold of Kai. See what his group is doing."

Jothi stood up again. "I'm going to go…Okay, I'm not going to make up an excuse. You two obviously need to chat. Let me know your decision later." They sped from the room like the tension might catch them. "Margot! You want to try a face mask?"

Talullah touched Dhal's wrist. "If it wasn't this mark, Renevelda would find some other way to find me. She wants the tapestry. Nothing will stop her from looking for it. If not you, she would use something else or someone else I—" She interrupted herself before she could say the word "love" — "care about. And while I'm obviously not happy she marked you this way, I *am* glad that you're with me. I would be lost without you."

He offered a weak half-smile that did nothing to assure Talullah she'd convinced him. "Are you sure about that? That I'm the one you want here?"

"Of course," she said. "Why wouldn't you be?" Her heart sped up at the thought that maybe he was thinking about Kai. That maybe he was jealous thinking she'd prefer to have Kai with her.

She and Dhal had been choosing each other for so long now she didn't know if she would ever be able to stop. Even if it ruined her.

Dhal shook his head. "We can't pretend our way out of this, Tules." He squeezed her hand. "Being around me is too dangerous for you. And like you want to protect me, I want to do the same for you. Let me take Margot home. Please. Let me feel at least a tiny bit useful."

"You're being stubborn." Talullah let go of Dhal's hand and crossed the room. They didn't fight often. She didn't like the way it made her lungs feel incapable of breath, the way it felt like he wanted to distance himself from her.

Maybe he did. Maybe all of this was too much for him.

"I'm being realistic." He said it gently. It seemed like for every fraction her frustration increased, his did the opposite. As she grew angrier, he calmed.

"You're being ridiculous."

"No, *you're* refusing to see that this is the right thing to do."

"How? How could it possibly be the right thing if we're apart?" Desperation threatened to unravel her right there. As much as she'd pushed him to stay in River Hill, the thought of parting now hollowed out her insides.

"It's not forever." He crossed to her and tipped her chin up so she had to look him in the eye. For a split second, she thought he might kiss her.

Instead, his words gutted her completely.

"Maybe this space will be good for us. I've been holding you back. Jothi can take Margot and me through the transport tree into Nainehta Forest, and then I'll take her the rest of the way home. I'll figure out a cure for this stars forsaken curse. And then I'll find you."

It was written in the lines between his brows, in the sharpness of his jaw—his mind was made up. There was no changing it.

"Fine. If that's what you want to do." Talullah hardened her emotions, trapping them like a fly in amber. She couldn't bear to fall apart in front of him. She turned away and busied herself sweeping the crumbs off the table and into her shaking hands.

Logic told her that Dhal and Jothi taking Margot home would be safer for her sister. She couldn't put Margot alone on a ship. Her sister had been lucky once crossing the sea, but that didn't mean a return trip would turn out the same.

Especially if anyone working for Renevelda found out who she was.

Still, it stung like a thousand angry hornets in her heart.

Yes, Dhal was going to take care of Margot. She'd be eternally grateful to him for that.

Selfishly, Talullah wished that someone, for once, would stay and take care of her.

CHAPTER 26

RENEVELDA

Renevelda tapped her pointed black nail on the desk in her divination room. She glanced at the open window. Then at the door.

She'd had enough practice waiting in the void that Katamai had trapped her in. That didn't mean she'd grown to tolerate it.

Tap tap tap.

She'd already exhausted her list of Seers for the day. Too many disappearing would raise suspicion. Plus, her magic begged her to let it rest. She'd been working nonstop collecting power in the Davabere Needle.

That, plus all the extra work required to sell her story to the Seers, had drained her energy.

So, instead of fiddling with her cards or looking at the star chart, she forced herself to wait. To be patient.

She checked the clock on the table in the corner of the room. They should be back by now. Unless they'd met resistance.

Renevelda stood up and slammed her palms against the table. So much for patience.

At that moment, the female guard tapped on the open door frame. "I have it."

"Bring it here. And Bodhi?" Renevelda asked as Ivo opened her cross-body leather satchel and deposited a square of fabric on the table.

The guard shook her head. "He was intercepted. I was focused on the mission."

Hmm. Interesting. Renevelda didn't much care what happened to him, though she should check that her Manipulation spell was intact. If he wandered too far and regained his faculties, he could make things difficult for her.

Renevelda placed her hand gently on the guard's back and tugged at her recent memories. She watched through the young woman's eyes as she approached the house. It was familiar only in the sense that she'd witnessed it in her exploration of Nadine's memory.

Her gaze caught on the soldier—Bodhi—in the yard. But he was not alone. The Seer who had given her trouble at the castle—the one with the headscarf and surprisingly strong magic—was there. And the burly guard Renevelda had assumed to be short a few brain cells. As she watched him take out her soldier, she realized maybe he didn't need to be. He could be the brawn. He didn't also have to have the brains. Exasperated, Renevelda finished the memory.

Now, she had a dilemma. If she left the guard with the rogue Seers, he could turn against her. Spill her secrets. The other option meant rescuing him.

Both left a bad taste in her mouth.

For now, she'd focus on the tapestry. What was one person in the grand scheme of things? Once she controlled the Source, they'd all fall at her feet effortlessly.

Renevelda dismissed the guard.

The sorceress's heartbeat sped up as she touched the fabric. Her magic recognized it immediately, warming through her body at sight of the green stitching in the shape of a tree, at the feel of the thread on her fingertips.

It was only one piece, but it was connected magically to the others. If she was correct, it could lead her to the rest.

Renevelda had used tracing potions before. Sometimes, she enacted the spell without it, but with something so delicate and important, it was best to be prudent and do the spell as thoroughly as possible.

Renevelda sniffed the potion she'd brewed earlier and watched as it changed to its appropriate, silver, partially translucent color. Her instincts told her she had brewed it perfectly. She laid the tapestry square flat on the table in front of her then filled a small dropper with the potion. With a big sigh, Renevelda closed her eyes and squeezed two drops of the potion onto the fabric.

She opened her eyes when it sizzled.

As far as she knew, it wasn't supposed to sound that way. The potion spread through all the fibers on the square, darkening them to nearly black. This had never happened before.

But then again, she'd never tried to trace such powerful magic before. She said the incantation three times and waited. In a split second, her vision darkened so she couldn't see a thing.

The spell had gone wrong somehow.

Had she measured incorrectly? Used the wrong ingredient?

Blind, Renevelda fumbled for the dropper. Maybe it needed more potion. In her haste, she knocked over something, which, by the crashing sound, shattered on the floor.

Her breathing grew shallow as her mind whirred, recalling every step of the process she'd taken. Every step she'd followed to the letter.

What happened?

The darkness continued. She was a prisoner of her own magic. Potentially the Suditzas' as well.

Perhaps they'd placed a protective spell on it. She should have been more careful.

The magic would wear off, eventually. It always did. At least, she hoped. Frustration bubbled insider her at her lowered confidence.

Get a hold of yourself.

She was a demi-goddess, for magic's sake. She simply had to wait for her mind to unfurl enough for her to figure out what to do.

Unfortunately, the magic had other plans for her.

She blinked, and instead of seeing the divination room around her, she'd entered a memory. Everything was awash in shades of purple.

With horror, she realized it was her own memory she'd been transported to, instead of the tapestry's memory of where it had been.

She gazed around the room, calming herself, assessing the situation. She was in her own body, much younger than her current self, and powerless to stop it from doing whatever she had done in the past. So young, in fact, that she hadn't yet moved into the castle. The way she was dressed and where she walked —through the side streets of downtown Viltresor City, with its dirt-caked stoops and pungent air—allowed her to be certain she hadn't yet met Eviliv.

Being back there, when she'd had only uncertainty and fear for companions, raised the hair on the back of her neck. She worked to push away the rush of adrenaline that always coursed through her at the chance someone might discover who she truly was. That they might take advantage of her.

Renevelda arrived in a place she recognized. The home where she'd briefly lived with the kind woman, Fideline, who'd taken her in when she'd first arrived in the city. Back before she'd trained with a Seer whose skill level she ultimately surpassed.

Deep in her soul, Renevelda felt she was supposed to notice something about this particular memory. Perhaps its location or the emotions it evoked. Her conscious mind tried to push through. Maybe this was a clue. Maybe the tapestry had once been in this woman's possession, or maybe she'd been one of the ones who had destroyed it so many years ago.

Renevelda moved through the home with comfortable ease. That home was the only place she could remember ever feeling that way. Like she belonged. Like she was loved.

The sound of a door opening broke her focus. She froze.

The memory ejected her with such force that Renevelda landed on the floor in an undignified heap.

What a useless spell. A useless memory.

It looked like she was going to have to find the rest of the tapestry pieces the old-fashioned way.

"Guards!"

Two Manipulated guards entered the divination room and bowed.

"Bring me another Seer."

CHAPTER 27

TALULLAH

Sunrise brought with it the worst kind of dread. Talullah pulled the blanket up to her chin as if it could shield her from the inevitable. For a moment she wondered if she should read the cards of the Potential, if somewhere in their images and relationships she could find an excuse powerful enough to convince Dhal to stay.

But the opposite might be true. Maybe they'd reinforce his decision to leave.

She scrubbed a hand over her face.

Today, she didn't want to know.

She wanted to leave herself with the slightest bit of hope that despite her internal turmoil, this would turn out okay. That Dhal would make it back to her somehow.

If the sorceress killed her before they could reunite, she'd have to haunt him forever.

The dark bit of humor made her wince, and yet, it provided

the levity she needed to fling off the covers, get herself ready, and walk out into Jothi's kitchen to face her future.

"Sleep alright?" Jothi's mother—Aizah—a short woman with Jothi's same smooth dark brown skin and easy smile, handed her a mug of tea as soon as Talullah crossed into the room. Cinnamon-scented steam swirled around her.

"As well as I do these days, thank you." Talullah sipped the tea. The warm spice scuttled through her throat and chest.

"Help yourself to breakfast. Everything's out on the counter." She putted around the kitchen, wiping the already clean counter with a wet rag, though Talullah could feel Aizah's concern for her. Jothi's mother kept her eyes focused on her task while she spoke. "It's difficult, parting from those we love. Whether days or weeks or months or years, it doesn't get easier to say goodbye. But, sometimes, we are lucky enough to say hello again. The hope of that always helps me."

Talullah's breath caught. She forced it back out.

"Would you like a hug?"

Talullah nodded. She couldn't speak. Holding the tears back took all her strength.

Aizah wrapped her arms around Talullah, creating a vanilla scented cocoon. The hug was warm and strong, yet not uncomfortable. Jothi's mother whispered in her ear, "It's okay to be afraid, dear girl. Bravery has no purpose without fear."

"Tuley, why are you crying?" Margot asked, entering the kitchen and effectively breaking the moment.

Talullah wiped her eyes before letting go of Aizah. "I'm having a hard morning."

Margot slid into a chair. "Well, I was thinking maybe you could show me around today. That could be a nice break, right?" The cheeriness in her voice made it even harder for Talullah to say her next words.

Talullah sat next to her sister. "Mar. I am so grateful you came here. I am so proud of you for being so clever and smart and brave, for getting yourself across the sea—even though I do not condone what you did you get here. And your Sight powers. You've grown up so much."

"Get to the bad news, Tuley." Margot's easy demeanor shifted. She folded her arms across her chest.

"Okay." Talullah took a breath. "Jothi and Dhal are going to take you home. Today."

Margot stood, her eyes flaming. "What?! No! You can't make me go so soon. Aizah said I'm welcome to stay!" She glanced at Jothi's mother for approval.

"I said it's okay with me, but the final decision rests with Talullah." She was gentle yet firm, a trait that Talullah remembered in her own mother. The aching chasm in her heart widened further.

"Mar. You have to go home. Father will be worried sick. Who's going to take care of him and Penny? Plus, if you're right about the Scry signal, once Dhal is"—Talullah's voice cracked—"gone, with you, I'll be able to Scry again. To talk with you and everyone else."

"This is so like you, you know? To push everyone away so you can have the adventure yourself."

"That's not what I'm doing. I have a responsibility to protect you. You have done an amazing thing coming to find me. And I'm going to need you to Scry me if you have any more visions, okay?"

"Don't I get a say in this?" Margot looked around the room. Jothi and Dhal had entered, their packs already hooked over their shoulders.

"Unfortunately not, Margot," Dhal said. "But it's like Talullah said. We're all playing our part. Talullah's job is to find the tapestry. You maybe have already helped with that. The information you gave might be important. My main job, right now, is to make sure you get home safely and to throw off

Renevelda's sense of Talullah's location. By coming with me, you'll be helping with that, too."

Margot's expression slowly morphed from indignation to thoughtful curiosity. "Hmm. So, we're leading the sorceress away from Talullah. That seems kind of dangerous for us." A spark of mischief brightened her green eyes. "And exciting."

A flash of adrenaline rolled through Talullah. She hadn't thought about that. That by being with Dhal, Renevelda would know her sister's location.

"We'd better go," Jothi said. "Not to cut the argument short, but we want to give Dhal and Margot as much daylight in Nainehta Forest as possible.

Talullah pulled Margot into a hug. "I'm sorry. I hope you'll forgive me someday. But I do love you, and I'm counting on you to look after Penny and Father, and maybe figure out how to mend the barrier? Or help Dhal break that curse."

"I'll do my best, Tuley. I love you." Margot let go first and met Jothi by the door, where their mother was shoving extra snacks into their pack.

Dhal hugged Talullah next, but instead of melting into him, her body stiffened, like it didn't want to give too much. "I'll try to Scry you as soon as I can," Dhal said. "Once I get Margot home."

"Okay," was all Talullah could manage.

And then they were off, leaving Talullah to figure out what to do next.

An hour later, Talullah's Scry bracelet rang.

She fumbled for it, pressing the sapphire, her body alive with anticipation. It was too soon for Dhal and Margot to have made it back to River Hill. Jothi wasn't even back from the transport tree yet. So who was calling her?

"Oh, thank the Suditzas you answered! Did I wake you?" Gwen Caprico said from the other side of the filmy circle.

"Gwen! No, you didn't." Talullah sat up and pressed her back against the headboard. She'd gone back to bed to sulk. "Is something wrong?"

Her Scry worked. Which meant Margot's intel was correct. Renevelda had been using Dhal's scar to track her location and block her allies from contacting her.

"Depends on how you look at it, I suppose." Gwen's blond curls bounced around her face.

"And how are we looking at it?" She sipped from the glass of stale water still on her maple bedside table from the previous night.

"I'm going to say positively. For now, at least. Your aunt told me you're looking for the Sudtizas' tapestry. There was a rumor about it when I was at Still Currents, many years ago. That it was buried on the Isle somewhere. Preceptor Hakaru will probably know more. Though I'd advise you speak to him in person, not via Scry."

"Why's that?" A slight breeze fluttered the gold linen curtains.

Gwen sighed. "Sometimes being in someone's presence helps them better understand your mission."

Colfax Caprico dipped into view. "Talullah, good to see you."

"Captain Caprico!" He'd finally stopped trying to correct her and rolled with it. He'd been a captain in the Terrapesian guard in the first timeline where he and Talullah first knew each other. In that one, she'd hated his guts until she realized he'd protected and ultimately saved her sisters by getting them out of the castle and away from the sorceress. This version of Colfax Caprico hadn't been part of the guard, but he and Talullah had worked together to escape the underground prison that had almost killed them both.

On the Isle of Salire.

"So, Gwen wasn't sure about this, and normally I defer to her. But I also have some connections that might be able to help in your search. It's likely to be dangerous, given the people involved."

"Darling," Gwen cut in. "Get to the point."

Captain Caprico rolled his eyes. "I'm coming to help. I can't do your fancy tree traveling magic, which Gwen has so helpfully informed me of, but when you get to the Isle, stay put. I'll meet up with you and tell you what I know."

"Got any ideas about lodging? I don't exactly want to go back to the dorms at Still Currents…" Being on the Isle was going to dredge up a lot of things Talullah had tried to bury. She didn't know if she could handle being back on the magic academy's campus.

Caprico nodded. "I have a working relationship with the proprietor of the Ocean's Crest Inn. It's the only inn on the Isle. Tell them James Drake sent you and everything will be taken care of."

"James Drake?"

Captain Caprico waved away the concern. "Nothing under the table or untoward, I promise. I have renounced that life completely, and I am an utterly respectable citizen now. Ask my wife."

Talullah looked to Gwen for confirmation of this. Gwen laughed while making a so-so motion with her hand, eliciting laughter from everyone. "I have approved this mission," Gwen said, "so I think you have nothing to worry about. Even still, be safe and be on your guard always. I don't think I necessarily need to tell you that for your sake, but as a mother, I need to say it for my own."

She hadn't known Gwen long, but Gwen had been close with Talullah's mother in their adolescence, before whatever happened on the Isle to separate them. Talullah still didn't know every detail about their past relationship and why they'd gone their separate ways, but she hoped she would learn it in due time, whenever Gwen was ready to share.

She did, however, trust that Gwen, and Captain Caprico, too, had her best interests at heart. And the relief that washed over her at having someone with her softened Dhal's absence a touch.

"When will I be seeing you, Captain?" Talullah asked.

"I'll meet you tomorrow night at Facet 59, the tavern in the inn."

Gwen cleared her throat. "How do you feel about returning to the Isle, Talullah?"

Talullah swallowed her apprehensions. They scratched her throat like cut glass. "Honestly? I'm nervous." She dragged herself out of bed to prepare her pack. "But if facing the Isle is what it takes to beat Renevelda, I'm willing to do it."

CHAPTER 28

TALULLAH

She arrived at high tide. Sand stretched from the shore where the transport tree grew to the Isle's rocky cliffs. Strong rays of afternoon sun beat down on the rocks, making them sparkle like quartz.

Talullah hadn't steered a Skimmer in a long time. She hadn't even finished her training. But the only way onto the Isle at this time of day was by water. She located a Skimmer tied to a wooden stake at the edge of the beach. The words "arrive precisely on time" were hand-painted in deep blue on the otherwise white side.

It belonged to the Katamians, then.

A pit yawned in her stomach.

The Isle raised all sorts of conflicting emotions. She had many fond memories of making friends when she first arrived, but loss would always shadow all of that.

Though she wore only her reusable Scry bracelet, the faint tinkling of metal on metal followed her on the breeze as she heaved her legs over the side and into the boat. The sound bolstered her. It was like Lynx was with her, offering encouragement.

She focused on that energy as she closed her eyes. Skimmers had to be guided by inner sight, not external. Talullah pressed the sapphire on Dunamai's Eye, then placed her hands atop the steering pole.

The boat roared to life, startling her. But within a few seconds, she'd grounded herself and focused her magic and energy on getting to the Isle.

Silver fish darted under the boat as it hummed along—not nearly as quickly as when Lynx drove. Talullah wondered whether the poisonous sand jellies hunted them now or whether they lay dormant, beneath the sand, waiting for land-walkers to stumble upon their hiding places.

At the base of the Isle, a man met Talullah. His red beard covered the bottom half of his face, and his eyes sparkled in the early afternoon light. "You have an appointment?" he asked.

"With Preceptor Hakaru," Talullah answered. She'd Scryed him as soon as she'd ended the call with Gwen and Captain Caprico. He'd agreed to see her.

The man checked a piece of parchment fastened to a thick plank of wood. "Name?"

"Talullah Bridgestone," she said.

The man nodded. "Very good. Up you go." He gestured to the stairs set into the rock. "It'll spit you out in the center of town. I'm sure you can find your way from there."

"Thank you."

"Welcome back," the man added as Talullah made their way to the stairs. "Thanks for everything you've done."

The scent of wet stone and salty air swirled around her as she climbed the staircase. Blue light from shell-shaped sconces illuminated the space.

When she got to the top, Talullah headed straight for Preceptor Hakaru's office, past Fideline's bakery, with its display of rainbow star pastries in the window.

"Come in," Preceptor Hakaru said when she knocked.

She entered, greeted by the scent of oranges. Preceptor Hakaru waved her in with a calm smile and gestured for her to sit in the chair in front of his desk. Behind the desk, the tank that used to hold a jellyfish was now home to a large snail, which was stuck to the glass.

"It's good to see you, Talullah." Preceptor Hakaru took a sip of something in a mug.

"You too, Preceptor. I like what you've done with the Isle."

Though high stone walls enclosed the Isle all around, the atmosphere breathed with a new sort of welcoming. Before, it seemed to scream, "Stay out." Now, though, the sentiments floating on the breeze whispered, "You are safe."

Preceptor Hakaru exhaled and placed his hands gently on the chest of his midnight blue robe. He'd earned new lines at the corners of his eyes, but the dark shadows that used to hang below them had faded. "Thank you. It has been hard work dismantling an entire toxic culture and rebuilding it from the ground up." He laughed softly. "I, of course, have not done it alone."

"I'm happy to hear that," Talullah said.

Memories of being in that office scratched at her attention, a cat's claws on a tree trunk. The longer they worked, the duller they would get, so when she finally acknowledged them, they wouldn't be able to harm her.

At least, that's what she told herself so she could ignore them for now.

Talullah cleared her throat. "Well, I know you're busy. I won't take more of your time than necessary. I'm here to find out what you know about the Suditzas' tapestry. My friend was a student here many years ago, and she heard that maybe one of the squares is hidden somewhere on the Isle."

"That is a legend," Preceptor Hakaru said in a nonchalant tone. "Impossible to prove either way."

Talullah let out a small laugh. "Seems like the myths around here are made of mostly truth."

A slight smile graced his lips. "I believe you have me there."

"I know for certain the tapestry exists. I've already found two pieces. And I believe the sorceress has one. Or at least she knows where it is. If it's the one on the Isle, I need to find it first."

Preceptor Hakaru straightened in his chair. "I see. Well, I will give you the small bit of information I have. It might not hold any weight, though."

"I'm grateful for whatever help you can offer," Talullah said.

He watched the snail in the tank as he thought. "There was a rumor that the Suditzas had a secret chamber in the tunnels and that their followers—before the divide—met there. If it exists, and you can find it, that would be my best guess as to where they would have hidden something of such importance."

Talullah suppressed a shiver. If her memories of Preceptor Hakaru's office were cat's claws, the ones lurking beneath the surface were lion's teeth. "Any ideas about how to find it? There seem to be a lot of paths down there."

"I'm sorry I can't be of more help." Preceptor Hakaru took another drink. He rubbed his round, hairless chin in thought. "I tend to stay aboveground if I can help it."

"That's okay," Talullah said. "You've given me more than I had before. Thank you for your time."

"Please let me know if there's anything else I can do for you while you're here." He stood, walked Talullah to the door, and held out his hand for her to shake.

"I will, thank you."

She exited Preceptor Hakaru's office and stepped into the city center.

Though the seasons had turned, the sun still warmed her face. It did nothing, however, to chase away the cold truth.

If she wanted to find the tapestry square, she was going to have to go back underground. To the last place she wanted to be.

CHAPTER 29

TALULLAH

Talullah found the Ocean's Crest Inn easily. It was a single-story building made of the same grayish stone as the rest of the Isle's establishments. It didn't feature as much stained glass or statues of Katamai as some of the others, but it looked well-kept, if a bit wind-weathered.

It must be difficult to keep building façades pristine with the saltwater blowing all over them.

The thick wooden door took a bit of muscle to open, but Talullah managed.

A skinny, pale, freckled boy, who didn't look much older than her, stood behind the large check-in desk. His red hair was rumpled. Perhaps, like Dhal, he had a habit of running his hands through it. "Welcome to Ocean's Crest," he said, his smile wide and genuine. "Do you have a reservation?"

"I don't," Talullah said. "But my friend, Col—James Drake —said you might have a room for me?"

The boy's eyes lit up. "You know Mr. Drake?"

"Yes," Talullah said. "I'm doing some sightseeing, and it turns out I'll be staying longer than I originally thought. Any chance you have availability?"

"Let me check." The boy—*Aran*, his name tag said—looked down at a ledger on the desk. His brows pinched together. "Thing is, we've been a lot busier lately. And we're a small place. I'm not sure—"

"Give her the suite," another deeper voice said. The person had come from down the hall and had appeared so stealthily Talullah hadn't even noticed. He was a tall man wearing suspenders over his fitted tunic. A stylish hat covered his head.

"Sir?" Aran squeaked. "There's already—"

The man held up his hand. "I know. I'll handle it." He turned his attention to Talullah, his head tipped in assessment. "Any friend of Mr. Drake's is a friend of mine. Welcome to the Isle of Salire. I'd invite you for a drink in the pub, but I'm guessing you're not of age quite yet. We do serve food, though, so if you're hungry later, head down." He turned on his heel and went back the way he'd come, disappearing through a door.

Aran tapped a fountain pen on the ledger, biting his lip.

"Are you sure this won't cause any issues?" Talullah asked. The last thing she wanted was to get this poor boy in trouble.

"Oh, no. Won't be a problem at all. The guest previously assigned to the room hasn't arrived yet. I'll move some things around. It'll work out fine." He scratched out the names on the ledger and offered the book to Talullah. "If you could sign your name here, I'll get your key."

She signed a fake name. Couldn't be too careful.

"If you need anything," Aran said, turning back around, "don't hesitate to ask. We have a few desk attendants, and all will be happy to assist in any way." He handed the silver skeleton key to Talullah. "Do you think—" The tips of Aran's ears turned red. "Well, I wouldn't guess…Will Mr. Drake be joining you at any point?"

"In fact, he will be," Talullah said. "I'm supposed to meet him tomorrow at a place called Facet 59."

"That's the pub. The one Mr. Milliner mentioned. He runs the place, Mr. Milliner. Prefers to keep to the pub most of the time. Through that door, and you'll be right there. It's gone through a bit of a renovation in the past couple of weeks, so pardon any dust you may encounter."

He pointed to the stairs next to the desk. "Straight up the stairs, turn right, and all the way at the end. That's where you'll find your room."

"Thank you so much," Talullah said. "I'm delighted to be here."

"Happy to serve." He bowed his head and gestured for her to head upstairs.

The suite was larger than Talullah had expected. It opened onto a sitting area with a small kitchenette. A single room with two beds was connected to a large washroom with a clawfoot tub.

Talullah set down her pack and plopped onto one of the beds, bouncing to test its springiness.

Now she had to wait until *Mr. Drake* arrived.

She distracted herself by bathing longer than necessary. By now, Dhal would have made at least five jokes to lighten the mood and raise her spirits. His absence echoed like a stampede in the quiet of the room.

Talullah never would have considered herself lonely.

She often worked long hours by herself at the antique shop, researching and cataloging, frequently forgetting to eat because she was so wrapped up in work. She loved to read in her free time, also a solo activity. Talullah relished being alone.

Even when she'd first left home to look for her amethyst, Dhal had been there. And Aunt Mirella and…her mom.

On her first trip to the Isle to find her sapphire, she'd found Lynx and Beck and Jothi. Dhal had come for her, then, too. Had saved her life even after she'd tried pushing him away.

The quest for the emerald had brought her Maeve and Silas, and *Kai*. And again, Dhal had been right beside her.

But now, in the inn room, with nowhere to go, the truth of it devoured her.

She was alone now, for real. And she was *lonely*.

She reached for the sapphire on her Scry, tears already brimming in her eyes. Calling forth her magic, she pictured the one place in the world she wanted to be more than anywhere else.

"It's Tuley!" Pennilyn squealed. She ran out of view, then appeared a second later, dragging her father by the hand, back into the living room of the Bridgestone cottage.

"For Founders' sake, Penny, hold on a moment," he grumbled, struggling to keep up with the use of his cane. He lifted his gaze to Talullah's favorite mirror and gasped. "My Talullah? Is it really you?"

"It's me, Father, for real."

"Are you safe? Where are you? Is Margot with you? Penny told me what happened."

Talullah's stomach constricted. "Dhal's bringing her. They haven't arrived home yet?" They should have been back by now. What if something happened to them? Her hands felt full of bees, warm and stinging and vibrating with anticipation.

"Not yet. I'm sure that if Dhalian is with her, she'll be okay. At least until she learns how long she's going to be grounded for. I can't believe her, pulling something like this." Her father gripped his cane tighter, his fingers clenching like the muscles in his jaw.

"She did it for me," Talullah said quietly, her gaze fixed on her sister's blond pigtails. "She thought she needed to help."

Some of the tension relaxed in her father's neck at that. "And you? You didn't answer my questions, I noticed."

"I'm...back on the Isle. Captain Caprico is meeting me tomorrow. Look, Father, I'm sorry about the barrier. I didn't know what else to do, and I—"

"Don't apologize, Talullah," he said, cutting her off. His voice was leaden. "I'm glad you're alright."

"I'm alive," she said. She wouldn't go so far as to say she was alright. Not with her loneliness engulfing her insides like wildfire. "I should be able to Scry you now. Can you let me know when Margot and Dhal show up?"

"Of course."

They talked until Talullah's voice grew hoarse, her eyes heavy. Her heart was nearly full.

"We'll let you rest now," her father said gently. "Stay safe, my Talullah. We can't wait for you to come home."

THE DREAM SWIRLED AROUND HER, fast at first, in shades of pink that deepened to a rich crimson. Stone walls surrounded her, with no windows in sight. Was she underground? In the prison again?

But no.

The prison cells were nothing but empty rooms. This place was built for a different purpose.

The stone clicked under her boots, but she turned her attention upward. The sky above, black as midnight, sparkled with bright white stars in purposeful groups.

Talullah took a few steps, assessing the pool of shimmering water ahead of her.

The ground rumbled. Blood smeared her palms. A flash of white light and then tree roots burst through the stone floor, snaking away from her.

Her mouth tasted like iron. Panic rose in her chest again, like in her previous dream. "Dhal?!" She pushed herself off the ground, leaving bloody prints in her wake.

"Dhal!" she screamed again.

An icy laugh cut through her core. "The Source's power will overwhelm you. You're weak. Unsuited for it."

Talullah's body tensed. "I guess we're about to find out."

Everything froze.

Her gaze snagged on something falling from the ceiling.

Red and gold. Soft.

A feather.

CHAPTER 30

TALULLAH

Captain Caprico was one of only two patrons sitting in Facet 59 when Talullah arrived. He'd chosen a dark wood table in the furthest corner of the room. Hints of mahogany peeked through a layer of white paint on the walls' paneling. The brighter color reflected the light from the teal sea-glass fixtures, which hovered above every table.

A tingle of magic ran through Talullah. Was the pub's appearance altered by Manipulation magic?

But she wasn't there to discuss interior design. The captain stood and gestured for her to join him at the table.

"Nice to see you again, Captain," Talullah said, choosing a seat to one side.

Colfax nodded from his chosen chair facing the bar. "You as well."

Talullah grabbed a single-page menu from the table and perused it. Her stomach growled loudly. "What's good here?"

"Fish is always fresh," Colfax said. He took a sip of amber ale from a sweating glass.

A server arrived promptly to take their order. A large-toothed clip featuring a gauzy decoration, part of which dipped over one of her eyes, held her shiny black hair away from her face.

Talullah ordered a fish dish that made her mouth water thinking about it. Colfax ordered a plate of chicken and roasted potatoes.

"Be back with that soon," the server said. Colfax gave the girl a tense glance.

Odd.

When the server turned away, Talullah startled at the back of her head. The clip in her hair was in the shape of a large spider whose legs had been pinned beneath it.

"Do you know her?" Talullah asked.

"We'll get to that in a bit," Captain Caprico said. He blew out a strong breath and gulped more ale. "I can't believe I'm about to do this. And I also can't believe I'm back here so soon. Though the situation demands a strong solution."

This seemed more of a personal pep talk than information for Talullah, so she held her tongue.

"Gwen heard some rumors when she lived here. Which aligns with some things I've heard. The problem is, pursuing these things means getting involved with people that I don't necessarily think you should be in contact with." He glanced up at the barkeep/owner—Mr. Milliner—who was drying a glass, his attention on his task. "As a father, I'm hesitant to do this. But as someone who wants to see that wretched sorceress go down once and for all, I have to make an exception. These people I'm talking about are members of the magical community who've played various roles throughout the years. Whether they be good or bad is up for interpretation. We need their extensive knowledge of the island's geography and its secrets and history."

"Like the underground prison?" Talullah asked. The one

they'd been trapped in together had held many secrets, including the illusions that made it difficult to escape.

Colfax nodded, rubbing the golden-brown scruff on his chin. "There are many more secrets to discover on the Isle. The people I'm talking about traffic in them. If what you seek is on the Isle, they'll know where to find it."

"When do we meet them?"

Colfax looked up again. Talullah followed his gaze to where the barkeep had stopped his glass polishing and stood with his full attention on their table. The server had rounded the corner from the kitchen with a tray in hand.

Colfax and the barkeep both nodded at each other. "Tonight. At midnight."

TALULLAH WRAPPED her body in her swirly cloak and took another look at herself in the mirror. She brushed her obsidian hair behind her ears as she lifted the hood up. Rather than spend hours cooped up in the room at the inn, she'd gathered all her courage and walked around the island, reacquainting herself with its landscape.

All Talullah could think about after her meeting with Colfax were the memories she'd made there and the friends, Beck and Lynx, she had lost. How quickly she'd become accustomed to the way of life on the Isle. It had felt like home almost immediately, not because of the island itself, but because of the people she'd grown close to.

She'd felt their spirit in the wind as the island had settled into its evening dress, a chill blanketing the landscape as the sun disappeared below the horizon made of glittering blue sea.

Winter would arrive soon.

Talullah didn't know if the weather or the memories had affected her more. Now, as she readied herself to meet Colfax's contacts, she tightened the cloak around herself, hoping it would shield her from both.

She could tell her amethyst to block her memories for her, at least for a short while. But remembering her friends and the tragedies that had occurred on the island and the strength and courage it had taken to overcome them fortified her. Remembering her struggles, and the fact that she'd prevailed over them, gave her hope that she could face whatever came next.

It was almost midnight. She didn't feel ready. Didn't know if she ever would.

Talullah locked the room behind her and descended the stairs past Aran, who was still at the desk. She wondered if he ever went home, or if maybe he had a permanent apartment in the inn. He seemed to always be there.

They acknowledged each other with a polite wave, and Talullah ignored his confused expression. Surely he was wondering why she would be leaving so late. The island didn't have a curfew anymore, now that the school was closed temporarily for reevaluation and restructuring.

And to let the shock and grief fade even a little.

Talullah still felt like she was breaking a rule, even though such a rule no longer existed.

She pushed the thought away and stepped out onto the inn's porch. Captain Caprico was already waiting for her, leaning against the rickety railing and looking out toward the sea.

The nearly full moon cast a silvery glow across his golden-brown hair. His jaw was clenched, and his eyes crinkled at the edges. It was a grim expression. One that reinforced what he'd said earlier. If he didn't think it was absolutely necessary, he would not be doing this.

"Good evening, Captain," Talullah said.

He shifted his stance slightly, choosing to take another moment to himself, with only the stars for company, before acknowledging her presence. "It is evening. That is sure.

Whether it's good or not remains to be seen." He turned to face her and rubbed his jaw with his open palm. "I'm having second thoughts about this meeting. I think it may have been unwise of me to contact them, especially on your behalf."

Talullah straightened up. "Don't back down now. This is the best lead I've had so far. And if dealing with these people means that I can find the piece of the tapestry I *know* is hidden here, then we need to do it. We need to find it before Renevelda does. She wouldn't hesitate to go through this group."

Captain Caprico let out a humorless laugh at that and returned his gaze to the sky. "I think the sorceress might have more leverage than any of us do. She'd easily be able to get herself out of a sticky situation."

"We've already decided to go forward with this plan, Captain. Are you going to facilitate the meeting, or are you going to force me to go alone?"

He sighed, exasperated. "I thought you might say something like that. Let's go. We don't want to be late."

They made their way in silence to a weather-beaten building. Its cream clapboard exterior had sustained more damage than the rest of the buildings on the Isle. Chips of paint and chunks of wood had been sloughed off nearly every thick board. The distress stood out—the rest of the buildings were in pristine condition.

Or no one had made an effort to Manipulate this one's appearance.

"The grocery shop?" Talullah asked, her eyebrows raised in question.

A ghost of a smile played on Caprico's lips. "That's what I said the first time I came here." Then his expression sobered. "But don't let outward appearances fool you in any way, shape, or form. Whether it's a building or a person, everything can be Manipulated to show you what it wants you to see."

Talullah knew that was true. Again, she thought of the prison.

The captain knocked twice on the wind-scuffed door. A rotund man answered immediately.

He had a warm, kind-looking face, but Talullah sensed toughness beneath it.

Everything can be Manipulated, by magic or by willpower.

Appearances, environments, emotions.

She pressed her sapphire to heighten her awareness of all those things as they entered the small grocery store. They followed the man, who didn't say a word, as he limped across the floor using a cane similar to one Talullah's father would have used.

Her father was one of the strongest people she knew.

They walked all the way to the back of the store in silence. The only sound was the slight creaking of the floor and the squeak of their boots on its freshly polished surface. The leader opened one of the cool case doors and stepped into it.

Talullah wished Dhal were with her, to share in her excitement and apprehension. They couldn't get enough of secret passages and hidden doorways. She tamped down the worry and ache of thinking about Dhal and focused. She followed Captain Caprico and the man down a hallway and into a room.

Hats hung on the wall in various patterns. Bowler hats, newsboy caps, monstrosities heaped with feathers and ribbons. Some types Talullah had only seen in history books, and others she'd seen on patrons walking around the Isle today.

Hats? Interesting.

A tall and sturdily built man with bronze skin and a gentle face said, "Ah, I see you've brought a friend this time, Mr. Drake."

"Let's get right to it," Colfax said. His arms hung easily at his sides, but tension made his hands rigid. "We're looking for something. And we think you might know where it is."

Talullah opened her mouth to explain what they were looking for, but Colfax put his hand out to stop her.

The tall man smiled, and his eyes glinted, the expression of a snake about to strike. "Please tell us more about the treasure you seek."

Colfax continued. "It's probably heavily guarded by old magic, and we'll need protection against whatever we might face. Talullah," he said to her, his jaw clenched so tightly she feared he might break it. "Tell them."

"It's a piece of a tapestry. With an embroidered tree."

A young woman's voice floated from one corner. "Tapestry?"

Talullah hadn't noticed her when they first arrived, which was probably the point. She sat in a rope chair that hung in a dark corner with barely any light. Though now that the woman spoke and moved, spinning slowly, the threads of the rope sparkled with magic. The young woman climbed out of the chair and approached, all leisure.

"It's you," Talullah said, surprised. "You're the server from the tavern."

The young woman offered Talullah a half-smile that seemed to say she was both impressed Talullah had noticed and also flattered she had been remembered. It would have been difficult to forget the woman's nearly black eyes and shiny dark hair, not to mention the spider that she still wore in her hair. The netting and spider's legs were now unfurled so that it covered half her face. "We know exactly what you're looking for and how to protect you when you get it, but, as I'm sure Mr. Drake has informed you, we don't do favors. We're going to need something in return."

"Of course, there will be payment," Colfax said. "What's your price?"

The young woman held out her hand to Talullah to shake, ignoring Colfax for now. "I'm Geomi."

Talullah shook her hand. It was ice-cold. "Nice to meet you."

Geomi flashed a sharp smile. "I think we would be remiss if we traded this favor for money." She nodded to both the men in the room, who returned the gesture. "It seems this young girl has some power that we could make good use of."

Talullah stilled. Had Colfax told them about her powers? No. He would never. Had her necklace somehow broken free? No, it was still tucked safely beneath her tunic.

"I can see things others can't," Geomi said, her smile widening to reveal pointy canine teeth. "Your magical aura is quite complex indeed," she whispered.

If Geomi knew she was Sezna Seer, there was nothing Talullah could do to mask it any longer. But still, she pushed her shoulders back. She refused to back down. People like this would happily push her around if she let them.

"Oh?" Talullah replied. She would be willing to do almost anything to get these people to help her find the piece of the tapestry. But they didn't need to know that.

"Yes." Geomi studied her through the spider's legs. "We'll help you find what you seek. But first, we'll need something from you."

Colfax growled. "That wasn't the deal we made. Your deal was with me."

The grocer smirked. "New information, new terms. Business requires adaptability. You know how it is, Mr. Drake."

"What do you want from me?" Talullah asked.

"Nothing much," said the strong-looking man. He shrugged, smiling, tasting the air for fear. "Just an old ring."

TALULLAH

"If you have a better idea, I'm all ears." Talullah couldn't hide the frustration in her voice.

Captain Caprico had been trying for the last hour to convince her not to do this favor for HAT, the group Colfax had introduced her to. Honor Among Thieves, that's what the acronym stood for. Though Talullah had to squint to find any hint of honor in the deal they wanted to make with her.

Not that she had any room to negotiate.

"There are any number of reasons they might want to send you into danger," Colfax reasoned. "We can't trust them. I shouldn't have brought you here." He paced back and forth in the small room the HAT members had allowed them to use to deliberate. Unlike the main area, the room they were currently in didn't have any sort of decorations. Not a single hat hung on the walls.

After some not-so-gentle coaxing, Captain Caprico had

finally revealed how the members of the HAT ring had both helped him to retrieve the sapphire that she now wore around her neck and also had potentially tried to kill him in the process.

"Their help comes with a lot of dangerous strings." He practically growled the words, more to himself than Talullah.

"You knew that going in," Talullah said. "So, why *did* you bring me here in the first place, if you were going to turn around and try to stop me from getting their help the moment they proved you right? Plus, I wouldn't have the sapphire without them, regardless of their shady methods. Renevelda might already have a piece of the tapestry. If we want to prevent her from getting this one, we need to move fast."

Captain Caprico grunted. Talullah could tell he knew she was right.

"It's going to be dangerous no matter what," she pressed. "But with their help, we might be successful. I think I need to do what they're asking."

"But what's their motive? That's what concerns me." Colfax continued pacing. He rubbed his thumbs along his fingers from pinkies to forefingers and back again.

"I don't know," Talullah replied. She blew out a frustrated breath. "Maybe you're being paranoid."

"Maybe," Colfax said. "I know these kinds of people better than you do." His words bit into Talullah. "Or did you forget I used to be one of them?"

Talullah blinked. Sometimes—most of the time—she did forget Captain Caprico used to be a criminal. She'd never thought of him that way. Would never group him with the other members of HAT. Not in a thousand lifetimes. Was her trust in him blinding her to the reality of this unsavory part of the world?

"You're right," she said. "You do know them better than I do. But I know the sorceress better than you. And I know that if she gets this tapestry and gains control of the Source, nothing else will matter. She'll burn it all to the ground to watch herself rise. I need to repair the tapestry and reunite the Sight factions before she destroys the whole community. It's the only way to beat her."

Colfax opened his mouth, but Talullah cut him off. "I've made up my mind. If you want to leave, I won't hold it against you. But, I'm doing this. With or without you."

Colfax sighed through his nose. Talullah imagined him as a dragon, smoke curling out and fanning around his face. "How do we know they haven't already made a deal with the sorceress? How do we know this isn't some kind of trap, that the ring is for her?" Colfax asked. He crossed his arms over his chest.

Talullah paused. She hadn't considered that. "We don't. But we're running out of time. And, if they do want it for her, then maybe she'll be distracted enough by it that I can find the final piece of the tapestry."

"They don't seem to despise Renevelda as much as we do. I wouldn't put it past them to take a good deal when they see one. I think we need to proceed with caution here." Captain Caprico paused his pacing and swallowed hard. He rubbed his stubbled chin.

Talullah nodded. "Using caution doesn't necessarily mean we do nothing. It also doesn't mean that I trust them. What if I pull a card? Would that help ease your concern?"

She should have done that to begin with, but she felt apprehensive about doing magic there, in HAT's lair. If it would get them to a decision, she'd risk it.

"Fine," Colfax said. "But, if your reading spells disaster, we walk away. Deal?"

"Deal." Talullah pulled out her deck and crouched on the dusty gray stone floor. She shuffled the cards and cleared her mind. "Should we move forward with this plan of securing the ring for HAT in exchange for their help finding the tapestry square?"

Talullah took a deep breath.

Flip.

The Scales.

Flip.

The Chariot.

Talullah's mind eased. Things were looking good so far. "I'm seeing an awareness of an event, that's the Scales. And the Chariot signifies willpower and triumph. One more."

Flip.

Talullah's heart stuttered.

The Tower.

Upheaval. A collapse. Isolation.

But it could also mean seeing things in a new way.

"So?" Colfax pressed.

Talullah forced a smile and focused on the promise of the Chariot. They would triumph, even if hardship came.

A knock came on the door. "Time's up." The voice slithered through the bottom of the door, which eased open. Olheiro's smooth demeanor did nothing to dull the hungry intensity in his gaze.

Talullah gathered her cards and cleared her throat. "I'll do it."

Colfax said, "It's shocking how alike you and Gwen are."

Talullah rather liked Gwen, so she smiled. "I'll take that as a compliment." She never would have thought of herself as assertive before, but that's how she felt.

Colfax and Talullah followed Olheiro back into the main room.

"How long will it take?" the Grocer asked, leaning on his cane.

"Not long," answered Talullah. "If it's where you say it is."

The Grocer laughed, his thumbs sliding along the black suspender straps straining against his girth, and nodded. "It is. We're sure."

"And," Talullah added. "While we're gone, you promise not

to tell anyone else the location of the tapestry piece or to assist them in acquiring it."

Again, the Grocer nodded. "Mr. Drake, it would have been useful for you to have her with you last time, no? Quite the negotiator. We have a deal, Miss Talullah."

"And, how can I trust you to keep your end of the bargain?"

Olheiro produced a contract written with shimmering black ink on a piece of smooth cream parchment. "There is honor among thieves, Miss Talullah. We uphold our agreements."

"So I've heard," she said, accepting the pen and signing the contract she'd read five times before deliberating with Colfax. "But I'm not a thief."

Olheiro flashed his dangerous smile. "Not yet."

CHAPTER 32

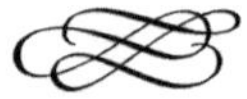

MARGOT

 argot dragged her feet in the dirt as she trudged a few steps behind Dhalian. Once again, she was being left out. She'd traveled across the stars forsaken ocean for Founders' sake, only to be turned away.

She still wasn't old enough or strong enough to help.

Her jaw clenched in time with her squeezing fist. The pulse of her fingers against her palm kept her from spiraling too far as she bit back the tears.

"Hey," Dhalian said quietly over his shoulder. He stopped to let her catch up. "I know this isn't what you expected, but Talullah wouldn't send you away without cause, especially when you went through so much to get to her. You know she appreciates what you did, right?"

Margot nodded slightly. Because, as much as she hated the situation, Dhalian was right. Perfect, responsible Talullah cared about her sisters. She would do anything to protect them. Would never hurt their feelings on purpose. For once, though, Margot wished Talullah would see her as anything other than the stubborn middle sister.

Margot sniffed. The peat smell in the air tickled the inside of her nose. "I know."

Knowing didn't make her feel any better.

They trudged through Nainehta Forest in silence, hearing only the chittering of the animals who dared to dwell within. Margot had heard rumors of ghost animals passing between worlds there, but she couldn't See them. Not without Urtha's Gift.

Yet another thing Talullah had that she didn't.

Maybe she was a tiny bit jealous of her sister after all.

Dhalian let her marinate in her own thoughts until she was soggy with them. They were nearly at the smoking trees that denoted the shift from traditional trees to magical ones when Dhalian stopped her with a gentle hand placed atop her shoulder. Though his expression belied pain. His eyebrows scrunched and his jaw clenched.

"Wait. Listen," he whispered through his teeth. His hazel eyes combed the area.

Voices.

Three of them, judging by the varied pitches ringing in Margot's ears. She darted her gaze left and right, looking for the source.

Dhalian pulled her behind a tree as people passed by them. He covered his bandaged wrist with his opposite palm and breathed shakily in and out.

Pure instinct guided Margot to reach for her magic. She cast a Concealment illusion over both her and Dhalian. It was growing, her power. She could taste it. Like sugar and cinnamon.

Though she was still nowhere near as skilled as she wanted to be. As she knew she could be. It was frustrating, the learning curve. But she would get it. And it seemed she was doing a good enough job now.

"The sorceress said the signal came from here," a tall woman barked out. She was built like a soldier, with defined arm muscles and quads that stretched against her riding pants. Her eyes swirled with blue, shimmering magic.

Well, Margot assumed it was magic. If not, that woman had better see an eye doctor pronto.

Dhalian stiffened beside her.

"If the girl and boy are here, we'll find them." The younger man with absolutely zero hints of hair on his deep brown skin stalked past on stilt-like legs. His gaze was altered in the same way.

"Spread out and find them." The woman swung her long, straight blond ponytail over her shoulder, and adjusted her black cloak. "The sorceress needs those other tapestry pieces immediately."

Margot inhaled sharply. They were looking for Talullah, and they had been tracking Dhalian's scar to try to find her. She'd been keeping tabs on their location so she could steal the pieces from them instead of finding them on her own.

At least Margot and Dhalian's misdirection had worked for now. Talullah was far away and could remain hidden. But they were sitting ducks.

Margot forced more of her intention into hiding them, reinforcing her Concealment spell.

Dhalian nodded at her. A cooler sensation mixed with the warmth of her own magic. So, Dhalian had a Gift too? That surprised her, though nothing should have surprised her at this point. Nonetheless, she welcomed the help in their current situation. "I've muffled our sounds, but I can't hold it for long. I haven't exactly been practicing," Dhalian said. "Impressive illusion, by the way."

His voice was dry and weaker than she was used to hearing.

"I'm going to try something else," Margot said. "It's a misdirection spell like what I used to trick the barrier. Hopefully it will buy us enough time to get out of here. She pulled the handheld mirror out of her bag and framed her and Dhal in it. She didn't have a spare teddy bear this time, so instead, she focused on a bush in the distance and projected her and Dhalian's likenesses onto it.

From this far away, she couldn't solidify the image all the way. But they needed a distraction.

She paused, forcing her feet to stay still on the fallen gold and silver leaves.

"I think I see them. Over there." The third of the group, a short woman with a square jaw and thick black eyebrows raced over.

"Let's go," Margot whispered. She encouraged her illusion to run in the opposite direction. The tall blond woman and the young man followed their companion in chasing the illusion.

Margot and Dhalian didn't waste any time. They sprinted out of the forest and all the way to the barrier near River Hill before they stopped to rest.

"How long do you think we have before they realize their mistake?" Dhalian asked between panting breaths.

"I'm not sure." Margot placed her hands atop her head and breathed in the cold air. "But we definitely need to figure out how to disable that thing in your arm."

"Do you think you can manipulate that spell you used? Make some kind of wearable deflection?"

Margot titled her head in thought. "I think I could do that. But I'm going to need my sister's help."

Dhalian frowned. His brows cinched together. "We just left Talullah, I don't think—"

"Not Talullah," Margot said, smiling, for the first time in days. "I have two sisters, you know. We're going to need some help from Penny."

～

DHALIAN HAD BEEN hesitant to go back inside the barrier. Margot wondered if he didn't trust that he'd be able to leave again. She'd assured him by practicing it herself. And after three times, he finally believed her. When they entered Margot's cottage, Penny saw them first.

She rammed into Margot with a hug so hard Margot nearly lost her breath. "Thank the Founders you're all right. I'm so sorry, Mar. I had to tell Father everything, and he's been trying to Scry with Aunt Mirella and we couldn't find you and—"

"Margot?" Her father's eyes were swollen and rimmed red, his pale cheeks splotchy. "Oh, Mar! I am so glad you're home." He scooped her up and squeezed like he'd never let go. "And angry, of course. I don't know what you were thinking, leaving and gallivanting across the sea like that."

"Father, can you punish me later? You can ground me for eternity. But first, Penny and I have some work to do."

"We do?" Penny asked

They worked all night, fueled by hand pies and potatoes and tea, to get the spell and the hardware right. Penny found some old metal and mirrors in their father's antique shop to fashion into a watch-like band Dhalian could wear over his scar. Margot spelled it, imposing the deflection illusion on it.

They tested it out by having Dhal wait in a separate room while Margot tried to Scry him. They couldn't replicate Renevelda's magic, of course, but the spell deflected enough that Margot couldn't pinpoint exactly where he was.

"And, if you turn the dial," Penny said proudly, "you can move the illusion further away or closer to you.

"I think I'll keep it at its furthest strength for now," Dhalian said. "I'd prefer she think I'm in a completely different country. This is fantastic. Thank you so much."

"Get back to my sister. Help her finish what she's started.

And for the Founders sake, come back home in one piece." Margot pushed the sapphire on the corner of the mirror in the living room and thought about Talullah, calling her image up in her mind. It only rang for half a second before Talullah's face appeared.

"Mar, are you home? Is Dhal with you?" All her words rushed together in a breathless blur. Margot nearly sobbed at the relief in Talullah's voice. It matched her own.

"Of course, Dhalian got me home safely. Like he promised. Now I'm sending him back to you."

"Where should I meet you, Tules?" Dhalian asked. Margot didn't miss the longing in his expression. She'd always suspected the two of them had been dancing around each other. Margot rolled her eyes.

"Hidden Market," Talullah said.

"I'll see you soon," Dhalian said.

"Talk to Father and Penny for a minute." Margot pulled Dhalian toward the front door, away from the others. The sun had started to rise already.

She opened her bag and grabbed the book and the star chart she'd been studying. "Give these to Talullah. I don't know if I'll be able to Scry with her to tell her anything I might discover. It's better if she has them." It physically hurt—a little twinge that ran from her fingers to her heart—to give away the little bit of independence and knowledge she'd accumulated. But it was for the best, like Dhalian had said. She'd done her part by telling Talullah about her vision and by helping Dhalian with his tracking problem. Maybe she didn't need to be in the middle of all the action to help.

"Thank you, Margot. For everything."

"Yeah, yeah," she said, and she shoved Dhalian toward the door playfully. "But you'd better not come back here until you've finally kissed her."

CHAPTER 33

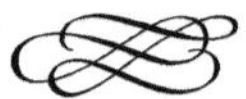

KAI

Guilt had wreaked havoc on Kai's nervous system in the last few days. He hadn't slept. Had barely eaten. Couldn't see how he was supposed to swallow cinnamon bread and sip tea like nothing had happened. Like he hadn't let Talullah and everyone else down.

He should have done something to stop the thief. Anything. Instead, he'd stood there, paralyzed by fear and indecision. Per usual.

Kai paused his sulking for half a second to steal a glance at Theresa and Veylan Marquet. They huddled close together under a tree looking at the ledger Kai and Edouard had compiled for King William. They'd become closer over the past few days. Something about the younger Marquet's presence seemed to calm Theresa, made her more sure of herself and their plan.

Kai had replayed his conversation with Veylan many times. Something about it felt...off. He couldn't quite name what it was about Veylan that made him wary. Could have been the tattoo on Veylan's neck, but plenty of perfectly pleasant people had tattoos. No, it was something in the young man's demeanor.

Theresa had spent less time with Kai recently, and he couldn't figure out why. Something had created a fence between Kai and Theresa. Not quite a wall, not yet. He could still glimpse her through the slats. Was it his lack of action, his inability to do his job and Scry Talullah? Whatever it was, Theresa defaulted to taking Veylan's advice over Kai's, even for small things like what flavor scones they should have at breakfast. It stung. He and Theresa had always been close. She'd been like an older cousin he could look to.

But now, Kai stood on the perimeter while Veylan commanded the inner circle of Theresa's confidence.

Would Theresa believe Kai if he shared his concerns about Veylan? So far, he'd kept his observations and feelings to himself. He didn't want to cause unnecessary conflict, to upset the group dynamic without certainty.

How would it go, if Kai challenged Veylan's authority in his own house?

Not well for Kai, he imagined.

It was bizarre, when he thought about it. When he let the reality of the situation sink in. It no longer felt like a dream.

It felt like war.

They even had a prisoner.

The guard they'd captured was being kept in the garden shed. Quentis had adapted it so the man wouldn't perish during the cold nights, and they'd been bringing him meals.

No one was sure what to do about him, especially now that Renevelda's Manipulation magic had worn off.

Kai hadn't been present when Veylan and Quentis had questioned the guard the first time. When he'd asked how it went, he'd gotten some vague replies.

It didn't add up. But, as usual, Kai was having a hard time putting the pieces together.

He needed help. To talk to someone he trusted.

And he yet didn't trust himself to talk to Talullah.

Instead, he slipped inside, past the mayhem of another card game, and closed himself in the room he now shared with Zinni, though his best friend wasn't there.

Kai lit the orange blossom candle on the bedside table and pulled out his pocket Scry.

It took all of two seconds before Alexander's face filled the mirror. "Kai Lin, why am I only now hearing from you? I've been worried sick, you know. I tried you a few times, but I couldn't get through. I assumed..." Alexander ran a hand through his golden brown hair. "I didn't want to believe you were...you know..."

"I'm fine, Alexander. We escaped through the tunnels beneath the castle. It took longer than expected to find the exit. Scry signals didn't work underground." Kai swallowed the lump in his throat. "I'm sorry. I should have contacted you the moment we made it out."

"I'm relieved you're alive." The prince blew out a long breath. "We're okay here, too. Me and Imogen and...my father."

That was a whole soup tureen full of conflicting emotions.

But at least they were safe.

Kai often wondered if there was anything more he could have done at the castle. He still felt immense guilt for the deaths of the three guards whom Renevelda had taken control of. Kai had tried to keep them safe, but had he done his best? Or had he only done what was best for him in that moment? The guilt would eat him alive if he let it.

"So...what's happening wherever you are?" Alexander asked.

For a moment, Kai briefly wished for the power of discernment that the Dunamarian Seers had. The opportunity to look into the future and preview what might happen if they took a specific path. It was dangerous, he knew, to get caught up in such thoughts and in such magic. Talullah had told him as much about her journey to the land of the Between.

Those paths were more pronounced and dangerous, of course, than a simple card reading. But in that moment, he couldn't help but wish for something to guide him on this part of the journey. He often wavered like this, when big decisions needed to be made, and anything that could ground him and provide a little more certainty would be welcome.

Like telling Alexander about Theresa's desire to have the prince lead the rebellion. Or divulging the fact that his cohorts currently held a man prisoner.

Kai cleared his throat. He breathed in the orange blossom scent, hoping it would be enough to solidify his nerves, which were currently the consistency of vanilla pudding.

"The thing is, Alexander, I don't know what I'm doing anymore." He sat on his pallet on the floor and leaned his back against the wall, relishing the support it offered.

"If this is about the girl—"

"It's not."

Alexander's teasing expression sobered. His eyes ceased their laughing sparkle, his lips curving down. "What's happened?"

"Things have taken a turn. Veylan's insisting we keep Renevelda's guard as a prisoner, even though the Manipulation spell has worn off. And we're not getting any information from him. At least, not that I'm hearing. Veylan won't let anyone else near him. Is that suspicious? Because it feels suspicious. And I'm afraid to bring this up to anyone else because how does that make me look? Like a traitor. Like I don't belong here. And there's so many people here, but are we doing anything? I mean, what are we even doing with all these Seers? It's all a bit too much, but where else am I supposed to go at this point?"

The words rushed out of him like red wine from an over-turned goblet. They matched the blood already on his hands from the people he couldn't save.

Had he made a terrible mistake following Theresa and Edouard?

His thoughts flashed to his family. How long would it take for news of the upheaval at the castle to reach the farm towns in Terrapese?

Would his family be proud of him, or would the knowledge that he had Sight powers overshadow anything remotely heroic he'd done?

Should he send them a message to let them know he was alive, at least? But then that might invite further questions, and he wasn't certain how long they would be staying at the Marquets' house if more messages arrived for him later.

"Kai? Are you there?" Alexander's voice pulled Kai out of his spiral.

"Yeah. I'm here. Barely." Kai closed his eyes and took a deep breath.

"I don't know much about the Marquets, but I have heard Veylan's name circling around. And not necessarily in the best of circles. Please be careful."

Kai's mouth went dry. "What have you heard?"

"Nothing concrete. He's been seen with some people with less than savory reputations. You could come here, if you want. There's enough space." Alexander's hopeful tone pumped more guilt into Kai's already overflowing supply. He wanted, more than anything he now realized, to be reunited with his friend.

But he couldn't leave. Not until he figured out what was going on with Veylan Marquet. If the young Seer was hiding something that could be dangerous, Kai owed it to himself, Zinni, Theresa, and fine, Edouard, too, to learn what it was.

He'd already let the tapestry piece slip through his fingers. He couldn't let the truth do the same.

"Kai?" Theresa knocked on the door. "Can you join us outside?"

He sighed and nodded to Alexander. "It seems I am required elsewhere. It's good to see you, Alexander."

"You, too. Take care of yourself, okay?"

Kai forced a nod, then disconnected the connection, already trying to think of a little white lie he could tell Theresa and Veylan to avoid them finding out he'd talked to Alexander without mentioning his joining the rebellion as its leader.

The irony of searching for the truth about Veylan while keeping secrets of his own was, unfortunately, not lost on him.

Kai arranged his face into an expression that could be considered calm and loped over to the blanket where Theresa and Veylan were sitting. Edouard loomed behind Theresa, standing instead.

"We've been discussing the sorceress's motive," Theresa said. "And Veylan has an interesting theory."

Veylan told a story about the Suditzas and how they'd divided their power into the tapestry, as well as put it together with the eye amulets as blessings. "The rumor is the Source controls magic, and only someone with all four Sights can access it. Or, if there are four Seers, one from each Sight faction, who have bonded themselves, they will be able to control the Source."

He paused for dramatic effect. "Or, they could destroy it."

"Destroy it?" Theresa said. "Why on earth would anyone want to destroy the Source of all magic? It would wipe out much of the community."

Kai added in a whisper, "It would be devastating for those with magic. That was why they were so terrified." Although the four sects of Sight magic had long since severed close ties to one another in favor of pursuing their own interests, a strong leader could bring them back together. "But if they reunited to control the Source, they could take over the world. They could oppress non-magic users like they've been oppressed in Viltresor for so long."

Veylan nodded. "They could do it easily. However, if that leader happened to be an evil sorceress, she could control the magic and everyone who possessed it."

"This is no longer about equal rights or freedoms," Theresa said. "If the sorceress gains control of the Source, then what we want won't matter at all. She'll be able to use us like little puppets, and *that* is why we have to oppose her."

"It's going to be a struggle," Veylan said. "Many have already joined her, believing she'll propel them to their rightful place."

Theresa picked up where Veylan left off. "We can't let the sorceress control the Source, but also we have to make sure that no one else controls it either."

"Wait a second." Kai pressed his fingers between his eyebrows. "Are you suggesting that we somehow bond and control the Source? I don't think we'd be powerful enough to control that kind of magic. What is the plan here?"

"We're not suggesting that at all," Theresa said. "We don't want to use the Source, just make sure no one can use it against us."

"Again, *how* do we do that?" A headache pounded in Kai's skull.

Veylan's eyes glinted. "We control the map to the Source. And we kill the sorceress."

CHAPTER 34

TALULLAH

"Why do they want this ring in the first place?" Dhal asked.

Talullah breathed in the scent of him. Honey and morning dew and so, so real. She almost couldn't believe it. He'd come back. Part of her—a bigger part than she dared to admit—had worried he might stay in River Hill.

But Dhal had kept his word. He'd come back. Margot—with Penny's help—had even created a device that could confuse the magical tracker spell, a perfect fusion of their talents. Penny had built the mirrored wristband now attached to Dhal's scarred arm. Margot had spelled the mirrors to send out multiple illusory signals, basically a more advanced version of what she'd used to trick the barrier.

Talullah had Dhal back and she could still Scry.

Her sisters were brilliant.

"It doesn't matter, does it?" She and Dhal stepped into the forest nearest the Hidden Market.

Though, it wasn't truly hidden anymore. Not now that the territories had combined. They no longer needed to hide their trade, especially since neither territory had solid enough leadership to stop the influx of contraband.

Instead, it was the opposite. There was nearly free reign to buy and sell and trade anything one desired. The Hidden Market had changed.

A wave of unease washed over her as she and Dhal entered the market. It used to bring her great joy to see the merchants calling out their wares amid the music and laughter contained by the magical barrier. The market was one of the only places in the two kingdoms where she'd felt truly safe.

Not solely because of the magical barriers, but because of the sense of cooperation that the Hidden Market had fostered. It had been less about defying the two kings' wishes, and more about the people forging their own paths, deciding what was most important to *them*. Breaking the rules ranked second back then.

But now, as Talullah regarded the market and all its changes, she could tell that things were different. Rule breaking, it seemed, had become the number one priority.

Before, brightly colored fabric and soft wind chimes had adorned the tents. Now, many were draped in dark, heavy fabrics to obscure whatever wares they held inside. There had always been a few tents like this before, at the far edge of the market. Talullah had avoided them. Back then, she'd distrusted all magic. Especially the dark kind those tents advertised, but even her own.

Now, things inside her were different, too. She trusted her own magic more than anything. The sight of all the dark tents told her that others did the same, whether for good or for evil.

Dhal squeezed her hand, and they moved forward through the market's cobbled streets. Talullah pushed her shoulders back and her head up high, making sure that the hunting knife holstered at her hip was clearly visible.

She hoped not to use it, but she wanted others to know it existed.

"Any idea where to start?" Dhal whispered in her ear, and a soft tingle crept up her spine. He was trying to be covert. But still, his closeness elicited a physical response.

"HAT gave me a description of the tent. We're looking for Documents, etc."

Talullah glanced over at what used to be Baako's stall. Her favorite place no longer existed. *Just as well.* She hated to imagine her gentle friend conducting business in such a shady environment. Still, selfishly, she missed him. Nothing would calm her more than to curl up on a crate and listen to one of his stories, like she used to do as a child. But, time had passed. That was no longer her reality.

She hoped he was off doing more fulfilling things and tried to focus on the fact that he hadn't been dragged into the darkness.

"I think that's the one we're looking for," Dhalian said. He pointed to a small stall huddled in between a few others. If they hadn't specifically been looking for it, they might have missed it. It looked to be part of its neighboring tents, not its own entity. But Talullah glimpsed the subtle differences in the fabric. With senses heightened by her sapphire, she noticed some of the magical wards that surrounded it.

All the tents had some kind of protection spells. Talullah could understand why. A place like this had to be rife with thieves and others who wished to do the merchants harm. They had a right to protect themselves.

This tent, however, had an extra layer of warding that Talullah couldn't quite understand. "Let's go," she said, and she pulled Dhal forward.

When they reached the door of the tent, a short, oily man

with thinning black hair poked his head out between the draped fabric. An equally thin mustache quivered above his sneering lips. "We're closed."

"You don't look closed," Dhal said, peeking in.

"We do a certain kind of business here." He flicked his creepy gaze over at Talullah. "Not the kind of business fitting for a young, upstanding lady such as yourself." His sad mustache twitched up at one corner.

Emboldened by her gems and her mission, Talullah smirked right back. It was time to throw this slimy, bottom-feeding carp back where he belonged. "You're mistaken."

Though she trembled a little inside, she projected the utmost confidence. That was one thing Captain Caprico had taught her: when dealing with these kind of people, it was important to feign authority, even if one didn't have any. "Are you prepared to turn away coin?"

Dhal shook the black velvet bag full of marbles from Praeteriti. Rare money would give them a better shot at getting what they needed, she hoped.

The man gaped. Carp-like, indeed.

Talullah raised her brow. "Should we spend elsewhere?"

The weaselly man stared at her for a moment. The wheels turned behind his beady rat-like eyes, but he nodded his head and opened the curtain for them to pass. "Don't say I didn't warn you."

In the corner of the tent, behind a plain, nearly black table sat a large, muscular man. He exuded the feeling Talullah always got when she walked into a dark room, like some kind of unknown entity was watching her.

He barely glanced up from his work, where his hands flicked back and forth across a metal object of some kind. "What do you want?"

The weaselly man spoke first. "They have money."

The large man lifted his eyes, assessing her and Dhal. "Oh?"

Talullah shoved all fear aside, knowing he would be able to smell it on her. She bolstered herself with her sapphire, and she and Dhalian approached the table.

"We're looking for a ring."

The merchant stood to his full height. If he and Kai were standing next to each other, this man would be at least five inches taller. He ran a hand through his pale hair and arched a barely visible eyebrow. "Look a bit young to get engaged."

A hot flush vined up Talullah's throat. But she refused to give in to embarrassment. "Not that kind of ring. It can be dangerous, you know. Making assumptions."

At this, the man sat back in his chair and looked at her straight on. His golden eyes swirled with some kind of magic Talullah couldn't identify. It wasn't the same kind as the Manipulation magic that Renevelda had used. That magic had turned the subject's eyes bright blue.

What had this man done to himself? Or had someone else done it to him?

Whether it was some kind of Manipulation spell to change his appearance or voice or something else entirely, Talullah waited patiently, not allowing herself to break away. The first one to blink would lose.

Maybe he sought something in her stare. Lies. Intent. Weakness.

Talullah held his gaze. She refused to be bullied. He wanted to know how far she would go with this and how easily he could dissuade her.

Finally, he broke eye contact and reached into a crate. He set out two wooden boxes big enough for cigars and opened them. Silver and gold circles glinted inside. Gems crusted some of them, while others remained bare metal. None emitted the hum of magic she was looking for.

"These are nice. But not quite what we want. What else can you show us?" She'd spent enough time negotiating with customers and with merchants herself to understand the power play he was trying to make. She would stand there all day if she had to, and it was likely she would turn away other important customers if he failed to get her out of there.

He leaned forward then. A black tattoo in the shape of a clover stretched on the skin of his neck.

She'd told him she didn't assume, but it was probably a safe guess that he was used to people being intimidated by his appearance. His biceps alone probably weighed half as much as she did.

"You know what?" he said finally. "I like you. You've got spunk. I'll bite this time. I think I can help you out."

He turned around and unlocked one of the many drawers behind him, returning with another wooden box, much smaller than the others. He lifted the lid. The brass ring Geomi had described smiled up at her. Like a feather twisted into a circle. But there were two instead of one. "Only question now is, can you afford the price?" The challenge lit his gaze as he assessed her.

Talullah's hand closed around the velvet pouch. The marble-like money from Praeteriti clacked together. People like this wanted rare items. He wouldn't be able to get these from anyone else. Hopefully that would be enough for him to make the trade.

She dropped the bag on the table in front of him.

"Sounds a bit light for pewters," he said.

"They're not pewters," Dhal said. He squeezed Talullah's hand again.

The merchant raised one barely visible blond brow. He was intrigued.

The man stuck his thick fingers into the opening of the bag and pulled it apart. Then he snatched a few of the marbles and held them in his palm. He'd grabbed one of each, a black Nokto, a silver Metait, and a white Luz.

Money from the world of the past should fetch a steep price in a place like this.

The man rubbed his jaw. "Where did a girl like you get these?"

"What matters is they're real."

The man peered into the bag. A wide grin spread over his face. "All right. I'll take this. But I want something else, too."

"That's more than enough," Talullah argued.

"Ah, maybe. But the thing about negotiations, doll, is you can't let your leverage slip. You're a Sezna Seer. Pretty famous one, too, I've gathered."

She startled at that, ready to deny it.

"The spell at the entrance reveals the magical auras of everyone coming into my tent. I knew from the moment you walked in that you have all the Suditzas' Sight magic."

"So, you wanted to see what else you could get out of her," Dhal said, bitterly.

The man shrugged. "I'm a business man." He leaned forward again. "As I see it, the only reason you'd need that ring is you're in big trouble. You need help from some dangerous people. They want the ring, and if you don't deliver, neither do they. Seems like you've lost your leverage. You want to make good on your promise, you take my deal."

The true weight of her Gifts settled on her chest as if the merchant squeezed her ribs with his unnaturally large arms. Empathy for her great-great grandmother and all the Sezna Seers who came before Talullah swelled inside her.

Had they all felt so used, like pawns in a twisted game of survival?

Everyone wanted a piece of their Gift, and they were shameless about it.

But he was right.

Talullah had nothing else to give.

She'd been hopeful she could get out of this without

revealing her identity. Apparently practicing her Sight hadn't smothered her naïveté.

"It's funny," the merchant said. "How sometimes we think we're so clever and that we're less noticeable than we are. I've got the upper hand now. Unless you're willing to walk away without the ring, I suggest you make it official." He produced a contract which would be a binding agreement of their deal sealed with enforcement magic. The second one she'd have to tether herself to in less than a day.

Talullah had no choice. She needed the ring to fulfill her deal with HAT and to receive their help finding the tapestry square. If she didn't, Renevelda could find it first.

"What else do you want from me?" Talullah's voice grated against her vocal cords, dry with defeat.

"You, my dear, are going to tell me my future."

Talullah exhaled and shook her head. "I haven't trained that much with predictions."

The man squeezed his fist around the quill. "Deal or no deal, Seer?"

"Tules," Dhal started. "We'll find another way."

"This is the only way." She locked her stone gaze on the merchant. "But, I want both rings." HAT had only asked for one. But Talullah wanted to know the ring's magic. To see if HAT could use it against her or if it could aid Renevelda.

The merchant chuckled. "Pressing your luck, eh?"

"It's called a negotiation. Do we have a deal or not?"

A sly smile revealed the merchant's yellowed teeth. "Alright."

Talullah accepted the quill from the merchant and met his golden gaze. "Where do I sign?"

CHAPTER 35

TALULLAH

Talullah scrawled her name. She ignored the way Dhal's jaw clenched as he watched her sign. When she'd finished, she left the quill on the desk and faced the merchant. "I don't have your birth chart or any star maps, and it seems you're fresh out of tea." She glanced around the stall. "So, if you want a reading about the future, you'll have to settle for a palm reading."

"Works for me." Interest glazed the merchant's spelled eyes.

"The problem," she continued, "with reading the future like this is that it won't be complete. I won't be able to tell you everything that will lead up to the moment that the magic reveals to me. It's a single point in time that I can access."

Hopefully. She hadn't exactly practiced much or experimented with her ruby's powers. Acid bubbled in her stomach.

The man rubbed his chin, then cocked his head to the side.

The way he smirked made Talullah's insides scramble, and she knew before he opened his mouth that he was going to try to alter the deal before they even started. "Well, isn't that what your other magic is for? Dunamai had a way of seeking out potential futures. Can't you find the end point and work your way backward?"

Talullah tensed. She'd tried that before in Enodia, the land of the Between. "That's not an option. It ends poorly for everyone involved. My offer stands. I will do a palm reading to answer one of your questions, and then you will relinquish the rings you promised to me, which, I'll remind you, you've magically bound yourself to uphold."

She'd made him sign the contract first, to be certain.

It was imperative for her to convince him to keep this arrangement as it was. She couldn't risk mixing her magic again, especially where the Potential was involved. The Between had recently stabilized, and she didn't have the time or the energy to go traipsing through the paths for this crook of a man.

"Alright. You know, if your current gig doesn't work out, I could use another assistant. I like your tenacity." He smirked again.

It sickened her how much he was enjoying torturing her like this. He was determined to make it as hard as possible for her to get what she needed.

"Let's begin. I don't have all day." She pulled up a wayward, slightly wobbly, three-legged stool and settled herself across from the merchant at the table. Her gaze flicked to the other weaselly man, who still sat at the doorway of the tent, watching with his beady eyes. Dhal had moved to the entrance at the merchant's request for privacy. But his eyes flicked back and forth between the oily guy near him and the merchant. Talullah's heart swelled at the support. She wouldn't have been able to do this alone. The two men would have easily overpowered or chased her off.

Talullah brushed her hair away from her face. "Give me your palm. Your dominant hand will provide the most accurate reading."

She hadn't had much time to read the palmistry book from Edda, but she'd have to work with the knowledge she had.

He placed his hand atop the table, close enough for her to see. "It's easier if I hold on to it. Is it alright if I touch your hand?" She would rather have been stung by a sand jelly than touch him, but she was eager to get this over with as soon as possible.

"All right." He shifted a little bit as if the request was foreign. She imagined he wasn't used to people touching him with care or kindness.

She slipped her hand under his large one and ignored the creepy-crawly feelings that wormed through her. It was the complete opposite kind of feeling from what she had when she held hands with Dhal. She fixed her gaze on his palm. "Now, what is it you want to know?"

"Hmm," he said, pretending to think about it, though eagerness made his palm rigid. He'd wanted to ask this question for a long time. "When will I become successful?"

"Can you make it more specific?" she said.

"How about, when will my hard work pay off and allow me to leave this behind?" He gestured around the tent.

She nodded. "That should do fine." She squinted at his hand, taking note of the lines and how they intersected. The marks here and there denoting certain events. She allowed her amethyst to give her a mental picture of the palmistry book she'd received from Edda.

"This line here represents your lifeline, the trajectory of your life, as well as its length. And this line represents your relation-ships. This other line represents your work life. We see here where these lines intersect, a triangle that could denote success.

And over here is an obstacle of some kind that you have over-come. And this here"—Talullah cut herself off.

She looked closer at the marking. It was a line broken into three, the part closest to the lifeline branching into two, with a dot between the forks. Talullah's stomach turned, and she suddenly felt lightheaded.

It could mean any kind of setback. But the way her ruby burned her throat told her this was a bad omen. Perhaps the worst kind. The kind that separated a person's soul from their body.

Talullah scrambled for a way to answer that would uphold her end of the bargain without sending the merchant into a panic. He was creepy and grumpy and a swindler, and she didn't like him at all. But that didn't mean she would tell him the details of his pending demise. Not liking a person didn't mean she had to cause them pain.

"What is it?" His voice and eyes were both lit with anticipation. "What did you See?"

Talullah switched her focus to a different, nearby mark. She swallowed the lump of fear. "I see a familial relationship that has been straining you lately. And over here is a work success that you've been hoping for."

The man straightened up and brightened at that comment. "Success, eh?" This was clearly the direction he wanted to go in, but by the placement of the worrisome marking, Talullah realized that the success in his work event would ultimately end his life. At his family's hand, by the looks of things.

What a terrible way to go.

But also, she was new at this. It would be so easy for her to misinterpret. This was why seeking the future was so dangerous. It was slippery. Amorphous. Easy to get wrong and ruin some-one's life.

"How soon will it happen?" he asked.

Talullah shook her head. "Like I said, I can't See—"

He cut her off with a slam of his opposite fist on the table. "You promised the truth, and you promised this reading in detail. So tell me—when will it happen?"

She opened her mouth, but he continued. "I know that you know. Don't pretend otherwise."

"Don't speak to her like that." Though he was across the tent, Dhalian's seething voice struck strong. His hazel eyes flamed.

The man looked up at him and laughed a little. "Or what? You gonna tickle me with your luscious curls?"

Dhalian tilted his head slightly, the picture of calm, unfazed by the threat. "You ever heard of a silk reaper?"

The man stiffened. "Only the deadliest spider on the continent. 'Course, I've heard of it. Everyone's heard of it." As tough as the merchant was on the outside, the tremble in his hand hinted at a weakness, a fear of spiders. In another context, it would have been humorous.

Dhal stalked over slowly. His focus never left the merchant. His voice whispered low and unfamiliar and authoritative. "I'm like that spider. Small, inconspicuous. You barely even notice me until you're dead on the floor from one tiny bite."

The man laughed, revealing two missing teeth, the rest yellowed.

Dhal remained stone-faced as he reached into his pocket and pulled out a capped syringe full of liquid. "If I can't do it with my bare hands, then this should do the trick. Concentrated venom. Extremely expensive, but worth it, I'd wager." His eyes flicked up to the merchant's, who had stilled like a statue.

"Where did you get that?" he whispered.

Dhal laughed, his tone devoid of mirth. He gestured toward the tent's exit. "Plenty of places around here that a guy could get such a thing. Convenient, I'd say, to have a stealthy supplier so close."

Talullah held her breath. There was no way that was silk reaper spider venom. He had to be bluffing. Though they'd been separated for a while. He could have purchased it when she was on the Isle.

The thought made her heart beat faster.

The man gruffed a non-reply.

"Apologize to her now, if you please," Dhalian said, his body still tense.

The merchant flicked his gaze from Dhal to the syringe and then to Talullah. "Begging your lady's apologies," he said to her.

Dhalian capped and pocketed the vial again. He nodded at Talullah and reclaimed his post by the entrance. The weaselly man scooted his chair another foot away.

"So," the man continued in a more polite tone. "Please continue your enlightening reading, my dear."

Talullah steeled herself and studied the man's hand again. There were scars here and there, which would tell her their own stories if she asked them to, even without her amethyst's magic. But he wanted to know about the future.

"I want to know about this here." He pointed to the marking that had made her pause. "What did you See?"

She tried again to explain away her feelings, but the man grabbed her other hand and forced her thumb onto the marking. With a searing burn to the backs of her eyes, Talullah was thrust into the vision of the future encoded in the man's palm.

He stood outside that same tent. It was late afternoon, and the sun beat down, relentless in its mission to singe the dry grass.

He was waiting for someone, muttering to himself, tapping his foot, shielding his eyes with his hand and gazing out into the market.

At last, a cloaked figure approached. Recognition lit the merchant's face. They knew each other. Was the other man the family member Talullah had mentioned?

They talked, all inaudible to her.

The hooded figure guided the merchant back inside the tent, where they stood alone, and clasped him on the back. "Thank you for your service. You've been instrumental in moving the sorceress's plan forward."

"So, I'm in for that promotion?" The merchant slapped the other figure on the back in a light-hearted manner, smiling.

It struck Talullah as odd to see him smile. He looked like a completely different person.

"Not exactly," the hooded figure said.

The sound of metal unsheathing sliced against Talullah's eardrums.

Two sets of gloved hands grabbed the man from behind.

A glint of silver flashed in the corner of Talullah's eye. She turned, but it was too late.

The merchant barely had time to gasp before the hooded figure drove a dagger directly between his ribs. The handle stuck out of the man's chest, blood running in rivulets down his tunic. Thin threads shimmered within the tunic's weave, a foreign material Talullah couldn't name which flashed gold through the red-stain of her vision.

The smell of copper tanged the air.

"It's unfortunate it had to be this way, cousin." The hooded figure twisted the knife and pulled it out.

Another flash of red pulled her from the prophecy.

Talullah was back in the tent, panting, her mouth dry, her eyes struggling to focus, her mind wild.

The merchant watched her with an intense expression.

She drew slow inhales in through her nose and pushed them out through her mouth.

Do not vomit all over the table.

Her hands shook, still grasping the merchant's. Tears welled up in her eyes. Though she had no particular love for this man, she did hold sympathy for him.

"Well?"

She knew enough to know never to predict someone's death, even if the lines pointed in that direction. It was unprofessional, and also it was of no use scaring them. Everyone would die eventually.

She tried to speak, but no words came out. She flashed her gaze over to Dhalian, and when their eyes met, he rushed to her side.

"I said I want to know what you Saw, Seer. This is what you promised." The man squeezed her palm until she cried out in pain.

"We're done here," Dhalian said.

The big man stood up and loomed over both of them. "She hasn't fulfilled her end of the bargain."

"She's done enough." Dhalian grabbed the rings and shoved them in his bag. He pulled the syringe out of his pocket.

"Wait, Dhal." Talullah took one last look at the merchant, whose eyes hadn't left hers. "Don't trust your cousin," she said. "He's going to betray you."

It wouldn't be enough. Talullah knew that. What she'd Seen was going to happen, regardless of whether or not she said a word.

But at least she'd tried.

She'd done as she'd promised, though it wouldn't change a thing.

"Come on, Talullah, we're getting out of here."

The merchant reached for her, his pores leaking desperation. "I need to know more."

"He's coming for you. Soon. With a big knife." Talullah's vision blurred.

The merchant stared at her, his jaw tense. But something had spurred the weaselly man into action. He rushed toward them. "I'm afraid I can't let you leave with those rings." Dhalian aimed the syringe and stabbed it into the man's shoulder.

He sank to the ground, still conscious, but a bit wobbly. The large merchant watched them go, his hands pressed flat on the desk, his jaw tense.

Outside the tent, Talullah gasped for air. "That wasn't really silk reaper venom, was it?"

Dhal shook his head, smiling sheepishly. "Of course not. It was a bit of the muscle relaxer Mr. Miscian gave me. We needed to buy some time. He'll live."

That was more than she could say for the merchant. Her stomach contracted. She forced the rising bile to retreat down her throat.

"Come on. We need to get back to the Isle."

When they reached the edge of the market, Talullah glanced back. The merchant stepped out of the tent, as she'd Seen in her vision. He shook out his arms and legs and rolled his neck from side-to-side. He'd changed his tunic. The new one glinted with hints of red and gold woven through the otherwise black fabric.

The sun was in nearly the exact same spot as in her prophecy.

Not far from them, a hooded figure headed toward the Documents, etc. tent. Talullah's insides clenched. She hadn't expected the prediction to come true so soon.

Dhalian pulled her focus back to him. "We've got to go, Tules."

She nodded. "I know." She couldn't look away from the merchant. The hooded figure had almost reached him.

"What's wrong?" Dhal asked.

"Does it make me a bad person, knowing what's about to happen to him and not trying to stop it?"

The smell of honey surrounded her as Dhal hugged her. "You fulfilled your contracted obligation. You warned him. What happens next is up to him and him alone. You can't stop every bad thing from happening."

Talullah clenched the fabric of her cloak in her hands, willing its smooth texture to ground her.

You've been instrumental in moving the sorceress's plan forward.

What had the merchant done? Encouraged Seers to go to the castle? Provided illegal documents or magic?

Whatever crimes he'd committed, he'd done so knowingly. He'd chosen this path.

And likewise, he'd chosen his fate. Whatever it was.

Talullah turned away and didn't look back.

CHAPTER 36

TALULLAH

"Jules." Dhal nudged her. "We're here."

Talullah had basically sleepwalked the whole way back to the transport tree. Her limbs weighed heavily from the loss of adrenaline. Guilt had stolen any words she might have said. Despite her earlier rationale, she couldn't completely erase it.

Dhal steadied her when the tree jolted to a start, and he didn't let go until it was time to step back out.

He'd been quiet ever since she'd stalked away from the Hidden Market. Did it change the way he felt about her, that she knew the merchant was going to die, and she didn't try to stop it?

She couldn't decide if it changed the way she felt about herself.

"It's not your fault, you know." Dhal's voice was low and smooth and wrapped her up like a summer wind. "You can't save everyone."

"I know." She did. It didn't make it any easier.

Gift or curse? What was her power, really? What was the point of knowing what was bound to happen? Why would anyone want to?

"Come on." Talullah guided Dhal to the water's edge, where Captain Caprico had docked a Skimmer for them. It was high-tide again. They couldn't walk across the expanse of sand. Couldn't swim either, unless they wanted to be jellyfish food.

A shiver ran up Talullah's spine. The scar on her ankle hadn't faded with time. If anything, it had grown more pronounced, darkening with age as if to remind her that the jelly had almost taken her, too.

It was also a reminder that it hadn't. That against all odds, she'd survived.

And it was her job to make sure her life was worth it.

Find the tapestry. Control the Source. Beat the sorceress. Save magic.

That's why she survived. She had to believe it. This was her destiny.

She and Dhal climbed into the Skimmer.

"You have enough energy for this?" Dhal asked. "I can help."

Talullah started to say no. That she had it under control. But exhaustion pulled her eyelids down. Her muscles shook as if she'd climbed a thousand stories up a rope ladder. "I wouldn't say no to a little help." She offered a weak smile.

Dhal looked surprised at first, then sprang into action. "Of course." He settled opposite her near the front, leaving their packs in the back as a counterbalance to their weight. Dhal placed one hand on the steering pole. Talullah stacked hers on top.

At the contact, relief crashed over her like a cold tidal wave. From Dhal's magic, yes, but mostly from *him*. From his support. His unwavering presence.

Together, they steered the Skimmer through the calm dark

water. In her mind's eye, Talullah saw fish scurry beneath them, chased by jellies of all sizes.

Were there more now than before? Or had Talullah never understood their numbers?

She and Dhal urged the Skimmer to go faster. Talullah was eager to be on dry land again, away from the delicate but strong tentacles that threatened to pull her to the depths.

Captain Caprico met them, along with the gruff-looking man with a bushy red beard. The two adults tied up the Skimmer, and then Captain Caprico, Talullah, and Dhal ascended the stairs.

There were fewer to go up, with the risen water level, but still Talullah's feet dragged.

It had been a rough few hours, physically and emotionally.

And she had the feeling it was about to get worse.

Olheiro greeted them at the door of the Grocer's place, that same ready-to-strike expression stretching his lips over his golden brown skin. The blue light from the sconces reflected off his teeth and eyes like a wild animal in the pitch dark of the forest.

A glimpse of danger.

Enough to make a point.

"Back so soon?" said the Grocer as they entered the lounge. The room's musty scent had intensified. "I assume that means good news."

"We wouldn't have come back empty-handed." Talullah accepted one of the rings from Dhal. "We're ready to trade."

"I'm impressed." Geomi unfurled herself from her rope chair and approached. "What did you have to do to get it?"

"Those details weren't in the contract," Talullah replied, pasting on a fake smile. "And we're short on time."

"Down to business," Olheiro said. "I like that." He went to a closet and brought back a wooden box full of small vials. "Remember these?" he asked Captain Caprico.

"All too well," Caprico replied, humorless.

"For protection," Olheiro said, handing Talullah two vials. One was full of blood-red liquid. Hopefully not actual blood. Talullah's stomach rolled at the thought. The other vial held a shimmering stick that reminded her of chalk.

"And the directions?" Dhal asked.

The Grocer handed over a crumpled parchment.

Dhal looked it over. "A map of the tunnels?"

"What? You think we remember all this stuff?" The Grocer laughed and pointed out a section of the tunnels. "This is where the tapestry would be. If it's still there."

"You're not certain?" Captain Caprico asked.

Olheiro shrugged. "We stay out of that area if possible."

"And why's that?" Caprico narrowed his gaze.

"We like to stay below the radar. A piece like the tapestry and the room where it's rumored to be? That's above our paygrade."

"Until now," Talullah said. "What's the ring do, anyway?"

Geomi raised a sculpted black brow as she accepted the ring from Talullah. Her eyes widened upon closing it in her palm. A satisfied smile twisted her lips. "Those details weren't in the contract."

"Right. Well, thank you, I guess," Talullah said.

Talullah hadn't expected them to tell her. Didn't need them to. She was used to uncovering objects' secrets on her own. Once, back before she'd known about her magic, a quest like this would have fueled her all night, the secrets and magic and consequences the stuff of her waking dreams.

But now, she knew the truth: this kind of adventure wasn't everything she'd thought.

"We'll thank them once we're out of the tunnels alive with what we came for," Captain Caprico growled.

"A pleasure as always, Mr. Drake," the Grocer said. "If you need anything else, you know where to find us."

Dhal, Talullah, and Captain Caprico hurried up and out of

HAT's headquarters before Talullah could question her judgment further.

What if HAT had tricked her? What if this map led to nowhere? What if they'd planned to trap them in the tunnels on the sorceress's order?

"Too late for all those questions bouncing in your head," Captain Caprico said. "What's done is done. And contrary to what I said before, I do think they're telling the truth. There is *some* honor among thieves."

"Hopefully enough to not get us killed," Dhal added in a falsely cheery tone.

Talullah wasn't convinced, but there was nothing she could do about it now. "Dhal, what's the map look like? Can you figure out where we are in relation to the section the Grocer showed you?"

"You want to go now?" Dhal asked, his expression both appalled and surprised.

Talullah shook off the lingering doubts and fixed him with a stare. "Do you have a more convenient time in mind?"

Dhal looked taken aback at first, but then he said, "Maybe when it's not the middle of the night and pitch dark and creepy. Perhaps after you've had some sleep and something to eat."

Talullah shook her head. "The sooner we find the tapestry, the sooner we can get off the Isle. The man who came after"—she couldn't force herself to say 'murdered'—"the merchant said the merchant had helped move the sorceress's plan forward. I'm assuming the hooded guy was in on that plan, too. We don't know how far along Renevelda's plans are or who's involved. I don't want to waste any more time. I'll sleep when I'm dead. Which, if all goes well, won't be for a very long time."

"At least eat something. You're going to need all the energy you can manage."

"Fine. A quick meal, and then we go." Talullah regretted snapping at him because he was concerned. She knew that with her whole heart. Urgency would dispel her anxiety, she hoped. If she sat or slept or waited too long, she didn't know if she could force herself to go down into the tunnels.

She'd read their history. She'd Seen their horrors.

Her friends had died down there.

It was the last place she wanted to be.

It was the only place she could go to atone.

Captain Caprico called in a favor from Mr. Milliner and got three fried fish sandwiches from Facet 59 to go. Talullah wondered what it would cost him later, if there'd be some scheme he'd get roped into because she needed to eat and nowhere else was open.

The food threatened to come back up with Talullah's nerves, but she forced it down with a swig of water.

She did feel better, stronger, after she'd polished off the whole thing. Could she use sleep? Sure. But she couldn't risk it.

Dhal met her eyes. He and Captain Caprico had finished also. They were waiting for her to give the order.

"It's time," she said. "Dhal, let's see that map."

CHAPTER 37

KAI

We control the map to the Source. And we kill the sorceress.

As if it were easy. As if it were moral. As if it would solve all their problems.

Kai couldn't predict the future, but he knew none of those things were true.

He had never felt so hopeless in all his life. Theresa seemed bolstered by Veylan's confidence, by his suggestion that they take the artifact Talullah needed.

If his group decided to follow this plan, that would put Kai and Talullah on opposing sides.

It would make them enemies.

The thought made Kai queasy. He certainly couldn't invite Talullah to come now, despite the *encouragement* from Veylan. Which would no doubt be increasing now that they had a spoken-aloud plan.

Was that why Veylan had orchestrated their heart-to-heart that day in the yard? Did he want Talullah around because she had a piece of the tapestry?

Suddenly the chirping birds' song turned shrill. His tea tasted too bitter.

He didn't want to control the tapestry. Didn't want to attempt to murder the sorceress.

So then what *did* he want?

He wanted things to go back to normal. Back to when his biggest challenge was helping Alexander pick out a suit or listening to him go on and on about the daily doldrum.

What Kai wouldn't give for a day so boring his eyes couldn't stay open.

That was all a daydream. He couldn't remember when he'd slept well-enough to feel rested.

Zinni appeared out of nowhere. Or maybe he hadn't been paying attention.

"What's wrong, Z?" he asked. Her face was pinched, and she looked vaguely sick, too. "Tell me, please."

Zinni didn't normally beat around the bush, and this time wasn't any different. "The guard talked."

"He did? When?"

"Just now, apparently. I overheard Veylan and Theresa talking to Quentis when I was chopping yet another potato in the kitchen."

A fleeting flash of hope dashed across Kai's mind. "What'd he say? Anything we can use?"

Zinni's expression soured further. "That Talullah agreed to help the sorceress."

And there went the hope. Kai's stomach dropped. "No way. He's lying. She'd never do that."

"Not even to protect her family?"

"I—" No. She wouldn't. Talullah loved her family more than anything, but she'd never agree to work for the sorceress, the murderer who'd threatened Talullah herself more than once.

Kai trusted her. "No. I don't believe it. He's trying to divide us. Distract us, even."

Zinni nodded. "That's what I think, too."

"What?"

Zinni worried her lip with her teeth. "There's something else he said that I'm not certain is a lie."

"Which is?"

"The attack that took place wasn't the Katamians. Well, technically it was, but they weren't under their own control. It was Renevelda."

Kai pressed his palms over his eyes. "Of course, it was." He sighed. He was so, so tired. "I thought that was obvious. Is this new information?"

Zinni shrugged. "The other factions didn't know. They barely know anything about her, and what they do know is what she's telling them."

"And they believe her."

"Yeah. It's easy to follow someone who seems like they know what they're doing when you're scared and fumbling for any scrap of certainty."

"So, what do we do about this?" Kai paced in a line, back and forth across the grass. "If we tell people the sorceress is using them, it's our word against hers. And who's going to believe us?"

"Especially because there's a reward on our heads."

Kai's attention snapped up. "What?"

"There are posters up all over the city, according to Quentis."

"Suditzas' sake. Well, I guess it was inevitable. But that means we can't walk into Castle Viltresor and expect to take her down. Not that that was ever a viable plan."

Zinni smirked, a bit of her normal sass returning. That spark of normalcy gave Kai a bit more confidence. Even when the world had gone to dirt, at least he still had Zinni. "You also think the younger Marquet talks a big game?"

Kai's exasperation flooded out of him. "Yes. I don't understand why Theresa is so enamored by him. I mean, okay, he's objectively handsome. But that doesn't make a person trustworthy. And I don't know how he expects us to get into the castle and kill a sorceress. It's madness." A thread of understanding tickled Kai's consciousness. "Unless he plans to Manipulate our appearances. Have you noticed he's changed?"

Zinni nodded. "His hair. It's much darker. His eyes, too. Yesterday he asked Theresa how she'd feel about making hers more red."

"That would solve the problem of our pictures being plastered across town." Kai bit his lip. "It still doesn't sit right with me. He's taken over."

"Theresa seems grateful for the break, though. Glad to be out of the leadership role."

It was true that Theresa had been more relaxed since arriving at the Marquets' cottage. The bags under her eyes weren't as pronounced. She, unlike Kai, had been sleeping better, it seemed.

"Something is wrong here," Kai murmured, more to himself than to Zinni.

She squeezed his hand. "I feel it, too."

"What are we missing?" Kai gazed around at the activity in the yard. People went in and out of their tents. There was constant activity, but all of it lateral. Never moving forward or toward anything. "Veylan's first plan is to control the Source, right?"

"So he says."

"What does that entail? We need more information. Does Quentis have any books in his study?"

Zinni raised an eyebrow.

"What?"

She laughed. "It's nice to hear you talking about books again. I think you're coming back."

"I never left, Zinni."

"Not completely. But I think we've all been a bit adrift lately."

That was the hollowness Kai had felt in his soul. Ever since he left the castle, he'd been wandering aimlessly. Without real direction. Without real purpose. But Zinni naming it reignited him.

"On second thought," he said. "I have a better idea. I want the truth. I'm going to talk to the guard myself."

CHAPTER 38

TALULLAH

*D*hal pressed his fingertips to the map's top right corner where the compass rose had been drawn and closed his eyes. Tiny blue sparks of magic trickled out of his fingertips and through the paper, revealing that there was much more to the map than had originally appeared. "I've learned a few tricks from watching you," he said. "I suspected HAT wouldn't reveal every secret."

The map now had two layers to it, the dark charcoal outline with some of the landmarks marked on it, and the layer Dhal's magic had revealed. Even more tunnels existed than Talullah could have imagined. "We're here." Dhal pointed. "If the Grocer is correct, the tunnel or room or hiding spot of the tapestry is over here, which means we need to take this route through the tunnels." He traced his finger over the path as he spoke.

Colfax shuttered. "I can't believe we have to go back down into that hellhole."

"Burying secrets seems to be a theme around here," Talullah said. "If it was easily accessible, anyone could have found it a long time ago."

Captain Caprico gathered some supplies from his room at the Ocean's Crest Inn, then they set off toward the nearest entrance to the tunnel, which happened to be a cellar door outside the HAT headquarters. It was hidden behind a large bush, and Talullah couldn't help but think of her family's safe place in River Hill, the cellar behind the blackberry bush outside Mabel Miller's teapot shop.

"Are you sure you're ready?" Colfax asked Talullah. "I'm sure waiting a few hours won't make a difference." His face held the fatherly concern she'd become used to seeing when he wasn't bossing anyone around.

"Let's go," she said. They stepped down into the dank stairwell and switched on their magic lanterns to light the way. The faint blue glow bounced off the weather-worn stones as they descended further underground. The lower they got, the tighter Talullah's chest grew.

She hadn't enjoyed the tunnels the first time she and Jothi had come down, and she liked them even less now that she knew their true purpose. She tried not to think about all the horrors these walls had seen, and she willed her amethyst to stay dormant. The last thing she needed was to be pulled into a memory.

There was a time to remember and a time to act. Now was the latter.

They walked in heavy silence for a while, breathing in the musty air latent with the stench of past atrocities and rotted seaweed. Gritty sand coated the bottoms of their boots.

A right here, a left there. Up a set of stairs, down half of another. So many twists and turns Talullah didn't know which way was north. It was like being trapped underwater and trying to find the surface, only to be fooled by the reflection of the sun.

At least in the tunnels she could breathe. Mostly.

Dhal's frustration raised his shoulders a fraction with each dead end. "That would have been good to mark," he grumbled.

Apparently his magic hadn't revealed every hidden layer.

Down a long hallway which Dhal swore had to be it, water dripped in her mind like a leaky faucet, and with each drop, her hold on her memories loosened, until finally it broke completely.

The first thing to surface were the last words Lynx had spoken to her before she'd jumped in the Fountain and sank to her death.

Nothing I do has an iota to do with you. Not anymore.

Talullah's ears rushed with blood that sounded like a crashing ocean. Her arm screamed with the memory of scraping against the rough edge of the Fountain's platform, trying to pull Lynx up and out. Cold, icy water stabbed her like thousands of needles. Salt water burned her eyes. Talullah pushed hard against the memory, trying to force it away, but it morphed into Beck's proud, round face as he told them all so jovially that he was going to graduate.

Talullah shoved her memories with all the willpower she could muster, pressed her sapphire, and took a deep, calming breath. *Focus on the now. The tunnels. The tapestry.*

When she finally came back to herself, she realized the loud echo was her own screams ricocheting off the walls.

Colfax watched her closely. His mouth was pressed in a thin line. Dhal had already wrapped his arms tightly around her. She inhaled the ever-present scent of honey and morning dew from his shirt and coat as he stroked her hair and whispered gently to her. "It's okay. You're safe. I'm here."

Talullah shook her head as if it could be that easy to cage the demons and their snapping jaws. "A bit of a snag." Her voice sounded like she'd swallowed sand. She wiped the tears from her cheeks with her fingers. "And now we move forward."

They didn't speak of her outburst, but she could tell her two companions wanted to. The concern in Dhal's expression was going to give him premature wrinkles. She almost told him as much, but then she'd invite conversation.

Later. She would address it later, after they had found what they were looking for.

When they reached the next break in the map, Dhal told them to stop.

An impossibly large mirror blocked the path. It stretched from the top of the ceiling to the floor and the width of the path.

"Odd place to store a mirror," Dhal said. "I'm going to bet it's not here for grooming purposes."

"Is there a wall behind it?" Colfax approached, trying to peek around the frame.

"I think it's an illusion," Talullah said. "Like before." In the prison, there had been an illusory barrier keeping her and Captain Caprico's cells separate. Once she'd Seen past it, she'd been able to dissolve it completely.

Talullah pressed her sapphire once more and called forth her Present Sight. She imagined the scent of cinnamon to ground her, chasing away all remnants of her troubling memories. She stepped up to the mirror. Her reflection—hair coming loose from her braid, sunken eyes the color of a fresh bruise—stared back at her.

"It's okay to be scared," a voice said in her mind. Her own voice. And as it spoke, her reflection's mouth moved. "It's okay to turn back. You don't have to be the savior everyone wants you to be."

It was true she'd felt the pressure building since she'd escaped the Firefall of the Unforgiven, winning against Renevelda for the first time. Like a river dammed by boulders.

It surged with more force after the incident on the Isle. After she'd failed to save her friends.

The paths in the Between had nearly broken her. She'd been

the only one who could save it. And even still, she couldn't save Corinne.

Now the dam had broken.

Find the tapestry. Control the Source. Save magic.

Why her?

Because she was destined? Because she chose it?

How could she ever know whether her choices had been her own or designed by the Suditzas long ago?

Did it matter how she'd gotten here or only that she had?

"It's okay," her reflection whispered. "To not want it. But if you do…"

An icy chill rolled over her head, like cold honey dripping in her hair. She snapped her attention to Dhal, who stood next to her, his hand lifted above her and the blood-red vial held up. Its contents streamed over her head, breaking the mirror's spell.

"I'm not even going to guess what this stuff is," she said, shivering as it oozed down her hair.

"Probably better not to know," Dhal agreed.

Talullah called her Present Sight further forward. "Show me your truth," she said to the mirror.

Her reflection smiled. The mirrored scene flashed red and her ruby took over.

"No, I want to get rid of the illusion," she called in vain.

But either the stones weren't listening or there was another layer of magic she hadn't noticed. Talullah watched herself fall to the ground next to a calm pool of water. It wasn't the Fountain. It couldn't be. This water seemed to be inside a cave of some kind, a circular room with a midnight ceiling, stars winking above. Like in her dream. Talullah's reflection dragged herself forward. She tipped her face toward the water. Rainbow ripples spread from the place her lips made contact.

A single, red and gold feather fluttered from above. It landed in a hand that didn't belong to her.

Dhal's hand.

Talullah's breath caught in the vise made of her ribs, each bone digging like talons into her soft lungs and stomach and heart.

The mirror shattered.

She threw her arms up to cover her face. But the sting of glass shards on her skin never came. Instead, the mirror burst into droplets of water and showered her, Dhal, and Captain Caprico with a harmless mist.

The path ahead was clear.

Talullah sucked air, crouched near the ground. The musty, fishy scent of it turned her stomach. She pressed a palm against her chest, feeling the rapid heartbeat thump.

"Tules?" Dhal stepped toward her hunched figure. His steps were light but sure. He kneeled beside her and tilted her chin up. "Hey."

At the contact, a shiver ran through her whole body. In her mind, her own panicked voice echoed his name.

She couldn't let herself think about what her vision meant, though whispers of it curled around her veins like smoke. Later she'd deconstruct the meaning of the phoenix feather, her desperation, Dhal's presence. But now she had to fold the vision and tuck it into a drawer.

"Let's keep going," Talullah said through gritted teeth.

Dhal studied her face for a moment more. His questions would have to wait in line behind her own.

Captain Caprico cleared his throat. "It looks like that's the way through." He pointed to a dusty door that'd been forced into the stone wall. He approached and pushed down the black handle coated with dark orange rust, nudging the splintered wood with his shoulder. "It won't budge."

"Let me try." Dhal joined him. They both heaved their weight against the door which looked like it should crumble to dust at the slightest touch.

Looks can be deceiving.

"If we came all the way down here and we need a key," Talullah said. Her anger at HAT bubbled on her tongue. As Talullah approached, a buzzing sound swarmed her like a nest of angry wasps. The door's frame shimmered red and blue and green and purple. "It needs magic. Let me do it."

She called forth her Present Sight as she curled her dust-coated fingers around the handle. A sharp sting sliced her palm. "Ouch!" She removed her hand, wincing.

A thin blade protruded from the handle. It had pricked her palm. Not too deep, but enough to draw blood.

Maybe it *wasn't* rust on the handle.

Talullah wrapped her hand in her tunic. The door hummed. It clicked and opened inward, like the transport trees.

"Needed a blood offering?" Captain Caprico guessed.

"Then why didn't it take ours?" Dhal wondered.

"It wanted Sezna Seer blood," Talullah said. She eased the door open further and crept in. Dhal and Captain Caprico followed closely behind.

Their lamps illuminated a small room. Black marble flooring with streaks of white stretched wall-to-wall. It shone, despite the neglect, obvious in the thick layer of dust on the tree-shaped wall sconces. Preserved by magic, perhaps. In the center of the room sat a white wood table large enough to seat twelve people. Scratches covered the surface.

The memories in the room called to Talullah.

Read the room, the voices of the Unforgiven had told her last time. She'd been terrified then.

She was terrified now.

Talullah pressed her amethyst and let the past speak to her, a welcome reprieve to be lost in what had already been instead of the fate to come.

A tall figure cloaked in a thick robe moved around the room, then stopped at the shortest wall. They scraped something across the stone, leaving symbols in their wake.

The shape was familiar, like a specific constellation. Talullah came out of the memory buzzing with anticipation. "Can I have that stick that HAT gave us?"

Dhal uncorked the vial and tipped the shining stick into her palm.

She moved to the exact spot she'd Seen in her memory. She closed her eyes and called forth the image so she could recreate it exactly. The stick spread smoothly on the wall, leaving shimmering white shapes in the pattern that she'd Seen in her vision.

As soon as she'd finished, Dhal inhaled. "That's it. The pattern we studied at Edda's."

"Why did you draw The Phoenix?" Captain Caprico asked.

"The Phoenix. Of course," Dhal said. "We figured it was a bird, but didn't know which one."

"I've seen it before," Talullah explained. "When we were searching for the Ceserites." She furrowed her brows, trying to connect everything. "And the Phoenix feather has been recurring too. On the chart Margot gave me. In my visions. So, why is it down here?"

"Nothing seems to be happening," Dhal said.

Talullah pressed her fingertip to the cut on her hand and traced the symbol with her blood. When she'd finished, the pattern glowed. White magic lit up the whole wall.

It shifted, revealing an accessible cove big enough for Talullah to reach a hand in. Dhal held up his lantern.

Talullah gripped a velvet pouch covered in so much dirt she couldn't be sure what color it had been originally.

The wall shifted back into place as soon as her hand was clear. Talullah's fingers twitched as she untied the ribbon and opened the bag.

When she touched the fabric within, her body hummed. Dunamai's Eye warmed, recognizing the magic inside. She lay it flat on the table. It was the piece they had been searching for—

Katamai's square of the Suditzas' tapestry. The blue thread was nearly pristine. It sparkled at her like a smile.

"We got it," she said. "I can't believe we got it."

The fabric sang in her hand, and as she tucked it into her bag with the other pieces, the three of them harmonized in her mind.

One more.

Dhal unfurled the map HAT had given them. An unlikely calm stole through Talullah's nerves. She'd been afraid they wouldn't find the piece, that the whole errand would have been for naught.

They took two steps toward the door.

Then the ground quaked.

CHAPTER 39

TALULLAH

The floor rumbled, a storm building beneath the stones. Dhal's eyes echoed the panic that raced through Talullah's own body.

"What was that?" he asked.

Captain Caprico cut in. "Maybe instead of figuring that out, we should get out of here. Before this whole place collapses on top of us."

They backtracked toward the hallway they'd come down, but an iron gate now stretched from ceiling to floor. Dhal gripped it and shook, but the bars held.

"This is real, right?" Captain Caprico asked. His words hearkened back to the illusions he and Talullah had faced while in the prison below ground on the Isle of Salire.

Talullah pressed her sapphire to ground her and to provide clarity amidst the chaos. A grating sound tried to snag her attention, but Talullah leaned into her sapphire's magic and pushed everything else aside.

The tunnel around her sharpened in focus. The stone bricks, crumbling with age, were rough to the touch. They shivered beneath her fingers. Everything else was as it appeared. A zap of disappointment shot through her. She'd hoped, however faintly, that this was somehow part of the reason she'd endured the horrors on the Isle of Salire. That it had been in preparation for this moment, so she could reach for that experience and use the same skills that saved her and Captain Caprico before.

No such luck.

"It's real," she said.

Dhal paced, his gaze trained on the walls. "There must be a switch to let the magic know that someone safe found the tapestry, like some kind of code or button or something that will alert the magic to stop its defensive measures."

"Would have been good to find that before we took the square," said Captain Caprico.

"It's not like anyone meant for us to find it," said Dhal. "Unless."

"Unless what?" Talullah asked.

"Unless they did," Dhal said slowly. "What if the original Seers meant for you to come here? What if your great-great grandmother knew you would?"

A whisper of a memory tickled the back of Talullah's mind.

Read the room. It has secrets it wants to share.

"You might be right, Dhal." Talullah pressed her amethyst and allowed the memory to envelop her. A tall woman with long white hair spoke to a short man with square spectacles. She stood on a stone tile that had been carved with a symbol.

"*...when she's found it...*" the woman said.

"*...if she finds it, you mean...*" the man countered.

"*No. I mean* when. *I have Seen this future. My great-great-*

granddaughter will come. She'll know what to do." The woman —Aurinia, her great-great-grandmother—stomped her foot.

The memory ejected her. That was it? Talullah *didn't* know what to do.

Yes, you do, Little Seer.

"The prophecy," Talullah said to Dhal and Captain Caprico. "The Spirit Fox mentioned something." Her amethyst brought the words back to her in Zeri's girlish yet sharp tone. Talullah relayed them in her own parched voice. "With blood shed on stars of sleight, power taken as foreseen." Dunamai's Eye warmed against her collarbone.

The quaking intensified. Blue-light flickered behind their tree-shaped shields. Pieces of rock and dust spilled from the ceiling down in front of them.

Captain Caprico dodged a rock the size of his fist. "Stars of sleight. Deceitful stars."

Talullah bent down and scrutinized the markings in the shiny black marble. They weren't random. Thin silvery lines connected white circles. "Deceitful stars. The floor is a map of the night sky. Help me find the phoenix."

Captain Caprico got down on his hands and knees. "How confident are you about this? Because it sure feels like the ceiling is coming down at any minute."

"I'm not exactly one hundred percent certain about anything at the moment," Talullah said. "But I'm leaning into optimism."

She, Dhal, and Captain Caprico searched the floor.

"Over here!" Dhal called.

Talullah wiped the sweat off her forehead with the sleeve of her tunic and met him on the other side of the table. In the exact spot where, in Talullah's vision, Aurinia had spoken to the short man.

Talullah's magic thrummed in her blood. Tingles chased through her fingers, up her arms, and to her collarbone.

"With blood shed on stars of sleight," Talullah said. She

reopened the cut on her palm and smeared it along the phoenix constellation's lines. The smooth stone was cool against the raging heat of her magic.

The rumbling stopped. A relieved breath burst through her lips.

"Well done," said Captain Caprico. "I guess we can be going now."

"Let's hope that's all the blood that needs spilled for a while," said Dhal.

Talullah heaved her pack onto her shoulder, shaking off the lingering dizziness. "Once we're out of here, Captain, I'm going to need you to tell me more about the phoenix constellation. I have a feeling this isn't the last we've seen of it."

In her mind, a red and gold feather fluttered down from the sky. Dhal's hand caught it. A sharp pain plunged its way into her heart.

"I'll tell you everything I know as soon as I see the real sky again," Captain Caprico answered.

"Then we'd better get out of here."

A bolt like lightning zapped the door.

"What was that?" Captain Caprico took a step toward the door.

The lightning flashed a second time in a swirl of purple. Like in the Mazuchawi, the magical maze in Praeteriti. Then, the lightning had appeared in the shape of part of her necklace. A later strike had taken her mother from her a second time.

But this lightning, though familiar, was not the same. Instead of anyone turning to dust, it pulled Talullah into another memory.

A thunderstorm raged outside the window. She stood in this same small room with a group of people all gathered around a table, each sitting in a high-backed chair. A tapestry lay flat in the center of the table. In each corner, an embroidered tree sparkled, their roots twisted together in a tangled knot in the center.

The Suditzas' tapestry, back before it was torn apart.

Words too small for her to make out wound around the tapestry's perimeter. Embroidered symbols dotted each quadrant, though Talullah didn't know their meaning.

A star chart lay next to the tapestry. It struck her amethyst's memory.

Margot's chart.

The one her sister had given her matched this one. But how had Margot gotten her hands on it? How had it ended up in River Hill?

Had Talullah's mother placed it there before she disappeared to Praeteriti? Had she known Talullah would need Margot's help?

She'd have to ask herself those questions later. The Seers in the memory were arguing.

"How can you be certain she's connected to the constellation?"

"How can she not be, based on what we've Seen?"

"Being wrong would be catastrophic."

"Being right still might be."

"It's preposterous to think that this star chart predicts what you've said to be true."

One of the other Seers placed two palms on the table, standing as she did so. Her poise made Talullah stand up straighter, though no one in the memory could see her.

Aurinia.

"Well, then maybe you should read the leaves and tell me what you see," Talullah's great-great grandmother continued. "Maybe you should conduct another star chart analysis. I'm telling you, I have done multiple calculations, and it all turns out the same. The sorceress will rise, and she will have the tapestry."

"And what can you tell us beyond that?" a square-jawed Seer asked with a sneer.

Aurinia sighed. "That is as far as I can See. You can choose to believe me or not. But that is what I have predicted."

"If what she says is true, we are destined to fail. How can we protect the Source?" The Seer tugged on one of her many rich brown braids.

"The prophecy tells of sacrifice. Of rebirth," the hunched Seer in the corner offered.

"But rebirth for good or for evil?" The Seer with tight curls flicked her wide eyes to Aurinia.

Aurinia's eyes closed. "Impossible to know for sure. All we can do now is try our best to keep the tapestry safe."

"We'll divide it," the oldest Seer said. He stroked his chest-length beard. "Make it harder to find. Delay as long as possible."

The Seers argued for long minutes. Some stormed off, unconvinced the tapestry should be sliced in pieces. That doing so went against the responsibility the Suditzas' had bestowed upon them. Some remained, repeating the only way to protect their magic was to divide it.

The oldest Seer opened a wooden box and revealed a shimmering spool of thread and a large pair of shears.

"It's for the best," he said. He slid his gnarled fingers through the shears' loops, lifted the tapestry to slide the bottom blade under, and snipped.

Talullah came out of the memory parched. She chugged half the water in her canteen.

The sorceress will rise, and she will have the tapestry. The sorceress will rise, and she will have the tapestry. The sorceress will rise, and she will have the tapestry.

Talullah couldn't stop the refrain from beating against her skull. Was Aurinia right? Was Renevelda destined to win, to control the Source? Was she destined to remake magic into her personal slave?

Was everything Talullah had done for nothing? Was she destined to fail?

"Tules?" Dhal asked.

Her watery eyes met his. "I'll tell you everything as soon as we're safe." Her words tasted like an empty promise. Telling the truth about what she'd Seen wouldn't change the outcome.

Talullah looked over his shoulder at the map with both layers, the original and Dhal's magical revelation.

Captain Caprico scratched his stubble on his chin as he studied the map. "Alright. Time to get us out of here."

CHAPTER 40

KAI

Kai sneaked out of the cottage late in the night. He'd gnawed his fingernails to the quick waiting for an opportunity to talk to the guard held prisoner in the converted shed.

But there always seemed to be someone around. He'd watched another new group member deliver the guard's dinner and waited some more. Zinni thought he was crazy. She was probably right.

It was insane to think talking to the guard was a good idea, but Kai needed to do something. He felt stuck. Like he'd been trapped in a bubble and couldn't get out.

The plans to find the Source's location were going slowly. Veylan had cornered Kai a few hours ago to ask him about Talullah. Whether Kai had contacted her yet. Whether she was coming soon.

Kai had lied through his teeth. Said he couldn't get ahold of her. The truth was, as much as he wanted to talk to her, he couldn't risk it. Veylan was pressuring him too much. He wanted the pieces of the tapestry Talullah had—however many that was. Kai wouldn't bring her into Veylan's orbit until he knew exactly what the younger Marquet was hiding.

And he wouldn't even start thinking about the plan to sneak into the castle to kill the sorceress.

It all felt juvenile.

Like it would get them all killed. Maybe that was Veylan's true plan.

Kai swallowed hard and looked up at the stars, wishing he knew their names so he could ask them for a favor. He settled for three bonfire-scented deep breaths instead.

Would he have preferred to speak to the scary and potentially magic-Manipulated guard during the daylight hours, when the sun was out and birds were singing and hope still seemed within reach? Of course. But life wasn't fair, and it was too dangerous to get caught.

He could have asked Zinni to come along, but if things went sideways, he didn't want to get her in any more trouble than he already had. It was his fault she was in this situation in the first place. The guilt of that gnawed at him daily, like a dog savoring a large bone.

He wouldn't risk her life on a hunch.

Look at him now, playing hero.

He couldn't delay it any longer. It was now or never.

Kai pulled the hood up over his head, feeling a bit silly stalking out into the night like a phantom. He double-checked the lawn was clear and everyone had turned in for the night before tiptoeing across the grass as skittish as a field mouse.

He held his breath the whole way, but he made it to the shed that served as a prison without incident. Quickly, he Manipulated the lock and let himself in.

The stench of unwashed body hit him immediately, and he covered his nose.

"Can't help it," the guard said from the corner where he'd been tied to a metal pole with magic-suppressing cuffs.

"Sorry," Kai said. "Reflex. It surprised me."

Glittering runes ran around the entire inside of the door frame. Kai hadn't studied runes. He didn't know a protection marking from a color-changing one. As far as he knew, not many Seers used them anymore.

Kai paused. There could be spells on there to alert Veylan to an intruder, to hear or see what was happening inside. His heart stuttered.

But if that were the case, Kai's position was already compromised. He swallowed hard and took a step in, closing the door behind him.

If he was going to get caught anyway, he might as well get the information he came for.

The palm-sized lantern near the door cast enough light for Kai to see the man who'd huddled himself into a ball to keep warm. The shed was even cooler than outside. Was that on purpose?

Kai shivered. He found the empty glass bottle that had been enchanted to Manipulate the temperature. He used his own magic to adjust it to a more comfortable one, both for himself and for the guard.

There was such a thing as human decency. This man deserved more than he'd been getting, according to how things looked in the shed. Why had they kept him here? What information did they think he could provide?

Though if they let him go, they risked him telling Renevelda where they'd made camp.

"Thank you," the man said in a gruff voice. His red hair was snarled, and dirt streaked his pale, freckled face.

Kai offered him two canteens. "One is water and one is spirits. I wasn't sure which you needed more."

The man tilted his head in question, assessing Kai and likely his motives. "They aren't poison. I wouldn't know how to do such a thing." He lifted the canteen containing spirits to his mouth first and took a small sip. It burned his throat and nose. He'd never had a taste for it. He chased it with a sip from the other canteen, dulling the sting with water.

"Point proven." The guard laughed, low and raspy. "To what do I owe the pleasure of a visit?" He accepted the canteen full of spirits, then took a long swig, wiping his mouth on his arm. He hadn't even flinched.

Kai took a breath. "Thought you might like to chat."

"Oh? What took you so long?"

Kai shrugged and sat down on the dusty floor. "Lack of courage, mostly."

The guard laughed again. "Can't do much damage in my current state now, can I?" He nodded at the cuffs.

"I've learned not to make assumptions. For all I know about the world, maybe you can breathe fire or shoot lightning from your eyes."

The guard took another swig. "Wish that were the case. Wouldn't be here still if it were." He shrugged. "What do you want to know?"

"What's life like at the castle now?"

"Bleak. Manipulation spells come out of nowhere and suddenly you're doing things you don't want to do and never thought you would. I almost wish she'd taken my memories too, so I wouldn't have to remember."

Kai paused. "But you do remember?"

The guard's jaw tensed. He took another swig of spirits and nodded once.

"Can you tell me anything about her plans or her strengths?"

The guard tilted his head. "I assume I'm as good as dead, whether or not I tell you. Won't be any going back to her now that I've been here. She'll probably kill me for failing to steal the tapestry square. And if not, she'll assume I talked and kill me for treason. If I can do one thing to help you survive, it might serve us all. Though I'm not in a position to grant favors." He raised a brow.

Kai laughed this time. "You're trying to make a bargain as a prisoner?"

The guard fixed Kai with a stare. "Either you get the information that you want and I die, or you don't get the information you want, and I still die. A man with nothing to lose might as well try."

"I respect that," Kai said. "What do you want?"

"My freedom, of course."

"Give me some good information, and I'll do my best to make it happen. I have a bit of sway."

The guard raised his brow.

"Not magical." Although, he did have that. "Despite how it may seem, I do try to uphold my morals. I don't Manipulate people." Not anymore. The scars of using the guards to escape the castle still haunted his conscience. They'd all died. Maybe they would have anyway, but there was no way to know for sure.

The guard paused for a moment. If there had been a window in the shed, he would have been looking out at the yard with his clear gray eyes. "How much do you know about the people you've invited into your circle, into your plans? How many people have you told you want to murder a sorceress?"

"I never said I want to murder anyone."

"Doesn't matter if you said it or not. You're with them now. Their plan is your plan."

Kai twitched at that. How could he be on both the right side and the wrong side at the same time? When had the lines gotten so blurred?

"If I were you, I'd beware how much you talk. And when

you listen, really listen. There's a spy in your midst." The guard looked Kai straight in the eyes, as if to prove he was telling the truth.

Kai drew a sharp inhale. His mind chanted *Veylan* over and over.

"Sometimes shadows lurk in the light." The guard's eyes took on a faraway expression. It couldn't be the spirits acting so soon, making a common man speak like a prophet. "Don't trust —" The guard's words cut off. He clawed at his throat as if he could no longer speak.

Kai rushed over to help him, offering him the water. The guard scraped at his throat, his eyes bulging out as pressure built. He gasped for air.

Kai did everything he could to help the man breathe, but it was no use. He looked in the man's eyes, fully aware this was his last chance. "Is Veylan Marquet the spy?"

The man wheezed one final desperate breath before he slumped in the corner. He had no pulse.

Kai panicked, looking around the small shed. His eyes fixed on the runes near the door. One burned red and black like a hot ember.

Flies buzzed around the remnants of the man's dinner near his boots. The oats had crusted on the rim of the bowl, hours old and cold. Kai leaned forward to look closer, feeling the pull of magic. The dried oats contained a fine red powder. At first glance it could have been cinnamon.

But the spice was too expensive to waste on a prisoner.

A matching rune, etched in black and red, glistened on the side of the bowl.

Someone had poisoned the guard. Spelled the room and his food to take effect if he told the truth.

Suddenly Kai became aware of how the situation looked. He was the last person to see the guard alive. It would look like *he* was the murderer.

In a frenzy, Kai took his canteens back and reset the room temperature to how it had been before he'd come in. He tried to erase his footprints from the dusty floor.

He couldn't leave any trace he'd been there. There were no witnesses to prove his innocence. Unless one of those runes had recorded their interaction like a Nemosyn. And if Veylan had put the runes there, as Kai suspected, Veylan wouldn't defend him.

In fact, maybe it was a trap. Maybe Veylan found out Kai wanted to talk to the prisoner. He was already frustrated that Kai hadn't delivered Talullah.

Kai crept back into his room at the cottage. He climbed into his bed and pulled the covers all the way up to his chin, as if the extra fabric could dampen the loud thumping of his heart.

Someone had poisoned the guard. Their only inside connection to the sorceress.

Just as he'd been about to reveal the spy's identity.

Kai's uneasiness had multiplied by ten.

Someone wanted to sabotage their plans. Someone was working for Renevelda.

And Kai would bet anything it was Veylan Marquet.

CHAPTER 41

TALULLAH

It took nearly an hour, but they finally made it out of the tunnels. A disbelieving laugh broke free from Dhalian's mouth and Captain Caprico took a deep breath. Talullah fell to her knees and pressed her hands onto the ground, willing her magic to keep her sane, to ground her in reality instead of letting her lose herself in the chaos.

She drew some shallow breaths and tried to make them longer and calmer as she finally allowed herself to accept that they'd succeeded.

Her Scry bracelet vibrated on her wrist. She pulled it off and pressed the sapphire. A big wave of relief washed over her when Maeve's pale face and puff of wild red hair filled the bubble. The seamstress/Seer had taught Talullah how to read the Potential and how to travel to the Between. Without Maeve, Talullah never would have found her emerald or saved the Between from collapse.

"Talullah! Thank the goddesses. I've been trying to reach you for hours."

Talullah could barely speak, so Dhalian nudged his way into the frame. "We were stuck underground in some tunnels. But we're alright now."

Maeve furrowed her brows and worried her bright red lip with her teeth. "Could you use a place to rest and recover? Come meet us at my flat as soon as you can."

"Us?" Talullah asked.

Silas poked his head over Maeve's shoulder. "Present and accounted for."

Another wave of gratitude washed over Talullah, loosening one of the many knots lodged in her chest.

She'd been so worried they hadn't made it or that they'd been caught. But this was proof they were okay. "We would love a place to clean up. Thanks, Maeve. Be there as soon as we can."

After they disconnected, reality caught up with Talullah. Maeve's apartment was in the heart of Viltresor City, not far from where Renevelda held the castle hostage. The sorceress could have spies everywhere. She could have Manipulated the whole city by now.

"You think it's a good idea to go back into the city?" Captain Caprico asked gently. "We could return to Ocean's Crest Inn."

Talullah gazed up at the stars, half-hidden by clouds, and let the cold night air clear space in her lungs. "We can't hide out on the Isle forever. Plus, if HAT did set us up, I don't want to wait around for them to find out we escaped. They might want to… you know. Finish the job."

"Especially if someone paid them to," Dhal added.

"Good point. I could get in touch with some of my former colleagues," Colfax said. He fiddled with the sleeve of his cloak. "A few of the old safe houses should be empty."

Despite the casual offer, Talullah heard the trepidation in his voice. Getting involved with HAT was already too much for him.

Dipping a toe back into the world of organized crime had already negatively affected him. She couldn't ask him to wade any deeper.

"We'll be careful," she said. "We'll make it there in no time. No problem."

They stopped at Ocean's Crest to collect their belongings. Luckily, Geomi wasn't working the desk. Instead, they said goodbye to Aran. The boy's bright eyes dimmed, his shoulders slumping as he signed them out on the ledger and hung their rooms' skeleton keys on the wall behind him. "Well, you know where to find us," he said, his voice falsely light. "If you ever need a place to stay."

"Thanks for everything, Aran," Talullah said. She wouldn't make a promise to return that she might not be able to keep.

The transport tree spat them out at the edge of Viltresor City. They'd taken tentative steps out when Dhal put his arm out to stop them. "I think we're going to have some problems." He pointed to a flyer posted on a tall oak tree.

It was a wanted poster with sketched images of Kai, Theresa, and the burly guard whose name Talullah hadn't caught.

Below their faces were pictures of Talullah and Dhalian.

Colfax furrowed his brows at the poster. "I could go meet Maeve and Silas to figure out what's going on, and then come find you. No one knows I'm involved. You can lie low at one of the old safe houses."

Talullah shook her head. "Renevelda saw you on the Isle last time. Even if she's not actively searching for you, if she sees you, she'll assume you're helping us. She'll torture you for information about our whereabouts."

"What do you suggest we do?" Colfax asked.

"Let's go back in the tree and think."

They shuffled back inside the transport tree. Talullah leaned her back against the door. She focused on the glittering threads of magic peeking through the tree's black walls. She pressed her sapphire and called the scent of lavender into the space, for calming and comfort.

"We could go back to Praeteriti," Dhal suggested.

Talullah shook her head. "Going there is a move in the wrong direction. We have three tapestry pieces. Renevelda likely has the other one, if what we've heard is correct. We have to figure out a way to get it from her."

"How do we get through the city, then?" Captain Caprico asked.

"There will be too many guards to Manipulate," Dhal said.

"Maybe making us invisible will be enough," Talullah suggested. Though she didn't know if she could hold the spell that long. "I've never practiced changing anyone's appearance. I think it's too risky to do it now for the first time."

"Let's go now, then," Captain Caprico said. "We still have a few hours of night left. Between the dark and your magic, we should be able to get to Maeve's before sunrise. And I'm giving you the locations of a few safe houses, in case we get separated at any point." He borrowed some parchment and a charcoal pencil from Dhal and scribbled some coordinates, landmarks, and a roughly drawn map for both Talullah and Dhal.

"Let me consult my emerald before we go anywhere," Talullah said. It was funny how not too long ago she wanted nothing to do with magic. Now, using her power brought her comfort.

She pressed the emerald and asked it to show her what might happen if they crossed the city under these plans.

When she came out of the vision, she nodded. "I think this is the best shot we're going to get."

Talullah stood in the middle of their line, holding hands with Dhal and Colfax. She Manipulated the air around them to make them invisible, bolstered by Dhal's added magic, and they stepped back out into the night.

CHAPTER 42

TALULLAH

The streets of Viltresor City were eerily quiet as Talullah, Dhal, and Captain Caprico made their way to Maeve's. Talullah could count on one hand the number of people they saw. All looked hurried and fearful as they rushed to their destinations.

The night itself held its breath, whether for Talullah and her friends or for the citizens caught in the crosshairs. Everything seemed so fragile. One wrong step could shatter the world.

Talullah opened the lime green door to Seldom as it Seams. She didn't need a key. The shop's wards recognized her magic, though Maeve had added extra protections since Talullah's last visit.

Good.

If they'd learned anything from Kai's accidental entrance, it was that their protection spells required specificity.

Especially now that it wasn't only non-magical folk who might be their enemy.

The scent of basil hugged her as she moved further into the shop, past half-dressed mannequins and bolts of silver tulle and iridescent silk that hadn't yet been put to sleep on their shelves.

Maeve practically tumbled down the stairs. Bare feet peeked out from beneath her gauzy blue pants. Her face was scrunched tight in concern.

Talullah dropped the Manipulation spell shielding her and her companions. She'd been struggling to hold it for the last few minutes, even with Dhal's magic reinforcing hers.

"Oh, thank the Suditzas," Maeve said. She jumped down the last two steps and pulled Talullah in for a hug. Her wooden bangles clanked together. "I've been so worried."

Talullah didn't have the energy to answer. She sank further into Maeve's embrace, not even minding the clump of wild red hair that covered her face.

"About time we saw you again, Miss Bridgestone." Silas, Maeve's pathwalking friend, spoke from two steps up. His warm voice calmed her. "Why don't you all come upstairs?"

In Maeve's apartment, Talullah sank onto the sofa. Her thoughts slammed against her skull like prisoners. "Water?" she whispered.

Silas appeared with a pint glass full. Talullah chugged the whole thing in one go.

She couldn't remember when she'd last slept. At Ocean's Crest? When was that? It had to have been days ago. Had they only just escaped the tunnels on the Isle?

She closed her eyes for a moment. To stop the room from spinning. Something warm and weighted settled on her chest. This time, though, it wasn't suffocating. It was comforting.

When Talullah blinked her eyes open again, two round blue ones stared at her. A fluffy gray tail flicked back and forth, tickling her arm. The cat that shared her name purred, the vibration echoing in Talullah's own ribs. "Oh. Hello, there."

"Sorry about that." Maeve's soft voice roused Talullah's brain from her sleep. "I turned away for a few seconds and—"

"It's alright," Talullah said. She stroked the cat's back gently. "Where's everyone else?"

"In the kitchen," Maeve said softly. "You slept for a while."

"I did? I'm sorry, I shouldn't have. There's so much to tell you." Talullah tried to sit up, but she got tangled in the blanket someone had carefully tucked over her.

"It's alright. You're safe now. We have time."

"We don't. The sorceress—"

Maeve sat down next to Talullah and patted her knee. "Eat first, save the world after. Come." She held out her hand, and with the other she untucked the blanket so Talullah could swing her legs over the edge of the sofa.

Cat Talullah—Tally, as Talullah had taken to calling her—hopped off Talullah's chest, shot her an indignant look, and stalked down the hall.

She must have looked as rough as she felt by Dhal's grimace. But he didn't comment. No one said a word as Talullah devoured two blueberry muffins, five sausages, three poached eggs, and a mug of cinnamon tea.

When she was sure she couldn't fit anything else in her stomach, she looked up. "So, about last night…"

She told them everything. "And that's why I think I need to walk the paths."

Silas crossed his arms over his chest. He swung his long black twists over his shoulders. "No."

"We need answers. We need context."

"No," Silas said again.

"Silas…" Maeve looked at him. And whatever silent conversation they had convinced him to change his mind.

"Fine. But again, I do not like it."

"You don't have to like it," Talullah said.

It's necessary. It will be worth it.

She needed to know which course of action might lead her to getting the last piece of the tapestry. If Renevelda had it already, Talullah needed a plan to steal it from her. And if the sorceress didn't have it, Talullah needed a hint about where to find it. Maybe it was hidden in the Between, like her emerald had been. If so, it might still be there. Maybe the Between could keep Renevelda out like Praeteriti could.

They all entered the lift still concealed in a closet in Maeve's tailoring shop, Seldom as it Seams, on the main floor. Talullah reached for the jar of black buttons to trigger it. Down they went until they stopped in the circular room below ground. Light from the black iron tree sconce bounced off the whitewashed wood panels covering the walls. Orange and bergamot scents slipped through the barely visible crack between the hidden door and the floor.

Inside the tapestry room, woven prophecies still lined the perimeter. There, Talullah had learned, not too long ago, how to travel to the Between. With her emerald, she could have used a transport tree to go there, like she did to get to Praeteriti, the world of the past.

But the thought of going back out into whatever web of traps Renevelda had woven gave her pause. If she was going to do something dangerous, she might as well do it surrounded by people she cared about and who cared about her.

She was safe here.

Maeve and Silas spread out the blanket with the emerald circle woven into it.

Talullah sat in the center of the circle with the small tapestry of the Between's gate in her lap and breathed.

Dhal lit the tapered candles Talullah used last time, one black, one white. They'd each been burned nearly halfway, but the moon and star symbols on each one remained intact, as if they'd shifted down rather than melt with the rest of the wax.

It would be fine.

The Between was stable now.

But what would it show her?

Silas, Maeve, and Dhal all sat around the circle with an equal amount of space between them. It was nice to know they were willing to be her anchors.

The threads of the Between's gate called to her, as if it had been waiting for her to return. Equal parts excitement and apprehension lit a fire inside her. No matter what it showed, things could be changed. But it was always easier to see with a sliver of light than in the pitch dark. A hint of what might come would help them prepare.

She knew well the power of the Between and the immense pull that the Potential could have on anyone. Especially on her.

Maybe someday she would be able to casually visit Triv, the Between's guardian. For now, she had an important job to do.

She grasped Dhal's hand, ignoring the jolt that passed through her, the same way it always did when they touched. Not only from their magic calling to each other, but from the love she felt for him.

At this point, she had to admit to herself that that's what it was. Deep and first love that she hoped would be her only. Love she'd been trying to ignore.

What about Kai? The treacherous voice in her mind wouldn't let go of what could have been.

It still could be.

Did she only want Dhal because he was familiar and safe and had already proved he would stand by her through whatever came?

Their shared history gave their relationship strength. But who was to say she couldn't also have that with Kai?

And what if Dhal didn't feel the same? It would rip apart the strongest friendship she'd ever had. Was she greedy for hoping that they could be more?

You could walk the path. That same voice called to her as she crossed into the Between. *You could get a glimpse of what life would be like with each of them.*

Talullah blinked the foggy thought away as she appeared in the alternate realm, standing next to the large iron gate that separated the paths of the Potential from the rest of the Between.

This was the first time she had ever appeared in this realm standing upright of her own volition, instead of gripping onto the iron bars as if they were a lifeline. She hoped that spoke of renewed strength and personal growth, but there was no way to know for certain.

She shook off the effects of entering the realm and headed for Triv's cottage.

The Guardian could change the Between's atmosphere at her will. A power so great it terrified Talullah. Today, Triv had chosen a calm forest setting. Sunlight dripped over lush green deciduous trees. The smell of earth and grass lulled Talullah into calm. It was the scent of her childhood, of the Before.

Before Renevelda.

Before Talullah knew she had magic.

Before her mother left.

But she wasn't there for personal reflection. She was there to stop the sorceress.

Talullah knocked on Triv's cobalt blue door. It opened immediately.

The Guardian of the Between blinked at Talullah, her golden brown eyes assessing. Her black hair fell in smooth, springy ringlets over her shoulder. "Back so soon?" Triv asked.

"It seems so," Talullah said.

"Any chance this is a social visit?"

"Can it be both social and business?"

Triv sighed. "One second."

Talullah waited on the porch while Triv pulled on a floor-length silk robe and cinched it at her waist.

Talullah stifled a laugh.

"What? You think I look funny?" Triv snapped, but a hint of mischief sparkled in her eyes. She was all bark and no bite.

"Not at all. I was marveling at the near-Divine gift of always looking perfect, even though I assume I woke you up."

Triv swatted away her comment, but then fluffed her hair and smiled. "It is quite a gift, isn't it? Now, tell me why you're here."

Talullah summarized what had been going on so far.

"You couldn't bring good news with you this time? I might have to revoke your traveling privileges."

"Only good news next time, I promise."

Triv rolled her eyes and grabbed the iron skeleton key off the hanger in the hallway. "All right. Follow me."

They walked side-by-side to the gate, Triv's sandals thwacking and Talullah's boots nearly silent atop the soft leaves.

"So, how have you been?" Talullah asked.

"Oh, you mean since you saved my entire realm from collapsing on top of me? Yeah, I've been pretty good. Keeping busy."

"Have you had many path walkers come through?"

"Some. More than usual." Triv smiled, remembering.

"You seem happier."

"It's easy to be happy when your world isn't falling apart."

"Are you still lonely?" Talullah's voice was quiet. She didn't want to pry. But she and the Guardian had gone through something formative together. That kind of bond bred a certain kind of intimacy.

Triv shrugged. "Sometimes. But I feel like something big is coming. Something that's going to change everything, you know? Maybe even allow me to leave this place on occasion."

"What gave you that idea?"

"Something one of the Wanderers said the other day. About magic changing."

"Changing? How?" Could that have anything to do with Zeri's prophecy or what the Seers of old had thought would come—the event that drove them apart?

"I'm not sure, kid. Maybe you'll find something about it out there." Triv unlocked the gate. "Good luck out there. Bring me good news." She winked.

"I'll do my best." Talullah stepped through, waved to Triv, then turned her attention to the paths ahead of her.

It felt strange to observe the paths as they'd originally been, before Corinne had overstayed her welcome. They seemed almost friendly, like they wanted to help her instead of devour her whole.

But the pull of the Potential could still have dire consequences. It could still manipulate her senses. Corinne's presence hadn't changed the Between's personality.

It wasn't necessarily a friend, even if it wore a friendly face.

She pressed her sapphire to ground her in her present choice, and she called her emerald forth. "Show me the three most likely ways forward as of now, in regard to the sorceress Renevelda's plan with the Source."

The paths all glowed a golden color, then green. They flash back to gold. Talullah asked her intuition to guide her to whichever path she most needed to See. Without hesitation, the rightmost path glowed brighter, and the other two dimmed to a silvery gray. "Bright one, it is."

She tucked her necklace under her tunic, pressing it as close to her heart as she could for good luck.

Then she took a deep breath and stepped onto the path.

CHAPTER 43

KAI

"**W**ould you stop fidgeting?" Zinni chastised Kai gently but sternly.

"How am I supposed to do that?" Kai turned back toward her. He'd been pacing in their room for nearly an hour. His hair stuck up like he'd run his fingers through it a thousand times, probably because he had. Maybe even more than that.

He'd needed to talk to someone. He'd twiddled his thumbs in bed, weighing the pros and cons of going to Quentis and confessing everything. But then he couldn't exactly tell the older Marquet what he suspected: that Veylan had murdered the guard.

Another thought struck Kai. What if Veylan had done it and Quentis already knew? What if they'd planned the whole thing together?

The uncertainty of it all made Kai's stomach turn. The list of people he could unequivocally trust had dwindled even further.

He didn't want to involve Zinni. If things went poorly, he

wanted her to have the benefit of ignorance. Eventually, Zinni had pulled the quilt off his head and told him to fess up, that she couldn't sleep with all his anxious thoughts clogging up the room. Edouard had given up on sleeping in there as soon as Kai returned. He'd probably claimed his own tent space outside rather than get dragged into Kai's drama.

Kai had been in the same position ever since Zinni involved herself, pacing back and forth with his bedside lantern on. He'd tried to walk in the dark, thinking it would calm him. It only made him see shadows that didn't exist. Plus, he stubbed his toe on the edge of the bed frame and opted to turn the light on.

If he was going to have an anxiety spiral, he might as well lean into as many comforts as possible.

Zinni touched his shoulder to still him. Her warm brown hand smelled like vanilla. "Yes, this is bad," she started. "But it's not the end of the world. It could be worse."

Kai stared at her. "How could this possibly be any worse?"

"Well, you could have killed the guard, on purpose or by accident. That would be worse. Then *you'd* be a murderer. And then we'd be trying to hide a body right now instead of worrying someone's going to find the man you watched die but didn't have a hand in killing."

Kai sighed and squeezed his eyes shut. "You're right. That would be worse. You'd help me hide a body?"

"Of course. If you ever murder someone, I'm sure they would deserve it."

"I don't know if your loyalty is reassuring or concerning."

Zinni shrugged. She shook her freshly braided black hair over her shoulder. "I trust you. I know you didn't do anything to that guard except help him. Anyone else will know that too."

At first, he hadn't wanted to tell Zinni anything, but eventually she weaseled it out of him, as she always did. She'd been shocked, and a little offended, that Kai had gone to see the prisoner without her.

"I still can't believe it," she said now.

"I think he was about to tell me who the spy is, and that's when everything went south. The runes sparkled and then he just…" Kai trailed off, letting his hands drop from his hair to his sides.

"Okay. So, it's obviously too late to help the guard. You did all you could. Now, what are we going to do moving forward?" Zinni sat on her floor pallet and propped her elbows onto her knees.

"My gut says Veylan did this. That he's working for Renevelda. We need to find proof. And we need to know who's helping him."

Zinni bit her lip in thought. "You don't think Theresa…"

Kai sighed through his nose. "As much as my heart tells me she wouldn't, I don't know anything for certain anymore." His head throbbed as he resumed his pacing.

A sharp knock sounded on the door. Kai and Zinni exchanged a look. "Who's knocking at this hour?" Zinni asked. "You have a lady friend I don't know about?"

She was trying to lighten the mood, and Kai was grateful for the attempt, but it landed flat in the moment. Especially after his mental back and forth about whether to contact Talullah.

"Edouard probably forgot something." Kai ignored her and opened the door.

It was one of the older members of the group. "Quentis is calling a meeting."

"Now?" Kai asked. "It's the middle of the night."

The guy shrugged. "When the master of the house calls a meeting, you show up. Plus, you're awake, anyway. Unlike some of us."

Kai tensed. "Of course. We'll be right there."

The guy nodded and rubbed sleep out of his eyes with a tawny, weathered hand. He'd clearly been lost in slumber, unlike Kai and Zinni.

"You think they found the guard?" Zinni whispered.

Kai clenched his jaw. "I can't think of anything else that would warrant a meeting between dusk and dawn."

They met in the living area, all huddling together. Their numbers had grown so much over the past few weeks that all the seats were taken and most of the floor was covered with people scrunched hip to hip.

Kai and Zinni stood at the back. A Katamian Seer lit a fire in the grate, but even its warmth couldn't chase away the chill that had settled over Kai.

Quentis clapped his hands twice to get everyone's attention. "I'm sorry for waking you all at this unmagical hour." He chuckled once and then resumed his somber expression. "But I have some disturbing news to share with all of you. An hour or so ago, we discovered that the guard in our care had died."

Gasps rang throughout the room. Kai and Zinni both tried to put on faces of surprise, but Kai's pulse fluttered like a caged bird in his body. His breathing quickened as he listened to Quentis explain the situation.

"We don't know yet what happened. It's possible the guard chose to leave this world."

More gasps and shocked explanations.

"We did our best to treat him humanely," Quentis continued.

Kai stifled a scoff, remembering the temperature in the shed and the meager food rations the guard had been given.

"It is a difficult time indeed for everyone, and we urge you all to comfort one another. Losing a prisoner from the opposite side of our conflict is a strange situation to be in. He was both a human being and leverage in our conflict. We had hoped to get more information than we managed in our time with him."

"Was it murder?" someone yelled out in the crowd.

Quentis scrunched his brows, and tension formed in his mouth. He swallowed hard. "We don't know the cause of death for certain, but we have no reason to suspect unsavory motives at this time."

Well, that was both a relief and a concern. At least Quentis wouldn't be accusing Kai of anything now. Unless Quentis was lying to the group to keep everyone calm. And if he was involved with Veylan's plan, he would want to turn away any kind of suspicion.

Kai swallowed. Everyone knowing about the guard tangled the web even further. He couldn't trust anything Quentis said. Not until Kai had proof Veylan had orchestrated the guard's death and Quentis was innocent.

"I urge you all to continue with your plans, and we will let you know as we discover more. Everyone may go back to bed. No one should enter the shed at this time."

"As if we'd want to," mumbled another person as they gathered up their blanket and trudged back to their room.

Kai breathed deeply. He hadn't been found out. Not that he had anything to be guilty of, other than ignoring a rule. All he'd done was talk to the guard, the same as Veylan and Quentis had done. Only perhaps Kai had done so with a bit more kindness. He'd wanted information, too, and he'd gone about it in a slightly different way. He'd found something too.

Something they—or at least one of them—didn't want him to know.

Even if they found evidence of Kai's presence in the shed, they didn't have proof he'd done anything nefarious.

Because he hadn't. There couldn't be proof of something that didn't happen.

He and Zinni shared a sidelong glance as they took a step toward their room. Veylan caught Kai's eye from a few feet away.

The younger Marquet lifted a recently-darkened brow. "Kai, if you have a moment, I'd like a word."

Zinni looked at Kai questioningly, and Kai nodded at her. "I'll be okay."

Or he'd pretend to be.

Reluctantly, Zinni went back to their room, and Kai followed Veylan out into the yard.

They were alone, and the crispness of the air woke Kai's senses. "Something you wanted to talk about?" Kai asked. He folded his arms over his chest to preserve his warmth, wishing he'd brought a blanket.

Veylan, however, seemed perfectly content in the icy air. He stared at Kai for a moment with his sharp gaze, then he leaned in and lowered his voice, though no one else was around. "I know you were in the shed before the guard died. You'd better start talking."

CHAPTER 44

TALULLAH

The doorway to her chosen path appeared almost immediately, its curtain made of heavy red velvet trimmed in gold. Talullah stepped through it, not daring to guess what she might find on the other side.

A courtyard. That's where she ended up. A woman with high cheekbones and sapphire eyes flicked her haunted gaze to Talullah from nearby. She wore scraps of clothing that Talullah could tell used to be a fine gown. A metal circle wrapped itself around her neck.

Her skin bordered on gray, but gripped enough color that Talullah could tell her heart still beat in her chest. She was alive, but barely.

On her forearm was a black tattoo.

Dunamai's Eye.

Instead of an amulet, the sign had been inked into her skin.

No, not inked. *Burned.*

The skin around the design flared up, reddish pink. Just like Dhal's scar.

She had magic, but judging by her physical weakness, much of it had been drained away. Had the woman been a Seer before? Or had Renevelda made her one?

Talullah had never heard of such a thing happening, of Seers without magic being branded with it.

But she wouldn't dare claim she knew everything there was to know about magic.

On the woman's bare shoulder, another faint mark called Talullah's attention. A circle with three stars inside.

Talullah gasped. Her mind flashed back to the story she and Dhal had read in Praeteriti. The one that had been ripped from Renevelda's book.

The sorceress's mark of the Divine had never appeared. That's why she'd been cast out of the Realm of the Divine.

So, this husk of a woman was Divine? Or used to be.

Talullah's stomach clenched, her mind racing to piece together this world she'd entered. A world that might come to be.

Two more women trudged into the courtyard, each with the same marks and metal collar.

Renevelda's mother and sisters.

They couldn't be anyone else. Not if Talullah knew anything about the sorceress. She'd wanted to get revenge on her mother, had told Talullah so when they'd met that first time inside the Firefall of the Unforgiven.

In this future, the sorceress gets her desire. She makes prisoners of her family in the mortal realm. What else had she done?

Talullah pressed her sapphire to ease her shallow breaths and still her shaking hands. She stepped away from the fallen Divine, forcing herself to remember none of this was real.

Not yet. But it could be.

She sped up, venturing outside the courtyard and into the city. Viltresor City. But it was unrecognizable.

The city Talullah knew sparkled with promise and magic and actual gems. The stone buildings surrounding her now were so devoid of hope not even the sun dared reach out to them.

Except for the castle.

Talullah shielded her eyes against the stone beacon. It towered over the city, drowned in liquid gold and rolled in crushed diamonds.

Her feet took her to the castle gate without prompting, the path moving her along.

Once she'd crossed the threshold, she blinked, and she was in the grand hall. She wished immediately she could turn back. That she wouldn't have to hear the words the Manipulated guard spoke aloud.

"The mortals are all dead, Sorceress."

Renevelda rose from her throne, her half-smile sharp as broken glass. "All of them?"

The guard nodded. "Every last non-magical being has been gifted to the seas."

"The jellies must be pleased. And the rest?" The sorceress adjusted the gold tiara atop her tightly braided, ice blond hair.

"Those who've sworn fealty remain in their assigned camps."

A brow flicked up. A question. A challenge. "And those who haven't?"

"Scheduled for draining."

Talullah swallowed, her bone dry throat working hard to keep her bile down.

"Except the ones you requested. I brought them here. Would you like to deal with them now?"

Renevelda looked over her shoulder, then flicked her wrist, as if tugging a leash.

Talullah gasped. She watched herself fling forward at Renevelda's magic. A golden collar circled her own neck. She expected Renevelda to have killed her already, maybe the moment she took control of the Source. Instead, Renevelda had made her a pet.

Future Talullah kneeled at the sorceress's feet, her gaze trained on the guard, her jaw clenched. The neck of her tunic was torn. Beneath it, Dunamai's Eye still hung. But it had been fused to her body. An angry red rash covered the nearby skin.

"Bring them in," Renevelda said.

The guard tugged on his own invisible leash, bringing crumpled people into the light.

Real Talullah stifled a sob, though no one paid her any attention. There, she was a ghost.

Maeve. Silas. Kai. Margot. Dhal.

And one more.

Her mother.

Renevelda stalked toward the group, who'd all been bound to the point of helplessness. She dragged Future Talullah with her. "Who'd like to go first?" Renevelda asked with a sly smile. Then she withdrew the Davabere Needle.

It's not real. It's not real. It's not real.

Talullah repeated it like a mantra, let it sink into the space between her too-fast heartbeats. Like it would save her.

She turned from the room and ran. She couldn't save them here, in the Between.

But she could still save them in the real world.

Tears blurred her vision as she streaked past guards and servants and Renevelda's own family members, as she raced back through the suffocating blood red velvet curtain and onto the quiet, deserted path of the Between.

If Renevelda controlled the Source, no one was safe. Not even the Divine.

If Talullah couldn't stop her, the whole world and beyond would be destroyed.

Talullah gasped for breath as she paused on the path of the

Potential, still gazing at the curtain that hid horrors of the sorceress's success.

It wasn't real.

Not yet, at least.

Talullah's neck burned as if a hot rope had wrapped itself around her. Remnants of the Potential version of her on a leash. Of her necklace scorching her skin. Her own power infecting her.

No, wait.

Talullah pressed her hand to her neck. It wasn't that. Dunamai's Eye had warmed again, her emerald blinking like a lighthouse beacon.

It was time to go back to the present.

And time to make sure what she witnessed never came to be.

CHAPTER 45

KAI

Kai could have lied to Veylan. He could have spun a story about how he'd never been to visit the prisoner. *Deny deny deny*, his inner voice urged. *Preserve yourself.*

But Kai was done pretending everything was okay.

Talking to the Manipulated guard was the only useful thing he'd done since he'd left Castle Viltresor. He had to follow through.

Kai licked his dry lips, then immediately regretted it as a swell of cold air threatened to freeze them. "I went to see him."

Veylan raised his brows. "Obviously. I found traces of your magic and you tripped the alarms. Did you not think we'd have security measures to let us know what was going on?"

Vaguely, in the back of his mind, Kai *had* known that. And he'd proceeded, anyway. Because it was the right thing to do. Someone had to find out the truth.

Kai shrugged and tried to hold his mask of indifference. "I wanted answers."

Veylan laughed. "Did you find them?"

"I did." Kai leveled Veylan with a challenging stare. His blood pumped hotter now, the adrenaline shielding him from the cold.

"And what exactly did he tell you?" Veylan asked.

Kai smirked, though his stomach rolled. "I think you already know the answer to that."

Veylan's pale jaw clenched. His hands tightened around the porch railing. The signs Kai had been looking for, that he'd been correct about Veylan and his intentions.

"I know more than you'd like me to, I think," Kai said. "So, I guess you're going to have to kill me, too."

What? Stop goading him! Kai's brain whirred, trying to stop him from taking things too far. But he'd been waiting too long to accuse Veylan of wrongdoing. His mouth ignored his mind.

"Though, unlike that poor guard, I have people here who will miss me, who will know *exactly* what happened and who was responsible. You're not going to get away with it, Veylan, so you might as well fess up and admit that you've been playing both sides for quite a while now. I don't know how deep you're in with the sorceress, but I do know you're somewhere in her confidence. I suspect you've been tinkering with changing your appearance for some reason other than to help us infiltrate the castle. And as soon as I find proof, everyone else will know, too."

A thrill ran through Kai as he spoke, less from the threatening words than from the way Veylan's eyebrow twitched. His generally pale, now obviously dark brown, eyebrow. Getting under his skin made Kai feel alive and purposeful for the first time in weeks.

What choice would Veylan make now that he knew someone was onto him? Kai didn't think the other Seer would attack him now, not where anyone could push open the back door or walk around the side yard and see their leader sticking a knife in someone's chest.

But now that Kai had lain his cards on the table, he would have to be more careful. The guard had been poisoned, after all. Queasiness overtook him now as his brain caught up.

He'd threatened a powerful man.

That was a terrible mistake.

Veylan, unarmed as far as Kai could tell, leaned closer. The tight ridges in his neck pulsed. "You think you've got it all figured out, do you? Let me tell you something, Kai. People see what they want to see. Right now, they see me as the person who has fed and clothed them and kept them safe from the sorceress's attacks. I've kept them far from the fights amongst the Seer factions. What have you done for them?"

Kai held his breath, afraid if he let go, his confidence and bravado would wheeze out with it.

"There's nothing you can do or say that will turn these people against me. They see what I want them to see, and I don't even need Manipulation magic to do it." He brushed a gentle finger over his brows. The hair faded to its normal color. "If you speak one ill word against me, you and your friends, Theresa included, will be out of this house and into the line of fire so fast you won't even be able to say *help*. So, I guess you have a choice now." Veylan continued gazing out toward the leafless deciduous trees crackling in the wind. "It's your word against mine."

Kai was about to respond with a half-formed, almost-witty retort when one of the other Seers, a young man with a mop of dusty blond hair and lanky build eased open the door and peeked out. "Sorry to interrupt, Mr. Marquet, but the newest arrival is here."

"No apology necessary," Veylan said. "In fact, the timing is perfect."

He nodded at the young man who loped around the side of the house, and a moment later, returned with two guards.

Between them, a woman who looked to be about his mother's age, walked with her head held high and defined brows set in determination. A long black braid hung down the back of her bright red tunic. A strip of cloth acted as a gag, and shiny rope bound her hands, but her dark brown eyes flashed with determination, so strikingly, sickeningly familiar.

"You never even tried to contact Talullah, did you?" Veylan asked Kai.

"No." Kai lifted his chin higher. "I didn't trust your motives for bringing her here."

Veylan laughed again, a puff of air from his lips which curled through the pitch night sky like steam. "I'm giving you one last chance to earn my favor and your place here." Veylan nodded at the new prisoner. "Contact Talullah and convince her to come here with the tapestry pieces. Or she can blame you for her mother's death."

CHAPTER 46

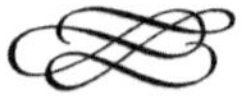

TALULLAH

alullah lay awake that night staring at the ceiling in Maeve's spare bedroom. She wished more than anything to be in her own bed, in her own home, with her father and sisters.

She wanted cinnamon pancakes and hours at the library and new artifacts whose stories she could discover.

The irony ground against her nerves. She'd always wished for an adventure, a way out of the spell that protected her town and the people she loved. She'd wanted to get away. And now that she had, she'd give almost anything to go back.

She couldn't erase the images she'd Seen on the path of the Potential. They'd been stamped onto her memory like the Divines' tattoos, painful and permanent.

Dhal had stayed up with Maeve and Silas to talk strategy for retrieving the last piece of the tapestry from Renevelda. They'd infiltrated the castle once before. But this time the stakes were higher.

Failure didn't only mean Renevelda would control the territory. It meant remaking magic into an ugly tool for revenge and spite.

It meant the end of humanity.

Talullah sat up and wiped perspiration off her face. She sipped from the glass of water Dhal had left by her bedside. Even her sapphire had struggled to calm her nerves.

But that was only one scenario. One path she'd walked. At any given time there were hundreds of ways life could pivot, change, morph into something new and unexpected. Enodia's paths could show the three most likely scenarios, and Talullah had only glimpsed one.

That meant there was still hope.

Talullah clung to that thought as she dug out her deck of cards and turned on the oil lamp just enough to see by.

Reading the cards wouldn't be as sensorial as walking in the Between, but it might bolster her confidence. Talullah grounded herself in the imagined scent of cinnamon and shuffled the deck three times. She cut it into three piles and laid them side-by-side.

Deep breaths inflated and deflated her lungs.

Breathe in possibility, breathe out anxiety.

"If there's a path in which we're successful in our goal to prevent Renevelda from controlling the Source, please show me."

She flipped the first card of each pile.

Chariot.

Lovers.

Sun.

A thin, sparkling emerald thread hovered above each card, then the top ends converged, twisting together in a knot.

Talullah took a deep breath and touched her emerald with one hand and the knot with the other. Like when she'd practiced with Maeve before she knew how to travel to Enodia, Talullah entered the foggy scene as a spectator.

Potential Talullah sat alone at a table in an unfamiliar kitchen. The air smelled stale, as if the home hadn't been visited in a while, its windows shuttered tight for months or years. She stared at the Suditzas' tapestry, all four squares still detached from each other.

Something glinted on Potential Talullah's right hand. Curiosity sparked in Present Talullah. She moved closer to get a better look. Surprise captured her breath. It was the second feather ring, the partner to the one she'd given to HAT.

Talullah returned to Maeve's spare room and stared at the cards in front of her.

The Chariot. Lovers. The Sun.

The Chariot could signify many things: Deep-seated fear that one could triumph over, willpower, victory.

Lovers indicated close personal relationships, perhaps romantic in nature. The need for support from loved ones.

And The Sun: joy, energy, simplicity, optimism, rationalism.

Talullah had asked the cards to show her a path in which victory was possible, and this was what they'd shown her. She needed to lean into the cards' meanings, especially the Sun's. Optimism and rationale plus support from her loved ones would lead her to triumph over deep fear.

Talullah abandoned the cards and took the ring out of her pack. Dhal had given it to her for safe-keeping. She admired the way the lamp's low light reflected off the silver-plated feather, which was streaked through with faint brushstrokes of gold.

She couldn't spend hours researching the origins of the newest arrivals at her family' antique shop, but she could still lean into her strengths. This ring was more important than HAT had let on. If her Potential self's hunch was right, she understood why the merchant didn't want to let it go.

Talullah placed it back inside her pack for now, trusting she would know when to wear it.

The silver and gold Scry bracelet slipped down her arm, trailing a coolness across her warmed flesh. The sudden urge rose to Scry her family. She could see their faces, hear their voices.

But then she'd risk telling them the truth of what she'd Seen. The horrors that would come if she failed to fix the tapestry and use the Source's magic to reunite the four Seer factions.

She held it in her palm, weighing the options when the bracelet vibrated in her hand. "Kai? Is that you?" A swell of relief washed over her, chilling her. "Where have you been? Are you okay? Four Worlds, I'm happy to see you!"

Dark circles shadowed his eyes. He looked like he hadn't slept in weeks. A smile cracked the tension pulling his lips tight. "It's so good to see you, Talullah. I've wanted to call so many times. To be totally honest, things have been better." His voice was scratchy, too. Like he'd been under a lot of stress.

"Where are you?" The room was so dark Talullah could barely see him.

"Storage room of some kind, I think. I needed a place to contact you where I wouldn't be overheard."

"Why? What's going on?" Talullah sat up further in bed and pressed her back against the wall.

Kai tugged his earlobe. "I should have Scryed sooner. Renevelda's guards broke into the cottage where we're staying. Goddesses, I don't even know how long ago that was. It feels like weeks. Could be only days. The important part is the guard stole a piece of the tapestry you're looking for. I can only assume Renevelda has it now. I'm so sorry. I couldn't stop them."

Talullah's blood turned cold. She was right. Renevelda did have a piece of the tapestry. Her shoulders tensed. One step toward the path Talullah had Seen.

"It's not your fault. And, at least now I know where to look for it."

"Did you figure out what they're for? How are you doing with the other pieces?" A desperate sort of hunger seeped through his words.

Talullah sighed. "Yes, I know what they're for. And I've found the other three. I need the one Renevelda has."

Kai shifted, his eyes locked on Talullah's "That is the best news I've heard in weeks. And, as for the last piece, I think I've figured out a way to get the tapestry piece back from Renevelda. My group has been spying on her. We've found a weakness in the castle's protections."

A spark of hope ignited in her. If Kai could help her get the last piece, she'd have all of them. She'd be able to fix it, show the Seer factions its purpose and power, convince them to reunite, and stop Renevelda.

"I can't give you details over Scry. Some people here have been questioning my loyalty. If they find out I've been talking to you, I don't know what they'll do."

"Can you leave?"

He nodded and rubbed the back of his neck, a gesture Talullah had never seen him do before. "I'm planning to. This isn't what I signed up for. Do you know where the old trading outpost is, near the border between Viltresor and Terrapese?"

Talullah nodded. Even if she didn't, Dhal would. "Yes, we can find it."

"Meet me there after dark tomorrow. I'll tell you everything. And, Talullah?"

"Yeah?"

"Be careful."

∽

M AEVE AND S ILAS had tried to convince her to stay longer, but Talullah's heart hadn't stopped pounding since she'd ended her Scry session with Kai. She was *this* close to getting what she needed. Of course, it wouldn't be as easy as that to stop Renevelda. She still needed to mend the tapestry, find the Source, use the magic, and convince four factions who didn't exactly agree to team up and trust her.

But nothing mattered unless she had the last piece of the tapestry.

She had to get it. Now.

"How did Kai seem?" Dhal checked their packs yet again, adding extra food supplies Maeve practically forced them to take. They hadn't stayed in one place for long since they'd escaped the castle.

All the running and moving and constant thinking had made Talullah's mind and body fatigued. She could see the signs on Dhal, too. The sunken eyes, the dull skin. Neither of them were well-enough hydrated or fed or rested.

But Talullah couldn't bear to idle any longer. Not if doing so gave the sorceress the edge she needed.

"He seemed…tired. Like the rest of us. I think he might have gotten a tattoo." She'd glimpsed a hint of black on Kai's neck, the place he kept touching, before they'd disconnected the Scry.

"A tattoo?" Dhal raised his brows.

"Yeah. On the back of his neck. There was something dark and swirly there, but it could have been shadow. He never seemed the type to me."

"Well, you haven't known him all that long. I guess we'll find out for certain soon enough."

Maeve knocked on the door frame and leaned against it. "You're sure I can't convince you to at least stay one more night?"

Talullah shook her head. "Kai said tonight. He seemed desperate. Like maybe this is his only chance. We can't risk contacting him now. And we can't abandon him. We need to help him get out of the camp, and we need the information he has for us."

Silas peeked his dark brown face over Maeve's shoulder. "I still think it seems a bit convenient that after all this time he'd Scry now."

"Or maybe it's good timing," Talullah said. "Plus, he couldn't get through before because of the tracking spell."

Silas scrunched his brows. "Maybe. But you should have a backup plan."

"In case what? He tries to hurt me? Kai would never."

People here are questioning my loyalty, he'd said. The anxious part of her brain locked onto that. What better way to prove his loyalty than to bring a Sezna Seer into the fold? Was Kai capable of using her like that?

She didn't want to believe so, but times like this did strange things to people. Thinned the line between right and wrong in their minds. People could convince themselves of anything if they were desperate enough.

Talullah shook that thought away. She trusted Kai. "No, he wouldn't do anything to harm me."

"We'll bring a backup plan, just in case," Dhal said to Silas.

Silas nodded, his jaw still tense. "Something feels off. I need to walk. Maeve, will you anchor for me? I don't think my emotions are stable enough right now to do it alone."

"Of course," Maeve said. She gave Dhal and Talullah hugs, then followed Silas down the stairs. Talullah and Dhal weren't far behind them.

Maeve and Silas took the lift down into the tapestry room, and Talullah and Dhal headed for the front door.

"You sure about this?" Dhal asked.

Talullah nodded, taking one last breath scented with Maeve's grounding basil. She cast a Manipulation charm over them, drawing some of Dhal's magic as well, to strengthen it.

At this time of night, the city streets were quiet. Dhal directed Talullah to the edge of the city, where the residential properties became fewer and farther between. Once they'd cleared the houses completely, Talullah finally let herself breathe deeply.

Getting out of the city was the hardest part. They wouldn't have to worry as much about Renevelda's spies all the way out there.

"It's right past this line of trees," Dhal said. "Norr and I mapped it last year. It has an interesting history, actually—"

"Talullah?" another voice called out.

"It's Kai," Talullah said. "Come on."

"Hurry," Kai called.

She and Dhal approached the horse-drawn cart. "Not exactly inconspicuous," Dhal grumbled. "Anyone could have heard you coming."

"I did the best with what I had," Kai said. His voice sounded strained still. "Get in. We need to get moving."

"Wait, how did you know we were here?" Dhal asked.

"I Saw you, of course."

"But we used a Manipulation spell," Dhal continued.

"I'm a Seer. I know how to break through those. It's not exactly difficult."

Talullah paused. This didn't sound like Kai. He'd never spoken of his abilities this way. He'd only just come to terms with having magic.

"What are you waiting for?" Kai asked. He turned and the glow of the moon illuminated a strip of skin on the back of his neck.

"When did you get a tattoo?" she asked warily.

Kai touched it gently with a few fingers as if he'd forgotten about it. "You don't like it?" He smiled and the shape it took was all wrong. It wasn't easy or charming, though it seemed like it was meant to be. It made Talullah shiver. "Look. We can stand here and talk about all the ways we've changed since we last saw each other, or we can get somewhere safe."

Dhal squeezed Talullah's hand in question.

"You know what? I'm going to need something else first," Talullah said, turning up the fake charm. Her gut told her this wasn't Kai. Not the one she knew. So who was it? And how had he contacted her?

"What's that?" Not-Kai asked.

"A hug, of course. We haven't seen each other. I thought you could be dead. Didn't you miss me?"

Dhal stiffened beside her. He whispered, "What are you doing?"

"Getting the truth," she replied, quietly.

Not-Kai slid open the door of the cart. A fake smile curled across his face. "Of course I did." He swaggered over and spread his arms wide.

Talullah leaned in. Immediately, her suspicions were confirmed. Kai—her Kai—smelled of parchment and had a freckle past the outside corner of his left eye. This person was a stranger.

She hugged him, feeling slimy and wrong as she rubbed his back and let her fingers pause on the back of his neck. "I'm so glad you're okay," she whispered in his ear.

Her amethyst's magic pulled her into the young man's memory. Purple smoke filled her mind's eye, and then she was in the past.

"This will do," Not-Kai said.

"You think it will be enough?" A tall blond woman built for battle opened the cart door.

"She won't have time to look too closely. It won't take much to convince her," Not-Kai said. "Not if she thinks I'm him."

A flash, and then she was elsewhere. The Hidden Market. Striding toward a merchant waiting outside his tent.

Documents, etc., read the sign.

He had a job to do.

The man hardened his heart, drowned out his feelings. It wasn't personal, just business.

Even the triumphant smile his target had offered so easily upon accepting his compliments hadn't been enough to sway the man in the end.

It was necessary. It would be worth it.

He drove in the blade, twisted it, to be sure.

He left his cousin bleeding on the ground.

One more body added to his count. Not the last, he was sure, before all this was over.

But one step closer to his glory.

Talullah came out of the memory, gagging, her eyes filling with tears. She stepped back, but the murderer wearing Kai's face squeezed her arms.

"Oh, I think there's been a misunderstanding, Talullah," the silky voice whispered in her ear. Where the likeness of Kai's shiny black hair had been, blond slithered through as the illusion faded.

"Dhal! Run!" she shouted.

An *oomph* came from Dhal's direction. Talullah caught a glance of him over her shoulder. He was doubled-over, his arms wrenched behind his back by the tall blond soldier from the imposter's memory.

Talullah's arms had gone numb from the pressure. She tried to kick the man, but he stomped the ground and her legs froze in place. He Manipulated her body to betray her. She couldn't move. He picked her up and shoved her into the carriage alongside Dhal.

Panic built in Talullah's chest. A sob threatened to break free. She'd been so desperate that she'd walked right into a trap. And her captor had known she would.

He'd Seen through her magic. He wasn't only a Katamian Seer. No, he had to be something more.

The young man, now fully himself again, tossed her and Dhal one last pitying look. "It's going to be a bit of a ride. I hope you don't get cart sick."

A gas seeped in through the cracks. Talullah and Dhal tried to cover their noses and mouths, but the space was so small that it filled quickly with whatever magic substance had been put into it.

"I'm so sorry," Talullah said to Dhal, her wide eyes locked on his, burning and watering from the gas.

"We're going to be fine." He coughed.

"By the way," the blond boy said. "Kai sends his regards." And he slammed the door to the carriage closed.

CHAPTER 47

TALULLAH

Talullah groaned. Her head throbbed like she'd been hit with something heavy, though she couldn't recall that having happened. Crust stuck to her eyelids as she fought to blink them open. She coughed, her lungs sore, and then tried to sit up.

Talullah found herself in a room alone. Her arms and legs had been bound to the stiff wooden chair. It was dark, but a sliver of silvery light peeked through a gap near the floor. It was enough light to reveal a smattering of boxes piled in all corners and papers strewn across the floor.

A storage room. That's where Not-Kai had said he was when they'd Scryed.

She could scream for help, but she'd lose any element of surprise. If her captor thought she was still unconscious, she had an advantage. But where was Dhal?

Saliva dribbled out the corners of her mouth and soaked the strip of fabric acting as a gag.

Magic sparkled all throughout the room, especially on the door. It had to be some kind of magical security system. Maybe to alert her captor if she moved or tried to escape.

She needed to get her bearings. Figure out what to do. How to get out of there.

First, she called on her amethyst, thankful that it was still hidden beneath her shirt, and grateful that the Suditzas had protected it with anti-theft magic so that no one would be able to take it from her. The tender skin at her throat suggested they had tried.

She called upon her memory magic to replay what had just happened in the room. The purple image faded onto the present. The young blond man had tied her to the chair. Dhal wasn't with him, so he must have put Dhal somewhere else first.

Adrenaline raced through her blood. What if he'd killed Dhal?

A flash of her prophetic vision bled into the memory. Sweat coated her palms. *Dhal!*

Was this it, the moment she'd glimpsed but never fully? The moment she dreaded because she feared it would be the end of them?

Dunamai's Eye warmed, bringing her attention back to the memory. Panic wouldn't help her escape or find Dhal. Because he was alive still. She sensed it in the part of her heart where she'd locked her feelings for him.

Talullah refocused on the memory, drowning out the red vision and letting the purple shine though. In it, the young man took Talullah's knapsack and dumped its contents on the floor. He rifled through them until he found what he was looking for.

The three tapestry pieces.

He left the room and sealed it with his magic.

Talullah let go of the memory.

She sobbed freely now. He'd stolen them.

Renevelda would soon have all four pieces.

She would control the Source.

The path Talullah had walked in the Between was coming true.

And it was all Talullah's fault.

TALULLAH WALLOWED for only a moment then forced herself to get it together. She could still change things. Nothing was set in stone. The Chariot, Lovers, and The Sun danced behind her eyelids. She'd glimpsed a path in which she would win, now it was up to her to fulfill it.

She scanned the room for anything she might be able to use as a tool to free herself from the chair. The rope rubbed against her wrists. There was something familiar about its texture, the way something smooth was braided with the rough. Dhal's wrists had been bound with the same kind when she'd found him in Nainehta Forest in the other timeline.

He told her then that magic laced the ropes, so nobody could cut them. They could only be untied. She could work with that.

Frantically, Talullah worked to get her wrists in a better position so she could try to loosen the knots with her fingers. The angle was terrible, and it shot pain through her shoulders, down her arms, and into every inch of her hands. But she pressed on. Wiggled one piece a bit, then another.

It was painstaking. She had no idea how long she had before her captor returned. If he returned. Maybe he'd leave her in the room to starve or dehydrate. By her dry mouth and beginning of a headache, it wouldn't take long.

Why hadn't he just killed her when he had the chance? She'd been defenseless.

Again her mind returned to the path she'd walked in Enodia.

The golden circlet around her neck. The invisible leash. The infection spreading from Dunamai's Eye through her chest.

Renevelda wanted to keep her. Torture her. Make her regret ever standing in the way.

Then she'd kill every last one of Talullah's friends and family members.

She'd make Talullah watch.

The grimness of the possibility fueled Talullah to work faster. She managed to get her hands undone and then got to work on her feet. The longer she worked, the more her thoughts turned to Dhal. She had to find him.

At last, her hands and legs were all free. She tossed her gag on the floor and ran her dry tongue around the inside of her mouth. She rolled her wrists and ankles, wishing she had some of Dhal's salve from Mr. Miscian to ease the pain.

Her bag was nowhere in sight, so her captor must have returned at some point before she woke up to get it. All the books and maps and resources she'd collected were gone. The feather ring, too. She stifled a cry.

All she had to rely on now were her wits.

Focus on The Sun. Optimism and rationale.

Her next objective was to get out of the room. She paced around the small space, careful not to touch anything. Anything could be a trap or a security trip to alert her captors of activity in the room.

There were no mirrors and a thick layer of dust coated anything that might have once been reflective.

She used her sapphire next to dial up her sense of hearing to see if she could hear anything going on outside the door. The protective wards on the room prevented her from hearing anything except her own erratic heartbeat. She approached the piles of objects and cast out a feeler for any magic within. Nothing there was usable.

Next, she used her emerald to read her likely potential

futures. She didn't have her deck of cards with her. They'd been in her bag with everything else Not-Kai had stolen.

Instead, she closed her eyes and reached. It wouldn't be as potent a vision without the cards or the actual paths in Enodia, but it would be something.

She opened herself to the possibilities in her mind's eye. Three paths came forward. Each one beckoned her in a different way. Her intuition pulled her toward the leftmost path. Maeve had always told her to trust her intuition.

Talullah leaned into that path and opened her eyes and mind to what the path had to show her. It showed her reuniting with Dhal.

They were in a room that seemed to be beneath ground, which would make a lot of sense if the people who had kidnapped her had taken her into one of the many tunnels.

Everything led back to these tunnels.

There was a way out of here. She just had to find it.

She traced her steps back on that path to see where it began.

Voices careened down the hall and yanked her out of the vision.

There was nowhere in the room to hide. She would play her situation down to her captor. Make herself seem weaker than she was.

Sweat slid down her forehead and stung her eyes. With her sapphire's help, she calmed her breathing and her pulse. She had to be prepared for anything.

She waited for a long moment until the door opened. Not-Kai looked at her, and a tiny smirk appeared on his face. He'd reapplied the illusion to disguise himself as Kai.

"Talullah. Please forgive the bindings." He flicked his gaze to her wrists. His smile morphed to a grimace. "Which I see you've already rid yourself of."

"They were uncomfortable. I have sensitive wrists."

"They were a necessary precaution."

"Take off the Manipulation magic."

"What?"

"I know you're not Kai. I knew the moment I saw you in the forest. Take off his face."

The Seer shrugged. "It served its purpose." He wiggled his fingers, and his appearance changed before Talullah's eyes.

She stifled the gasp of horror that pressed against her mouth as he pulled down his hood. The clover neck tattoo peeked out from behind the black fabric of his cloak. She'd read his past, had watched him murder his cousin in cold blood, twice.

Her pulse thundered once more in her ears.

How did this man even know Kai? Had her friend been in league with him all along?

"I figured you might not trust me if I showed up like this. Borrowing your friend's likeness was an occupational necessity. You have made quite the name for yourself in the Sight community over the past year, Miss Bridgestone. It's made planning quite difficult. But, I found a way."

"Why did you choose her side?" Talullah's hoarse voice scraped her reed-dry vocal chords.

"Sometimes we have to side with the lesser of the evils."

She laughed, mirthless. "And you think the sorceress is less evil?"

"Her offer was the best at the time." He shrugged as if it was no big deal.

"Why do you trust that she'll deliver anything she's promised you? I don't understand."

The Seer laughed, but it was also void of any humor. "I don't expect you to understand at all. What I do expect you to do is play your part and fix the Suditzas' tapestry."

"You've already given the tapestry to Renevelda, right? Why would she need me to fix it?"

"She wouldn't need you to fix it. *If* my plan involved handing it over to her. Things change." He reached into Talullah's bag and pulled out the pieces she'd collected…and an extra one. The one Renevelda had found first. He'd stolen it from her. The pieces were there. *All four of them.*

Talullah's brows shot up. "You want me to fix it for *you*?"

"I don't want you to, Talullah. Unfortunately, I need you to. And, I'm confident once you see whom I have to offer you as repayment, you'll be compelled."

Whom. Not *what.*

Talullah's heart galloped. Which of her loved ones would pay the price this time for being close to her?

Her captor pulled out a small mirror from inside his shirt pocket and turned it toward Talullah so the glass shimmered under the newly illuminated light.

He pressed the sapphire inlaid at the top of the mirror. Cerulean smoke filled the glass like any other Scry. Talullah held her breath, not daring to guess whose face she was about to see.

A voice from the past shook her to her core. "Where is my daughter?" her mother asked in the mirror. "Let me see her."

CHAPTER 48

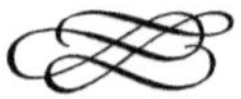

TALULLAH

Talullah's breath caught in her throat as she took in the image of her mother in the Scry. Immediately, her mind went to all the ways that this could be a trick. Her captor could be using Manipulation magic to show her what she wanted to see.

He could have done any number of spells on the Scry, any number of mental Manipulations on her while she was unconscious. Or one of his allies could be disguised as her mother, like her captor had used an illusion to change his own appearance. If she chose to believe him, then what would happen?

"Mother?" She tested the word tentatively. It hung in the air, suspended between hope and suspicion.

"It's me."

Talullah narrowed her eyes. "Prove it."

The corner of the woman's mouth ticked up, the prelude to a smile. "You've always been so intelligent, Talullah. That's why I knew you could do this." She sighed and pressed the tips of her fingers to her forehead. "I've been gone so long. What could I possibly say?"

Talullah's captor leaned in toward the mirror. "This is taking too long."

Another figure appeared behind her mother in the Scry. The tall female soldier from her vision, the one who'd questioned her captor's illusion abilities. She moved Talullah's mother's hair behind her shoulders.

Talullah inhaled sharply. A golden metal collar gleamed around her mother's neck.

"We used to bake together. Cinnamon was always your favorite spice." Desperate, frustrated tears leaked from her mother's eyes. "I planted a hazelnut tree in our front yard."

As much as Talullah wanted to believe her mother was alive, she couldn't trust her captor. Not after he'd tried to deceive her once. But collecting information had always been her strong suit. Gathering the data, reading the clues, and then using her logic to come to a conclusion.

"I made you practice weaving, even though you always preferred to sew."

Talullah sat up straighter, shifting in her hard seat. That wasn't a detail anyone could have guessed. "Was this why? Did you know I would try to repair the goddesses' tapestry?"

Her mother nodded, dark brown eyes brimming with things unsaid. "Use your heart, keep your mind, Talullah. We don't always see with our eyes."

Her mother was right. Talullah had always clung to knowledge like a lifeline. But now she also had other strengths at her disposal. She had her Sight powers, all of them strengthened by her stones. Dunamai's Eye sat against her collarbone with warm comfort, encouraging her to use everything she had learned so far.

She called forth her intuition, anchored by her emerald, and let it guide her.

A stone landed in her gut when she realized that the image in front of her was the truth and not the result of a Manipulation.

"Do I have your attention now?" Talullah's captor locked her in place with his frigid blue gaze. "Your mother is now my prisoner. And if you refuse to fix the tapestry, as I have so politely asked of you, I have no qualms about killing her."

"Wait!" Talullah reached for the Scry, but her captor was too quick. He pressed the sapphire to disconnect it.

Talullah reached again for her own magic, intending to Manipulate her way out. She found a void in its place. The humming that usually tickled her blood had stilled.

She darted her gaze left and right, a caged animal ready to fling itself against its bars. Her limbs tingled as she stalked around the room.

"I let you use your magic before," her captor said. "I needed you to confirm you truly saw your mother. But now it's time to decide. I don't like to wait." He stepped toward Talullah.

A rumbling sound came from out in the hallway.

The door creaked open, and another young man poked his head in. Before Talullah could make a run for it, the man at the door collapsed, hitting the floor with a loud thunk.

Her captor drew a long blade from a sheath at his hip and stalked toward the door. "I'm certain I said no interruptions."

A large, muscular man with a black tattoo on the back of his neck appeared in the doorway.

A man who shouldn't be breathing, let alone attacking people.

"Hiltrud?" Not-Kai froze, his eyes widening like he'd seen a ghost.

The merchant withdrew a syringe from his pocket. "Hello, Veylan." He plunged the needle into his cousin's neck.

Talullah's captor—Veylan—raised his knife, but his muscled arms shook as if fighting resistance. Talullah watched, unable to move, to think, to scream, as one by one, Veylan's limbs seized. His fingers released the knife. It clattered onto the ground. Sweat ran down his face as he struggled. The merchant held him tightly, even as Veylan's knees buckled. He held on until the full contents of the syringe had been emptied into his cousin's body. Then he let go.

Veylan, wide-eyed and foaming at the mouth, tried to speak. He gasped once, twice. And then…nothing. His face went slack, his body still.

Finally, Talullah breathed. Shallow and ragged. Sweat and dirt and salt from tears coated her face. Her stomach heaved, but there was nothing in it. Her hands quavered at her sides, useless. She'd watched a man die. Again. For real this time.

"What was that?" Talullah rasped.

The merchant lifted his eyes and winked. "Silk reaper venom. Thanks to your friend for the idea."

Talullah paled even further. She'd predicted his death. She'd watched Veylan stab him, twist the knife, spill his blood. "I saw you…die."

"I'm harder to kill than I look."

No, she'd predicted his cousin would *attack* him. She didn't see the before or the after. "What are you doing here?"

"You saved my life with your prophecy. I always repay my debts." He gestured around the room. "Did you want to stand around and have tea, or can we go? Grab your bag."

Talullah inhaled sharply.

She chanced a glance at her captor. If that was silk reaper venom, he'd never wake up. She'd witnessed a murder for real this time. Her stomach clenched again.

If Veylan had stolen from the sorceress, Renevelda would have killed him as soon as she found out. Knowing his death was inevitable didn't soften the swell of nausea.

The merchant waved her on, stepping over the unconscious guard at the threshold. "Follow me."

"How do you know where to go?" Talullah asked, shouldering her bag. Having it close to her body wrapped her in comfort.

"Old habits." He left it at that. Talullah didn't press.

"We need to find my friend. He's here somewhere."

"No time, sweetheart."

She doubled her pace to keep up with his long, purposeful strides. "We can't leave him."

"You want to go back there and see what they meant for you? Be my guest. My business is done here, and I'm not waiting around."

Talullah hesitated for half a second. "I'm going back for him."

The merchant—Hiltrud—shrugged. "Suit yourself."

"Thank you. For saving me, I mean."

"Came to visit my cousin, and here you are. Two birds, one stone. Consider us even."

Coming from a guy in his line of work, Talullah would take "even" any day of the week. They parted ways, and Talullah started back toward the room where she'd been. Dhal must have been nearby in one of the other rooms. Behind one of the tens of closed doors.

But how could she find him?

Trace him.

Obviously. It's what she should have done the moment she stepped out of the room. She hadn't been thinking properly.

She gripped the clay rose in her pocket, the one she'd been careful to pack. He was her compass, and she was his.

Talullah called her amethyst's magic forward, searching for Dhal's path. It led down a long hallway.

"Amethyst," a voice echoed down the hall. "That way. She can't have gotten far."

Four Worlds. They'd Seen her magic.

How many of them were there? Her captor had Seen through her Concealment spell. What if the others could too?

She couldn't risk waiting around to find out. The footsteps came from the direction her magic had indicated Dhal was being kept.

But she couldn't go that way.

She'd have to find another.

And fast.

Talullah reached for her intuition again. "Help me get out of here safely," she whispered to the magic.

It tugged her again toward the sound of the voices. The ones who wanted to keep her, to use her for Renevelda's plan.

There must be something wrong with her magic. Veylan's wards had scrambled it, or witnessing his murder had confused it. Why would it be safer to go toward her enemies?

Her mind whirred with confusion.

What do I do?

She followed the hallway in front of her. Fresh air would help her think clearly. If she could get outside, regroup, she could plan.

Her breathing sounded too loud, the rasps of the air on her dry throat like an alarm drawing Renevelda's guards to her. Or that's what her mind convinced her.

What would Dhal do?

He'd come for me. No matter what.

She turned on her heel. They were in this together. She had to find him.

Dhal! Where are you? she screamed in her mind. Panic spread its wings in her chest.

She doubled back. This hallway looked the same as all the others. She hadn't turned, had she? Then why was she staring at a path with three forks? Musty air clouded her thoughts.

If we get separated, we meet at the safe house, Caprico had told them. But she couldn't bear to leave Dhal. Her heart picked up the pace, keeping time with her feet. If she left and he died, she'd never forgive herself.

Her emerald tugged at her attention, begging her to listen, to read the Potential and make a logical choice.

Talullah ducked into an alcove, panting hard and shaking. She pressed her emerald and imagined herself standing at the paths in the Between.

What will happen if I keep looking for Dhal? She held her breath as the paths fell away, leaving only one, the most likely. In her mind's eye, she stepped onto it. The Between's iron gate and weatherless sky dissolved into a long hallway, the same one she'd been running down.

Two Manipulated guards with swirly blue eyes paraded away from her, each clutching a fistful of their captives' tunics. Dhal and Talullah dragged their feet, weighed down by the irons clamped onto their ankles.

Dhal looked at the Potential version of Talullah. His gravelly voice broke her. "You promised to go to the safe house. You promised."

Talullah let go of the vision. She wanted to glimpse the other two paths, to convince herself there was a chance she could still leave this place with Dhal.

But footsteps echoed toward her. She'd run out of time. There might be a chance she could change that outcome, tip the favor to her side and guide them to safety.

The risk was too great. In the current situation, if she stayed any longer, both she and Dhal would be caught.

As much as it gutted her to admit, the best thing she could do now was leave. She swallowed the bile inching up her throat.

Talullah followed her amethyst's memory of the hallways until she reached a dead end. The door that would grant her freedom and maybe doom her best friend.

No. Those thoughts would eat her alive. She'd come back for Dhal. They always found each other.

Talullah touched the doorknob and gritted her teeth as she forced her own magic to overpower the locking spell that had covered the door.

She eased it open, sneaked outside, took a deep breath, and checked the coast was clear.

Then she called her amethyst's memory once more and ran.

CHAPTER 49

KAI

*V*eylan had been gone for hours. Kai paced in his room, sweating bullets and ripping the petals from as many end of the season flowers as he'd dared to pick from the garden and smuggle into his room. He, of course, hadn't given Veylan what he'd asked for. He couldn't in good conscience tell Talullah to come to the Marquet home.

Not now that Kai knew for certain Veylan was up to something nefarious, likely in league with the sorceress. On the other hand, Kai couldn't stomach Veylan's threats.

After what happened with the guard, Kai was convinced Veylan would keep his promise to kill Talullah's mother.

Which was why he and Zinni had taken turns watching the cabin at the edge of the property over the past few hours since Talullah's mother's imprisonment.

If Veylan had gone to the trouble of locating and kidnapping a woman who had been missing and thought dead for nearly a decade, he had bigger plans than driving a wedge between Kai and Talullah. Veylan needed Talullah's mother as leverage against Talullah.

He wouldn't kill her mother until he'd made his threat.

It was likely that's where Veylan had been for the past few hours. Hours that were too late to be considered night and too early to be considered morning. The time of day when nothing made sense but possibilities seemed endless.

After Kai had refused Veylan's offer, he and Zinni—cloaked under a less-than-perfect Concealment spell—had followed the young man charged with settling Talullah's mother. The scent of pine surrounded the abandoned shack of a cabin. At least she'd been given better lodging than the guard.

Though Kai figured that had more to do with Veylan wanting to keep his new prisoner a secret. It would have been more difficult to convince Quentis and the others that Talullah's mother could cause them any sort of harm.

Kai plucked a few more petals off the half-dead white flower and dropped them in a bowl on his desk. He'd stopped asking them questions a few hours ago. He knew what needed to happen. His hands needed a way to stay busy until it was time.

Zinni, Kai, Theresa—who, thank the stars, had finally seen reason after Kai explained everything to her—and Edouard were leaving the Marquet estate.

First, they had to save Talullah's mother. Now. Before Veylan returned.

Finally, Zinni knocked on the door, and Kai rushed to open it. She gave him one terse nod, her face set in determination.

Leaving Quentis was the only part of this plan that made Kai feel the slightest bit bad. The older Marquet was genuinely a kind person. He'd been welcoming and open and led astray by his manipulative son.

A pit formed in Kai's stomach when he realized the older

Seer would one day have to reckon with the fact that his own son had taken advantage of him.

"Are Theresa and Edouard ready?" Kai asked.

Zinni nodded. A length of thick brown leather held her mass of tiny black braids out of her face, and she had chosen a pair of closely-fitting riding pants and a practically-cut tunic.

"Then it's time." Kai threw the rest of the flowers into the bowl on his desk. He shouldered the bag that held his meager belongings.

Outside, only the crickets made a sound, chirping a chorus so loud it rivaled the beat of Kai's heart. He and Zinni met Theresa and Edouard at the edge of the property where the evergreen trees thickened.

"He has security precautions set up," Theresa whispered. "He showed me. I know how to disable them, but they'll still trigger an alert that someone has done so. I'd guess we have about five minutes before Veylan finds out about this."

Kai squeezed Theresa's hand. "I'm so glad you're here. I couldn't have lived with myself if we'd left you behind."

Theresa returned the gesture. "Turns out not everyone is who they say. I'm only sorry I didn't see it sooner." She let go of Kai and used both hands to skim the bark of the nearest tree. "Found it. Ready? Go."

A line of blue magic traced the front door of the cabin. Kai turned the handle and pushed it inward.

The musty scent of neglect and rotted wood enveloped Kai's senses as he stepped inside. Talullah's mother lifted her head from her spot tied to the lone wooden chair in the center of the room. Her eyes flashed angrily and dangerously.

Kai approached her slowly. "We're not here to hurt you. I'm a friend of Talullah's, and we're going to get you out of here."

CHAPTER 50

TALULLAH

Once she'd entered the safe house, locked the door, and added an extra layer of illusion magic to keep her hidden, Talullah gave herself five minutes to wallow in despair.

How could she leave him?

Even knowing what she did about the Potential, her body ached with the wrongness of knowing he was there somewhere and still walking away.

Her sobs would have echoed had the foyer and living area not been stuffed with squishy sofas and armchairs in mismatched prints. The yellow and orange plaid cushions folded in on her like an awkward hug when she sank into it. It was a poor substitute for a friend, but it didn't seem to mind the puddle her tears left on its dusty pillows.

Despite the cozy furniture, it was obvious this place was not a home. Perhaps it had been, once upon a time. Maybe then, portraits of children and their parents or groups of friends or lovers just getting to know each other hung from the empty nails that jutted through the peeling, yellowed wallpaper like fangs searching for prey.

Maybe then, the air had smelled like nutmeg or fresh bread or roasted duck instead of the sickly tang of neglect perfuming the air.

The building's walls and roof, bolstered by magic, provided protection. But there was more than one form of shelter, and Talullah wouldn't consider this place safe in all the ways that mattered.

It will be okay, she tried to convince herself. It had to be. She'd trusted her magic to get her out, and it had. She had to trust it would lead her back to Dhal, too.

And Dhal was strong in his own right. He was clever. He'd figure out how to escape.

She dried her tears and searched the galley kitchen for a glass. She dusted one off with a musty beige cotton towel she found in a drawer. Ignoring her splotchy face and swollen eyes in the glass's reflection, she filled it to the brim with water she hoped was drinkable.

After three full glasses, her mind had cleared enough to rummage for something to eat. It was hard to tell how long ago anyone had been in the house. She found a sack of nuts still in their shells that didn't smell rancid and spent the next fifteen minutes cracking them open and eating them.

It wasn't nearly enough to fill her up, but it was better than nothing. Now, semi-fueled, she let herself think.

Was Dhal okay? How was she going to get back there to save him without being discovered? Was the merchant's cousin dead, or did he have the same kind of power that had saved the merchant?

Right now, she had to focus on fixing the tapestry.

At the wobbly kitchen table, Talullah unfurled the squares on the scratched surface.

She'd been so worried about finding the pieces of the tapestry, but now she understood that hadn't been the most difficult part of this process. Now, she had to fulfill the prophecy and, therefore, her destiny.

She had to repair it.

Talullah's hands shook as she flattened the cloth. Her mind flashed to the tabletop loom her mother had given her when she was a child. Talullah had always preferred sewing to weaving. She'd never understood why, except the needle and thread had fit more naturally in her fingers than the larger needles used for weaving.

Her mother had insisted she practice. Had badgered Talullah about it relentlessly.

This, of course, was why.

Her mother had known all along this day would come. That the fate of magic and beyond would fall on her skills.

This was the vision her mother had of her so long ago, the one that set all their lives on this path. The one that had taken her mother away from the family, had convinced her mother that leaving was the right thing to do. But of course, there was no way to know whether her mother had set this event in motion by making that decision, or whether she'd preserved this future with the choices she'd made. That was the difficulty in having Certain Sight. The end scene was the only guarantee, but the path to get there was fuzzy.

If only her mother had had the gift of Potential Sight as well and had been able to see the events leading up to now, maybe they could have avoided missing each other for so long. Maybe there was more than one path that led them to this moment.

It was too late to know that now. Talullah could go back and change it, if she wanted to. But she knew better than to Alter the past. The consequences were too steep. Too many unknowns could set the world off-kilter.

Gratitude washed over her, keeping her fear company and chasing away the ghosts of past hurt. Despite the struggles, Talullah's mother had done her best to prepare Talullah for her task.

Talullah traced the braided thread in shades of blue and red and green and purple that wove around the perimeter, echoing the covers of the books in Praeteriti. The ones that held a person's life story. The threads of Time existed all around if one had the skill and patience to look. To See. They'd spellbound her when she'd been trapped inside Igdrasil, the largest transport tree in Nainehta Forest. That first glimpse, the first time she Saw, changed everything.

Awe overcame Talullah as she grasped the honor she'd been Gifted being able to not only notice them, but touch and change them.

In a way, this tapestry was a life story, too. About the Suditzas and their plans for magic, their hopes of sharing it with others.

Gillie was right. It could be used for ill, yes. But it could also be used for good.

Magic crackled in the air. Her amethyst glowed in Dunamai's Eye.

Read the tapestry.

It has secrets to reveal.

Talullah tried to push the memory's call away, to focus on her task. But the memory insisted. It knocked on her subconscious with desperate, pleading fists.

Her intuition told her to listen.

She let herself be pulled into the memory.

Four women bent over a loom in a cozy cottage room. Fire crackled in the stone grate. The faint scent of woodsmoke tickled the inside of Talullah's nose. Her eyes snagged on the gazing globes and mirrors, the forgotten mugs next to plates of tea dregs, and a large panel on the wall that showed the position of the stars.

The Suditzas.

CHAPTER 51

TALULLAH

In the purple haze of the memory, Talullah stepped closer. Warmth from the fire spread up her face and hands. She tuned her hearing up with her sapphire so she could more clearly make out the Suditzas' words.

"You think that's wise?" Katamai said to her sisters. She shook her curtain of sleek black hair over her shoulder, her sharp eyes questioning. The Goddess of the Present was the only Suditza Talullah had ever seen, though she could guess the others' identities.

"Why don't we ask her?" The one with poppy-red curls and a satisfied smirk on her pale face must be Cesera.

The other three Suditzas paused. Then, as one, all four turned to stare at Talullah.

"Well? Are you coming or not?" The goddess with rich brown skin and straight, chin-length lavender hair pierced Talullah's gaze with her own. Urtha.

"You can see me?" Talullah whispered.

Dunamai rolled her eyes. "Yes, dear." She turned to her sisters. "I told you we should have warned her."

"And risk everything?" Katamai argued. She gestured at the black panel on the wall. Its painted white stars glistened as if freshly applied.

"Didn't matter anyway, did it?" Cesera said smugly. "She made it here, like I said she would."

Talullah took another few steps closer. The scratched wood floors creaked under her worn leather boots. "But this is a memory." She looked at Urtha, the Goddess of the Past for confirmation.

Urtha tilted her head a bit. Her purple hair swayed. "Yes and no."

"Okay?"

"It's our memory, mine and my sisters'. But time is fluid for Sezna Seers, remember?"

"So, I'm visiting you in the past?" Another step forward and Talullah met them on the thick cream rug near the brick hearth.

"For ease of discussion, yes," Cesera said.

"And why exactly am I here?" Talullah glanced around the cottage again.

"Because in this moment, you need our help. And perhaps our permission," Katamai said. "You're fighting your instincts."

"The tapestry," Urtha continued, "is just a tool." She gestured to the cloth on the loom in front of her. It's what the pieces she'd found would look like if she'd been able to reunite them.

Silver symbols flecked the background, some shaped like constellations, others less identifiable. The four trees' roots snaked and twisted until they met in a knot in the center. Gold thread showed the rivers borne of the Source. Silver and gold words marched across the perimeter. Words Talullah hadn't seen on the squares she'd collected.

"Why don't the squares I've found have words?" She

glanced at each Suditza in turn. "They only appear when the tapestry is whole?" Talullah asked. Her body hummed with new understanding. "But why?"

"There is danger in being divided," Katamai said.

"This isn't just a map to the Source," Talullah said. "It can't be. Because even if a person found the Source, they wouldn't know how to use it." A flare of heat bloomed behind her ribcage as understanding rooted there. "The tapestry holds instructions for how to use the magic."

Talullah's eyes roamed the symbols again. Her attention snagged on the spatial relationship between them. A rhythm existed there in the lines and swirls and stars, a cadence of harmony and life. A pattern of existence. "These represent your followers, right? The humans and other creatures you've Gifted. This is how we're supposed to work together within magic."

Dunamai nodded. Smoothed her shoulder-length, dark brown hair. "We have felt the vibrations of change through the Four Worlds. There are many paths forward. Some are poisonous. Some speak of hope."

Talullah looked to Cesera, the Goddess of the Certain. "And what do you See for the future of magic?"

Cesera's eyes welled with tears. "All I have Seen is *you*."

A sharp breath lodged in Talullah's lungs. "Is that good or bad?"

Cesera shrugged. "This is one area where I cannot divine. The future of our magic in your world remains a mystery."

"So, why call me here now?"

"To remind you that you have our knowledge," Urtha said. At her words, Talullah's amethyst glowed.

"And our grounding influence," added Katamai. The sapphire lit up.

"And our intuition." The emerald glowed as Dunamai spoke.

"And finally," Cesera added. Talullah's ruby sparked to life. "The confidence to move forward as you feel is necessary. The stars chose you long, long ago, Talullah Bridgestone. They do not make mistakes."

The constellations on the Suditzas' chart dimmed, except for one. The bird Talullah had seen everywhere. The phoenix. A symbol of life and death, of beginning and end.

Cesera smiled, her eyes tinged with sadness. "Some things must end in order to begin."

A white flash of light enveloped the room. Talullah blinked.

The cottage faded, along with the goddesses, leaving Talullah alone once more in the safe house.

The tapestry pieces beckoned her. But Talullah needed one more thing first, before she fixed it. Something she'd Seen in her exploration of the Potential path in which she could win.

The feather ring barely weighed anything in her hand but as she slipped it on, the magic warmed its way around her finger.

"Zeri!" Talullah called.

"Hello, Little Seer," a high voice said. Zeri, the Spirit Fox, hopscotched along the perimeter of the dining area. Her black boots landed soundlessly on the cracked terracotta tile.

"You said something when I fought Renevelda the first time. You said you owe me a favor for freeing you."

Zeri's golden yellow eyes sparked with mischief and something else. Pride. "Ah, finally. So, what do you want from me, Little Seer? Choose carefully. There are no do-overs. Not this time, anyway."

A half-smile graced Talullah's face at life coming full circle. "My loom, needle, and thread."

"You could ask for anything at all, and you want your loom?"

"Yes." It was time to lean into her skill instead of away.

Zeri nodded once, disappeared, then reappeared seconds later. She held the object of Talullah's past out and the girl took it, almost reverently.

Talullah gripped the edges of the loom. Hours upon hours of her life had been spent with this object. And all for this. "Thank you," she whispered. To Zeri. And to her mother, wherever she was now.

"What do you plan to do?"

"I'm going to fix what's broken. I'm going to prove the prophecy isn't about Renevelda destroying magic as we know it."

The Spirit Fox cocked her head. "Oh, Little Seer. I thought you'd have figured it out by now. That prophecy *is* about the destruction of magic. But not at Renevelda's hands."

Talullah's stomach dropped in anticipation of Zeri's next words. Somehow she knew them before they slithered through the spirit's pointed teeth.

"The destruction comes from *your* hands, Little Seer. *You're* the one destined to change Sight magic forever."

Some things must end in order to begin.

Was that why Cesera had been upset? Had she foreseen Talullah destroying magic? If that were the case, the Suditzas wouldn't have trusted her. No, she had to mean the end of something else. The end and rebirth.

What if the Seers had assumed destruction when the prophecy foretold change? Of how the world handled magic? And what if to make that change, Talullah had to use the Source?

"You're wrong." Talullah stared at the tapestry on the table. What if she wasn't strong enough? What if she did destroy magic?

"All four Gifts and still you fight what they tell you." Zeri's bright red ponytail swung behind her. "You're not paying attention, Little Seer. You're not listening."

Anticipation made Talullah's fingertips tingle, but Zeri was right. She still hesitated for some reason. Talullah took her deck of cards from her bag and shuffled them. She cut them three times, then stacked them on top of each other. She would draw one card, and if all her Sights agreed, she'd accept this was what Fate had in mind.

The stars had chosen her. The Goddesses, too, in their own way, had chosen her. And now she had her own choice to make.

"Am I supposed to take control of the Source?" She took a deep breath and flipped the top card.

The Spirit Fox, too, stilled.

The Phoenix.

The card of destruction and rebirth. Of accepting the end of one thing to move forward with something new.

The ring on her finger glowed red and gold.

Margot's voice rang in Talullah's memory then. *In my dream, you grabbed a feather.*

A flash of her own, red-stained vision came next. A red and gold feather fluttered from above.

The star symbol she'd seen everywhere. On the wall of the tunnels where she'd found the blue tapestry square. On the way to the Ceserites' compound. On the ceiling at Edda's café.

Alluded to in the prophecy Zeri had spoken to her about sacrifice and resurrection.

The phoenix.

Phoenix feathers are supposed to have protective powers, Leo, Edda's son, had said.

Some things must end in order to begin.

Sometimes things were as simple as they seemed. Sometimes all it took was a person getting out of their own way to step in the right direction. The signs had all been there. She just hadn't wanted to accept what they meant.

Sacrifice, Seer, and master of flight, in unity prevail.

And transform magic with immortal light, in control of threaded grail.

No matter what Zeri said, Talullah had to try to fix what had been broken. She secured the four squares onto the loom and pinched the needle and the glittering silver thread.

In and out she wove the thread, stitching the panel of the past to the panel of the present. Zeri watched with interest.

The balance must be restored.

Weave and sew, weave and sew.

The refrain had haunted her before, in what seemed like another life entirely. Back before she knew much about her own magic or her great-great-grandmother's grand plan for her, or the prophecy that had torn her family and the Sight community into pieces.

Now, the words comforted her. She knew how to weave and to sew. It was as natural as breathing. Talullah stitched faster, attaching the panels of the potential and the certain futures.

A confident smile spread across her face as she cinched the final knot and snapped the thread with her teeth. Words—the Suditzas' instructions—seeped up through the fabric, the spell of separation finally broken after so long.

Talullah read the words, let them sink deep into her marrow.

Where she expected fear, she found only resolve, the willpower to face it and emerge victorious. Decisiveness. And most of all, trust in herself. The Chariot incarnate.

Sacrifice, Seer, and master of flight.

The phoenix feather ring emanated a warmth that ran up her arm, through her collarbone, and to the place where Dunamai's Eye rested. "Maybe you're right after all, Spirit Fox. Maybe I will destroy magic as we know it. But I'm also going to save it."

Even if it costs my life.

CHAPTER 52

TALULLAH

Zeri's yellow eyes widened in understanding.

For the first time, when her mouth split into a grin bearing pointed teeth, Talullah didn't flinch or feel an ounce of fear. Instead, a wave of something like admiration washed over her.

"You, Talullah Bridgestone, are not the same girl I first met in Nainetha Forest." The Spirit Fox snapped her fingers, the sound muffled by the black leather gloves she wore. A red and gold iridescent feather appeared in the spirit's clasped fingers. She twirled it once, studying it.

Talullah's hand cooled and she looked down at it. The ring was gone. "What did you do?" Panic surged through her veins.

Zeri offered her the feather. "Phoenix feathers have been protecting mortals for centuries, usually as symbols meant to ease worry. Sometimes woven through fabric or encased in metal. But they are strongest in their pure form."

"So the myths are true?" Talullah accepted the feather, surprised its warmth lingered. "Phoenix feathers can save someone from death?"

The Spirit Fox looked up at the ceiling, as if searching the cracked material for stars. "Yes."

"Can I ask you another question?" Talullah asked. She stared at the gold running through the red feather.

Zeri nodded. "I think you've earned the right."

"How do you deal with Seeing the future and knowing you can't change it?"

"I am not like you, Little Seer. It's difference for spirits."

"Then how am *I* supposed to deal with it?"

"Seeing it doesn't mean it will be exactly so. Perhaps you've experienced such a thing already. Prophecies are clues. The rest is up to you." She stared at the ceiling a second longer. "Best of luck, Little Seer. Consider my debt paid."

Zeri vanished.

Talullah watched the spot where she'd been for a moment. Would she ever see or hear from Zeri again? Though the Spirit Fox's visits always brought layers of confusion, Talullah had also come to appreciate them. In her own way, Zeri had been guiding Talullah.

And now, as Gillie had said, it was time to work her magic. She gently tucked the feather into the front pocket of her trousers.

Relief and excitement encouraged her, tinged with a hint of fear. Change was always scary, and the unknown was scary, too. It was the reason so many people sought to learn about their futures. They thought knowing what was coming would prepare them. But often the opposite happened.

People learned the inevitable future and adjusted their decisions and lives accordingly, seeking to either avoid or ensure that event would happen. Talullah had seen this firsthand with her own mother. She was trying hard not to blame her mother for those decisions. It was impossible to know what Talullah herself would have done in the same situation. If *she* had a child whose destiny had been written in the stars.

Would she do everything in her power to avoid it? Or would she, like her mother, try to give her daughter every opportunity to succeed, even if that meant disappearing from her life?

If Talullah had known her life and her quest for magic would end here, with an attempt to control the Source, would she have run away and never looked back?

She shook away the philosophical questions, because now that she'd chosen her path forward, she focused on the feel of the threads and what she planned to do with them.

From the first touch of her fingertips to the colored threads, it was like coming home. She focused on how the threads tickled her hands and how they connected to one another.

The few times she'd been in Gillie's house, she hadn't realized the trees on the bottom were stitched upside down. But now it made sense why: the roots of each tree met in the middle of the image in a tangled, twisted circle. A symbol for how each phase of time was inextricably linked with the others.

She closed her eyes, used her sapphire to infuse the air with the grounding scent of cinnamon, and reached for the wisdom the Suditzas had granted her.

All I have Seen is you.

Cesera's visions, her prophecies, always came true. But not always in the way one expected. Talullah may not be able to save magic, but she was going to do her best to try.

She stitched the phoenix constellation over the ball of roots, a way to write herself into the Suditzas story.

Talullah shrugged her bag over her shoulder. If things went poorly, this might be the last house she ever stood in. She was sad it wasn't her own.

Nausea rolled through her stomach. She glanced at the front door. Her heart ached to wait for Dhal a little longer.

But now that she'd repaired the tapestry, she had to get to the Source.

Talullah had waited as long as she could.

Hating herself for leaving Dhal yet again, Talullah exited, locked the door, and conjured a Concealment spell over herself.

IN THE DANK TUNNELS, Talullah's ears filled once more with the sound of rushing. Not blood, this time.

Water.

Following the tapestry map, she descended another set of stairs. At the bottom, she paused, dialing up her senses.

Her heart pounded in her dry throat as she looked around. Three paths branched off from her current location. Which one would lead her to the Source?

Though the sandy damp stone and dark enclosed space didn't resemble the paths in the Between at all, Talullah couldn't ignore the similarities of choosing the way forward.

Her intuition tugged her toward the middle path. She confirmed with a glance at the tapestry that it would be the quickest way.

A zap of magic pinned her back to the rock wall. Her head smacked against it. A trickle of blood rolled down the side of her head, dripping onto the tapestry in her hand. Angry blue light exploded around her body and illuminated the hall.

The breath froze in her lungs as she made eye contact with her assailant. Not Veylan back from the dead. Not another guard.

Ice blond hair coiled into a crown atop her head and her smile could slice to the bone. It was the sorceress herself.

Renevelda.

CHAPTER 53

DHALIAN

*D*hal woke up in the closet-like cell, dizzy and confused. He struggled against the zapping pressure in the air, a magical suppression spell which made it difficult to sense the shadow of magic lurking in his veins.

The lantern near the door flickered twice from his efforts. But all he managed to do was confirm his worst fear: he was alone. Which meant Talullah was somewhere else, likely in danger at the hands of the impostor who'd pretended to be Kai. That cleared Dhal's mind enough to think.

He had to get out of there. To find her.

What if the sorceress got to her first?

Dhal wiggled his wrists back and forth, wincing as the rough jute rope laced with something smooth and cool rubbed against his scar.

His scar.

It was exposed again. Which meant Impostor Kai had

removed the device Margot and Penny had made for him to confuse the tracking spell. Renevelda would know exactly where he was. And when he found Talullah, the sorceress would find her, too.

Unless she already had.

Dhal spiraled for seconds into minutes. Too long spent on unproductive thoughts. He tried again to access his magic. To do what, he hadn't yet decided. He hadn't trained long enough to create strong illusions. The best he could do was strengthen Talullah's and enhance his already-sharp navigational skills.

The door to his prison burst open.

Dhal's eyes locked onto the intruder. He prepared to do whatever he could to fight. To make it out the door.

The last person Dhal expected stepped inside, bringing with him a gleaming beam of light.

The merchant Dhal had threatened at the Hidden Market. The one whose death Talullah predicted.

The one who was supposed to be dead.

He stalked over to Dhal. Was he working with the impostor? Was he here to exact revenge on Dhal for his ill-advised threats?

The merchant squinted as he bent down behind Dhal's chair. Blue sparks crackled on the tips of his fingers. "She went that way. Door at the end of the long hallway." The ropes loosened then fell from Dhal's wrists. The merchant locked eyes with him. "You'd better hurry."

Dhal nodded. "Thank you." He stood and wobbled before regaining his balance. He had so many questions, but he chose the one that mattered most to him in the moment. "Why'd you save me?"

"Your girlfriend saved my life. And in your own strange way, you had a hand in that. I tried to leave you. Turns out my conscience isn't completely hollowed-out yet." The merchant strode back to the door and peeked out. "Coast is clear. Good luck, Silk Reaper." He left without another word.

Dhal took his chance and followed. The merchant pointed toward the hallway opposite the one he himself took. Dhal was on his own, now, apparently. Not that he was complaining. The merchant may have saved his life, but the guy still gave Dhal the creeps.

No one patrolled the halls. Dhal moved as quickly and quietly as he could. What had the merchant done to all the guards?

Never mind. He didn't want to know.

At the end of the hall, Dhal found the door. It hung nearly closed, but not quite. As if someone had gone through and hadn't pulled it shut behind them.

Dhal eased it open enough to slip through. Outside, he exhaled, then headed for the safe house they'd agreed upon.

He sprinted the whole way there. But he was too late. Talullah had been there. He found stray strings of her hair on the porch and prints from her boots on the lawn.

If she'd gone without him, she had the tapestry. She'd gone to the Source. And he would find her.

DHAL TRACKED Talullah's boot prints to a building big enough to hold a set of stairs. The door hung wonky on its hinge, but he eased it open without it falling off and closed himself into the darkness.

The cavern smelled of desperation and anticipation. Or maybe that was the nervous sweat running down his forehead.

He reached again for his magic, enough to light his way. A circle of blue the size of a grapefruit appeared on the floor. He released the breath that had been wheezing in his chest since he'd awoken. So far, so good.

On light feet, he descended the stone staircase.

He clung to the slight hope that things could still work out okay. Even if that hope resembled a hesitant smudge of charcoal on a piece of parchment, the beginning of an idea, rather than a confident, thick, intentional stroke.

Still, he never thought about backing out for one second. Talullah needed him. And, selfishly, he needed her. Always had.

And maybe it was pathetic hoping she'd someday look at him the way he looked at her. Maybe it was pointless longing for their friendship, which had been forged in the fires of early childhood and solidified with every difficulty they faced together over the past decade, would suddenly turn from platonic to something more.

Hell and a half, maybe she'd choose Kai.

If that was the case, fine. The gut-wrenching pain he felt knowing he couldn't have her the way he wanted, knowing someone else did? He could live with that.

But if she *died*?

He'd never survive it. He wouldn't want to.

Dhal wove his way through the tunnels, relying on his innate sense of direction and the small tells Talullah had left behind. Traces someone else might miss, if they didn't know her the way Dhal did. The scuff marks her boots had trailed in the dirt. The obsidian strand of hair caught on the rough stone wall, as if she'd brushed against it.

Everything about the rightmost path urged him that way, like an invisible string connected him to his best friend, or like they were magnets drawn to each other.

He could almost imagine Talullah walking through there, dragging her boots through the dirt. Could almost smell the lavender that clung to her hair after she wore the cloak she'd inherited from her mother.

They knew each other better than anyone on the planet. They'd protected each other their whole lives. Had weathered every storm.

The sorceress could burn the world down for all he cared.

All that mattered was getting to Talullah.

He had to let her know she wasn't alone. Had to tell her he was proud of her. That she'd always been his true north to purpose and joy.

And that, no matter what happened in the past or present or potential or future, he loved her.

CHAPTER 54

RENEVELDA

Renevelda relished the sight of the pitiful teenage Seer in front of her. Finally, the little pain in her side would get what she deserved.

Renevelda didn't trust anyone to do this for her. She'd waited too long and had worked too hard to watch her victory slip away at the hands of a child.

This victory was going to be so sweet.

When Renevelda had first heard her spy in the rebel camp had succeeded in finding Talullah and the rest of the tapestry squares, she'd praised him. The girl had been secured. And yet, it had taken too long for him to turn the squares over to her. She'd gone looking for them.

And found the cell empty, the girl and the squares gone, and her spy's blood staining the cell floor.

It didn't take a genius to figure out the girl would head for the Source. Renevelda had assumed the gnat of a boy would be with Talullah. She'd traced the boy's scar, but on her way, Renevelda had gotten lucky. The girl had walked right into her hand, delivered by destiny.

Renevelda summoned the tapestry from Talullah's hands into her own. She'd even fixed it, the poor, naïve dear. The girl tried desperately to hold on to it. But, her weak hands were no match for the sorceress's magic. The mended fabric slipped through her fingers and glided to Renevelda, who snatched it from the air.

The power in the threads pulsed in her hand, and she savored it like fine wine. Renevelda pressed the fabric to her chest. She drank in the moment and the look of utter despair on the girl's face. Renevelda could have goaded her, and maybe in the past, she would have. But she didn't want to waste more time. Instead, she rolled up the tapestry and clutched it in her hand, leaving Talullah to slump to the ground.

The sorceress reached for the Manipulated guards' minds. She'd left a few of them at the entrance to the tunnels in case she needed backup. Now, she compelled them forward, leaving a thin trail of blue magic for them to follow.

She couldn't afford any disturbances from unwanted visitors, should anyone find their way to her.

Cleo screeched, then fluttered down, regarding the unconscious young Seer with her beady black eyes. Renevelda gestured for her bird servant to follow, and they made their way toward the Source.

The newly powered tapestry's threads glowed gold as she got closer to the center, where the tangled web of roots formed a knot in the center of the tapestry.

With each twist and turn and set of stairs descended, Renevelda's anticipation built. It pounded in her chest and arteries and stung her veins. Though she'd gone further below ground, the air became fresher the longer she walked. Cleo's wings beat above Renevelda's head as the bird circled, as impatient as the sorceress.

Finally, Renevelda reached the center of the map. In front of her loomed a wall made entirely of twisted tree trunks and vines. She approached with caution.

Embossed symbols protruded from the trunks, but Renevelda didn't bother to read them.

Entry to the Source would require proof of magic, a blood sacrifice.

Renevelda unsheathed the dagger at her hip. It gleamed bright silver in the tunnel's low light. She pricked the tip of her finger with the clean blade and smeared the blood on the wall.

Creaking sounds filled the dead-end hall as the tree roots snapped apart and retreated to reveal a doorway large enough to walk through.

The sorceress placed the dagger back in its sheath and stepped through the doorway, Cleo following close behind.

Renevelda had envisioned this place many times, had dreamed of it. Nothing could have prepared her for the splendor that awaited her.

It was like an underground palace. The ceiling hovered fifty feet above, tiled to look like the night sky, complete with constellations. White marble pillars stood on either side of the hallway entrances, which branched off from the main area, and a colorful mural ran the entire circumference of the circular space.

Against one curve, four waterfalls, each stream the thickness of Renevelda's arm and each a color of one of the Suditzas' magic, ran side by side until they trickled into the pond.

Renevelda held her breath. The place garnered more awe and respect than she'd ever given to anything else.

She couldn't, however, muster much reverence for the Suditzas themselves. They had created a wondrous, sacred space to honor magic. But they'd abandoned her in her time of need. They could have helped her all those years ago when she still believed them to be benevolent.

She'd asked them to restore her power or bestow upon her the power which she deserved. They had refused her.

And so, she'd taken it upon herself to fulfill her own destiny by whatever means necessary.

Renevelda ran her hand gently through the waterfalls' spray, not daring to graze the waterfall itself. She knew better than to touch the font without offering something in return.

The power was so pure and untainted.

And she deserved to wield it.

She spread the tapestry on the black and white tiled dais floor next to the clear pond. The waterfalls' droplets bloomed into rainbow ripples on the water's surface.

The sight reminded Renevelda of the day, so many years ago, when her tears had created ripples of her power in a puddle on the streets of Viltresor City. That day had changed her life; she'd met Eviliv.

But looking back had never moved her toward her destiny. She squashed the memory before it could fully form.

This day would change her life, too, but for the better.

Today, she'd take her power into her own hands, instead of offering it to someone else.

After all this time, she had been right. The Source was not a myth. And everyone who had told her otherwise was about to get the surprise of their lifetime.

Each of the woven trees on the tapestry glowed in their respective colors. Renevelda's own power throbbed in her veins, waiting to be amplified and released so she could finally prove to herself and everyone else that she had overcome her human blood, the tainted part of herself. She intended to replace that human part with this magic and make herself a full goddess worthy of reigning in the realm of the Divine.

Her mother and sisters would pay for their refusal to accept and acknowledge her.

She would repay their mistreatment in kind. How would they

like to be cast out from their Divine home, as they had cast her out when she was a young girl?

The Goddesses had thought they were so clever when they created the tapestry, thinking it would protect their magic from harm. But Renevelda knew the truth: it had hindered them. By hiding the tapestry for so long, they had stunted their own followers' progress. They could have been so powerful.

Renevelda had to thank them for being afraid.

And she had to thank the other Seers who had attempted to destroy the tapestry so many years ago, because they too, had only stopped themselves from gaining enough power to defeat her.

Nothing and no one could stop her now.

The instructions woven into the tapestry cautioned against using the Source's magic. They warned the magic should only be used in the direst circumstances. Renevelda had decided that she met those qualifications. What could be more dire than a half-goddess who deserved to be more?

The magic she'd painstakingly collected bubbled within the Davabere Needle like a kettle about to scream. It was a wonder, this magical object. She almost wished she had been there during its creation. Back when the group of humans who were unblessed decided to do as she was doing now and exploited their every advantage to create their own form of power.

The power pulsed. The Suditzas wanted proof she deserved to wield the Source? She'd give them proof.

Sacrifice, Seer, and master of flight, remake magic in immortal light. The prophecy had always been about her. She was sure of it. *Sacrifice*—the magic she'd collected. *Seer*—the magic she'd taught herself. *Master of flight*—who else had taken on the challenge of pushing their Manipulation magic so far as to shape-shift?

And, *remake magic in immortal light*—her aim had always

been to remake her magic, to snuff out the weakness and make herself truly immortal.

Renevelda stabbed the Needle into the tapestry, weaving her name among the symbols, solidifying her contract with the magic. It was difficult for her to get the needle in and out, as if the fabric itself was fighting her. But she gritted her teeth and persevered, weaving in and out, in and out in a steady rhythm, even as sweat beaded on her brow and her muscles quaked. Even as her fingers grew numb from the magic or exertion, or both.

Perhaps even frustration.

Renevelda Anaideia was nothing if not determined. She guided the Needle through the fabric despite the pain seizing her fingers.

With immense effort, she pulled through the last stitch, tied it off, and snipped it.

The tapestry glowed and burned and rippled, now imbued with the power she had stolen from all the Seers who had defied her and all of those who had tried to stand in her way.

The blood of her enemies would fuel her rise to the top.

Vindication was but a breath away.

Cleo hopped over, bringing the pouch of ingredients to Renevelda.

Renevelda lay the tapestry on the altar next to the pond and removed the vial of shimmering powder from her pouch. As she recited the protection spell she'd found in one of the old tomes during her decades-long research on the Source, she sprinkled the powder on her hand.

Then, she grabbed the gold-plated goblet and gently put it underneath the trickling water of the waterfall. She filled the cup to the brim with rainbow swirled liquid.

Dipping her fingers into the cup, she sprinkled a few drops on the tapestry. It sizzled at first but nothing else happened.

So far, so good.

For the next step of the spell, she folded the tapestry into fourths, rolled it like a scroll, and plunged it into the pond. An offering to the Source of the magic within, to introduce it to her name and magic.

The cavern shivered.

Water wept down the walls from nowhere.

Tree roots crawled down the sides and toward her.

Something was *very* wrong.

Renevelda didn't feel full of power at all. Her limbs wobbled. A cold sweat broke out across her hot forehead. She shivered, feverish. Even her vision blurred. She felt as if she had given everything to the Source instead of receiving from it.

She glanced around for an exit. But the roots came from every direction. They'd already grown over the doorways and knotted together.

Renevelda attempted to Manipulate them. She reached for her power, breathing hard, and bid it to slice through the roots and vines.

But in place of strength, Renevelda found a hollow nothingness.

Her mind cycled back to the day she'd stolen power from the first Ceserite. She'd spat a prophecy right before she breathed her last breath. *Sacrifice.*

The sorceress's breathing hitched. What if any sacrifice wasn't enough. What if she'd misinterpreted?

Tree roots slithered like wooden snakes toward her, ready to wrap her up and strangle her.

Cleo squawked and rose off the ground, shooting the sorceress a look.

Renevelda wanted nothing in the world more than power, than proving her worth to herself and to those who had doubted her, to those who told her she was not enough.

A twisted root reached the corner of Renevelda's boot. She stepped back to get away from it.

Her heart panged.

She'd sacrificed a great many people in her quest for power.

But nothing about her sacrifice had belonged to *her*.

What would be enough to appease the old magic?

What could she possibly give up that would be worth something to the goddesses of old? That could prove she was worthy of the power they previously denied her?

"What do you want?" she called out to no one. "More of my blood?" She tore her nail across the flesh of her arm in a frenzy. Blood welled in the scrape. She flicked the droplets into the pond.

It hissed, but the walls still wept and the roots still crawled toward her.

In her lifetime, she had valued nothing except her own ambition.

And her most loyal servant.

"You want my only companion? A true sacrifice?" She choked on the words as she shouted at the magic.

Cleo flapped higher, but Renevelda latched onto the bird's leg. Cleo struggled to get away, kicking her free leg and beating her wings in a panic, but Renevelda couldn't think straight.

Tears welled in the sorceress's eyes. Hair fell from her twisted updo across her forehead.

"Is this what you want, Suditzas? You want me to sacrifice the only creature I trust? To prove I'm willing to shed my ties to humanity?" She was screaming now, with strands of icy blond hair plastered to her face. But she'd come this far. What was a little further, if it got her what she wanted, what she deserved?

She locked eyes with the bird and her breath caught in her chest. A second of hesitation.

Cleo screeched, a plea.

Renevelda's grip tightened around the bird's leg.

Could she do it? Could she give up the one connection she had left?

CHAPTER 55

TALULLAH

Talullah woke in a groggy fog. Her head throbbed. She vaguely recalled hitting it. A touch of her fingers to the aching spot on the side of it revealed a sticky substance she assumed was blood.

Rock walls surrounded her. The air smelled like the aftermath of a fall rainstorm.

Pieces of recent events scuttled into place like ants lining up to march. She'd fixed the tapestry. And then, Renevelda.

The sorceress's icy glare was seared to the back of Talullah's eyelids, stamped in a shock of purple light. Talullah fumbled around her in search of the tapestry, though she knew it was futile. As soon as Renevelda had attacked her, she would have taken the tapestry.

Maybe she'd already used it. Maybe all of Talullah's effort had been for nothing. Maybe everything and everyone she loved had already been destroyed.

Don't give up yet, Little Seer. The Spirit Fox's voice echoed in Talullah's mind.

Talullah slipped her hand into her trouser pocket, moving her arm with care. It was sore and probably scraped and bruised, but it didn't feel broken. Her fingertips grazed along the soft phoenix feather. She still had it. The sorceress hadn't found it.

She drew a deep breath. If there was any chance Renevelda hadn't enacted the spell, Talullah had to force herself to get up. To find and stop the sorceress. To see this plan through to the end.

But she didn't have the map to navigate her to the Source.

We don't always See with our eyes.

How right her mother was.

Talullah pushed herself to standing, wincing as pain lanced through her shoulder and she wobbled on her feet.

Her stomach turned at the motion, but she forced herself to breathe. In and out. In and out. In and out.

In her wrist, her pulse beat a reminder that she wasn't yet dead. And that meant she still had a chance. The path she'd Seen with her emerald and cards could still come true.

A prickling sensation worked its way through Talullah's palm. Faint fingers of purple light crept into her field of vision from ahead. A trail.

Faint footprints streaked through with blood—her own, Talullah realized—led down the center path. She bent down and touched the nearest print to her, calling her amethyst again. She may not have the map, but she could trace the sorceress's route.

The hallways carried her through wide and narrow passages, down stairs, and around sharp corners until she came to a dead-end.

Gnarled black tree roots and vines covered a portion of the wall. They'd been braided together to seal off a doorway. Threads of colored light wove through them.

Talullah held her breath and willed her heart to slow.

Renevelda shouted on the other side of the blocked door. Cleo screeched as if struggling. Had someone else beat Talullah to the Source in hopes of opposing Renevelda?

She pressed her sapphire to strengthen her vision. Blood smeared across the silver plaque in the middle of the tree root wall. Runes pushed their way out of the roots like the first green shoots of spring breaking, too early, through the last frost of winter.

They reminded her of the runes on Igdrasil and all the prophetic trees in Ragnatri. Each tree held its own messages in its own language.

She touched them with gentle fingers like one might pet a newborn kitten.

The runes arched into her touch, making themselves more pronounced. Talullah's mind reached back to all the days she'd spent absorbing the languages of worlds she wished to visit. And she recognized these.

She translated, a bit clumsily, as she scrutinized the symbols. "Tules!"

Talullah turned, her entire body going up in chills. "Dhal! Thank the goddesses you're okay!"

Dhal ran to her and tugged her into a fierce hug. He pulled back slightly, his eyes scrutinizing every inch of her face. He ran his hands along her jawline and back up to her temple, grimacing when he touched the dried blood on the back of her head. "Who did this to you?" he growled. His eyes flashed with danger, like when the merchant had threatened her at the Hidden Market.

"Renevelda. I'm fine. I'm sorry I didn't wait longer at the safe house. I had the tapestry and I couldn't lose any more time—"

"I'm glad you didn't wait. You *had* the tapestry? Is Renevelda...?" Dhal asked. He nodded at the root-blocked door.

"She took it. She's in there with it and the Source. And I'm going to be honest. I don't know what's going to happen when I go—"

"We." He squeezed both her hands and forced her to look him straight in the eyes. "When *we* go in there to face her. You've tried pushing me away for too long. You've known me long enough to figure out I'm as stubborn as you are. I'm not going anywhere."

Talullah smiled a little. "When *we* go in there. Just be prepared."

It took her a few tries, but eventually she got all the words in the right order. The most recent prophecy Zeri had spoken to her.

Twisted roots like night, four in harmony convene.

With blood shed on stars of sleight, power taken as foreseen.

Sacrifice, Seer, and master of flight, in unity prevail.

And transform magic with immortal light, in control of threaded grail.

Death relinquished by a heart of might, an ancestor restored.

The sky weeps its blight, then will rise a new sense of accord.

As soon as Talullah finished speaking the words aloud, the branches crackled and retreated enough to make a large enough hole for her and Dhal to step through, side-by-side with hands clasped.

In the center of the room, Renevelda stood, her eyes locked on Talullah. Shock flickered over the sorceress's expression. She let go of Cleo's leg and the bird darted upward, landing on a ledge halfway up the wall. Then her lips curled into their sinister smile. "Oh, dear. I really think you should have stayed dead."

Renevelda used her magic to collect water from the Source, then sent a whip of it toward Talullah. Talullah dodged and rolled. The memory of King Eviliv being dragged into a frozen wave gnashed at Talullah's mind.

Out of the corner of her eye, Talullah glimpsed Dhal duck behind a rock and disappear. Apparently he'd learned a few more tricks.

"Don't waste everything the goddesses have built, Renevelda." Talullah breathed hard. She'd landed on her already injured shoulder, but she wouldn't show any weakness. She needed to distract the sorceress long enough to make her way up to the Source. To finish this once and for all.

"Waste it?" Renevelda laughed. "I have spent nearly my whole life looking for the Source."

Magic wrapped around Talullah's throat. It lifted her off the ground, and her feet dangled in the air. Talullah's eyes went wide as she gasped for breath.

It's an illusion. Talullah pleaded with her airway to respond to her thoughts instead of the sorceress's magic.

"I thought I only needed power to prove to the Source I was worthy. Turns out, I needed something—someone—personal."

Talullah's gaze caught on Dhal who had reappeared behind the sorceress. Gray-brown dirt coated his dark brown curls. And his hazel eyes, normally full of mirth, flashed with pure lightning.

The sorceress's magic suffocated Talullah's attempts to urge him away.

Cleo, who watched from a perch high above, studied Dhal with interest. But she didn't screech to her master. She did nothing to warn Renevelda.

The sorceress pressed the Davabere Needle ever so slightly to Talullah's fingertip, drawing out her raw magic.

Despite herself, Talullah buckled under the magic's force. She bit the inside of her cheek to keep from crying out.

The power trailed up the Needle in a golden thread. Her vision grew hazy.

The ceiling above shone bright with familiar constellations.

"You have been a scourge on my life ever since your birth, Talullah Bridgestone. And I will waste no tears at your demise." She pushed Talullah's tired body with her booted foot until she was at the edge of the water, her nose nearly touching the surface.

This was the moment Talullah had been waiting for. Time to give herself to the Source and steal the magic right from under Renevelda.

Talullah dragged her hand across the back of her head. Red blood painted her fingertips.

Just before she heaved herself over the edge, the water's reflection showed a shadow leap from behind the sorceress and connect with her body.

Talullah hit the water first, followed by two more splashes. The water wasn't deep, not nearly as deep as the Fountain on the Isle of Salire. But it was freezing. She struggled to the surface with a gasp.

Not quickly enough.

Renevelda, soaked through and seething, held Dhal up by the front of his shirt. "It seems you have a death wish."

Dhal locked eyes with Talullah. "I would die to save the girl I love."

A flash of red light illuminated behind Talullah's eyes. A glimpse at the next five seconds.

Sacrifice.

"No!" It was supposed to be her.

All Talullah could do was react. Cleo swooped down over her head. Talullah held up the phoenix feather. Cleo grabbed it and dropped it in front of Dhal, who caught it, a flash of surprise in his eyes.

Right as Renevelda's blade pierced him through the heart.

CHAPTER 56

TALULLAH

Talullah's scream echoed through the cave, reverberating off the walls. Or maybe it came out silent, the sound trapped inside her mind.

What if Zeri was wrong? What if her visions weren't literal, but metaphorical? What if the phoenix's protective magic was a myth?

It has to work. It has to. Please let it work. Please let it work.

The prayer took over every conscious part of Talullah's body. The world moved in slow motion as the sorceress dropped Dhal's body on the platform by the Source, his blood seeping out in a perfect ring around his body, and turned her attention to Talullah.

Talullah hauled her own body out next to him, her instincts triumphing over frozen limbs. "Dhal! Dhal, wake up!" She located his pulse in his neck, weak but detectable. Just barely.

Frantic energy coursed through her body. What could she do? She wasn't a healer. *Dhal's bag.* Where was his bag? It would have the salves from Mr. Miscian. One would stop the bleeding. It had to. But the sack lay abandoned somewhere beyond where Talullah's tear-blinded gaze could reach.

She pressed her hands over the wound as hard as she could. The phoenix feather, now completely red with blood, stuck to Dhal's chest.

"A sacrifice made of love," Renevelda said. "How quaint. And yet, how convenient."

Renevelda's voice brought Talullah back to the cavern. She tore her gaze away from Dhal.

Rainbow liquid from the waterfall flowed toward the sorceress, like an insect drawn to light. It climbed up her limbs and over her face until all Talullah knew was the suffocating feeling of grief and shattered hope and dreams left unfulfilled.

She'd failed.

Dhal was dead.

The sorceress had won.

"Talullah!" Kai's voice carried from somewhere down one of the blocked hallways. "Are you in there?"

"We're coming!" Another voice, so familiar and comforting Talullah held her breath. Could it be?

Five people barreled through the door. Kai led the charge, his hair a mess, his face streaked with dirt, and his clothes torn and stained. "I came as fast as I could." He bent over panting. The second of hesitation cost him.

Fibers of sparkling gold magic zapped from Renevelda's fingers and formed a golden cage illusion over him and Zinni before they could move out of the way. The woman with the headscarf and the burly man always with her—Theresa and Edouard, Kai had told her—ran in opposite directions, drawing Renevelda's focus away from the Source.

The fifth arrival rolled behind one of the marble pillars just in time to dodge another cage spell. But Talullah didn't miss the way her long black braid swung like a thick rope over her shoulder.

Talullah's breath hitched. "Mother?"

She ran to Talullah, breathless, up the steps to the Source. Her long black braid swung behind her. Renevelda tried to freeze her, but she dodged the spell and stopped by the water, crouching next to Talullah.

Theresa gritted her teeth while her fingers flexed and curled, her Manipulation magic pulling rocks free from the wall with thin but strong strands of blue magic. She hurled them at the sorceress with a guttural yell.

"What are you doing?" Talullah asked.

"We came for you. You are not alone, Talullah."

"We're here, too!" shouted Silas as he entered the room, followed by Maeve. Two guards chased them, their eyes swirling light blue.

Renevelda held her hands outstretched toward them to try to take back control. But she couldn't split her strength into so many pieces. The clench of her jaw and the way her arms quavered told Talullah the sorceress was reaching her limits.

Silas took one guard down and bound him with a length of rope. "When this is over, we'll make sure you're safe."

The second guard came toward Maeve, but Silas slipped behind him and tied him down next to the other one.

Sweat trickled down Talullah's forehead and mixed with the layer of water on her skin. Her own strength was waning from using so much magic.

"Enough." Renevelda compelled the gold-plated goblet on the cavern floor to zip into her hand. She dipped it into the Source. The water swirled with rainbow magic and smoke rose above it, making it seem as if it were hot instead of the icy death-trap it truly was.

"Your love's sacrifice won't be in vain." The sorceress smirked then tipped the cup to her lips.

Talullah's mother grasped Talullah's hand and new energy surged into Talullah's limbs. With as much strength as she could muster, Talullah manipulated the cup in Renevelda's hand so it melted, then reformed it in her own.

"No. It won't." She'd do everything in her power to bring down the sorceress.

"The Source's power will overwhelm you." Renevelda smiled.

"I guess we're about to find out." Talullah's body protested, but she let go of her mother's hand and crawled her way to the edge of the pool. She shoved her bloody hands—Dhal's blood and her own mixed together—into the water.

For Dhal.

Talullah gulped the water. It ached like death, at first. A sharp pain that faded to nothingness in an instant. Blackness loomed in the corners of her vision as pure magic entered her system.

At the same time, Renevelda cupped her hands and dipped them into the Source. She brought the water to her mouth and drank. "Now we'll see who's really worthy of the magic."

Talullah wobbled on shaky legs. Vaguely, she heard Dhalian calling her name. That couldn't be right. Dhal was dead. The sorceress had killed him.

A frantic sob escaped her.

And now Talullah would make Renevelda pay.

Guided by the Source's magic and her own, Talullah squeezed her hands into a fist and willed Renevelda's illusions to release her allies.

Renevelda stood taller, flexing her fingers. Her eyes glinted like a rainbow refracted in broken glass. "Tell me, Little Seer. How do you feel? Because I could conquer a world."

Talullah's limbs vibrated with power, maybe too much of it. Could she hold it all inside her or would it burn her to ash from the inside out? The heat was almost too much to bear. It was like fire and ice in her veins all at once.

She needed to focus. Talullah reached for Katamai's magic to ground her, to help her think.

But Renevelda wasted no time. Hands splayed wide in front of her, the sorceress conjured a wall, separating Talullah and Renevelda from Talullah's allies. "It's just me and you now, Little Seer. Let's see who the Source deems worthy."

The ground beneath Talullah's feet shook. Talullah's knees hit the ground, but no pain shot through her bones. The Source's magic bolstered her.

You've been here before, her amethyst reminded her. The first time she'd faced Renevelda, the sorceress had tried to isolate her inside the Firefall of the Unforgiven. Had forced the spirits inside Talullah's mind to drive her mad.

But it hadn't worked. Because Talullah wasn't alone.

She wasn't alone now, either.

"That's where you're wrong," Talullah gritted out. The Source's magic scalded her blood. She formed a fist, fighting the pressure the sorceress applied against her body.

But instead of sending the magic at Renevelda, Talullah hurled it at the illusory wall the sorceress had erected.

The crackle started in the ground beneath Talullah's feet. It shot at the wall and climbed it, rainbow magic spreading like ivy until it covered the whole illusion. It shattered like the mirror Talullah had broken in the hall.

"What a sweet trick," Renevelda said. "If you'd like to watch your friends die, who am I to stop you?"

"Talullah!" multiple voices called as they rushed toward her.

Renevelda lazily wiggled her fingers and blackened tree roots crept across the floor toward each of Talullah's allies. One-by-one, the spelled tree roots captured them. The roots wound up Theresa's legs first, then Edouard's, and Kai's.

"No!" Talullah called. She used her own magic to pull the roots back, to convince them to retreat. But she wasn't strong enough.

"Ready to give up?" Renevelda asked.

Roots claimed Talullah's mother next, capturing her near the edge of the platform. The magic trees pinned Maeve and Silas to the wall.

Talullah sent magic to each of them, but she couldn't splinter herself and save everyone. It would take all her concentration to free even one of them.

"Should I kill them first and put them out of their misery?" The sorceress stalked around Talullah. "Or should I entomb them in the trees and let them suffocate slowly? Which would you prefer for yourself?"

Gnarled roots inched toward Talullah, too. She clenched her jaw against the pain of the Source's power surging through her, begging to be let out. Instead of running away, she let the roots come. The first one wrapped around her right boot and curled over her leg, like the jellyfish that had tried to drown her.

She'd survived then by using her Gifts.

Talullah touched the root. The runes grazed her fingers and sucked her into a vision.

Her future-self studied the stitches she'd added to the tapestry—the phoenix pattern—as they glowed bright as the clear night sky. Above her head, the constellations illuminated.

The rest of the Suditzas' tapestry glowed as well. All the extra markings that represented everyone the Suditzas' had Gifted.

It clicked, then, what Talullah needed to do.

The vision released her to the chaos of the cavern. Renevelda approached Talullah now, where the spelled roots held her in place, seemingly helpless and beat and halfway to death.

Looks could be deceiving.

The Suditzas created the tapestry to unite their Gifts and to make magic stronger by doing so.

The Source's magic pounded against her skull, coursed too hot through her body, made it hard to think and breathe. It was never meant to be wielded by one alone. That's why it was trying to push its way out of her. Not because she was unworthy of using it. To warn her, because she *was* worthy. Because she understood it was meant to be shared.

Renevelda was right. It could consume her, if she let it. If she refused to understand its true purpose: to unite instead of divide.

Like turning on a spigot, she eased off the hold on the Source's magic and let it drain into the root, emptying it from her body. The rainbow trail slithered along the root and away from Talullah, toward the roots trapping her allies.

The roots of all the magic trees connect just as the magic waterways all connect to the Source. Edda's words echoed in Talullah's mind as the magic spread and illuminated the roots across the cavern. It loosened the bindings and covered her allies in a rainbow sheen.

"What are you doing?" Kai called.

"What she has been destined to do since birth," Talullah's mother said. "Changing magic as we know it."

"It has always been meant to be shared."

Renevelda scoffed. Her eyes swirled with a frenzied rainbow of magic and elation. "You're stupider than I thought. You're giving up everything you've worked to find. Your once chance of coming out of this alive."

"If you don't let it go, it will consume you," Talullah whispered. "It already is." The sorceress's already pale skin looked translucent. "I saw a bit of myself in you, Renevelda, as much as I never wanted to admit it." A bone-deep exhaustion settled over Talullah's body and into her voice. "I read your story in Praeteriti. What your mother and sisters did to you…you didn't deserve it."

Slowly, Talullah's allies drew nearer to her until they stood in a line opposite the sorceress.

Renevelda sneered. "I took my life into my own hands and molded it into my destiny. I gained the power of the Source through my own willpower, and I am strong enough to hold it. Stronger than you could have ever hoped to be. Your pity doesn't serve me."

"That's part of the problem. You believe everything and everyone exists to serve you. And if you don't release the power, it's going to take your life." Talullah held up the Suditzas' tapestry, soaked through with Source water and stained with blood. "They never meant for it to be like this."

"It doesn't matter what they wanted. And I'm tired of your lecture." Renevelda raised her hand to cast magic at her, perhaps to finally pierce her through the heart, but a shimmering shield appeared in front of Talullah.

Her line of allies held strong, their hands all held out in front of them, using the magic she'd given them to protect her.

The gnarled roots crept across the floor.

Renevelda attempted to turn them back, but they only moved faster toward her. The first one curled up her left leg then wrapped around her hips. She struggled against it for a moment, and then a sickening smile curled her lips. "The roots are all connected, aren't they?"

The sorceress dug her nails into the root and stripped away the top layer, exposing the threads of magic beneath. She pressed the threads and inhaled, drawing the magic into her fingers.

Her veins turned red, blue, green, and purple, all the colors of the power. She looked like one of the transport trees with its threads of color winding throughout it. For a moment, Renevelda's eyes sparkled with the surge of power.

The root, now drained, fell to the floor.

Renevelda studied the veins in her hands, then looked up at Talullah. "You were too weak. But I am strong."

Talullah took a step back. She joined hands with her allies, forcing her remaining strength into the shield they'd created. Sweat trickled down her forehead as she touched the root Renevelda had scraped and tried to give the magic back to it. Back to the trees, back to the Source. Back where it belonged.

The root curled under Talullah's touch and reclaimed its hold on the sorceress's ankle.

The smile faded from Renevelda's face, morphing to a grimace. She doubled over and heaved.

Still, the sorceress straightened upright. Fought against the heat Talullah knew was burning inside her.

The power turned on her, consumed her from the inside, like the illusions she'd used on Dhalian and countless others.

Finally, Renevelda shrieked.

She crumbled into a pile on the floor, breathing shallow, ragged breaths. A rainbow lightning strike shocked the sorceress's body. It turned her form into a pile of shimmering dust.

Talullah's whole body shook. Another death. Tears flowed from her eyes as she sank to her knees, her body so spent it couldn't hold her upright any longer. She couldn't believe it was finally over. When she and Dhal got home—

Oh.

There was no "her and Dhal."

There never would be again.

Talullah approached the lifeless body of her best friend. The boy she loved.

Dhal looked so small and fragile, though Talullah would never think of him that way. Not after he'd proved his friendship and loyalty time and again, especially in the last hour.

He'd found her. Had died for her.

She crouched at his side.

He'd always been her true north, guiding her toward the best version of herself.

And now?

Now, she was completely lost.

A tree root curled around his hip, as if cradling him. At Talullah's touch, it released its hold. The phoenix feather clung to Dhal's chest, right where Renevelda's blade had gone through. Where blood had stained his shirt, rainbow colors shimmered.

Everyone present gathered around her, the smell of dirt and blood and sweat tangible evidence they'd come to help. People who loved her, others whom she barely knew. But the only person she wanted couldn't hug her back.

"I kept tabs on him while I was gone," Talullah's mother said softly. "I always knew he loved you."

The steady stream of tears turned to rapids wracking her. Talullah sobbed. "*I* killed him." Dunamai's Eye heated against her chest. "I could go back. I could take it all back." She wiped her eyes, the wild fervor of possibility thawing her blood. "I could change it. I *have* to change it. Now that I know what she's going to do, I can stop her before it gets this far. Someone can intervene. I thought the vision—but I must have been wrong— but I know better now—" She fumbled with her necklace, seeking the amethyst. But she'd need to go to Praeteriti. Get a book to change. But whose book? Her own? Dhal's?

A cough broke through the flurry of her panic, then the sound of spilled water.

Talullah looked up, eyes wide. Her breath stopped in her throat. Fresh tears spilled down her face as Dhal's eyes flickered open.

"Tules. Don't. You. Dare."

Talullah's whole body flushed with heated disbelief. Maybe she'd wake up in a second and find this was a dream, and she'd have to return to the nightmare of real life without Dhal.

Maybe the sorceress had knocked her unconscious, and this was all a nightmare.

"Dhal, are you really here, alive?"

"I think so?" Dhal coughed out, his lungs wheezy and breathless. On shaking hands he clumsily pushed himself upright into a seated position. "What happened?" He blinked as if he'd just woken from a dream, and his eyes widened as his gaze darted around the cavern, at all the people. They'd all stepped back to give Talullah and Dhal some space. "Where's Renevelda?"

"She's gone, Dhal," Talullah said. "We won."

Dhal exhaled, his shoulders dipping. A slight smile curved his cracked lips. "Of course we did. I never doubted you, Tules. Not for a second."

"It wasn't me. It was all of us. You especially."

Dhal's smile faded. The glint in his eyes dulled. "I remember now. She, ah, well, she stabbed me, didn't she?" He placed his hand right over the wound, covering the phoenix feather. He ran his other hand through his hair, like he always did when he was nervous. "Look, about what I said before Renevelda, you know, killed me." His voice strained on the words, rumbled with fatigue and embarrassment. He inhaled sharply and exhaled with a pained hiss, his face taut. "I hope this doesn't make things weird."

Talullah's mouth split into a smile so large it tugged on her wounds. But she didn't care about the pain. "Dhal?" she said softly.

"Yeah?" His gaze landed on the ground.

"Look up."

He did, his hazel eyes meeting hers.

She kissed him.

He kissed her back.

And it was the answer to so many years of questions. The exclamation point at the end of the chapter she'd been hoping to finish and the turn of a fresh page into something new and better and, hopefully, with fewer threats of death.

Though their love had somehow, already, conquered that too.

Dhal pulled away first, slowly, and enough that he could use his lips to speak. "Maybe we should continue this conversation

at another time. Without an audience. And perhaps when I've
had a chance to wash off the smell of the afterlife?"

Talullah's cheeks burned at remembering they weren't alone.
"Right. Wait. You went to Praeteriti?"

Dhal touched his forehead to hers, his eyes once again alight
with mischief. "Cece says hi."

CHAPTER 57

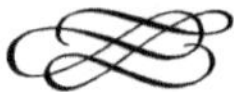

KAI

*K*ai couldn't make himself look away. The chemistry between Talullah and Dhalian was undeniable. And if he'd had doubts before about their feelings for each other, their kiss sure cleared all of those up.

Talullah stepped away from Dhal, her reluctance to leave him evident in the way her eyes lingered on him, as if she blinked he might disappear, and approached Kai. She tucked her shiny black hair behind her ears. "Can we talk?"

"Yeah. Of course." Time for the dreaded breakup speech. Anyone with eyes could see it coming. Though could it be a breakup if they were never truly together?

Kai chanced a glance at Dhalian, but he was busy being checked over by Talullah's mother, Silas, and Maeve.

Talullah led him to a little alcove away from everyone else. Kai laughed to himself on the inside. If he hadn't witnessed her and Dhal kissing, he might feel differently about the coming conversation. Like it could be going his way.

"Look," Kai said, "you don't have to do this." His defenses were already up, a steel shield to fend off the inevitable heartbreak.

"Can you please let me talk? I owe you an explanation." She took a deep breath. "I liked you, Kai. I need you to know that my feelings for you were real."

Liked. Were.

"But the truth is, I gave away most of my heart a long time ago. I wasn't sure how Dhal felt, especially after I changed the timeline. I tried to bury my feelings for him."

"Those things always come to the surface eventually," Kai said, a sad smile appearing on his face, surprising him. "And honestly, the guy literally took a blade to the chest and came back to life for you. There's no room to compete with that."

Talullah sighed heavily. She glanced at Dhal, then back again. "I don't want you to think I was leading you on. I guess maybe I was. But I didn't mean to. It wasn't intentional."

Kai shivered from the chill that swept through the cavern. "I know, Talullah. I don't blame you. And I hope you know that I would never have joined Renevelda's side. I didn't know about Veylan's plans until it was too late."

"I believe you. And for what it's worth, I'm sorry for any pain I've caused you." Talullah's dark brown eyes met his.

Though his heart hurt—and likely would for a good long while—at knowing she didn't feel the same anymore, he wouldn't let the pain consume him. "You gave me a gift, you know?"

She cocked her head to the side. "What's that?"

"I learned that I can share my true self with someone. Other than with Zinni, I've never had that before. So, thank you. For truly seeing me."

"You're welcome. I hope you use all your Gifts for good. What will you do now?"

Kai blew a breath through his lips. "I'm not sure. I guess regroup with Prince Alexander and King William. The territories still need leaders."

"Maybe the prince will need an adviser?"

Kai nodded, smiling at the ground. "I think I may be in the position to ask for that promotion."

"Thank you for everything, Kai. I have a feeling we'll be working together again. As long as you're not opposed." She raised a questioning brow.

"I'm not opposed at all." As the words left his mouth, he tasted their truth. He'd still be coming to terms with this new normal for a while, but Talullah had wiggled her way into his life, and he wasn't ready for that to end. "Is this a feeling or something you've Seen?"

She shrugged, a smile that matched his winding its way through the dirt on her cheeks. "Maybe a little bit of both this time. Take care, Kai. Scry sometime, okay?"

"I will. What are you going to do now that the sorceress is gone, and the prophecy has been fulfilled?"

Talullah's eyes sparkled. "I've got a few ideas in mind. But there is one thing I have to do first."

CHAPTER 58

TALULLAH

As Talullah approached the outside of the magical barrier that had both protected and suffocated her as a child, nerves sent tingly pokes through her entire body. She'd been waiting for this moment ever since she cast the reinforcement spell on the town. Ever since she'd first decided that she needed to protect everyone inside.

She recognized now the irony of the situation.

Didn't regret it, though. She understood now what the Founders of River Hill must have felt when they decided to isolate their community because of their fear and desperate need for safety.

They'd sacrificed everything for the slim chance that they could remain hidden. But as the prophecy had stated, they were always destined to be found, whether by Renevelda or someone else. Their secrecy couldn't last forever.

With Prince Alexander ruling one of the territories and a

council of Seers and non-magic users being formed, it was time to fulfill the final part of the prophecy. It was time to reintroduce River Hill and its inhabitants to the rest of the world.

Many of the townspeople living inside the protective spell had never been outside of it. They'd never gone to the Hidden Market or ventured into Viltresor City or Terrapese.

They'd never experienced anything outside their small community. Talullah drew a sharp inhale at the knowledge that doing so might terrify some of them.

But she'd finally come to trust her visions and herself, and she'd Seen that this would be good for her community. They no longer had to fear Renevelda or the rule of people who sought to destroy them for their ancestors' treason.

It was time to face their fears and discover who they could be without the barrier. The magic had protected them long enough.

Dhal gripped her hand tightly. Now that she knew his true feelings, and he knew hers, the gesture filled her with joy. They had always been meant to be. Even if neither of them had seen it, they had certainly felt it. Stepping over the line between friends and more was like crossing their own barrier.

The ghost of their first kiss still lingered on Talullah's lips as she squeezed Dhal's hand and took a deep, cold breath, her eyes fixed on the shimmering glow of the barrier and the rip her sister had made.

"Are you ready?" he asked her.

She nodded. "It's time." She removed her supplies from her bag and arranged them on the ground next to her.

Soft footsteps and the faint scent of lavender urged Talullah to look over her shoulder. "Sorry, it took me so long," her mother said. "I had to pack up a few extra things."

"That's okay," Talullah said. "We haven't started yet."

To say things had been uncomfortable between them over the past few days would be to ignore all the nuances of their relationship and situation.

Talullah had chosen to forgive her mother's absence during her childhood and early adolescence. Knowing what she did now about her own power, her mother's power, and Sight magic in general, there were too many variables to hold blame and grudges. She'd spent half her life alternating between wishing her mother would come home and seeking a true reason to hate her.

Her mother's intentions had been good. Talullah didn't want to punish her anymore.

Besides, Kai and his group had only been there to help because her mother had Seen Talullah's future. She'd known how to navigate the tunnels because of the prophecy that had haunted her for her whole life.

Talullah's mother opened her recipe book and propped it up on a stand. The same book that had failed young Talullah in the search for her mother. The same one that had given her the key to creating the spell they were about to reverse. In time, she would ask her mother how much she'd known about Talullah's journey to this moment.

For now, they had a job to do.

Talullah handed Dhal the Davabere Needle. He gripped it carefully by its middle. After this spell, Talullah would give it to the council so it could be kept safely in a vault.

Talullah's Scry bracelet buzzed on her wrist. She slipped it off and pressed the sapphire. Her sisters' and father's faces appeared in the shiny bubble. They walked toward her from the other side of the barrier. It was completely opposite the vision she'd had in the Between. When her sisters had walked away from her, lamenting her absence at the upcoming Winter Festival. Goosebumps prickled Talullah's arms. How close were they to that reality? To one where Talullah never came home?

She blinked back the hot tears forming in the corners of her eyes.

"You don't think you're going to do this without us, do you?

Because, as I recall, we were pretty integral in this whole thing being successful," Margot said, not allowing their father to get a word in edgewise.

"Wouldn't dream of it, Mar," Talullah said. "I was about to Scry you. Nice mirror, by the way."

Margot preened. "Turns out Great Aunt Mirella doesn't play favorites."

"I got one, too!" Penny yelled, trying to push her way in front of Margot.

Margot rolled her eyes. "Even though she can't use it on her own. She's not like us."

"Sight powers or no, everyone has a place. And who knows? Maybe her Gifts haven't expressed themselves yet," Talullah said. "But we can talk about that later."

Dhal and Talullah's mother stood in line with Talullah, the three of them mirroring her father and sisters on the other side.

From beside her, Talullah's mother breathed in sharply. "They're so beautiful. I hope—"

Talullah squeezed her mother's hand. "It will be okay. It might take a while, but they'll warm up."

"Ready?" Dhal said into Talullah's Scry.

"More than ready," said Talullah's father.

Dhal pricked his finger first with the end of the Davabere Needle that took power. A quick touch. A bead of bright red blood with a slight silvery sheen welled on his fingertip. His encounter with the Source had strengthened his Sight powers. They still weren't on par with Talullah's, but only time would tell what he was capable of. Maybe Sezna Seers could be made after all.

Talullah pricked hers next, not even feeling the sting. Talullah's mother did the same.

On the other side of the barrier, Talullah's family each poked their fingers with individual sewing needles.

The sight made Talullah think of when she'd pricked herself

while making Penny's dress for the Sunflower Festival. She'd been worried about bleeding on the fabric, about permanently changing it.

Now, everyone present had willingly sacrificed a part of themselves to stain the fabric of Time, to permanently alter River Hill by reintroducing it to the greater world.

Margot handed a glowing vial of golden liquid—the antidote to Talullah's spell—to Penny and her father, keeping one for herself.

"Margot," her mother said with pride and awe, "that looks perfect."

Margot blushed. "I just followed the instructions." But Talullah could tell the compliment hit her sister deep inside her heart.

In tandem, Margot, Penny, and Talullah's father all squeezed their fingers over their vials. The red blood dipped into the gold, swirling into striations but never fully mixing, until the solution glittered like the phoenix feather.

Talullah's mother presented matching vials to Talullah and Dhal, keeping the last for herself. They performed the ritual too.

"On the count of three," Talullah said. "One…two…three."

They all flung the contents of their vials at the barrier. A sound like thunder boomed as the potion hit the magic, as if it were a large hammer striking solid stone instead of liquid touching spell.

Overhead, the sky turned dark red. It shifted to blue and green and purple before finally settling on gold. It shimmered for a moment before it exploded in a shower of drops. It wasn't rain, though, because it wasn't wet.

The barrier peeled apart like petals from a flower or leaves from a tree. Like the ashes that had descended when the Between had started to disintegrate.

They floated down, down, down, and Talullah watched with bated breath as the centuries-old magic faded away.

The sky weeps its blight, then will rise a new sense of accord.

And then there was nothing standing between her and her family anymore. She rushed forward as fast as she could and wrapped them all in a tight hug, intending to never, ever let them go again.

Her mother and Dhalian gave her the moment she needed to collect herself. She didn't even try to stop the tears from flowing. Months of pent-up guilt and regret spilled from her eyes. She let them all come, allowing the tears to cleanse her, leaving only love.

Her father stepped forward finally, gazing at her mother with a look of overwhelming relief. He pulled her into a strong hug and wept. "I'm so glad you're finally home."

It was starkly different from the reunion Alexander's parents had. Talullah knew then that she was so lucky to have parents who cared for and trusted each other as much as hers did. Her father had never given up hope that his wife would come home. Even in the darkest moments of loneliness and struggle, he had unwavering faith in her and in Talullah's ability to bring them all back together.

He had to have known more than he let on throughout these last years, but he had done as Talullah's mother had asked and hadn't revealed anything that could upset her chance of success.

He'd made a great sacrifice. They all had. And they would continue to do so. Because that's what they did to protect the ones they loved.

EPILOGUE

TALULLAH

Talullah stepped out the front door and onto the porch of her family's cottage. She breathed in the crisp morning air and stretched her arms high overhead. She'd slept well last night. She'd been sleeping better over the last few months, now that things with the Council were starting to even out.

It had taken months of contacting Seers across the territories, of explaining the sorceress's intentions and the use of the Source. Of showing the memories stored in Talullah's amethyst and convincing the world the Suditzas' tapestry was real, not created out of political ambition. Of meetings and negotiations to come up with a structure that suited each of the Sight factions, as well as included nonmagical humans and nonhuman magic users.

Gillie hadn't been interested, at first, when Talullah approached him about the idea of participating. Had used the word "Wrecker" more times than Talullah could count. But after gallons of elderflower honey and pots of tea shared during weekly visits, he'd finally warmed to the thought of considering her request.

He'd sat in on his first few meetings via Scry, and just last week, he'd joined in person. Sure, the Wood Faerie had scowled the whole time with his arms crossed, but progress was progress.

Kai and Alexander had visited from Terrapese once a quarter. They'd offered to give the Council the ledger Kai had helped create under King William, but the Council representatives had all agreed they wanted to start their governing term with transparency and free will. The ledger's signees had offered their information under duress.

The Council burned the book instead.

It hadn't been easy, by any means, and it would continue to be difficult. Arguments abounded during Council meetings and agreements were hard-won. Change required discomfort, discussion, concession, and compromise. But the near-fall into a world without autonomy grounded them all in gratitude. At the end of the day, they were all fighting for the same things.

Talullah could hardly believe it had been nearly a year since she and her friends had faced off against Renevelda for the last time. She didn't need her amethyst to recall that day in immense detail, but she preferred to keep it at bay as a dull memory.

There was no need to revisit it, especially not now, when things were finally settled. She couldn't remember the last time she'd been content and complete without having to use her sapphire.

She put a hand over her eyes to shield them from the sun. It was already getting warm. Her gaze landed on the silhouettes of the figures she sought in the near distance. She slipped her feet into the worn leather boots she kept on the porch and made her way over to her family.

Her mother greeted her first with a wide smile. She flicked

her long braid over her shoulder. "Well, look who decided to join us."

Déjà vu shivered over her like cool rain. This felt familiar, like one of the visions she'd had in the Between when she'd walked her paths of the Potential. In that path, her mother teased her about going to a dance with Dhal.

Talullah marveled at how much and so little of a future could be the same. She hadn't gone to a dance with Dhal last night.

She couldn't stop the smile from spreading across her face. They would be going to one that night, though.

The Seers' Council was throwing a celebration to commemorate the first anniversary of its establishment, which happened soon after Talullah helped to rewrite the future of magic for not only herself, but the rest of the world.

It had taken nearly the full year to come to agreements that would sustain the territories and ensure peace reigned between the Sight factions as well as non-magic users, but it had been work that was well worth it.

King Alexander and his adviser, Kai, had spearheaded many of the policies.

Talullah had served as an advisory member of the council, representing her age group. The Council recognized the value in hearing opinions spanning demographics.

"I hoped I'd find you out here," she said to her mother. "What are you planting?"

"Russian Sage and Geraniums," Penny answered. She wiped her forehead, leaving a streak of fresh dirt on her light brown skin.

"And we're going to put an herb garden over there." Margot pointed to the hazelnut tree Talullah and her mother had planted long ago. "Maybe some lavender."

Talullah kneeled on the earth while her mother and sisters rattled off the names of plants Talullah had never heard of.

"I'm surprised you two got such an early start today." Talullah raised her eyebrows.

"They were up with the sun," their mother replied, laughing. She used her sleeve to gently wipe the dirt from Penny's face.

Penny pretended to squiggle away, then leaned in and rested her head on her mother's shoulder.

"Are you excited to start your apprenticeship, Penny?" Talullah asked.

Penny nodded, and her blond hair fell forward. She brushed it out of the way. "But I still have a few years of studying to do before then. Though, the master mechanic said I can sit in on some classes, if I want to. He even gave me plans for some simple machines that I can practice on my own."

"What about you, Mar? Any thoughts about the future?" Talullah asked her middle sister.

Margot shrugged, but then a shy smile replaced her frown. "Mother offered to teach me to make some of the things in her potion book."

Thick gratitude welled up in Talullah's throat as she observed her two sisters getting to know their mother.

Tallulah had known her for seven years before she'd disappeared, but they had no memories of her, other than what Talullah and their father could tell them. A new kind of warmth spread from her heart outward. Joy. Genuine and complete joy at her family becoming whole again.

Talullah's father came around from the back of the house with his new shiny cane in hand. His legs were much stronger now, thanks to some tonics from the healers they'd met in the city and the ones who'd come to the new not-so hidden market.

"Are you headed to the market now?" Talullah's father asked.

"Yes. I want to check that everything is running smoothly and to see Baako, of course."

"And Dhal will meet you there?" Talullah's mother asked.

"Actually," a rich baritone said, from behind Talullah. "I thought I'd surprise you, and we could go together."

Talullah whirled around and threw her arms around Dhal, her best friend in the world, and as of a year ago, her boyfriend. "I thought you weren't getting back until later."

Dhal shrugged. "I left a few hours early. Norr couldn't be mad. I've been putting in overtime lately. Plus, Norr is a romantic, so he let me go without much of a fuss."

Talullah beamed, then took the bouquet of yellow sunflowers out of Dhal's hand and went inside with him to put them in a vase of water.

Afterward, they walked hand-in-hand to the place where the magic barrier used to separate River Hill from the rest of the world. A phantom tingle shivered over her as she passed through, even though the barrier no longer existed. Maybe that was a hint at another timeline. A time in which she'd failed. Or a time in which they'd never been threatened by Renevelda at all.

She counted the stumps out loud until they reached the edge of the market. It had become a large gathering place between the two territories for open trade and community. It was bustling now, and though the market used to meet only quarterly, under guise and bribes, it was now open almost every day.

The sun shone on her face as she and Dhal strolled through the market with their hands clasped together. It would turn cold soon, but Talullah didn't mind. Each season brought its own challenges and celebrations and opportunities for joy.

She thought back to the day when she'd bought fabric for Penny's dress for the Sunflower Festival, when she'd met Gwen Caprico for the first time at her tent and had purchased the heart-shaped compass that had ultimately led her to this place in life.

Over the past year, she'd often wondered which decisions had changed the direction of her life. The old habit of focusing on the past and what-ifs died hard, but she'd gotten much better at acknowledging them and letting them pass, instead favoring the Katamian magic in her that helped her stay in the moment. There were times, of course, to use her other powers to recall the past or look to the future.

They made their way over to the familiar tent with brightly colored fabric swaying at the entrance. Baako was a man of habit and hadn't changed a thing about his stall's appearance, despite how much his business had grown.

Talullah stopped in the fluttering doorway and watched silently for a moment as Baako spoke to a young man who looked to be about Margot's age. Baako pointed and gestured with his hands as he explained something. The boy nodded, his pale brows furrowed in concentration against his pinkish skin. Talullah could tell he was absorbing every single word the old man said.

Talullah knocked gently on the post holding up the fabric door. Baako looked over. He grinned at her, and with a twinkle in his eye, gave her an exasperated sigh. "Not here to buy more cinnamon, are you? Because I'm sold out."

She laughed. "Are you sure about that? Because I see about ten vials right there." She pointed at the dark red powder in their glass tubes with wooden stoppers.

Baako harrumphed. "Those are reserved for my favorite customers."

Talullah gave a mock-affronted look, then asked, "Who's this?"

The boy walked over to her, pushed his shoulders back, and stretched his hand out for her to shake. "Marius Hardy, ma'am. I'm going to be apprenticing with Master Baako."

"Apprenticing," Talullah said, shaking the boy's hand. "Aren't you a little young to apprentice?"

He nodded, his nearly-black hair flopping across his forehead, but then broke out with a smile revealing three gaps where he'd lost baby teeth and his adult teeth had yet to grow in. "Yes, but Master Baako said that if I mind my business, I can watch and learn. And since I'll be living with him, it makes sense for me to come to work with him. He can't have me making mischief at the house."

"That's a direct quote," Baako said, his expression serious but his eyes laughing.

"Oh, that's wonderful. Pleased to meet you, Mr. Marius. I'm Talullah. I learned a lot from Master Baako myself. You're in good company." Talullah directed her attention to Baako.

"Turns out this young boy is my great-nephew, and his parents are no longer with us, goddesses rest their souls. He needs a place to stay, so my wife and I offered to look after the little rascal, as long as he promises to behave." The older man gave the boy a stern look, but there was no strength behind it.

Talullah's heart warmed at the thought of Baako getting to be a father of sorts to the boy, like he'd been a grandfather to her.

"Well, I think you would do well to listen to Master Baako," she said to the boy.

He nodded seriously. "Of course, ma'am. I wouldn't dream of doing anything out of the ordinary."

Talullah patted him on the shoulder. "Oh, now, I didn't say that. Sometimes, doing things that are out of the ordinary can bring you the greatest kinds of adventure."

She winked at Dhal and said goodbye to Baako with a long hug. "I'll be back to visit. It is my job, after all."

Baako waved them away.

"Where should we go now?" Dhal asked as they exited the tent into the cool but sunny day.

"Well, you promised me an evening of romantic dancing. I probably should find a dress to wear."

Dhal leaned closer and whispered in her ear. "You already have one. It's back at your house. I hope you don't mind."

Talullah's heart fluttered. "What did you do?"

"Oh, it wasn't just me. You'll see."

~

BACK AT TALULLAH'S HOUSE, she opened the front door, and Dhal followed her inside.

"Finally!" said Margot. "Did you buy something from every stall or what?"

"We thought you were never going to come back," Penny said. Her emerald eyes shone brightly with anticipation.

"What's going on?" Talullah asked.

"Dhal here has been scheming," her father said.

"And we are his willing accomplices," her mother added, coming into the room carrying a garment bag.

"Open it," Dhal said, with a shy nod to the bag.

Talullah's mother laid it across the sofa. Talullah unfastened the bag and let it fall away. She stood speechless.

It was a dress—which she'd expected—but she hadn't expected this.

A magnificent silky gown in a stunning shade of silver. When the light reflected off the fabric, it shimmered like a rainbow.

She picked it up.

"Do you like it?" Dhal asked.

"I absolutely love it," she replied. "Where did you find it?"

"We made it," Penny said. "Me and Margot and Mother."

"Based on Dhal's design," Talullah's mother said.

"I've never seen anything like it." Talullah held it out so she could admire the sweetheart neckline and the way the fabric cascaded to the ground like water.

She turned to Dhal. "This is exquisite." Her hands trailed over the silky skirt until they dipped in between layers. She gasped. "It has pockets?"

Dhal's face broke into a wide, wild smile. "It has many, many pockets."

Talullah squeaked and threw her arms around him. "How did you even come up with this?"

"It came to me in a dream. When I…died. Everything went black and then suddenly, there you were. In this dress. You held my hand and told me to wake up. And I did."

A memory that couldn't possibly have been hers flashed in her mind. In it, she and Dhal danced by the lake while she wore a dress made from a rainbow. He twirled her and they laughed.

Talullah blinked herself back. "It's beautiful, Dhal. I can't wait to wear it."

THAT NIGHT, they danced in the Castle Viltresor ballroom. It looked different now that Alexander was king. He'd done away with the stuffy decor and the heavy curtains in favor of something lighter and fresher. He'd kept Theresa busy, though there had been fewer galas.

They swayed to the soft music provided by the string quartet. One of Talullah's hands rested on the feather embroidered on Dhal's suit jacket. Right over his heart. Talullah pressed her lips to his. Their status wasn't new anymore, but every day still felt exciting and full of potential. Like a true gift.

He kissed her again, a little more deeply this time, before pulling back and looking at her in the eyes. "I can't believe you haven't traded up now that you're a fancy Council member." He wiggled his eyebrows. He'd done his best to tame his bouncing dark curls, but a few still fell over his eyes.

She laughed and playfully swatted his shoulder. "You know, I don't have time to orient anybody new to my quirks. I have a lot of them."

"Lucky for me." He pulled her in for a hug. Like always, she breathed in his sweet scent of honey and morning dew that had become synonymous with comfort and joy and home.

She kissed him once more before saying, "So. If you could change one thing about the past, what would you change?"

Dhal's hazel eyes fixed her with a look made of love and conviction. He brushed her hair out of her face and kissed her softly. "Not a single thing."

I HOPE you enjoyed the conclusion to Talullah's journey! Please leave a rating/review. Reviews matter so much to authors, especially independent authors, like me. They help other readers find our books and encourage us to keep writing them!

If you haven't already, sign up to my newsletter at https://kier stenlillis.com/newsletter and get access to all of the series bonus scenes PLUS an exclusive, free short story set in the Sezna Seer universe, about the mysterious Suditzas and the creation of the first Dunamai's Eye amulet. You'll also get occasional updates, book recommendations, and sneak-peeks at what I'm working on!

ACKNOWLEDGMENTS

This section is always difficult to write because there is no limit to the number of people I could include, but there is a page limit…so, I'll do my best to be succinct.

Thank you so much to my husband for literally every single thing you do for me and our family. Without your support, this book—and all my others—would not exist.

Thank you to my parents who fostered my love of reading from a very young age and who always told me I could be anything I wanted to be. I believed you—and now I'm doing what I always wanted to do.

Thank you to my daughters. You constantly amaze me with your creativity, excitement, and infectious joy.

My editor, Fiona, you are truly a gift. Every time we work together I learn something new and grow my skills as a writer. I couldn't ask for a better person with whom to trust my words. You push me to dig deeper and polish the words until they sing. My work is always better after you, as you say, "get your muddy paws all over it."

To Rachel at Blue Raven Book Covers, you've revitalized this series with your designs and have made me fall in love with the stories all over again. Thanks for bringing my visions to life.

To every person who has encouraged me while writing this book or any of the others, thank you for your support. You have no idea how impactful your words are.

And, finally, to you, my readers. Thank you for joining me

on this journey and seeing it through to the end. Though Talullah's story is over, there are still so many more bouncing around in my head. I hope you'll come along for those, too.

ALSO BY KIERSTEN LILLIS

ABOUT THE AUTHOR

Kiersten Lillis writes fast-paced, no spice, mythology-inspired fantasy for teens and young adults. A pinch of mystery and something ghost-shaped always seem to work their way into her stories, whether or not she plans for them. Before publishing books, Kiersten edited wedding and event videos, spending hours crying alone at her computer while trying to bribe the author muse.

When not writing, she can be found improvising silly songs and bedtime stories for her kids, singing off-key to Taylor Swift, and sipping sweet tea while hiding from the Colorado sunshine.

Follow her on social for updates!

facebook.com/kierstenlillisauthor

instagram.com/kierstenlillis

bookbub.com/authors/kiersten-lillis

tiktok.com/@kierstenlillis

amazon.com/author/kierstenlillis